LONGING TO LOVE

"What do you want from me?" she asked, a slight tremble in her voice.

"This," he said, bending his head and kissing her aggressively.

Her arms went about his neck, as she responded with a fervor equal to his. Somewhere in the back of her mind, her better judgment cried out a warning, but she willed it to go away.

"Sweetheart," Cade murmured, planting taunting little kisses along one cheek, then the other. "Marry me. Let me take care of you."

His words, like a cold gust of wind, brought back her senses. "Take care of me!" she snapped, pushing out of his embrace. "I am perfectly capable of doing that myself!"

In an instant, Cade had her back in his arms. "I'd never hurt you, Jodie. I only want to love you, but you won't let me."

She longed to tell him what was in her heart, and to confess the fear she carried deep within, but the words wouldn't come. . . .

DESERT WIND

Rochelle Wayne

Zebra Books
Kensington Publishing Corp.

http://www.zebrabooks.com

ZEBRA BOOKS are published by

Kensington Publishing Corp.
850 Third Avenue
New York, NY 10022

First Printing: May, 1997
10 9 8 7 6 5 4 3 2 1

Printed in the United States of America

Chapter One

Jodie Walker's eyes stared unyieldingly into her aunt's. The woman knew that look; she gave up, and turned a pleading gaze to the man standing beside her. He stepped to Jodie, took her hands into his, and cleared his throat. But before he could say anything, she drew her hands free, and remarked willfully, "I'm going and that's that!"

"You must listen to reason," he argued.

"Reason can go to the devil!" she returned. "Besides, I'm only doing my job."

"Your job?" he quipped. "That badge you carry doesn't mean you're supposed to chase after killers. Good Lord! You're a woman! Just because your father was the sheriff and made you a deputy doesn't mean he intended for you to do something like this. His swearing you in as his deputy was a farce—a joke—and he was never really serious about it. I think he did it because he thought it would come between us. You know your father didn't especially like me."

Jodie was fully aware that her father had reluctantly

accepted that Bill Lawson was courting her. He never came right out and voiced a firm objection, but he told her once that he had misgivings concerning Lawson's character. She had asked that he explain, but he had no solid reason for feeling that way. He never again brought up Lawson's character; however, he remained lukewarm toward his daughter's beau. Lawson suspected the sheriff was waiting for an opportunity to discredit him in Jodie's eyes, which he believed was his reason for swearing her in as a deputy—the sheriff figured he would be shocked and infuriated. As indeed he was, but he didn't fall for the sheriff's ploy. Quite the contrary, he successfully hid his anger and disapproval; after all, he knew her job was only temporary. He was sure Jodie would soon be his wife, and then he would put his foot down and demand that she turn in her badge. That the woman he loved was a deputy was embarrassing enough; he'd not be further humiliated after they were married.

Now, as he looked into Jodie's angry eyes, he wondered if he had gone too far. He wished he could retract his words.

"A farce . . . a joke?" she said sharply.

"I'm sorry." He was quick to apologize.

"My father made me his deputy because he knew he could depend on me." Her face was flushed with anger as she brushed past him and strode swiftly across the parlor.

"Where are you going?" Lawson asked.

She paused, turned back, and said curtly, "To my room. I need time alone."

"Dinner's at six," her aunt reminded her.

Jodie crossed the small foyer, and hurried down the narrow hall to her bedroom. Closing the door soundly, she stood in the center of the room and looked around as though she wasn't sure why she was here. Normally, she didn't spend a lot of time in her bedroom—she preferred the outdoors. But she wanted to be alone, and her room afforded the refuge she needed.

She moved to her dressing table and gazed thoughtfully into the mirror. Her reflection stared somberly back at her. She was dressed in solid black, from her bonnet down to the slippers peeking out from beneath her floor-length gown. She hated black, and only wore the color at funerals. She had worn this dress four years ago when her mother passed away, and now she had donned it again for her father's services.

She pulled out the dressing stool, sat down, and continued staring at her reflection. Despite her grief, her luminous blue eyes were shining with vitality, defiance, and character. Hair, the color of chestnuts, tumbled from beneath her bonnet in a mass of unruly curls. She combed her fingers through the ends as though she could somehow force the stubborn curls to fall obediently. But the effort was futile; the natural curly tresses had a will of their own. She gave up on her hair and returned her attention to her face. The delicate features in the mirror were arresting, for sharply defined brows accentuated sky-blue eyes and prominent cheekbones. Her sultry lips were full, and her jawline was strong, yet beautifully feminine. She had a lovely, vivacious smile; it could totally captivate an admirer.

She got to her feet, took off her bonnet, and placed it on the dressing table. She then unbuttoned her dress and removed it with a flourish. She pitched it aimlessly and it fell on the floor beside the bed. She stood clad in her black petticoat, still staring at her reflection like she expected it to come alive. She almost wished such a thing were possible, and that her other self could temporarily bear her grief until she had time to deal with it herself. But reflections didn't come alive, nor could she afford the luxury of giving in to her feelings. Her father's killers were still at large, and she intended to find them.

She turned away from the mirror, went to her armoire,

and took out a dressing gown. She dropped it on the bed, quickly removed her petticoat, then slipped into the soft, sheer robe. As she carried the mourning gown to the armoire, she was unaware of the mirror picking up her reflection. But even if she had happened to look that way, she would have given her mirrored image only a cursory glance, for her inveigling beauty would not have caught her attention. Although she wasn't vain, she also wasn't blind, and she knew she was far from unattractive. But she didn't spend time admiring herself, for vanity was not part of her character. Therefore, the lovely image in the mirror escaped her notice. But an observer would certainly have admired her graceful frame, full breasts, and tiny waist. Her hips, though narrow, were femininely curvaceous.

She delved into the back of the armoire, retrieved a box, and crammed the mourning dress inside it. She closed the lid, then shoved the package into the farthest recesses of the wardrobe. She gave it a final, angry shove, as though the garment were somehow to blame for the grief it portrayed.

She returned to the bed, sat on the edge, and stared down at the floor. Tears threatened as she thought about her father. She almost surrendered to her sorrow, but her innate strength prevailed. Crying wouldn't change anything; if it could, then the tears she had shed for the past two days would have made a difference. No, crying didn't ease her pain, nor did it bring about justice. A hard, determined expression came to her eyes—her pain would lessen in time, and when her father's killers paid for their crime, justice would be served. She was intent on bringing in the murderers—dead or alive!

Her thoughts turned to Bill Lawson. She refused to believe Bill when he said that her father had made her his deputy simply to cause a rift between them. That her father didn't especially approve of Bill was apparent, but he wouldn't have used such drastic means to separate them. Her chin lifted stubbornly. He made her his deputy because he knew she was capable—she wouldn't believe otherwise. To accept Bill's explanation would be the same as admitting her father had made a fool of her. He would never have done that!

Her musings remained on Bill Lawson. She had met him two years ago when he inherited his uncle's ranch, the Double-L. The prosperous spread was five miles south of Crystal Creek—the small town where her father had been sheriff for as long as she could remember. Bill's uncle, James Lawson, had rarely spoken of his nephew. Jodie had lived in Crystal Creek all her life, and never in that time had Bill visited his uncle. James had a wife and son; his wife died four years ago, and shortly thereafter, his son was killed accidentally during a cattle drive. James lived a year following his son's death, then after a short illness, he passed away. Bill Lawson was his next of kin, and he inherited his uncle's estate.

Bill was exceptionally handsome, suave, and exuded an aura of confidence. Jodie found him extremely attractive and enjoyed his company; nevertheless, she refused his proposals of marriage. He had asked her more than once to be his wife, and each time she had told him she wasn't ready to give him a firm answer. Actually, she wasn't sure of her feelings, and she felt she needed more time. At first Bill had been patient, but lately he had begun pressing her. She didn't blame him; after all, she couldn't expect him to keep waiting for her to make up her mind. A frown furrowed her brow. Making a decision anytime soon was now out of the question. Marriage was not on her mind— she could think of nothing except finding her father's killers.

She left the bed and returned to the mirror. Studying her reflection, she tried to see herself objectively. Could she possibly apprehend two men who were cold-blooded murderers? She was, after all, a woman. Was she asking too much of herself? Was such a mission impossible?

She cast the nagging doubts aside. She was a woman, true, but that didn't mean she wasn't capable. Pursuing killers wasn't necessarily a man's job—she had already trespassed on male territory when she became a deputy, and she saw no reason to turn back now. She didn't have a man's physical strength, but she did have the cunning and the competence of a hunter, and she intended to use these skills to capture her prey.

In the parlor, Bill Lawson was pacing back and forth. Jodie's aunt, sitting on the sofa, watched him. Widowed six months ago, Doris had moved herself and her daughter from St. Louis to Crystal Creek, and into the sheriff's home. She finally waved an exasperated hand in Bill's direction, and said firmly, "Honestly, Bill! Will you please sit down and stop pacing like a caged lion?"

He sat in the chair that faced the sofa. However, he wasn't relaxed, but remained poised on the very edge, as though he expected to jump to his feet at any second.

Doris Talbert was very fond of Bill, and she offered him a sympathetic smile. "I know how worried you must be. But Jodie has a mind of her own. She doesn't always think like most women. My sister and brother-in-law were not firm enough with Jodie. I can understand why a father might fail raising a daughter, but for the life of me, I can't understand why my sister wasn't more strict. Of course, our parents objected to Margaret's marriage. They considered Cole Walker too wild and irresponsible. But Margaret married him anyway. After three years of wandering from one town to another, they ended up here. Cole was elected sheriff, and Margaret gave birth to Jodie. They had a son too, but he died in infancy."

Bill was finding it hard to curb his patience. He wasn't interested in the woman's rambling; he had only one thing on his mind—stopping Jodie from pursuing the men who had killed her father.

"You know," Doris continued, "When Jodie was a child her nickname was cute, but now that she's a grown woman, you'd think she'd want to be called Joanne. I mean, Joanne is such a feminine name, and Jodie is . . . is . . ."

Bill's patience snapped, and bounding to his feet, he remarked testily, "Mrs. Talbert, I really don't care about all that! Don't you understand what is happening here? We must find a way to stop Jodie. If she goes after those men, there's no telling what might happen to her."

"You'll not stop her," a woman's voice sounded from the foyer. "When Jodie makes up her mind, that's it."

Bill turned and watched as Doris's daughter came into the room. She was quite beautiful. Her figure was voluptuous, and auburn tresses, shining with reddish highlights, fell past her shoulders in silky waves. She had worn a black dress to her uncle's funeral, but had changed into a powder-blue gown that tastefully defined her every curve.

Bill's masculine gaze was admiring; a man would have to be blind not to notice her seductive beauty. If he wasn't in love with Jodie, he would certainly take an interest in Doris's daughter. Well, if Jodie didn't change her ways, he might do just that.

"Did you take a nap, Laura?" Doris asked.

She shook her head. "I couldn't sleep."

"Laura," Bill began, "maybe you could try talking to Jodie. She might listen to you."

Laura almost laughed in his face. She and her cousin could barely tolerate each other. They were two totally different personalities, and they continually rubbed each other the wrong way. But Laura's dislike for Jodie went further than that; she was bitterly jealous of her. From the first moment she set eyes on Bill Lawson, she wanted him more than anything on the face of this earth. He was handsome, and he had inherited a fortune—those were the two qualities she wanted most in a husband. If he wasn't foolishly smitten with Jodie, she was certain she could convince him to marry her.

Doris rose to her feet. "I must see about dinner." She turned to Bill. "You'll stay and eat with us, won't you?"

"Yes, thank you," he replied.

As Doris left the room, Laura went to the liquor cabinet and poured herself a glass of sherry. Sitting on the sofa, she patted the cushion next to her. "Sit down, Bill, and relax. There's no reason for you to let Jodie get you so upset."

He sat beside her, but he was again perched on the edge of his seat, ready to pounce at a moment's notice. "I just can't believe Jodie is really serious about this. Whoever heard of a woman chasing killers? Good lord! She must be out of her mind. That must be it—she's so grief-stricken she isn't thinking rationally."

"Oh she's rational, all right. That is, for Jodie. She's always been a little strange. Even when we were children and our families visited, Jodie was different from other girls. She acted more like a boy."

"A lot of girls are tomboys, but they outgrow it."

"Not Jodie," she replied. She favored him with a sugar-coated smile. "Has it ever occurred to you that Jodie may not be the right woman for you?"

"Yes," he sighed reluctantly. "It has crossed my mind, but I still love her. I can't help myself."

Laura was disappointed with his answer, but not overly so. Jodie would certainly pursue her father's killers, and Laura doubted that her cousin would survive such a reckless mission. However, if Jodie did somehow survive, Laura didn't think Bill would want her back. She couldn't imagine him marrying a woman who tracked criminals and engaged in such degrading behavior.

She patted his hand as though she sympathized with his feelings. "Try not to worry, Bill." She faked an angry frown.

"Shame on my cousin for doing this. You deserve so much better."

He was inclined to agree with her, but dismissing Jodie from his life was easier said than done. She was not only lovely, but her independence, willfulness, and vitality set her apart from other women, which inexplicably made her more desirable. He wasn't sure why, for her strong character often frayed his patience. But maybe that was the magical answer—he couldn't control her, and Bill Lawson was a born manipulator, which made Jodie Walker a challenge he couldn't turn away from. He considered marriage the ultimate victory, for then he could gain the upper hand and squelch her rebellious ways.

Cade Brandon rode slowly into the town called Crystal Creek. This was his first visit, and he was impressed with the small New Mexico settlement. The streets were clean and the buildings were in good condition. The citizens obviously took pride in their home. A steepled church was located at the edge of town; behind it lay the town's well-manicured cemetery. A freshly dug grave had caught Cade's attention when he passed the church.

He rode past the livery, blacksmith's shop, a mercantile, and a barbershop, which advertised baths as well as haircuts and shaves. The town wasn't very crowded; the sidewalks were mostly empty, and he passed only one buckboard and two riders on the main thoroughfare.

The sheriff's office was located in the center of town; across from it was the stage depot that also served as a post office. A restaurant was next door; on its front window were painted the words "Homecooked Meals Just Like Mom's." Above that was the establishment's name—Caroline's. A two-story hotel bordered the restaurant; next to it was a dress shop. Crystal Creek's only saloon, The Silver Dollar, was at the far end of town. Three horses were tied at the hitching rail; the saloon didn't get many customers during the day. Nights were busier, but weekends brought the most traffic, for several ranches surrounded Crystal Creek, and from Friday night till Sunday morning, the nearby wranglers frequented the saloon. Poker, blackjack, liquor, and five prostitutes brought them to the establishment in droves.

Cade guided his roan stallion to the hitching post in front of the sheriff's office. A man, ensconced in a rocker, his hat pulled down to shade his eyes, was sitting by the front door.

Cade dismounted, and moved to stand before the man, who appeared to be sound asleep. A deputy's badge was pinned to his shirt.

"Excuse me," Cade said, pushing aside his black vest so the man could see his own credentials.

The man slowly pushed back his hat, and squinting against the sun's bright rays, he looked up at the stranger. Suddenly, he bounded to his feet as though propelled by an invisible force. The stranger was impressive, for his tall frame was muscular, and the Colt revolver strapped to his hip appeared well-used. But it wasn't the stranger's formidable presence that had sent the deputy leaping from the rocker; it was the U.S. Marshal's badge pinned beneath the man's vest. They were both lawmen, but the stranger's federal position set him far above a town's deputy.

"Can I help you, sir?" the deputy asked.

"I need to see the sheriff."

"The sheriff's dead. He was killed two days ago."

"I'm sorry to hear that. Who's in charge?"

"Deputy Walker."

"Where can I find Deputy Walker?"

"At the sheriff's house." He pointed back down the street. "It's the first house before enterin' town."

Cade remembered passing the home. He mumbled a quick thank you, went to his horse, and mounted. As he rode toward the sheriff's house, he let his mind wander. He didn't normally indulge in daydreams, but today he made an exception. Ten years of working as a bounty hunter and a U.S. Marshal was about to become a part of the past. He intended to make this quest his last assignment. He had a ranch outside Abilene; he bought the spread two years ago, but he now had enough money saved to increase his herd of cattle. A small cabin sat on his property; for the next year or two it would suffice as a home, but as his spread prospered, he planned to build a house befitting his ranch, which he had named the Diamond Star.

Cade neared the sheriff's house, and he cleared the Diamond Star from his mind. The home was small, but in good condition. It had been freshly painted, and a white picket fence surrounded the front yard. He dismounted, flung the reins over the hitching rail, opened the gate, and strode up to the door. He removed his black hat, and slapped it against his thigh to shake loose some of the trail dust that had accumulated on its wide brim. He then knocked on the door.

Jodie, dressed for dinner, was leaving her room when Cade's knock sounded. "I'll get it," she called in the direction of the parlor. She wasn't sure if anyone was in there, but more than likely Bill was still here. Doris probably asked him to stay for dinner.

She opened the door, and came face to face with a man she had never seen before. That he was a stranger was not nearly as surprising as his striking appearance. At first, Jodie was only aware of his impressive height, and the strong muscles outlined beneath his tightly fitting shirt. But as she gazed into his face, his swarthy good looks held her mesmerized. Hair so black and shimmery that it seemed blue grew to collar-length, and dark blue eyes, shadowed by thick brows, were watching her with a glint she couldn't define. A well-groomed moustache lent him a roguish air, and his features were handsomely sculpted.

Cade was equally impressed with Jodie. She had changed into a dark gown that complimented her graceful frame, and her long, curly tresses fell past her shoulders in silky ringlets. Eyes, a shade lighter than his own, were staring curiously into his.

"I hope I'm not intruding," Cade began. He moved his vest so that she could see his badge. "I'm Marshal Brandon, and I'm looking for Deputy Walker."

U.S. Marshals didn't frequent Crystal Creek, and Jodie could only recall two Marshals ever visiting the town. Crystal Creek was usually a quiet, peaceful settlement, and the jail cells were normally empty, except on Saturday nights when a drunk, rambunctious wrangler or two were locked up for the night, then released in the morning.

She stepped out onto the porch, closed the door, and asked, "Why have you come to Crystal Creek?"

"Actually, I'm looking for two men, but I think this is something I should discuss with Deputy Walker. I understand the sheriff is dead, and that his deputy is now in charge."

Jodie's heart picked up speed. "Can you describe these two men?"

"One's a big half-breed, and the other one has red hair and a scar on his left cheek."

The description fit the men who had murdered her father. "They killed the sheriff," she said. "Two days ago in the saloon."

"I don't suppose you'd know if the sheriff received a wanted poster on them?"

"The poster came in the mail the day after my father was killed."

"The sheriff was your father?"

"Yes, he was."

"I'm sorry, ma'am. And forgive me for intruding at a

time like this, but I need to talk to Deputy Walker right away. Will you tell him I'm here?''

"You are talking to Deputy Walker," she replied.

Cade took a backward step, his eyes raking her from head to foot, as though if he got a better look her answer wouldn't be so incredulous. The woman standing before him was lovely, vulnerable, and totally feminine. He decided he must have misunderstood what she said. "I don't think I heard you correctly."

Her eyes flashed defiantly. He had heard correctly; he was simply too arrogant to believe his own ears—just like a man. "I said, I'm Deputy Walker," she replied firmly.

"Good God!" Cade exclaimed. "You're a deputy? That's the craziest thing I ever heard in my life!"

"You might consider it crazy, Marshal Brandon, but I take my job very seriously."

His shock turned into humor, and he replied with a devilish grin, "I could take you seriously in a lot of jobs, but a deputy is not one of them. That's a man's line of work. Where can I find the mayor? I'll talk to him instead." He quirked a brow. "He is a man, I hope."

"Yes, he's a man," she replied. Her temper simmered, but she kept it under control and gave him directions to the mayor's home.

Cade donned his hat, tipped the brim, and said courtly, "Good day, Miss Walker."

He started to leave, but her sudden question deterred him. "Mr. Brandon, do you plan to pursue those two men?"

"Yes, I aim to do just that."

"I'm going after them too. Why don't we ride together?" She didn't relish his company, but she could use his expertise.

Cade gaped at her incredulously. "Are you out of your mind? You can't chase after two killers! Ma'am, these men are cold-blooded murderers!"

"I'm perfectly aware that they are murderers!" she retorted angrily. "I just came from burying my father. So don't tell me what these men are capable of! I'm going after them and that's final! And I take back my offer to let you ride with me!"

He laughed tersely. "You're unbelievable!"

"And you're very rude!" She whirled around, and was about to go in the house and slam the door in his face, but he placed a halting hand on her arm. She brushed him aside.

His blue eyes pierced hers, and their expression was now very serious. "I'm going to give you some advice, and I hope you take it. Turn in your badge, find yourself a husband, and dedicate your life to raising a family. That way, you'll live a lot longer!"

"When I want your advice, I'll ask for it!"

Bristling, she watched as he strode to his horse and mounted. She went into the house and slammed the door with a resounding bang.

Chapter Two

Mayor Wrightman showed Cade into his study, served him brandy, then sat in the leather-bound chair behind his desk. Cade was seated facing him, and he studied his guest across the span of the desk-top. He was not only impressed with Brandon's appearance, but with his credentials as well.

Wrightman offered Cade a cigar; he declined. Wrightman took one for himself, lit it, then asked, "What can I do for you, Marshal?"

"I'm looking for two men—a half-breed and a man with a scar on his left cheek. I understand they were in Crystal Creek."

The mayor saddened. "They sound like the men who killed Sheriff Walker. Cole was a fine sheriff, and also a good friend. He'll be sorely missed."

Brandon took a drink of his brandy, placed the glass on the desk, leaned forward, and regarded the mayor intently. Wrightman, in his early fifties, was distinguished looking. His hair and goatee were dappled with gray, and his dark suit was expensive. Cade couldn't understand why a man who was obviously well-bred tolerated a woman as the town's deputy. Why would any man allow a young lady to hold such a dangerous position?

"Mayor," he began, "I met Deputy Walker. I don't need to tell you that I was shocked. How you run this town is none of my business. However—"

"I know what you're about to say," Wrightman cut in. "I was against Cole making Jodie his deputy. But as sheriff, he had that right. Sheriffs are elected, not their deputies." He suddenly smiled, for he considered the situation temporary. "But a new sheriff will be elected, and I'm sure his first order of business will be to dismiss Jodie Walker."

"Why would a father place his daughter in such jeopardy?"

"I don't think Cole thought she was in danger. Crystal Creek is a quiet, peaceful town. Before Walker's murder, we hadn't had a murder in over four years. At one time, Crystal Creek was lawless, but Cole cleaned up this town and made the streets safe for its citizens. As Crystal Creek's reputation grew, ranchers and homesteaders came here in droves. However, getting back to Miss Jodie. You must realize that she isn't exactly helpless. Her father taught her skills a man normally teaches to a son."

"Did you know that Miss Walker plans to pursue her father's killers?"

Wrightman was obviously surprised. "No, I didn't. Is she out of her mind? She can't do that!"

Cade picked up his glass and took a long drink. "Mr. Wrightman, if you have any influence with Miss Walker, I suggest you use it. I got the feeling she meant what she said."

The mayor, puffing on his cigar, replied, "I'm afraid I have no influence with Miss Jodie. But Bill Lawson certainly has. I'm sure he'll talk her out of this nonsense of tracking down the murderers."

"Who's Bill Lawson?"

"He has a ranch about five miles south of here. He and Miss Jodie . . . Well, they aren't officially engaged, but I'm sure it's only a matter of time."

A knock sounded on the study door, and the mayor's wife peeked inside. "Excuse me, dear," she said to her husband. "Emmett Bradley is here. He says he must see you right away."

"Send him in," Wrightman replied. He turned to Cade. "Bradley owns a large spread, and is one of the wealthiest ranchers in these parts."

A moment later, Emmett Bradley strode into the room, his demeanor imperious, as though his presence alone deserved immediate respect. He was tall, heavy-boned, and dressed in a tailor-made suit. His features were arrogant, and a haughty sneer hovered over his moustached lips.

The mayor bounded from his chair with the quickness of a soldier whose commanding officer had just arrived. It was obvious to Cade that Bradley was the power behind Crystal Creek. He decided to stand, and rose slowly to his feet.

Before Wrightman could make introductions, Bradley blurted out, "My son is missing."

"Which one?"

"Dirk. He hasn't been home for two days."

"Dirk's always going on binges. You'll probably find him at the Silver Dollar sleeping off his drunk in some woman's bed."

"I already checked there. No one has seen him since the night Sheriff Walker was killed. I'm afraid that the men who shot the sheriff have kidnapped Dirk."

"Could your son be staying with friends?" Cade asked.

Bradley cast him an lofty glance. "Who are you?"

Wrightman spoke up quickly. "This is Marshal Brandon. He's searching for the men who killed Cole."

"Are you a U.S. Marshal?" Emmett asked Cade.

"Yes, I am."

"I've searched everywhere for Dirk. No one has seen him."

"What makes you think these men kidnapped him?"

"He disappeared the same time they left town. Marshal, I'm a wealthy man, and these men could demand a high ransom."

"I take it, you haven't received a ransom note."

"Not yet."

"If they kidnapped your son, by now they would've gotten in touch with you."

Bradley raised his chin arrogantly. "You don't know that. I could receive a ransom demand at any moment. Marshal, I insist you find these men and return my son."

Cade's dark eyes narrowed. "I don't like your tone, Mr. Bradley."

Wrightman, fearing an unpleasant scene, quickly intervened. "Emmett, have you spoken to Miss Jodie about Dirk?"

He laughed harshly. "You can't be serious. It'll be a cold day in hell before I discuss a man's business with a woman. But I did speak to Jonas. He hasn't seen Dirk."

Wrightman turned to Cade. "Jonas is also a deputy. He's had the job for years. He's not much of a deputy; he spends most of his time getting drunk. I don't know why Cole didn't fire him. I guess he felt sorry for him. Jonas wasn't always a drunk; there was a time when he was as good as Cole with a gun. He helped Cole clean up this town. But four years ago, his wife and two children died in a fire; after that, he turned to the bottle."

"Regardless of his drinking," Bradley said, "I want you to swear him in as sheriff until one can be elected. You need to do it now before Miss Jodie convinces you to make her sheriff."

Wrightman seemed insulted. "I would never swear a woman in as sheriff."

Emmett was through with the discussion; he had a more pressing matter on his mind. He spoke to Cade. "Marshal, I am sincerely worried about Dirk. If he wasn't kidnapped, then I'm afraid he might be dead. Those men could have robbed and killed him."

"I'll keep an eye out for your son, Mr. Bradley."

"When do you plan to leave?"

"In the morning."

"Why wait until morning? Every hour you spend here, those men are getting farther and farther away."

"I've been on the trail for days. I need a bath, a good meal, and a night's sleep. And my horse needs rest, along with a bag of oats." He took a last sip of his brandy, said a terse good day, and left.

"Some marshal he is," Emmett complained to the mayor. "He puts his own welfare and his horse's above my son's. I should have Jonas round up a posse and search for Dirk."

Wrightman hoped he wouldn't go through with it, for he seriously doubted if Jonas could arrange a posse. Dirk Bradley was a troublemaker who had no true friends. The men from this vicinity would most likely refuse to search for him; in fact, once they learned he was missing, they would probably hope he never came back. However, Wrightman was not about to speak his thoughts aloud; instead, he said, "Emmett, I don't think a posse can do any good. Dirk's been gone too long. Jonas's jurisdiction is limited, you know."

Bradley was inclined to agree. "I guess you're right."

"Leave the job to Marshal Brandon. I'm sure he'll learn what happened to Dirk."

"He'd better!" Bradley remarked. "If he doesn't, I'll

see that his badge is revoked if I have to go all the way to the governor!''

Jodie saw Bill to the front door, and walked out onto the porch with him. Dusk had fallen, and gray shadows fell across her face as she gazed up into his eyes, which mirrored his concern.

"Bill, try not to worry. I'll be all right.''

With a flourish of his hand, he waved aside her words. "Oh, that's easy for you to say. For God's sake, Jodie! You're behaving as though you have no sense at all.''

"Don't talk to me like that.''

"What the hell do you expect me to say? Surely, you don't expect me to send you off with my blessings.''

"No, but if you're so worried, you can come with me. I could use an extra gun.''

Taken off guard, he stepped back as though she had slapped him. He swallowed deeply, and a trace of perspiration dotted his brow. Bravery was not a part of Lawson's character; in fact, he had spent a lifetime avoiding trouble. He valued his life above all else, and he was not about to risk it in order to accompany Jodie. He loved her, but he loved himself more.

"Jodie," he began calmly, "if I go with you, that will be the same as encouraging you. I refuse to give you any encouragement whatsoever. Furthermore, if you're forced to go alone, you'll come to your senses much faster and return home.''

She eyed him somewhat skeptically; she had a feeling he wasn't being totally candid. But the impression was too fleeting to leave a permanent mark. "Bill, I'm not afraid to go alone. Don't misunderstand me; I'm fully aware of the dangers involved. But those men killed my father, and I intend to bring them in dead or alive.''

"My God! Do you realize what you just said? Dead or alive? Women don't say things like that!"

"This woman does." Her eyes held his steadfastly, and her face was as determined as it was beautiful.

"When do you plan to leave?"

She intended to leave first thing in the morning, but she decided not to tell Bill. He'd certainly arrive with the dawn and attempt to talk her out of it. It was a scene she preferred to avoid; therefore, she replied, "I don't know. Maybe tomorrow around noon."

"I'll be back before noon. I intend to do everything within my power to dissuade you." He planned to bring the mayor with him. Surely, between the two of them they could convince her to stay. If not . . . well, the mayor could always order Jonas to lock her up until she came to her senses.

He brought her into his arms, kissed her lips softly, and murmured, "I love you, Jodie."

She didn't return the endearment, for she wasn't sure of her feelings.

Keeping her in his arms, he asked, "Do you love me?"

At that moment, a man cleared his throat, causing Bill to release her abruptly. He turned and watched as Cade Brandon came through the gate and sauntered up to the porch steps.

Jodie regarded the intruder irritably. "What are you doing here?" she asked.

"I stopped by to ask you a few questions about Dirk Bradley."

"Dirk?" she questioned. "Why do you want to know about Dirk?"

"He's missing."

"This is Mr. Brandon," Jodie said to Bill. "He's a U.S. Marshal, and is searching for the men who killed Papa."

"How do you do," Bill said, extending his hand. "I'm Bill Lawson."

Cade shook the man's hand.

"Marshal, are you aware that Miss Walker plans to pursue her father's murderers?"

He grinned wryly. "She mentioned it."

Bill resented the man's smile. Apparently, he didn't take Jodie seriously. "I do hope you'll order her to remain here."

Cade arched a brow. "If that's what you want." He turned to Jodie, and said with a twinkle in his eyes, "Miss Walker, I hereby order you to keep your pretty nose out of a man's business."

"You have no right to give me orders!"

"Of course, he does," Bill remarked. "He's a U.S. Marshal."

She knew Bill's point was valid, but she wasn't about to concede. "He might have the right to order me to stay if I'm a deputy, but he has no rights over me as a citizen." She eyed Cade defiantly. "If you want my badge, I'll gladly hand it over."

"Miss Walker, I really don't care what you do with your badge. But I'm leaving in the morning, and I don't want to come across you on the trail. I have enough on my mind searching for two killers; I don't need a woman getting in the way."

Their eyes locked in a battle of wills. "Get off my property! Now, before I run you off!"

"I'll be glad to oblige, Miss Walker, as soon as I ask a few questions about Dirk Bradley."

"Then ask them, and be fast about it."

"Emmett thinks the men who killed your father have kidnapped Dirk. However, there's been no ransom note."

"How long has he been missing?"

"Two days."

"Did Emmett check the saloon?"

"Yes. He isn't there, and no one has seen him. Does Dirk disappear often?"

"He's been known to. But Emmett usually finds him at the Silver Dollar. But there have been a few times when Dirk left town. He goes to Mexico, stays a couple of days, then comes home."

"Why does he do that?"

"Because he likes to raise hell, and Mexico is a good place for that. Crystal Creek is too civilized for Dirk's taste."

"Do you think he was kidnapped?"

"I seriously doubt it."

"Thanks for answering my questions, Miss Walker."

"It's Deputy Walker to you!"

He smiled, tipped his hat, and said, "Good-bye, Deputy Walker. And remember what I said—stay home and out of trouble."

"I'm not afraid of trouble, Mr. Brandon."

He turned, saying over his shoulder, "That's Marshal Brandon, ma'am."

Jodie steamed inwardly as she watched Cade open the gate and leave. His horse was at the livery and he moved away on foot.

"That man's intolerable!" she said furiously.

"He might not be very tactful," Bill remarked. "But he's right."

She threw up her hands. "I've had all I can take for one day! You and Marshal Brandon have tried my patience. I'm going to bed. Goodnight!"

She whirled around before he could stop her, went into the house, and closed the door.

Jodie went to her room, but she didn't go to bed. Instead, she hurried to her armoire and took out two sets of riding clothes and a carpetbag. She packed one set, along with extra undergarments. She quickly removed her gown and exchanged it for riding attire. She put on her favorite pair of boots, went to the dresser, drew her curly tresses away from her face, and secured them with a pearl-adorned comb. She then grabbed her hat, picked up her carpetbag, and strode down the hall to the kitchen. There, she packed a supply of food.

The house was quiet, for Doris and Laura had retired. Jodie moved silently; she didn't want to disturb her aunt or cousin. She especially hoped to elude Doris, for she knew her aunt would try to stop her. She was determined to leave, and nothing Doris could say would change her mind; nonetheless, she preferred to avoid an unpleasant scene.

She went to the parlor, stepped to the gun cabinet, and removed her Winchester and extra ammunition. She intended to leave a note, but as she turned away from the cabinet, she found Laura watching her.

Laura jealously looked her cousin over from head to foot. Jodie was striking, for her stylish attire fit her graceful frame perfectly. Her riding skirt, split so she could ride astride, was a dark shade of violet. Her matching vest, worn over a lilac blouse, was embellished with gold buttons and intricate embroidery. Her skirt barely covered her knees, and a peek of bare legs was revealed above her high-topped boots. Laura sneered inwardly—she knew her cousin well enough to know that she wasn't even aware of her own sensuality. She was certain Jodie had thrown on her clothes without even bothering to admire herself in the mirror.

"Are you leaving us?" Laura asked, her expression concealing her inner jealousy.

"Yes. I decided not to wait until tomorrow."

"Oh? Why not?"

"There's a U.S. Marshal in town. I had the misfortune of encountering him twice in one day. He's looking for the men who killed Papa. I'm sure he plans to leave in the morning. That's why I'm leaving tonight. I intend to get a head start. I also hope to avoid him."

"Bill will be furious, you know. He thought he could eventually talk you into staying."

"Well, he'll just have to get over being furious. I have a job to do, and no one is going to stop me."

"Is that the message you want me to give him?"

Jodie moved past Laura and started toward the kitchen. Turning back, she said, "You don't have to give him a message; he knows why I'm doing this. Tell Aunt Doris . . . tell her I said not to worry."

"I'll tell her, but she'll still worry."

"I know," Jodie murmured. She didn't enjoy upsetting her aunt, but it was unavoidable. "I don't know how long I'll be gone."

Laura smiled. "Good luck."

Jodie went to the kitchen, out the rear door, and to the stable at the back of the house. She stopped at the second of the four stalls, opened the gate, and coaxed out a magnificent Appaloosa. Her father had given her the stallion when it was only a colt. She had trained it herself, causing horse and trainer to be perfectly tuned. Gray, with a splattering of black dots on its rear, it was fine-looking. Spirited and powerful, it was more a man's horse than a woman's, but Jodie controlled the strong steed with ease.

She quickly saddled the Appaloosa, sheathed her rifle, and attached her carpetbag. She was about to leave when she suddenly remembered her bullwhip. It was hanging on a nearby peg; she grabbed it and looped it over the saddle horn. She could hardly believe she had almost forgotten her whip, for she might very well need it.

She rode out of the stable, past the house and down the main street. She intended to head south, for she figured the men who killed her father had gone to Mexico to hide out until they considered it safe to cross back over the border. She stopped at the sheriff's office to let Jonas know that she was leaving. She only stayed a moment, and as she came back outside and mounted her Appaloosa, she was not aware that she was being watched.

The hotel was across the street, and although it sat at an angle from the sheriff's office, from Cade's upstairs window, he could see Jodie clearly. It was merely by chance that he had happened to step to the window at the same moment Jodie was mounting her horse.

A deep frown creased his brow as he watched Jodie ride down the street and out of sight. With a ragged curse, he whirled away from the window, gathered his belongings, and stormed out the door. He had never encountered a woman so stubborn and reckless! He was terribly riled, but allowing her to be a victim of her own foolishness was not an option. Chivalry drove Cade down the stairs, outside, and toward the livery. He intended to catch up to Jodie and convince her to go back home and let him take care of finding her father's killers. Evidently, the woman had no inkling of the dangers involved, for he couldn't imagine any rational female chasing after two murderers.

Cade kept his roan stallion at a slow pace. He didn't want to catch up to Jodie until later. Figuring she would stop, make camp, and get a few hours' rest, he planned to slip up on her while she was asleep. He intended to put a good scare in her that would persuade her to go back home. Once she realized how easy it was to wake up with a gun pointed at her head, she would undoubtedly be only too glad to give up her quest and leave the job to him.

As Cade expected, Jodie stopped and made camp. The secluded area was surrounded by trees and thick foliage. It was past midnight when Cade approached, a full moon lighting his way.

He rode in closer, then dismounted and moved stealthily into camp. Jodie's bedroll was beside a small fire that had burned down to glowing embers. He paused for a moment as he envisioned the delicate curves outlined beneath the top blanket. What chance, he wondered, did this vulnerable woman think she had alone in the wilderness? He noticed her Appaloosa tied close by; the horse, distrustful of a stranger, snorted and whinnied loudly. Cade looked quickly back at the bedroll, thinking the horse had surely awakened its owner. But she didn't even stir. Slipping up on Jodie was going to be easier than he thought.

He withdrew his pistol, and was about to step to the bedroll when, suddenly, a loud crack sounded and his gun went flying out of his hand. Cade recognized the sound and knew a whip's lash had stolen his pistol with the speed of a striking snake. He turned about swiftly and found himself looking down a Winchester's loaded barrel.

Jodie had dropped her whip and was now holding him at gunpoint. Hidden in the shrubbery, she had waited for the right moment to step forward and strike.

"Why did you follow me?" she asked angrily.

He was filled with admiration; Jodie Walker was indeed unique. Furthermore, she was far from a helpless female. His pride was a little wounded. "I was planning on giving you a good scare," he said. "I thought if you woke up with a gun pointed at you, it would convince you to go back home." He indicated her spread blankets. "Stuffing a bedroll to look like someone's in it is an old trick, you know."

"It worked, didn't it?"

"Only because I wasn't expecting it."

"The next time you intend to sneak up on someone, stay downwind. My horse picked up your scent. I've been waiting for you to make your move."

He waved a hand toward the Winchester, which was still pointed at him. "Do you intend to shoot me?"

She lowered the barrel.

"I underestimated you, Miss Walker. Next time, I won't make that mistake."

"There won't be a next time. We're parting company

right here. I'll stay out of your way, and you stay out of mine.''

He wasn't about to leave her alone, and he now knew he couldn't convince her to go back home. He didn't see any choice but to ride with her. "I think we should stay together," he said.

"Well, I don't! You see, Marshal Brandon, I don't like you. I think you're overbearing, opinionated, and rude. I would rather keep company with a nest of rattlesnakes."

"Rattlesnakes be damned. You might find yourself keeping company with a band of Apaches. The farther south you travel, the greater your chances of encountering them."

"And I suppose you think you can protect me."

He grinned roguishly. "Maybe I think you can protect me."

Although she was opposed to Brandon's company, she was smart enough to know that she might need him. "Very well, Marshal," she decided. "We'll ride together." She bent over and picked up her whip.

"You're very good with that whip," he remarked.

"I suggest you keep that in mind, Mr. Brandon."

"You know, you're about as friendly as a riled bobcat."

"And my claws are just as sharp!"

"Put your whip away and sheathe your claws, Deputy Walker. Your virtue is safe with me. This is strictly a business arrangement." With that, he picked up his pistol and left to get his horse.

Chapter Three

Jodie went to her bedroll and removed the inner blanket that she had twisted and folded to resemble a body. She sat and watched as Cade secured his horse. He then took his own bedroll and spread it on the other side of the fire from hers. Although Jodie found Cade insufferably rude, she couldn't help admiring his strong physique and handsome face. His snugly fitting shirt emphasized rippling muscles and the wide breadth of his shoulders. Black trousers clung to his slim hips and long legs; a Colt revolver, strapped to his thigh, was worn low for a quicker draw.

He suddenly turned to her with a devil-may-care smile. "Are you measuring me as a possible opponent, or as a partner?"

"Neither," she replied.

"Why don't you get some sleep?" he suggested. "I'll stay awake and keep an eye out for predators."

She had a feeling he was finding their situation somewhat humorous. She wondered if it was possible for him to see her as an equal. She seriously doubted it. Men like

Cade Brandon were too set in their ways to change their views.

"Wake me in a couple of hours, and I'll take the second watch," she said. She started to lie down, but she knew sleep would probably elude her, for she had too much on her mind. "Marshal," she began, "exactly what are your plans?"

"Pardon?" he asked.

"How do you intend to find those two men?"

"I figure they are either in Mexico, or headed in that direction. It's like looking for a needle in a haystack. It's going to take a lot more luck than skill."

"I agree," she replied. "But I don't plan to stop looking for them, even if it takes a lifetime."

"A lifetime?" he questioned. "Your determination is admirable, but don't you think you're taking this to the extreme?"

"Those men murdered my father, and I'll not rest until justice is served."

"Sometimes, Miss Walker, regardless of how much we want something, there may come a time when we have to let it go, put it behind us, and go on with our lives."

"Are you talking from experience, Marshal?"

It was a moment before he answered, and the lingering glow from the dying fire illuminated his face. His expression was somber. "Yes," he murmured. "I'm talking from experience. Twelve years ago, my sister was captured by the Comanches. For two years I searched day in and day out. I thought of nothing else; finding Alison was all I lived for. But every lead I followed took me to a dead end. It was as though Alison had vanished from the face of the earth. Finally, I managed to find a Comanche chief who told me that a white woman had lived in his cousin's village. He described the woman, and she sounded like Alison. He said that his cousin's village was nearly wiped out by diphtheria. He remembered that the white woman had died. I'll never know for sure if the woman was Alison, but she probably was. I still continued the search; however, it was no longer an obsession. Finally, I stopped looking, and went on with my life."

"Twelve years is a long time. You must have been very young when Alison was captured."

"I was nineteen, and she was fourteen."

"What about your parents?"

"My mother died when Alison was ten, and my father died the year following her abduction."

"After you gave up your search, what did you do?"

"I became a bounty hunter, then a U.S. Marshal."

"You've led a very exciting life."

"Not nearly as exciting as you think. But this is my last assignment. I have a ranch outside Abilene. My uncle is living there, and taking care of it for me. Once this mission is over, I plan to retire my gun. But enough talk about me. What about you? Do you plan to marry Bill Lawson?"

"Why do you ask that?"

"Wrightman said you two are . . . a couple, so to speak. When I interrupted you two earlier this evening, you weren't exactly shaking hands." As the memory of Jodie in Lawson's arms flashed across his mind, it sparked a feeling of jealousy. The emotion was a little startling; after all, he barely knew Miss Walker.

"I don't know if I'm going to marry Bill," she replied honestly.

"Why is that?"

"I'm just not sure of my feelings."

"How long have you two been courting?"

"Almost two years."

"And you still aren't sure of your feelings?" he asked. "You know, that should tell you something."

"Oh? What does that mean?"

"If you aren't in love with him by now, then you'll never be in love with him."

"I don't believe in rushing into something as important as marriage." She regarded him somewhat peevishly. "I don't want to discuss Bill, or my feelings for him. My personal life is just that—personal."

"Whatever you say, Deputy Walker. I'm not here to give you advice on matters of the heart, but I do hope you'll take my advice concerning this mission. If I give an order, I want you to obey it."

"I have no argument with that," she replied. "As long as you're not ordering me around just because I'm a woman. I expect you to treat me as though I were a man."

"You've got to be kidding me."

"You either treat me as an equal, or we'll split up right here and go our separate ways."

He knew she meant what she said. However, treating her as a man was out of the question. She was undoubtedly skilled, but she was still a woman—and a very beautiful one. But he was not about to let her go on alone, and he replied with an askew smile, "We'll be equal partners, Miss Walker. But you aren't a man, and you can't expect me to treat you like one."

"I just want to be treated with the same respect."

"You have certainly earned my respect, Miss Walker."

She settled for that. "Since we're going to be riding together, you might as well call me Jodie."

"And I'm Cade."

She lay back on her bedroll, pulled up the top blanket, and murmured, "Goodnight, Cade. Don't forget to wake me up so I can take the second watch."

"Don't worry. I don't intend to lose a whole night's sleep. After all, we're equal partners."

She turned her back to him. She still found his attitude nettlesome, and if she didn't need an extra gun, she'd get on her horse and leave right now. She set her jaw firmly; she'd simply have to be tolerant. Just because they were partners didn't mean she had to like him!

* * *

Jodie took the second watch, but waking Cade wasn't necessary, for he was up before morning's light. They ate a quick breakfast, and were on the trail before the sun cleared the horizon.

The weather was warm, but not uncomfortably so. Summer was still weeks away, and the spring temperature was pleasant. They rode south toward the Rio Grande, maintaining a good pace, but not an arduous one. Tiring their horses could prove a fatal mistake, for their lives could very well depend on the animals' speed. Renegade Apaches often crossed the river to plunder and sometimes to murder in the process. Their possible presence was a real threat, and Cade, as well as Jodie, didn't take the possibility lightly.

Afternoon shadows were falling across the landscape when up ahead a flock of circling vultures caught their attention. They couldn't see what lay below the hovering predators, for a small rise stood between them and the birds' discovery. Drawing their rifles, they ascended the hill with caution, reined in, and looked down at the vultures' find. They saw a stagecoach, its horses gone, except for one that lay dead in its harness. Two bodies were sprawled beside the coach, and inside a man's body lay on the seat, his head hanging lifelessly out the open door.

"Apaches?" Jodie gasped, but it was more a statement than a question.

"Probably," Cade replied. They rode down the hill, dismounted, and checked the bodies. The three men were dead. Looking over the area, Cade recognized the tracks left behind. "It was Apaches, all right," he said. "About a dozen of them."

"Why do you suppose they killed these men? Why didn't they just take the horses and weapons and go?"

"I imagine the men fought back. If they had surrendered, the Apaches might have let them live, but there's no way to know for sure." He watched her closely, looking for a feminine reaction. The death infested area was enough to make a lot of women faint, or at least lose their composure. But Jodie remained poised.

Inwardly, however, she was somewhat shaken. She was too compassionate not to feel something for these men who had died. Also, knowing renegade Apaches were in the vicinity was enough to put anyone on edge. But she didn't consider turning around and going home. She had a job to do; she knew it was dangerous, but she was willing to take her chances.

"There's a way station about five miles from here," Cade said. "This coach would have stopped there to change teams. We'll let the people there know what happened. They can notify the army. I'll put the bodies inside the coach so they'll be safe from the vultures until someone can come for them."

"I'll help you," Jodie offered.

"Thanks, but I can manage." His admiration grew, for he knew she would have helped without a moment's hesitation. He moved to the first body, but before he could heft it over his shoulder, Jodie was there, ready to lift the man's legs.

She eyed him unwaveringly. "If I were a man, you would have accepted my offer. I don't want special treatment. What do I have to say or do to get that through your head?"

"My mother always said I was thick-headed."

"So are mules," she mumbled. "Let's get these bodies sheltered, then get to that way station. We're wasting time."

He lifted the dead man's shoulders, and Jodie picked up the legs. As they carried the body to the stage, Cade's respect for Jodie deepened considerably.

* * *

The way station was a one-story, adobe structure. A large corral, filled with horses, was nearby. There was also a log-constructed livery. Outbuildings were located behind the house, and a distance behind them were penned pigs. Chickens, running free, clucked loudly as Jodie's and Cade's horses sent them scrambling in different directions.

Two hounds had been resting on the front stoop, but they now stood their ground and barked rapidly. Their owner was alerted, and he came outside carrying a rifle. The man, middle-aged, was short and overweight. He silenced the dogs with a firm command, then invited his guests inside.

Cade and Jodie took their rifles with them. With a band of hostile Apaches in the vicinity, they weren't about to leave their weapons behind.

A long table built to serve stagecoach passengers and employees filled the center of the front room. The man propped his rifle beside the door, then gestured for Jodie and Cade to be seated. His wife quickly served coffee and hot biscuits dripping with honey. Like her husband, she was short and plump.

Over the simple fare, Cade told the couple about finding the coach and its dead occupants.

The man sighed heavily. "I was afraid somethin' like that happened. It ain't like the stage to be this late. You know, I heard rumors that a band of Apaches was comin' across the border, stealin' and a-murderin'. The damned heathens! If the army finds 'em, they'll hang 'em for sure. It's a sight I'd like to see. By the way, I reckon we oughta introduce ourselves. My name's Hector Graham, and this-here is my wife, Madeline."

"I'm Marshal Brandon," Cade returned. "I was here about five years ago, but back then this place was owned by a man named Browning." He was about to introduce Jodie, but she beat him to it.

"I'm Deputy Walker from Crystal Creek."

Hector's eyes widened with surprise, and his wife actually gasped aloud. "You know," Hector began, "I heard tell that Crystal Creek had a woman deputy, but I didn't believe it, not for a moment."

"Well, it's true," Jodie replied, her tone defensive.

Graham cackled heartily. "I reckon I've seen everything now. Why, ma'am, you're just a scrawny little gal. You ain't got no business wearin' a badge."

"Hector!" Madeline said sharply. "Miss Walker's life is none of your business." She reached across the table and patted Jodie's hand. "Don't you pay no mind to him. There ain't no law that says a woman can't wear a badge if she's got a mind to."

"Well, I reckon I'll go notify the army about the stage-coach ambush," Hector said, pushing back his chair.

"Do you want me to ride with you?" Cade asked.

"Naw, that won't be necessary. The fort's only a couple of hours from here. 'Sides, I reckon you have business of your own to tend to."

Cade described the men he and Jodie were hunting, and asked Hector if he had seen them. He said that he hadn't. "If you don't mind," Cade continued, "we'll stay here awhile, water our horses, then be on our way."

"Make yourselves at home," Hector replied, heading for the door. As he reached for his rifle, the hounds, still on the stoop, began barking viciously. He quickly opened the door and looked outside. "My God!" he groaned. He called the dogs inside, then closed and bolted the door. Turning an anxious gaze to Cade, he exclaimed, "Apaches! At least a dozen or more!"

The windows were hastily shuttered. Three windows, each with a shutter sporting a hole designed to fit a rifle's barrel, faced the front. Cade and Hector each took a defensive position behind a window, as did Jodie.

Again, Jodie's willingness impressed Cade. She had moved to a window as though holding off Apaches was a common occurrence, and no reason to get overly excited.

The Indians whooped loudly, but they didn't charge the way station; instead, they opened fire from a safe distance. The rapid shots startled Jodie's Appaloosa and Cade's stallion. The horses whinnied, stamped the ground with their front hooves, then, breaking free from the hitching rail, they galloped away with their reins dangling in the wind.

The Apaches ceased their firing, and raced after the runaway horses.

Opening his window, Hector said with relief, "Thank God, they was only after your horses. I was afraid we was dead, for sure."

Jodie opened her shutter with a solid bang, for she was angry about losing her horse. "Mr. Graham," she said, "I need to borrow one of your horses and a saddle. I'm going after my Appaloosa."

"Ma'am, you don't want to do that! Why, them Apaches will kill you!"

"Hector's right," Madeline put in. "Honey, your can't risk your life for a horse." She turned to Cade. "Marshal, you must stop her."

He grinned. "I'd probably find it easier to stop a tornado."

Jodie glared at him. As usual, she had a feeling he was finding her amusing. "Are you coming with me?" she asked. "Or do you intend to just stand there and grin like this is some kind of joke?"

"I don't consider having my horse stolen a joke. But I do wonder if you know what you're doing. I mean, there are at least a dozen Apaches, and only two of us."

"I can count, Marshal!"

He turned to Graham. "It seems Miss Walker has made up her mind. Can you loan us two horses and saddles?"

"Yeah, I can spare 'em, but I don't like it! I got a feelin' I ain't ever gonna see you two or them horses again. You two are ridin' into certain death."

Cade didn't say anything, but he knew Hector's prediction had a good chance of coming true. Nonetheless, he had decided to go after his horse before Jodie had said anything. He had hoped, however, that she would feel otherwise, and would agree to remain. He sighed testily. He should have known better.

Following the Indians' trail was easy; no attempt had been made to cover their tracks. Cade and Jodie kept a safe distance between themselves and the Apaches, for they had decided not to make their move until the band stopped for the night. They hoped to sneak into camp and steal back their horses.

At dusk, they trailed the Apaches across the Rio Grande and into Mexico. The renegades were apparently heading back to the Sierra Mountains.

The Indians traveled two more hours before making camp. Cade and Jodie spotted smoke from their fire, and stopped a short distance away. Vegetation surrounded the camping area, making it possible for Jodie and Cade to advance stealthily on foot. Hidden by night and foliage, they inspected the Indians' camp. The Apaches' horses were grouped close by, and were guarded by three sentries. The Appaloosa and Cade's stallion, still saddled, were with the other horses.

Cade looked on as the Apaches began passing around bottles of whiskey. "We're in luck," he whispered to Jodie. "They've stolen liquor. In a couple of hours, they'll be drunk. That's when we'll sneak in and get our horses."

"But what about the guards?"

At that moment, a warrior handed a bottle to the sentries.

"Does that answer your question?" Cade asked.

She smiled.

"Let's get back to our horses. We can come back when they've had time to pass out from too much whiskey."

They moved furtively back through the foliage. When they reached their borrowed horses, Cade unpacked the bread and cheese that Madeline had insisted they take along. Jodie grabbed a canteen, and finding a grassy area beneath a cottonwood, they sat down and did justice to the fare.

"When we go back," Cade began, as soon as they had finished eating, "I want you to stay in the shrubbery and cover me. I'll slip into camp and get the horses."

She regarded him suspiciously, for she had a feeling he was trying to minimize her part in this. He probably preferred to make himself an open target, while keeping her hidden in the bushes. Well, she wasn't entirely against his plan; one of them had to stay behind and cover the other. But she thought the roles should be reversed.

"Cade, is your horse skittish around people it doesn't know very well?"

"Most of the time, he's as friendly as a puppy."

"Well, my Appaloosa isn't friendly. Even though you aren't exactly a stranger, he's still liable to balk. If he does, he'll rouse the whole herd, along with the Apaches. Our best chance is to take back our horses without detection. Therefore, I'll sneak in and you can cover me."

"I don't want you taking that kind of risk."

"Stop it!" she muttered angrily. "Stop treating me like a helpless female! Your gallantry is admirable, but under these circumstances, it's inappropriate."

He knew she was right; if her horse was skittish, then she should be the one to go after it. But knowing she was right didn't make it any easier for Cade. She might not be helpless, but she was still a woman, and he hated putting her life in jeopardy.

"Well?" she persisted. "Are you too stubborn to admit I'm right?"

"No," he conceded with a sigh. "I know you're right. But you might try thinking about someone other than yourself for a change. How do you think this makes me feel?"

Her eyes flashed defiantly. "Is your male pride wounded?"

"You know, I get the feeling you harbor a lot of bitterness."

"Maybe you're right," she returned, bounding to her feet. She went to her horse, removed a blanket, and spread it on the ground. "I'm going to get some rest. Wake me when those Apaches have had time to get drunk."

She lay down and turned her back to Cade. His accusation had hit a sensitive chord deep inside her. She did feel bitterness; it had taken root when she was still a child. Implanted deeply, her bitterness had grown with the years. But she didn't want to think about that; the cause behind it was still too painful.

"Cade?" she murmured, her back still turned. "Do I go after the horses or not?"

"I can be practical, Jodie," he said quietly. "I'll cover you."

A faint smile touched her lips; she was beginning to like Cade Brandon.

Chapter Four

Jodie didn't think she'd actually fall asleep, but she drifted off and was awakened by Cade's hand on her shoulder.

"It's time," he said softly.

She turned over, for her back was facing him. He was kneeling, and his face was mere inches above hers. She looked up into his dark blue eyes, and, for a moment, his piercing gaze held her mesmerized. An urge to lace her arms about his neck and press her lips to his struck with a startling force. However, it jolted her back to her senses. Although she was beginning to like Cade Brandon, she didn't intend to let her feelings go any further than that. She got up quickly.

"I'm ready," she said, her even tone belying the desire his proximity had stirred.

They got their rifles, and moving quietly through the thick foliage, made their way back to the Apaches' camp. They covered the last few feet on their hands and knees, parted a full-branched bush, and peered cautiously at the

Indians. Most of them were sound asleep, but a few were still guzzling what was left of the whiskey. Too inebriated to stay on their feet, they were lying on their backs, holding the bottles over their mouths; most of the liquor was missing its target and dripping down onto their faces.

Cade turned to Jodie. "We could wait until they're all asleep."

"You know that more Apaches are liable to show up. We can't wait any longer. Will you please stop trying to protect me?"

"Damn it, Jodie!" he uttered quietly. "You might as well tell me to stop being a man."

She frowned impatiently. "You're mother was right—you are thick-headed."

"One of these days . . ."

"One of these days, what?"

"One day, Jodie, the right man's gonna come along, and when he does? Well, he's going to make you damned glad he's a man."

"And I suppose you think you're that man."

"Not me," he replied, a teasing twinkle in his eyes. "I've got too many plans for the future, and taking time to awaken your passion isn't one of them."

"My passion doesn't need awakening!" she remarked petulantly.

"You and Lawson must be more involved than I thought," he said wryly.

She blushed; she couldn't help it. "That's not what I meant. And this conversation has gone too far. I was just beginning to like you, Cade Brandon, but I was mistaken. My first impression of you was right—you're intolerable, and if I didn't need your help, I'd leave you right here." She gestured toward the grouped horses. "I'm going to circle around, then slip up to the herd. I hope I can depend on you to cover me."

"With my life," he replied.

She felt he was finding her amusing; her temper rose, but she suppressed it and moved away furtively. The area was completely surrounded by vegetation, and stepping soundlessly, Jodie made her way through bushes and past cottonwoods and mesquite trees. Praying the horses would remain calm, she crept into the small herd. Two sentries, lying side by side, were passed out on the ground, an empty whiskey bottle between them. Jodie couldn't see the third sentry; she hoped wherever he was, he was also sound asleep.

Cade's stallion and the Appaloosa were in the center of the herd, and Jodie had to brush past Apache ponies to reach them. Some nervous whinnies greeted her presence, but, for the most part, the horses stayed calm.

When she reached the stallion and her Appaloosa, she sheathed her Winchester, for she needed both hands to guide the horses back through the herd. She took their reins, turned, and found the third sentry standing in her way. He was inebriated, and swayed drunkenly on his feet. But the liquor he had consumed didn't cloud his vision, and the unexpected sight of a woman breathed life into his loins. He had foolishly left his rifle behind, but he carried a knife, and he quickly unsheathed it.

Jodie backed closer to the Appaloosa. She hoped if Cade could see her and the warrior, he wouldn't fire, for the shot would wake the entire camp. She eased next to the Appaloosa, and watched as the sentry, his stride unsteady, advanced one awkward step at a time.

Her hand slid stealthily up the Appaloosa's side and to the bullwhip still looped about the saddle horn. She grasped the whip, then moving with incredible speed, she stepped away from the horse, snapped the lash and sent it snaking about the warrior's ankles. She jerked back her whip hand, and the lash tightened, causing the sentry to fall heavily to the ground. Grabbing her rifle, she dashed to the warrior; he lay sprawled, his knife still in his hand.

Jodie's foot came down hard on the man's hand; then, before he could yell for help, she hit him in the head with the rifle's butt. The powerful blow knocked him unconscious.

She hurried back to the horses, put away her bullwhip and rifle, grabbed the reins, and started back through the herd. She had taken only a couple of steps when Cade showed up, holding a bowie knife.

He grinned somewhat hesitantly, and toyed with the knife as though he were trying to figure out its purpose. Actually, Jodie's competence had taken him off guard. He slipped the knife into his belt, and murmured an explanation. "A rifle shot would have brought a dozen Apaches to deal with instead of just one."

"Thanks for trying to help, but you shouldn't have left your post. I had the situation under control. Come on; let's get out of here."

Taking the reins to his stallion, he followed behind her and the Appaloosa. A hint of anger shone in his eyes—Jodie Walker was about as warm as an iceberg!

They rode throughout the remainder of the night, and reached the way station at midday. The Grahams were surprised to find that Cade and Jodie were not only alive and well, but had actually stolen back their horses.

As Madeline prepared lunch, Cade explained why their quest had been a success. There was admiration in his tone as he recounted Jodie's confrontation with the sentry. He was proud of the way she had handled herself. It wasn't her skills that aggravated him; it was her temperament.

Madeline put lunch on the table, and as the four of them sat down to eat, Hector suddenly exclaimed, "Those men you're lookin' for was here! They stopped early this mornin', paid for breakfast, then went on their way."

"Did they say where they were headed?" Cade asked, filling his plate.

"Nope, they didn't," Hector replied. "They got a third man with 'em. They called him 'Dirk.'"

"Bradley's son," Cade remarked. "Did he seem to be traveling with them willingly?"

"What do you mean by that?"

"They might have kidnapped him."

Hector shook his head, swallowed a mouthful of food, then said, "I didn't get the feelin' that he was bein' held against his will. The three of 'em seemed real chummy."

Cade turned to Jodie. "Why do you suppose Dirk's riding with murderers?"

"I don't know. Maybe he's rebelling against his father. Emmett has two sons. Dirk is the younger. His older brother, Garth, has always been his father's favorite. But then Garth is a replica of Emmett. I think Dirk's jealous of Garth, and does things like this to get his father's attention."

"That seems awfully childish. How old is Dirk?"

"My age," she murmured.

"And how old is that?"

"Twenty-three," she replied, hoping no one would remark that by now she should be married.

It wasn't to be, for Hector said heartily, "By the time Madeline was your age, we had three younguns. 'Course, they're all grown and married. How come some man ain't claimed you yet?"

"Hector!" His wife chastised him. "Can't you see you're embarrassing Miss Walker? Now, you just stop that kind of teasing."

"That's all right," Jodie said. "I'm not embarrassed. However, I don't intend to be claimed. I'm not a piece of property."

"I didn't mean it like that," Hector said apologetically.

Cade didn't say anything, but his earlier suspicion that

Jodie harbored a lot of bitterness deepened. He wondered what was behind the pain she tried so hard to conceal.

"Dirk often visits a Mexican town called Villa de Lazar," Jodie said, steering the conversation away from marriage. "It's not far from the border." She spoke to Cade. "I think we should go there."

"I'm familiar with the town. It's an outlaw's paradise. That's where most men go when they're on the run."

"I know that town too," Hector intervened. "And it's no place for a lady."

Jodie was through eating; she stood, and said, "I'm not going there as a lady; I'm going as a deputy." Her gaze went to Cade. "Are you ready?"

He quickly washed down a mouthful of food, got to his feet, and mumbled, "A man could lose weight keeping up with you."

She let his remark pass, and said to Madeline, "We'll need to buy a few supplies."

"I'll get you what you need."

"Add a bottle of whiskey to that list," Cade said. He turned to Jodie. "I enjoy a drink every now and then."

"I have no problem with that," she replied. She left with Madeline to get the supplies.

Hector chuckled. "That little gal's somethin' else."

"Yes, she is," Cade agreed thoughtfully, his eyes following Jodie. "I've never met anyone like her." He turned back to Hector. "I'd like to buy a pack mule if you can spare one."

"Sure," he replied. "I got an extra mule I can sell ya."

Villa de Lazar was a six-hour ride from the way station. Cade and Jodie expected to reach the town at dusk. They crossed the Rio Grande, and rode back into Mexico. They traveled three more hours, then stopped to water the horses and the mule. As Cade gave the animals water from a canteen, Jodie moved to a small boulder and sat down. The terrain was desert-like, and the scenery consisted mostly of sage brush and intermittent mesquite trees. Scattered puffs of clouds skimmed across the open sky, and the sun's rays bathed the land with dazzling light.

Jodie stared vacantly into the distance, her thoughts filled with the job that lay ahead. In a few hours she would confront the men who had murdered her father. Now that she was so near her goal, she began to feel nervous and her stomach felt as though it were tied in knots. These men were undoubtedly skilled, and arresting them would be extremely dangerous. A confrontation was imminent, for she couldn't imagine them surrendering their guns to return to Crystal Creek and face a hangman's noose.

Cade came to the boulder and sat beside her. "You seem deep in thought. Is something bothering you?"

She almost told him that she was frightened, but she considered that a weakness, and couldn't bring herself to admit to it. "Nothing's bothering me," she murmured.

Cade wasn't convinced, but he decided not to press her. "Do you mind telling me about the day your father was killed? I had intended to ask the mayor about it, but Bradley showed up before I had the chance."

"He was killed at night. I was at home. Jonas, who is also a deputy, was at the office with Papa that night. A customer from the Silver Dollar came to the office and told Papa there was trouble at the saloon. Papa didn't take Jonas with him; I'm not sure why. The trouble started over a poker game. One of the men we're looking for was accused of cheating. By the time Papa got to the saloon, the man had viciously beaten his accuser as the other man held the customers at gunpoint. Papa told the men they were under arrest. They handed over their pistols, but the half-breed had a derringer hidden in his boot. As Papa was about to escort them out, he drew the derringer and shot him. The men retrieved their weapons and began

shooting wildly, which sent everyone ducking for cover.
Papa wasn't dead, so on their way out the door, they put
two bullets in his head.''

"No one in the saloon did anything to stop them?"

"It was a weeknight, and the saloon wasn't very crowded.
The customers were too concerned with saving their own
lives to help save Papa's.''

"The mayor said your father was a fine sheriff. I'm surprised that he let the half-breed get the drop on him."

"So am I," she admitted. "He made a mistake, and it
cost him his life.''

"That's why a sheriff's job is very dangerous. That goes
for a deputy's job too." He gazed deeply into her eyes.
"Jodie, why do you insist on putting your life in jeopardy?
You have so much to live for. Why do you want to risk your
life this way?"

"Why do you risk yours?" she returned. "A U.S. Marshal's job is even more dangerous than a sheriff's, or a
deputy's."

"It's different for a man."

"Why is that?" she asked sharply, bolting to her feet. As
she glowered down at him, she suddenly became aware
of an intruder. Involved, they had missed spotting the
slithering rattler that had climbed the boulder. It was
coiled and ready to strike.

Cade heard the ominous rattle simultaneously with
Jodie's warning. He leapt from the boulder, but the snake
was faster. It sank its venomous fangs into Cade's hand.
Drawing his pistol, he shot the rattler; the powerful impact
sent the snake flying into the air. It dropped back onto
the boulder and slid lifelessly to the ground.

Taking his knife, Cade quickly made an incision across
the bite; then he sucked out the poison, spitting it onto
the ground. "Jodie, get that bottle of whiskey."

She hurried to the pack mule and got the bottle.

"Pour it over the bite," Cade told her.

She uncapped the bottle, took Cade's hand, and poured a large portion over the two punctures.

"We'll have to camp here," he said. "I'll be feverish for awhile. By tomorrow morning, I should be all right." Taking note of Jodie's pale face, and the worry in her eyes, he added gently, "I won't die."

"I know most people don't die from a rattler's bite, but it can be pretty bad."

"I know," he replied.

"I'll fix you a bed," she said, leaving to get his blankets. Her heart was beating rapidly, for she feared for Cade's life. She spread out his bedroll, then went in search of branches. It took several trips, for the area was mostly barren. Finally, she located enough kindling to make a fire that would burn for hours.

By the time she had coffee brewing, and a can of stew warming, Cade was running a fever. She had watered down the stew to make broth. She dipped a small helping into a dish, sat beside Cade's bed, and told him that he should try to eat.

He reached for the dish, but the fever had weakened him considerably. The simple feat of feeding himself seemed too strenuous.

Jodie fed him, and he accepted a couple of mouthfuls before brushing her hand aside. He hated being helpless, and he had no patience with his condition. He had ridden with Jodie to take care of her, and here she was taking care of him. It was a terrible blow to his pride.

She could sense his feelings, and she didn't insist that he try to eat more. She bathed his face with a wet cloth, and stayed beside him until he fell asleep. She then ate dinner and drank a cup of coffee.

Dusk gave way to full night, and Jodie spread her blankets close to the fire. But the blankets were for comfort, for she didn't intend to fall asleep; she needed to stay awake in case Cade's condition worsened. Also, they were in unsafe territory, and keeping a vigil was necessary.

Clouds rolled in from the west, and the land was shrouded in pitch black darkness. Although the plains were open, Jodie couldn't see beyond the glow of the fire. If an enemy approached, she wouldn't see him until he was upon her. She knew she had to rely on the horses for an advance warning.

The night remained quiet except for a distant coyote's periodic howl. Finally, the howling ceased, and an eerie silence ensued.

Jodie checked on Cade, and found that he was now sleeping peacefully. She touched his forehead; his fever had cooled a little. As she bathed his brow, the light from the fire shone on his face. She allowed herself the privilege of secretly admiring him. He was indeed attractive, and she found herself tracing his handsome features with her fingertips. The caress was sensual, and when she touched his lips, she was again struck with a desire to kiss him.

The Appaloosa, along with the stallion, suddenly whinnied softly. Bounding to her feet, Jodie turned a careful eye to her horse; it snorted, whinnied again, and pricked its ears.

She quickly got her rifle, built up the fire, then awakened Cade. "Can you stand?" she asked.

"I think so," he murmured. "What's wrong?"

"The horses are skittish. It might not be anything more dangerous than a coyote. But I think we should take cover behind the boulder."

He managed to get to his feet, pick up his rifle, and place an arm about Jodie's shoulder. She helped him to the boulder, then returned to the bedrolls, and molded the blankets to look as though someone were sleeping in them. Pressed for time, she did not do a very good job, but it would have to do. She hurried back to Cade; he was peeking over the boulder, his rifle cocked and ready to fire. His fever was breaking, causing perspiration to form heavily on his brow and drip into his eyes. He had to keep brushing away the sweat in order to see.

The area was well-lighted, for the fire was burning brightly. An intruder would make an easy target.

Jodie knelt beside Cade, cocked her own weapon, and waited for the unknown. The Appaloosa and the stallion were visibly nervous, and Jodie was certain that the predator was now very close.

An Apache warrior emerged from the darkness and into the light of the fire with the quickness and stealth of a ghost. He carried a rifle, and he opened fire, sending bullets into the two bedrolls.

Jodie, moving so fast that she took Cade by surprise, leapt to her feet and called out a warning to the Apache, "Drop your gun!"

That he had been tricked barely had time to register before he turned his rifle in Jodie's direction.

He left her no choice but to shoot first, and as he spun toward her, she pulled the trigger and fired. Her shot was accurate, and the warrior fell to the ground, his body barely missing the fire's leaping flames.

She moved quickly to see if he was still alive. He was, but the wound was grave. She recognized the warrior; he was the sentry she had confronted at the Apaches' camp.

Cade came to her side and looked down at the Indian. "Isn't he the same one . . . ?"

"Yes, he is," she cut in. "He's still alive. I wonder if there's a doctor in Villa de Lazar."

"Even if there is, he wouldn't tend to an Apache."

At that moment, the pounding of several horses vibrated the earth, their beating hoofs carrying through the quiet night like a multitude of drums. The sounds came from every direction; the camp was being surrounded.

Jodie's heart seemed to stand still. "My God!" she cried. "The other Apaches are with him!" She knew hiding behind the boulder wouldn't save them this time. But she wasn't about to give up without a fight, and grasping Cade's arm, she said quickly, "We have to take cover!"

But it was too late, for the riders suddenly broke through the darkness. They had the small area completely surrounded.

Jodie and Cade were confronted by over a dozen rifles bearing down on them.

Chapter Five

As Jodie stared at the intruders, her fear began to ease somewhat, for these men were not Apaches. She and Cade were surrounded by Mexicans. The man in charge ordered his men to lower their weapons; then he and two others dismounted and came forward. The leader cast the wounded Apache a look of contempt, then turned his gaze back to Jodie and Cade. He appeared to be in his early fifties; tall, swarthy, and distinguished-looking.

"Hello, Antonio," Cade said, shaking the man's hand.

Jodie was taken by surprise. It hadn't occurred to her that Cade and this man might know each other.

Antonio gestured toward the Apache. "He is still alive, amigo. Maybe your aim is not as good as it used to be, sí?"

"My aim's still deadly. I didn't shoot him." He indicated Jodie, and continued with a note of admiration, "She shot him."

Antonio's eyes traveled boldly over Jodie; her riding attire tastefully defined her graceful frame. He then gazed into her face. His scrutiny was intense, and Jodie began to feel as though he were measuring her worth.

"Jodie," Cade began, "this is Antonio Morelos. He has a hacienda not far from here." He said to Morelos, "I'd like you to meet Deputy Walker from Crystal Creek." A hint of amusement shone in Brandon's eyes as he awaited his friend's response.

Antonio was flabbergasted. "You are a deputy?" he asked Jodie, as though he had heard the impossible.

She frowned testily. "Yes, I'm a deputy," she replied, her tone defensive.

The patron, along with the vaqueros who spoke English, guffawed heartily. Between chuckles, the vaqueros translated for the others, adding even more guffaws.

Jodie was infuriated.

"Forgive me and my vaqueros," Antonio apologized, quelling his laughter. "But we were taken by surprise."

Jodie turned to Cade, and was even more enraged to find that he was smiling. Apparently, he was amused at her expense!

Cade was indeed amused, but by Antonio, not at Jodie. If the man knew how competent she was, he wouldn't be so quick to laugh. But Cade's smile faded suddenly as he wiped a hand across his sweat-laden brow. He was still weak and somewhat feverish.

Antonio, becoming aware of Brandon's condition, asked, "You are not well, amigo?"

"I was bitten by a rattler," Cade replied. "I got most of the poison out, but I'm still a little weak."

Antonio was immediately concerned. "You must stay the night at my home."

"Thanks, but . . ."

"I will not take 'no' for an answer," he insisted. Turning to a vaquero who was standing beside him, he waved a terse hand toward the wounded Apache, and ordered gruffly, "Get rid of that pile of dung!"

The vaquero drew his knife; he intended to cut the Apache's throat.

"Wait!" Jodie cried. "What do you think you're doing?"

The vaquero hesitated, and turned to the patron.

"The Apache must die!" Antonio said to Jodie, his voice harsh. But he suddenly shrugged his shoulders as though the situation wasn't very important. "He is dying anyhow. This way, he will soon be out of his misery."

The Apache understood English, and he listened passively as the patron ordered his immediate death.

"You have no right to decide that this man should die," Jodie argued. "I won't let you kill him!"

Antonio chuckled. "You are a spitfire, sí?"

"Don't patronize me, Mr. Morelos. I shot the Apache; he's my prisoner, and I won't let you murder him."

"It will not be murder, but a mercy. He is probably in a lot of pain."

"You don't care if he's in pain. You want to kill him because he's an Apache. If he wasn't wounded you'd still kill him!"

"The Apaches are Mexico's enemies. They plunder, rape, and murder. Any Apache who crosses my path is a dead Apache. We picked up this Indian's tracks and followed him here. We followed him to kill him, señorita." Antonio's patience had wavered; he was not accustomed to explaining himself to anyone, much less a woman. He gestured for the vaquero to carry out his orders.

Jodie still carried her rifle, and she aimed it at Antonio. "I meant what I said."

Morelos's mouth dropped open. No woman had ever pointed a gun at him. His vaqueros reached for their weapons.

Cade placed a firm hand on the barrel of Jodie's rifle, and lowered it so that it was aimed at the ground. He regarded her sternly. "You might be willing to risk our lives for an Apache's, but I'm not." He spoke to Antonio,

"Like you said, the Apache's dying anyhow. So why don't you pacify the lady and leave him be?"

"I don't need to be pacified!" Jodie spat.

Cade gritted his teeth. "For once, will you please control that temper of yours?"

Antonio suddenly laughed gustily. "Amigo, you need to take the señorita over your knee and show her who is boss."

Cade, his blue eyes smoldering, mumbled, "Someday, I just might do that!"

Jodie didn't say anything, for Antonio and his men would undoubtedly find her retort amusing!

Morelos turned to Jodie, bowed mockingly from the waist, and said, "Very well, señorita. I will respect your wishes. The Indian will be left to his fate."

The Apache, still listening, breathed a sigh of relief. However, he knew his survival was unlikely. His enemies would certainly take his pony, and he was too gravely wounded to travel on foot. He could only hope that his brother would come looking for him. But even that possibility didn't give him much hope, for he would probably be dead by the time his brother got here. His thoughts turned to the white woman; if he survived, he would owe his life to her. He had come here to kill her, for she had injured his pride. Not only had she used a whip on him, but she had also knocked him unconscious. But he was now in her debt. He hoped someday their paths would cross again so that he might repay her somehow.

Jodie quickly broke camp as Cade gathered up her bedroll and his. The blankets were soon on the horses, the campfire was smothered, and they were ready to leave.

Jodie mounted her Appaloosa, and watched as Cade went to his horse and swung into the saddle. He didn't look well, and she wondered if he was about to take a turn for the worse.

"Jodie," he began softly, so they wouldn't be overheard.

"I have some advice, and you had better take it. Don't threaten men like Antonio Morelos. They don't take kindly to threats."

"Really?" she quipped. "Well, let me give you some advice. Don't ever order me; ask me!"

"You know, Antonio was right. A sound spanking is just what you need."

"Try it, and you'll be plucking buckshot out of the seat of your pants for days!"

Antonio was anxious to leave, and he motioned for Jodie and Cade to join him. They rode to his side, and with the vaqueros following, they galloped away from camp. Jodie took one last glance at the Apache; he was lying motionless and she wondered if he was dead. That she had most likely taken another's life made her feel sick inside. But she had shot in self-defense. This land was violent, and so was her job. She didn't like it, but she could handle it.

The darkness of night shadowed Antonio's hacienda, preventing Jodie from seeing it clearly. But the night didn't completely conceal its grandness, and she was impressed as they rode up to the hitching rail that overlooked an immaculate lawn. A path led to a veranda that ran the full length of the white adobe house. The two-story structure had many windows, plus a lofty terrace bordered by an intricate iron railing. Antonio Morelos was evidently a wealthy landowner.

Antonio and his guests dismounted, leaving their horses in the vaqueros' care. As they approached the front door, it was suddenly opened, and the light from inside the house silhouetted the lovely woman standing in the open portal.

"Pápa!" she exclaimed. "I was beginning to worry. I expected you home before now."

That she spoke English to Antonio surprised Jodie. The woman's accent was obviously Mexican.

Before Antonio could explain his tardiness, the woman recognized Cade. Smiling radiantly, she threw herself into his arms, and embraced him enthusiastically.

"Cade, I am so happy to see you!" she cried, clinging as though she never intended to let him go.

Jodie experienced a pang of jealousy; it arrived without warning and took her totally by surprise. She forcefully repressed the feeling. Why should she care that this woman was in Cade's arms? He was nothing more to Jodie than a fellow law officer.

"Hello, Lucinda," Cade murmured, gently disentangling himself from her clutches.

"Miss Walker," Antonio said, "this is my daughter, Lucinda."

The young woman looked at Jodie for the first time, her gaze that of a rival's.

Jodie read her look and was tempted to blurt out that if she wanted Cade, she was welcome to him. But, instead, she honored the amenities and politely murmured hello.

Lucinda did likewise, but her heart was overflowing with jealousy. She had known Cade Brandon for years, and never in that time had he brought a woman to her father's home. She was worried that Miss Walker might be someone very special to Cade.

Antonio and his daughter led their guests inside. The moment Lucinda learned that Cade was ill, she quickly ushered him upstairs to the east bedroom. Antonio summoned his housekeeper, and sent her to help Lucinda tend to Cade. He then showed Jodie into the parlor.

The spacious room was grandly decorated. Expensive paintings adorned the walls, the furniture was plush, and floor-length curtains draped the windows. The hardwood floor was highly polished, and a colorful woven rug covered the center of the room.

As Jodie sat on the sofa, Antonio stepped to his well-supplied liquor cabinet and poured himself a snifter of brandy and a sherry for his guest. Joining her on the sofa, he handed her the drink.

"Do you mind telling me why you and Señor Brandon are in Mexico?"

She didn't mind, and told him their reason for being there.

"I think the men you seek are in Villa de Lazar," he said. "I was there earlier today. There were three hombres at the cantina who sound like the ones you are looking for."

"Did you speak to them?"

"No, señorita. But I did overhear the one with red hair tell the others that they should leave town in the morning."

"Darn!" she mumbled. "They'll be gone before Cade and I can get there."

"I am sorry, señorita. But if my vaqueros and I should come across them again, I will hold them, and send a wire to Crystal Creek."

"Thank you," she replied. "But I don't plan to return home without finding them."

He was surprised. "You cannot mean that. Mexico is vast, señorita; they could hide here for years. You may never find them."

"I don't think they'll stay here for years. Especially not Dirk."

Antonio shook his head with wonder. "You are very determined. But I think you are also very foolish, señorita."

Her eyes flashed. "Why do you say that?"

"A woman as beautiful as you should spend her time making some man very happy, not chasing after murderers. You do an injustice to yourself, and to the man you would love."

Jodie sighed wearily; battling such views about what a woman like her ought to do was becoming tiresome. Sometimes, she wondered if it was worth the effort. She decided that, this time, it was not.

She finished her sherry, then said she would like to retire.

Although Antonio desired her company, he was nonetheless considerate. Showing her upstairs, he escorted her down a long hallway. She asked which room was Cade's, for she wanted to check on his condition.

Antonio knocked softly on Cade's door and received permission to enter. Lucinda and the housekeeper were fussing over their patient, who, in return, was asking them to leave, assuring them that he was perfectly all right.

Although Cade was lying on the bed, he was still fully dressed. The women had encouraged him to get undressed and under the covers, but he was determined to wait until he was alone. He might be weak and a little feverish, but he wasn't incapacitated. His eyes lit up as Jodie came into the room with Antonio. Her presence alone was rejuvenating, for there was an aura of energy and spirit about her that started his own blood flowing. Also, her unpretentious beauty was as refreshing as a cool breeze on a summer's night.

She came to his bedside. "How do you feel?"

"Better," he replied; he almost said that her presence was all the care he needed. But he swallowed back the words, for he wasn't sure if she wanted to hear them; he had encountered a self-constructed barrier about Jodie that he wasn't sure any man could penetrate.

"Antonio saw the men we're looking for at Villa de Lazar," Jodie told Cade. "He said he overheard their plans to leave in the morning. They'll be gone by the time we can get there."

"No, they won't," he said. "We'll leave now." He sat up and swung his legs over the side of the bed. But his head was spinning so crazily that he couldn't get to his feet. The effort caused his brow to break out in a cold sweat.

"You aren't well enough to leave this room, let alone ride to Villa de Lazar," Jodie said firmly.

"You're right," he admitted, albeit reluctantly. He lay back down with a testy sigh, for he had no patience with his condition. He silently damned the rattler and his bad luck.

"Try to get a good night's sleep," Jodie told him. "By tomorrow, you'll feel a lot better."

"We'll leave in the morning," he replied. "At least that way, their trail won't be cold."

Jodie bid him a quick goodnight, and left the room with Antonio.

As he led her down the hall to her own quarters, her thoughts were racing recklessly. She had decided not to wait until morning; she intended to leave tonight. Her father's murderers were within her reach; if she waited until tomorrow they might elude her for days, weeks, or even months. She knew leaving without Cade increased the danger, but she didn't see that as a reason to change her mind. After all, she had started this mission alone, and she might as well end it that way.

Antonio showed her into a bedroom that was decorated in Spanish style. A red spread, which matched the drapes, covered the four-poster bed. Dark furniture with intricate inlays complemented the wall hangings and a multiple-colored rug.

"I think you will be comfortable here, señorita," Antonio said, indicating the room with a wide sweep of his arm. "As soon as a vaquero brings your carpetbag to the house, I will bring it up to you."

She had no intention of remaining here long enough to enjoy the room's comfort. However, she was not about to tell this to Antonio, for he would certainly try to stop her.

"Exactly how far is it to Villa de Lazar?" she asked, sounding vaguely interested.

"About a three-hour ride."

"In which direction?"

"From here, it is straight east. Why do you ask?"

"I was just curious."

"I will see if your bag is here."

"Thank you," she said, as he left the room. As she waited for his return, she paced back and forth. She wondered how difficult it would be to slip away from this hacienda. It might be impossible. Although she was a guest, she wouldn't put it past Antonio to keep her here by force. He would, of course, think he was doing it for her own good.

A light knock soon sounded, and Jodie admitted Antonio, who carried her bag. He placed it on the bed. He said with a chuckle, "The vaquero who delivered your bag said that your Appaloosa is very unfriendly. He said it took three men to unsaddle the beast." He arched his brow questioningly. "It is not the kind of horse a woman would choose."

"I raised him from a colt."

"And like his mistress, he is spirited and unmanageable, sí?"

"Yes, he's spirited, but I have no problem managing him."

"That is because he loves you. Maybe someday, señorita, you will love a man who will tame you as you tamed the Appaloosa. Maybe that man is Señor Brandon?"

"Cade and I are riding together as law officers."

"Then you are not in love with him?"

"Why do you ask?"

He smiled charmingly. "Maybe I hope to be the man who will tame you. I realize I am years older, but I am still young in many ways."

"I'm flattered, Mr. Morelos. However, no man will ever

tame me. He will have to accept me as I am. Now, if you don't mind, I'm terribly tired."

"Forgive me, señorita. I didn't mean to be inconsiderate. I will see you in the morning."

"Goodnight, Mr. Morelos."

"Please call me Antonio."

The moment he left the room, she returned to pacing. Knowing it was still too soon to slip away, she resigned herself to waiting for an least another hour. It was already late; surely by then the hacienda would be shut down for the night.

The housekeeper left the room, and Cade found himself alone with Lucinda. He liked Antonio's daughter, for he had known her since she was a child. That she had a crush on him was evident, but he had hoped in time she would get over it, because he could not return her feelings. His travels often brought him into Mexico, and whenever possible, he stopped at the hacienda to see Antonio. Morelos had befriended him years ago when he was still a bounty hunter.

Lucinda was sitting beside his bed, and she now asked, "The woman riding with you, is she someone very special?"

Cade smiled tenderly. "Yes, Lucinda, I think she is special. But I'm not sure exactly what you mean by 'special.'"

"Are you in love with her?"

"Don't you think that question is a little personal?"

"You are in love with her. I can tell!" Her sullen pout failed to flaw her beauty.

"Lucinda, even if I were in love with her, it shouldn't matter to you."

"But it does! Cade, you know that I have always been in love with you!"

"I'm sorry, honey. But I think of you as a sister."

Tears came to her eyes. "If you will not marry me, I will

have to marry Miguel Huerta. Pápa has already chosen him for me."

"Tell me about Miguel Huerta."

"I do not know much about him. I have never seen him. Pápa and Miguel's pápa do business together. Miguel and his family live in Mexico City. Pápa went there last winter, and the plans were made for me to marry Miguel."

"But arranged marriages are common among your people. You must have realized Antonio would choose your husband. Will you see Miguel before the ceremony?"

"He is supposed to come for a visit. He will be here soon."

"Maybe you two will fall in love."

"Sí!" she spat angrily. "And maybe the sun will fall from the sky!"

"Your father's marriage was arranged, and he and your mother were very happy together. When she died last year, he was devastated."

She nodded solemnly. "Sí, they were very much in love."

"Lucinda, I do hope things work out between you and Miguel. But you must get over your crush on me. My feelings for you could never be more than that of a brother's."

She got up from her chair, leaned over the bed, and taking Cade by surprise, she pressed her lips to his. She tried to turn the kiss into one of passion, but he gently pulled away.

"Goodnight, Lucinda," he said, his tone brooking no opposition.

"I will not give up on you, Cade. Someday I will make you love me. Just wait and see!" With that, she whirled around and left the room.

Chapter Six

Jodie slipped quietly down the stairs and out the front door. The night was still overcast, but as she stepped onto the veranda, the moon peeked out from beneath a cloud, its aureate glow illuminating the large stables located nearby. She hurried in that direction, thinking that at any moment she would probably be discovered. But she didn't encounter anyone between the house and the stables; the hacienda was asleep for the night.

She found the Appaloosa; her saddle, rifle, and bullwhip were stored beside the stall. She saddled the horse, mounted, and left quietly. The bunkhouses and the small adobe homes that housed the married vaqueros were located farther back, and she didn't have to pass them on her way out. She did, however, have to ride past the manor house. She hoped no one was looking out the window. But the structure remained dark, and no voice called out to her.

When she reached open ground, she allowed the spirited Appaloosa to break into a gallop. Now that she was actually on her way to Villa de Lazar, she let herself think about Cade. She had never seen him really angry, but she knew that was about to change, for she didn't doubt that he'd follow her to Villa de Lazar. Her resolution wavered, but only for a moment; by the time Cade reached town, she'd have her father's murderers restrained, or ready for burial. Furthermore, there was no reason for her to dread Cade's anger; he wasn't that important in her life. He would return to Abilene, she'd return to Crystal Creek, and they would probably never see each other again.

Maintaining a steady pace, she made the journey cautiously and without fear, for she had confidence in herself and her skills. Dawn was two hours away when she neared Villa de Lazar.

The Mexican town was fairly quiet as Jodie rode down the main street. She passed two hungry-looking dogs, and watched as they darted into the alley behind the town's restaurant to hunt for garbage. A few Mexican men, their sombreros pulled down over their faces, were sitting or lying in doorways, sleeping off a night's consumption of tequila. She passed a couple of pedestrians, but the two men didn't bother to look her way. They were used to people entering Villa de Lazar at all hours of the night. That she was a woman would have caught their attention, but they let her pass without notice.

She stopped in front of the town's cantina. Horses were still tied at the hitching rail, and she could hear voices coming from inside. The establishment was well-lighted; the smells of alcohol, spicy foods, and unwashed bodies drifted past the bat-wing doors and outside. The odors mixing with the stench of clumps of animal dung that were piled heavily in the street made Jodie a little nauseated. The night shadowed the town's filth, but she could well envision how dirty it must appear in daylight.

When her stomach settled, she dismounted, got her rifle, and flung the reins over the hitching rail. Reaching into her skirt pocket, she removed her deputy's badge and pinned it to her vest.

She moved to the swinging doors, pushed them aside, and entered the cantina with the confidence of an experienced gunfighter. The place wasn't very crowded; only five customers, the bartender, and two prostitutes were present to gape at Jodie, her presence rendering them speechless. They could hardly believe that a woman carrying a rifle and sporting a badge had suddenly appeared out of nowhere.

There was one customer, however, who wasn't quite as astounded as the others. He sat alone at a corner table, but getting to his feet, he stared at Jodie, who was staring back at him.

She crossed the room, went to his table, and said, "Hello, Dirk."

"Jodie!" he gasped. "Good God! What are you doing here?"

"I'm looking for the two men you're riding with."

As he motioned for her to sit down, he returned to his chair. "Damn it, Jodie! You don't have any business in a town like this one. Do you want to get yourself raped, even killed?"

"I don't intend to get raped or killed. Your two friends murdered Papa."

He was genuinely surprised. "I didn't know! I swear, Jodie! I had no idea they killed Cole."

"Why are you riding with them?"

The people inside the cantina were staring at them and no one was saying a word. Dirk lowered his voice so they couldn't overhear. "I met Red and his friend at the Silver Dollar. Red calls his friend Breed, because he's half Comanche. I played cards with them, lost most of my money, then went upstairs with one of the girls. Later, I left by the rear entrance. I wasn't in any hurry to get home, so I was taking it real slow. Red and Breed caught up to me, said they were going to Mexico, and asked if I wanted to ride along. I figured, why the hell not? I knew Pa would learn that I lost money playing cards, and I didn't want to hear another lecture. So I left with them to avoid facing Pa. I figured I'd give him a few days to cool off."

"Where are Red and Breed?"

"They left hours ago. I was just waiting for daylight to start back home."

Jodie leaned back in her chair and heaved a sigh of disappointment. She had come so close, only to end up empty-handed. She looked at Dirk, who was watching her intently. She wondered if he was telling the truth and didn't know that these men had killed her father. She decided in his favor; she had known him all her life, and although he was selfish and insensitive, she couldn't quite picture him knowingly teaming up with two murderers. She suddenly found herself feeling a little sorry for Dirk; he was handsome, educated, and had the backing of his father's wealth, yet, he seemed determined to ruin his life. But her pity dissipated, for he didn't really deserve it. He had no one to blame for his troubles but himself. A frown hardened her face as she reminded herself of all the times she had discouraged his affections and thwarted his advances. Once she had even threatened to shoot him; that had seemed to cool his passion, and thereafter he had left her alone.

She cleared his faults from her mind, and asked, "Do you know where Red and his friend are headed?"

"Farther into Mexico. Are you going back to Crystal Creek? If you are, we can ride together."

"I'm not going back."

"Surely, you don't intend to keep on with this. If you ride farther into Mexico, you might never come out."

"I won't be alone. I have Cade Brandon with me. He's a U.S. Marshal."

"A Marshal!" he exclaimed. "Where is he?"

"I left him at Antonio Morelos's hacienda. It's due west from here, and is about a three hour's ride."

"Why did you leave him behind?"

"He wasn't feeling well. What time does the restaurant open?"

"Early, I think. Why?"

"I plan to have breakfast before I leave."

"They sell food here at the cantina, but it's a little spicy for breakfast."

"I'll wait for the restaurant to open."

"If you don't mind, I'll join you. I'll be heading west for a few miles; we can ride together until I veer north."

She had no objections.

"I got a room at the hotel across the street," he said. "That's where my belongings are. I bought a change of clothes and a carpetbag before crossing the border. You wait here, and I'll get my things."

"If you have a room, why aren't you there sleeping instead of here?"

"I was earlier, but I woke up and couldn't fall back to sleep." He pushed back his chair and got to his feet. "I don't think anyone will bother you while I'm gone, but just to be on the safe side, you'd better keep that rifle close."

She didn't scoff at his advice, for she didn't see any reason to be unnecessarily rude. However, she didn't need someone like Dirk telling her how to take care of herself.

She ordered a tequila; the bartender delivered the drink, and she drank it slowly as she waited for Dirk's return. The liquor wasn't especially to her liking, but considering she was in the cantina, she figured she might as well be a paying customer.

* * *

Dirk hurried into the hotel, which was as shabby inside as it was on the outside. He climbed the rickety stairway, moved down the lighted hallway, and knocked on a door.

"Whoever's banging at this time of night better have a damned good reason!" a gruff voice bellowed from within the room.

"Red, it's Dirk. Let me in."

The bedsprings squeaked as though they were in pain, footsteps shuffled across the bare floor, and the door was swung open. A man's brawny frame, naked except for a pair of undershorts, filled the doorway; his mussed hair was bright red, and a jagged scar stood out clearly on his left cheek. His face, like his eyes, was granite hard.

Dirk brushed past him, and lit the bedroom lamp.

Closing the door with a loud bang, Red asked irritably, "What the hell's goin' on? How come you woke me up?" He belched loudly; the tequila he had drunk earlier, coupled with a spicy dinner, were playing havoc with his stomach.

"I think you should know there's a U.S. Marshal looking for you and Breed."

"Oh yeah? What's his name?"

"Cade Brandon."

Interest flickered in Red's bloodshot eyes. "Brandon, huh?"

"Do you know him?"

"I ain't never met him. But he wasn't always a U.S. Marshal. He used to be a bounty hunter. A few years back, he hunted down a friend of mine and turned him over to the law. The poor bastard was hung. I got a score to even with Brandon, but I ain't never had the pleasure of meetin' him. But I reckon that's about to change. Where did you see him? At the cantina?"

"I didn't see him. The deputy from Crystal Creek is here. Brandon is at a hacienda about three hour's ride from town." Dirk watched Red a little warily. "Did you and Breed kill Sheriff Walker?"

"Yeah, we killed the bastard. What's it to you, boy?"

Dirk took a backward step, as though he expected Red to reach out and grab him. "It . . . it's nothing to me."

"How come you came here to warn me? You're goin' home in the mornin', ain't you? Why didn't you just high-tail it back across the border?"

Dirk answered somewhat hesitantly, "You've been a good friend to me, Red. And I don't have any friends, not really. These last few days, we've had some good times together. I guess I figured I owed you a warning. Besides, I never liked Sheriff Walker. He was always locking me up for getting drunk and disturbing the peace. I'd have to pay a fine to get out of jail. If he wasn't arresting me, he was lecturing me as though he were my father. But I didn't come here just to warn you about Brandon. I thought you should know that the deputy is determined to stay on your trail. I was hoping as a favor to me, you and Breed would leave right away and ride into Texas. You see, I told the deputy that you and Breed are riding farther into Mexico. If you head for Texas instead, Brandon and the deputy will be hunting for you in the wrong direction."

"Your plan sounds good to me, but why do you consider it a favor to you? Are you trying to protect the deputy? Is he a friend of yours?"

"Not exactly, and the deputy isn't a man. It's Jodie Walker, the sheriff's daughter."

"A woman?" Red exclaimed. "Well drop my drawers and kick my bare butt! I've heard everything now!"

"Jodie and I grew up together, and I don't want anything to happen to her."

"You got the hots for her, boy?"

"I'd give anything to crawl into her bed, but Jodie's got a man, and I guess he's crawling under her covers. Bill Lawson. He's one of the richest ranchers in these parts."

Dirk hadn't told Red and Breed that he was also wealthy; he pretended to be nothing more than a poor wrangler. He was afraid his wealth would come between them, and he wanted to share in their adventures for a few days. It had been fun, but he was now ready to return to the comforts of home, even at the cost of facing one of his father's stern lectures.

"Is this lady deputy headin' back to the hacienda?"

"Yeah. I'm going to ride part way with her, but we're having breakfast first. The hacienda is due west, and I'll be riding in that direction for a few miles. While we're having breakfast at the restaurant, you and Breed can slip out of town."

"Good idea," Red said. He placed a hand on Dirk's shoulder, and patted it in a friendly fashion. "Thanks for your help. Maybe someday I can do you a favor."

For a second, it crossed Dirk's mind to ask Red to kill his father and brother. If they were dead, the ranch and all his father's wealth would be his. But the thought was fleeting; although he hated his father almost as much as he hated Garth, he couldn't quite bring himself to plan their deaths. The thought alone sent a chill up his spine, and caused nervous perspiration to form on his brow. His eyes darted crazily, as though he half-expected his father to suddenly materialize and admonish him for even thinking such a thing. He hurried to the door, moving as though his father's ghost was on his heels. He went to his room, got his packed bag, and rushed out of the dingy hotel.

Despite the rancid odors that hung heavily over the town, a deep breath calmed his nerves. He could hardly believe that he had actually considered asking Red to kill his father and brother. Until this moment, he hadn't realized just how deeply he hated them. But murder was going too far—besides, what if he were caught? Envisioning himself hanging at the end of a rope was terrifying. He quickly wiped the image out of his mind, and started across the street to the cantina.

Jodie was still at the table; the customers and employees had returned to talking and drinking. They had grown accustomed to her presence.

Dirk pulled out a chair, sat down, and put his bag at his feet. "The restaurant should be open soon."

"Good," she said. "I'm hungry."

Red knocked softly on Breed's door. The man was a light sleeper, and he awoke instantly. "Who's there?" he called, reaching for his pistol, which was hanging on the bedpost.

"It's me," Red replied.

Breed slipped on his trousers, and as he lit the lamp, the soft glow fell across his bare chest and stocky frame. His shoulder-length hair was ebony black, and his facial features were Comanche. He bore very little resemblance to his white father. "What's up?" he asked Red, upon opening the door.

Red recounted his visit from Dirk. "I got a way for us to make some good money," Red finished.

Breed didn't say anything; he merely waited for his friend to continue.

"Since this woman's lover is so rich, I think we oughta kidnap her. We can send Dirk back to Lawson with our demand. In the meantime, we can hole up with the Comancheros. If we promise Lopez part of the money, he'll let us stay until it's time to collect the ransom."

"How do we know Lawson will pay to get her back?"

"We don't. It's just a chance we'll have to take. If Lawson won't pay up, we'll sell the woman to Lopez. That should keep him from gettin' too upset."

Breed didn't fear any man, but he came very close to fearing Hernando Lopez. He didn't simply ride with the

Comancheros; he led the band of fugitives and rebels. He wasn't a man Breed cared to cross, for he didn't think he would live to talk about it.

"We will kidnap the woman," Breed agreed. "But when we see Lopez, we tell him there may not be a ransom. I will not try to fool Lopez. He must know that the woman may be the only prize."

"I hear ya. Pack up, and let's get out of here. We'll waylay Dirk and the woman a couple of miles out of town."

Red started to leave, but Breed placed a deterring hand on his arm. "You will not rape the woman."

"Hell, Breed, we might as well enjoy her."

"If she is a virgin, she will be more valuable to Lopez."

"Yeah, but what if she ain't?"

"When I see her, I will know."

"That's horse dung! You can't tell simply by lookin'."

"I will know," he insisted, his expression one of certainty.

Red didn't argue. He had learned from experience that Indians could sense things that went beyond a white man's perception. Besides, money was more important to him than having his way with their captive. Furthermore, Breed was right—a virgin was more valuable.

Following breakfast, Jodie and Dirk left the restaurant and started out of town. The sun had fully risen, and the daylight revealed Villa de Lazar's extreme poverty and filth. Jodie was glad to leave the place behind in exchange for the fresh air of the open prairie.

They had ridden a couple of miles when up ahead a good-sized boulder could be seen. Jodie considered making a wide sweep past the boulder, for danger could be hidden behind it. But at that moment, Dirk spotted a jack rabbit, and drawing his rifle, he spurred ahead, shouting that he intended to have rabbit for dinner. Jodie forgot the boulder and followed behind, smiling as Dirk's shot entirely missed its mark. She knew she wouldn't have missed.

He reined in beside the boulder, sheathed his rifle, and waited for Jodie to catch up. His face was red with embarrassment. "I wasn't really trying to hit it, you know."

"Lucky for the rabbit," she said.

At that moment, Red and Breed edged their horses from behind the boulder; Red's gun was on Dirk, and Breed's was aimed at Jodie.

"What the hell?" Dirk asked, gaping at his friends.

Breed rode to Jodie, and took her Winchester and bullwhip. Anger, mingling with disgust, shone in her eyes as she came face to face with the men who had murdered her father. She silently cursed herself for riding into their trap.

His gun still aimed at Dirk, Red told him, "I'll let you keep your weapons if you don't give me no trouble. I want you to ride back to Crystal Creek and tell Lawson that we got his woman. If he wants her back, he's to pay us two thousand dollars. You bring him and the money to this spot one week from today. We'll meet you here at noon. If Lawson's got the money, we give back the woman."

"I wish you wouldn't do this," Dirk said in a voice that resembled a whine. "I thought you and Breed were my friends."

"We are," Red replied. "We ain't killed ya, have we?"

"Enough talk!" Breed intervened. "Leave now, Dirk, or I will forget the ransom and settle for your scalp!"

Although Dirk liked Breed well enough, he found him intimidating, and he wasn't about to say or do anything to anger him. "All right, I'll leave," he said. He turned to Red, and added, "You aren't going to hurt her, are you?" He wasn't sure why he cared one way or the other; after all, Jodie had never been especially receptive to him.

"We ain't gonna do nothin' to harm her," Red assured him. "We just want the money."

Dirk knew it didn't matter whether he believed Red or not; he had no choice but to leave Jodie behind. He slapped the reins against his horse and left at a fast gallop.

Red holstered his gun and rode to Jodie's side. He ogled her, looked at Breed, and asked, "Well? What does that Indian second-sense you got, tell ya?"

"It is still too soon for me to know."

"For you to know what?" Jodie asked. She couldn't imagine what they were talking about, but she had a feeling it had something to do with her.

It was Red who responded. "Whether or not you're a virgin."

She blushed; she couldn't help it.

Breed took careful note of her embarrassment, before saying to Red, "We'd better leave. If Marshal Brandon is riding with her, he's liable to show up at any moment."

"Yeah, I guess you're right. As much as I'd like to kill the Marshal, I got better things to do. But I reckon our paths will cross sooner or later."

Keeping Jodie between them, they turned their horses about and started south. Neither man noticed their captive slip a handkerchief from her pocket and drop it on the ground.

As they traveled at a brisk pace, Jodie kept her eyes straight ahead as though she and her Appaloosa were alone on the prairie. Outwardly, she appeared calm; inside, however, she was very tense. But she was also angry with herself for letting these men take her so easily. She knew better than to blindly approach a large boulder, but her mind had been on Dirk's missing the rabbit. She had made a foolish mistake, and now she was paying for it.

She wondered if Cade would find her handkerchief; she didn't doubt that he'd go to Villa de Lazar, and when he didn't find her there, he'd certainly start looking for her. But he could easily miss seeing the handkerchief.

Although she hoped for Cade's help, she knew she might have to depend on herself. She cast both men a cautious glance. They were experienced and skilled; escaping them might be impossible. She wondered where they were taking her, but, most of all, she wondered what would happen to her after they got her there. Fear struck without warning, winding its way down into her stomach where it coiled up like a snake. She hated this feeling of fear, for she considered it an intolerable weakness. She tried to will it to go away, but it held on tenaciously.

Chapter Seven

When Cade went into the dining room, he found Antonio and Lucinda having breakfast. That Jodie wasn't there surprised him. He had thought she'd already be up and ready to leave.

"*Buenos dias,* amigo," Antonio said, gesturing for him to sit down. "You are feeling better, sí?"

"Yes, I'm almost as good as new," Cade replied, pulling out a chair. He looked at Lucinda, who was seated across the table. "Good morning, Lucinda."

She smiled warmly. "I am glad you are no longer sick." A bell was beside her plate; she rang it, and a moment later the cook entered from the kitchen. "Bring Señor Brandon whatever he wants for breakfast," Lucinda told her.

Cade placed a hearty order. "All I had for supper last night were a couple spoonfuls of broth," he said to Lucinda and Antonio. The memory brought forth a vision of Jodie feeding him and washing his fevered brow. She had been gentle and caring; her concern had touched him deeply.

Lucinda poured Cade a cup of coffee. "It is strong, the way you like it."

"I'm surprised Jodie is sleeping so late," Cade said, turning to Antonio.

"It is not that late," he replied.

"I figured she'd want to get an early start. Catching her father's murderers is all she thinks about."

"Sí, I got that impression when I talked to her last night. She is not like any woman I have ever met."

"I know what you mean. I've never met anyone like her either."

Lucinda detected admiration in Cade's voice that sent her heart plummeting. Was he in love with Miss Walker? She wondered if the señorita felt the same way about him.

The cook returned, followed by a vaquero, and spoke to her employer in English. "Patron, Juan has something to tell you."

"What is it?" Antonio asked him.

The man responded in Spanish. Cade's grasp of the language was limited, but he caught a few words here and there. He tensed as a spark of anger coursed through him like a swift current.

Antonio turned to Brandon. "Juan said that Miss Walker's horse is gone. So is her saddle, rifle, and bullwhip."

"Lucinda," Cade began, "will you go to Jodie's room and see if she's there?"

She left the room and rushed up the stairs to check.

Cade pushed back his chair, got to his feet, and began pacing angrily. "I can't believe she took off by herself!" He suddenly paused, waved his arms with exasperation, and muttered irritably, "Hell, why should I be surprised? Nothing Jodie does should surprise me! She's willful, stubborn, and totally independent! But, damn it, she's still a woman, and it's about time she started acting like one!"

Antonio chuckled. "I think you have fallen in love with

a spitfire, amigo. But she is like the Appaloosa she rides;
you will have to tame her with love."

"What makes you think I'm in love with her?" Cade
asked.

"Are you not?"

"I'm not sure," he admitted. He frowned testily, and
added, "Hell, it doesn't matter—Jodie's not interested in
me. She'll probably marry Bill Lawson."

Lucinda returned and announced that Jodie was not in
her room, but that her belongings were still there.

"If she left her things behind," Cade began, "then she
doesn't intend to go any farther than Villa de Lazar. If the
men aren't there, she'll be on her way back." He looked at
Antonio. "Do you mind asking Juan to saddle my horse?"

"No, of course not. Juan and I will ride with you." He
gave the order to his vaquero in Spanish.

"You will eat breakfast before you leave?" Lucinda asked
Cade.

"Thanks, but I've lost my appetite."

Jodie's captors stopped to water and rest the horses. In
the distance, mountain peaks looming toward a cerulean
sky formed a picturesque view. Jodie wondered if they were
heading for the mountains; she hoped not, for she knew
the region harbored Apache bands, all of them hostile.

She dismounted, checked her canteen, and found it
half-full. She took a drink of the tepid water, then poured
some into her hat and offered it to the Appaloosa. The
horse drank thirstily. She then recapped the canteen and
donned the damp hat. She turned and looked at Red. He
had finished watering his horse and was watching her with
a lewd expression. This renewed her fear, and sent a cold
chill up her spine. However, she kept her feelings well
hidden; she'd not let him know that she was afraid.

She breathed deeply, maintained her poise, and asked, "Are we riding to the mountains?"

"We sure are, Missy."

"Are you out of your mind?" she asked sharply. "The mountains are filled with Apaches."

"Don't worry your pretty head about no Apaches. We ain't gonna be in their neck of the woods. You see, them mountains don't belong only to the Apaches. The Comancheros live in them mountains too."

"Comancheros!" she exclaimed. She considered them as dangerous as the Apaches, maybe even more so.

"Breed's ridden with the Comancheros. He'll get us to their camp, and that's where we'll stay until it's time to meet with Lawson. That man of yours—he will pay the ransom, won't he?"

"Yes, of course he will," she replied, not doubting it for a moment.

Red grinned coldly. "Well, you better hope he does, 'cause if he don't, things don't look too good for you."

"What do you mean by that? Do you plan to kill me?"

"Why, I wouldn't kill a pretty little gal like you. Not unless I had no other choice."

Breed moved away from his horse, and as he pointed at a cottonwood, he said to Jodie, "You better step behind the tree, for we will not stop again until dusk."

She blushed, and hated herself for it.

Again, Breed noted her modesty.

Brushing past her captors, she walked to the cottonwood and darted behind it, thankful for its wide trunk.

As Red and Breed unbuttoned their trousers to relieve themselves, Red asked impatiently, "Well? Is she a virgin or ain't she?"

"I do not think she has been with a man."

"But you don't know for sure, do you?"

"I am sure enough."

"Well, maybe that ain't good enough for me!" Red grumbled nastily.

Breed's sudden glare was murderous; Red's courage wavered, for he knew he was no match against his companion. He had seen the half-breed kill too many times.

"You will not touch the woman!" Breed ordered. "Lopez will find her more valuable if she is a virgin."

Red buttoned his pants, and moved back to his horse. Mounting, he said with an amending grin, "Don't get so riled; I ain't gonna touch the woman. I agree with you; we gotta save her for Lopez. But if Lawson pays her ransom, she won't go to Lopez. Then I can stick it to her 'fore I give her back to Lawson."

Breed shrugged indifferently. "By then, it will not matter to me."

Jodie stepped out from behind the tree; Breed waited until she was mounted, then swung up onto his horse. They galloped away from the area, and headed toward the distant mountain range.

Cade was deeply worried as he left Villa de Lazar with Antonio and Juan. Asking around town, they had learned that a woman fitting Jodie's description had been at the cantina, and that she had eaten breakfast at the restaurant with a gringo. Cade suspected that Jodie was in some kind of trouble; otherwise, they would have come across her on their way to Villa de Lazar. The restaurant's proprietor had described the man with Jodie, and Cade knew he wasn't one of the men who had killed her father. She had been seen leaving town with her breakfast companion.

"Who do you think is the man with Señorita Walker?" Antonio asked Cade, as though he had read his thoughts.

"I don't know. Dirk, maybe."

Cade had told Antonio about the two fugitives and that Dirk Bradley was riding with them.

"Maybe Dirk is taking the señorita to see the men she hunts," Antonio speculated.

Cade's worry deepened even more so. "God, I hope not! What chance does she have against two cold-blooded murderers?"

"These men you pursue, what are they called?"

"I only know them as Red and Breed."

"Have you ever seen them?"

"No, I haven't had the pleasure," Cade grumbled.

"I have heard of the one called Breed. He has ridden with the Comancheros. I think he is half Comanche."

"He's wanted for three murders, and Red is wanted for two."

"What are your plans, amigo?"

They were nearing the large boulder where earlier Red and Breed had hidden. Cade considered Antonio's question for a minute or so, for he wasn't sure of his next move. He only knew that he had to find Jodie. But he didn't know where to start looking. He reined in beside the boulder, causing Antonio and Juan to do likewise.

"I intend to find Jodie," Cade finally answered. "But I don't know in which direction I should go. Every road leading into Villa de Lazar is so heavily traveled that distinguishing Jodie's tracks from the others is impossible." He waved an impatient hand at the ground beneath him. "She could've been in this spot, and I wouldn't know it. There are horse prints everywhere, but there are no signs of a horse being here recently. These prints could be hours old, or even days old. But they're all I've got to go on, so I guess I'll start here." He pointed at the tracks going south. "Three horses headed that way, and that's the direction I'll take." At that moment, he spotted something white on the ground beside the southern bound tracks. Dismounting quickly, he hurried over and picked up a lace handkerchief.

Antonio rode up to him. "Does that belong to the señorita?"

"I can't be sure, but I'd be willing to bet my last dollar that it does. She's in trouble, and she left it here hoping I would find it. She's heading deeper into Mexico with two other riders."

Cade returned to the boulder, and examining the ground beside it, he tried to make sense of the many horse prints that had been left behind. He noticed that a lone rider had ridden west; he wondered if it could have been Dirk. To cross the border at Crystal Creek, he would have to ride west before veering north.

Cade turned to Antonio, who was watching him. "I think Dirk may have led her into a trap. I've got a bad feeling that she's with Red and Breed."

"If she is with Breed, then he is probably taking her into the mountains and to the Comancheros."

"I'm going to ride back to Villa de Lazar, buy supplies and extra ammunition, then try to pick up their trail."

"I will go with you," Antonio said.

"I appreciate your offer, but I wonder if you realize the danger involved."

"If they reach the Comancheros before you find them, there is no way you can rescue the señorita. But I think I can get us into Hernando Lopez's camp. He has his own band of Comancheros. We must hope that is where Red and Breed are taking the señorita. Maybe we can negotiate with Lopez for her release."

Cade had heard of Lopez. "Do you know the man?" he asked with surprise.

"Sí, I know him." Antonio didn't elaborate; instead, he turned to Juan and sent him home, telling him to let Lucinda know that he was accompanying Cade.

As Juan rode away, Morelos and Brandon mounted their horses. Cade turned to his friend, and said, "Antonio, I'm grateful for your help. But our chances of coming out of this alive don't look good. Maybe you'd better reconsider."

"Our chances are better than you think, amigo."

"What do you mean by that?"

"I will explain later. Now we must hurry before the trail grows cold. Sí?"

Cade agreed, and they started back to Villa de Lazar to buy supplies and ammunition.

Dusk was cloaking the landscape when Breed gave the command to stop. The mountain range was now very close, and its rocky bluffs stood out clearly against the darkening sky. It reminded Jodie of a looming fortress sheltering its occupants from advancing predators. Sentries hidden in its many ravines could see for miles around.

As soon as they had dismounted, Breed collected kindling and built a huge fire. The leaping flames shot upwards as though they were trying to light the heavens. The heat from the inferno was intense.

Jodie, watching the blaze, asked Red, "Why did he build such a big fire?"

"There's Comancheros in them mountains who will see that fire, and they'll know by its size that we're a-wantin' to meet with 'em. I was with Breed once before when he made contact with 'em, and not long after the fire was blazin', a bunch of 'em showed up, armed to the teeth. But Breed's friends with their leader, and we was taken to their hideout and treated real sociable-like. We stayed 'bout two weeks." He laughed deeply. "I hope you ain't scared of bein' blindfolded."

She looked at him questioningly.

"They ain't gonna let you see the way in to their hideout. If you saw the way in, they'd never let you back out. Hell, I'll be blindfolded too."

"And Breed?"

"Naw, he knows the way in, but they trust him to never tell anyone. He won't even tell me. Them Indians can be real close-mouthed, you know."

Jodie moved away from Red, went to a mesquite tree, sat down, and leaned back against its trunk. That she was about to enter the Comancheros' hideout seemed incredible. She had listened to stories about the renowned bandits for years, but never in her wildest dreams could she have imagined that someday she would meet up with them. The stories she had heard were enough to put fear in the most stout heart. The Comancheros were known for their thefts, rapes, and murders. It was even rumored that they often sold their captives to Apaches and other bandits.

Jodie willfully cast such atrocities from her mind, and turned her thoughts to Cade. Did he find her handkerchief? She almost wished she hadn't left it behind, for there was no way Cade could save her from these men and the Comancheros. He would most likely get himself killed trying. His death would be her fault, for she had left him behind only to fall into a trap. She was suddenly angry with herself for placing Cade's life in jeopardy; she was also very concerned—the realization that he might die hit her with a heartrending force. Her eyes smarted with tears, and she felt sick to her very soul. A terrible sense of remorse swept over her; she should never have left the hacienda. She silently cursed her stubbornness and independence, for they might very well cost Cade Brandon his life.

Time passed slowly for Jodie as she waited for the Comancheros to arrive. Worrying about Cade was so depressing that she tried to keep him out of her thoughts, but the effort was in vain, for his life had become too important to her.

Full night had fallen by the time a group of riders could be seen in the distance. The moonlight shining down upon the land was like a golden beacon guiding their way.

Breed stepped forward and greeted the men. From

Jodie's position beneath the tree, she couldn't hear what they were saying, for they spoke in soft tones. The dozen riders were heavily armed; most of them appeared to be Mexican descendants, while the others bore strong resemblances to the Comanches.

Breed turned her way, and motioned for her to come to him.

She got up and moved to his side.

Two Comancheros handed him bandannas; he tied one around Red's eyes, then put the other one on Jodie. Taking her arm, he led her to the Appaloosa and helped her into the saddle. He quickly smothered the fire that was now a much lower flame. Mounting his own horse, he rode to Jodie, took her reins, and led her behind him. One of the Comancheros had the reins to Red's horse.

They rode away at a fast canter, and traveling blindfolded was a little unnerving for Jodie. Such pitch blackness was like being in a void that had swallowed her into its infinite depths. There was no escape; she was trapped in darkness.

Later, when the Appaloosa began to climb, Jodie knew they had reached the mountain. As they ascended higher and higher, her nerves grew even more taut. More than once she felt her horse's hooves slip on the loose terrain; each slip sent her heart lurching, for she had a feeling the trail was bordered by a sheer drop off.

Jodie's instincts were right; a high cliff did indeed pose a serious threat. But the Appaloosa was surefooted, and Breed's guidance kept the horse controlled and relatively at ease.

Red, however, was not so fortunate. A small rock slide, caused by a curious cougar investigating the procession, came tumbling down the mountainside. The pebbles were harmless, but the disturbance panicked Red's nervous horse. It suddenly reared up on its back legs, its front hooves pawing at the air. The steed's unexpected lurch tossed Red from the saddle. He released a blood-curdling scream as his body was hurled over the cliff. Death awaited at the bottom, silencing him forever.

"What happened?" Jodie asked Breed.

"Red's horse panicked and threw him over the cliff, "Breed replied, as though nothing important had happened. The others were now talking in excited tones. A couple of them had even dismounted to look over the cliff. Breed, however, remained eerily calm.

"Is he dead?" Jodie gasped. Blindfolded, Red's chilling scream had terrified her.

"Not even Red could survive a fall like that one." Breed's voice was still devoid of grief.

"You don't sound very upset. I thought he was your friend."

"I don't have any friends," he replied. "You are probably thinking that you now have one less man to arrest and take back to Crystal Creek to face a hangman's noose."

"I don't think I could ever take you back to Crystal Creek alive. You'd die before surrendering."

"You are wrong. I am not the one who would die; it would be you."

The procession moved onward, and Jodie held tightly to the Appaloosa's mane, praying that her horse would not panic like Red's. She felt the steed tremble beneath her, and she leaned forward and spoke to it soothingly. Responding to its owner's comforting voice, it settled down and followed obediently behind Breed's horse.

The passage up the winding cliff seemed interminable to Jodie, but finally they began their descent. The downward trek took less time and they were soon on even ground.

Breed coaxed the Appaloosa to his side, reached over, and removed Jodie's blindfold. The moon was still shining brightly, and she could see huts and tents in the distance. The savory aromas of food cooking over campfires filled the air, reminding Jodie that she hadn't eaten since morning. An adobe house, built upon a small hill, overlooked the compound. As the Comancheros turned their horses around to return to their posts atop the mountain, Breed, still holding Jodie's reins, headed for the main house.

Men, women, and children stared at Jodie and the half-breed as they rode past their homes. The sight of children surprised Jodie; she had never imagined them in a Comancheros' camp.

The encampment was located in a fertile valley protected by towering cliffs on every side. A trickling waterfall, cascading down the mountainside, furnished water for the valley's occupants.

Three quick rifle shots suddenly rang out from somewhere in the compound, taking Jodie by surprise.

"What's going on?" she asked Breed.

"That's a signal to Lopez. He knows to expect us."

They soon reached the house, and as they reined in, the front door was opened. A tall, majestic figure in splendid boots, white ruffled shirt, and black trousers lined with silver thread, stepped outside. His complexion was dark, and his brown eyes were almost effeminate in their beauty. He stepped up to the Appaloosa, and Jodie gazed down into a face that was exceptionally handsome.

"Buenos noches, señorita," he said, his smile revealing strikingly white teeth. "Welcome to my humble home." He reached up, placed his hands on her waist, and lifted her to the ground. He held her against him, and the message in his eyes was starkly sensual. "I can hardly believe such a beautiful woman has come into my life."

She pushed out of his arms, and said sharply, "I'm not here by choice."

It was then that he noticed the badge pinned to her vest. "Who are you, señorita?"

"Who are you?" she came back.

"Hernando Lopez," he replied.

She had heard of Lopez, but hadn't imagined him so

young. He looked to be in his late twenties. "I'm Deputy Walker from Crystal Creek," she told him, meeting his gaze without a flinch.

"Are you here to arrest me?" he joked.

Breed, dismounting, said to Lopez, "This woman is my prisoner. I am holding her for ransom, but if her man does not pay up, you can have her—for a price."

"Just name your price, Breed. I will pay it."

"I'm not for sale!" Jodie spat, her eyes glaring at Breed, then Hernando.

Lopez laughed heartily. "I am afraid, señorita, that you have no say in this matter."

She spoke fiercely. "I'd kill you before letting you own me!"

"Words like those, señorita, can have serious consequences." Lopez's dark eyes penetrated hers with an intensity that she was incapable of defining. Was he threatening her life, or merely trying to intimidate her? She couldn't tell simply by looking at him.

Chapter Eight

Lopez led Jodie and Breed into the house. They passed through a small vestibule and into the parlor. The room bore only the bare essentials: a sofa, two matching chairs, and three scarred tables. A well-supplied liquor cabinet occupied a corner of the room; across from it was positioned a huge gun repository filled with weapons. The floor, though clean, was bare of rugs, and no hangings adorned the walls. Jodie found the room as cold and as impersonal as its owner.

Lopez took Jodie to the sofa. "Sit down, señorita. I will fetch my housekeeper, and she will take care of you."

He left quickly, leaving Jodie alone with Breed, who was helping himself to Lopez's liquor. She watched as he poured a glass of whiskey and drank it in one gulping swallow. He refilled the glass, and downed the second drink as greedily as the first. He was filling the glass for the third time when Lopez returned, followed by a young woman wearing a combination of Comanche and Mexican garb. Hair the color of ebony fell over her shoulders in two long braids. The black tresses complemented her large eyes, which were as green as emeralds. Heartache and years of abuse were etched deeply in her face, hiding the beauty that had once been there.

Hernando went to Jodie, took her hand, and drew her to her feet. "Grass Woman will take you to the spare bedroom. I think you will be comfortable there. Later, you will join me for dinner."

Jodie didn't relish his company, but she was looking forward to dinner, for she was very hungry. Grass Woman motioned for her to follow, and they moved down a narrow hall and to the last door on the left. Grass Woman opened it, and stepped aside for Jodie to enter first.

The interior was dark, and the housekeeper promptly lit the bedroom lamp. Like the rest of the house, its decor was bare: a feather bed adorned with a colorful quilt, a badly scratched wardrobe, and a table holding a pitcher and a basin.

"If you would like to bathe," Grass Woman said, "I will have the tub brought in."

A bath was too tempting for Jodie to refuse. "Thank you," she replied. "I'd appreciate that."

"I can bring you a change of clothes. Tomorrow I'll wash what you are wearing."

"That's very nice of you, but I don't want to add to your chores. I'll do my own laundry. That is, if I'm allowed out of this room."

"I don't think Hernando will make you stay in here. There is no escape from this valley."

"Is there only one way in?"

"Yes, the way you came. The road in is heavily guarded. If you try to escape, you'll be caught—perhaps even killed. Hernando said that you are Breed's prisoner, and he can be very cruel. For your own sake, don't anger him."

The woman's civility and warmth was an unexpected

surprise that Jodie welcomed. "I appreciate your concern . . . Grass Woman. That is your name, isn't it?"

"It is my Comanche name. They called me Grass Woman because my eyes are green like the grass."

"My name is Jodie Walker. Your English is flawless. You weren't raised by the Comanches, were you?"

"I lived with them for many years." She moved to the door quickly, as though she were anxious to terminate the conversation. She left, closing the door quietly behind her.

Alone, Jodie began pacing the small room. She knew she was trapped in this valley and totally at the mercy of her captors. She didn't think Breed would harm her as long as she didn't cross him, but she wasn't so sure about Lopez. His intentions were obvious; and, as long as she was unarmed, thwarting his advances might be as futile as holding off an advancing storm.

Cade and Antonio made camp a couple of miles from the area where Breed had built the huge fire. A golden moon, surrounded by a myriad of twinkling stars, cast a soft light upon the mountain's high cliffs and towering peaks.

The men had eaten supper, and were now sitting at the campfire drinking coffee. Cade was staring vacantly at the distant mountain range. He wondered about Antonio's plans. The man seemed quite confident and self-assured, as though confronting the Comancheros was an every day occurrence and nothing to be concerned about.

Antonio was sitting across the fire from him. He looked at Cade closely; it was obvious to Antonio that Cade was deeply worried. He decided it was time to try to ease his friend's mind.

"You are worried, sí?" he asked softly.

"Of course, I'm worried. I don't know how the hell you intend to get us into the Comancheros' camp. You act as though they'll roll out the red carpet and welcome us with open arms."

Antonio chuckled tersely. "There will be no red carpet and no open arms; however, I think Lopez will agree to see us."

"He'll probably agree to see us all right—as his men hang us from the highest tree." Cade was impatient with Antonio's hedging. If he had connections to the Comancheros, he wished he would just come out and admit it.

Morelos put down his coffee cup, reached into his shirt pocket, and withdrew a cheroot. As he sorted out his thoughts, he lit the small cigar and inhaled deeply. What he had to say was confidential, but he was hesitant to reveal his personal life, even to a friend like Brandon. He knew he could trust Cade not to tell anyone, but that didn't really make it much easier. Antonio was a private person and unaccustomed to explaining himself, but under the circumstances, he felt he had no other choice.

"Amigo," he said, "I will try to make a long story short. I speak to you in confidence." He paused, puffed on his cheroot, sifted through his thoughts one last time, then began.

"Nearly ten years before I married Lucinda's mother, Adela, I was in love with another woman. Her name was Rosita. I was very young, and so was she. She was not an aristocrat. She was a peasant, and descended from peasants. She was very beautiful, and although I knew she and I could never marry, I could not stay away from her. She was in my blood, and I was intoxicated with her beauty. I do not know if she loved me too. Maybe she did, or maybe she only wanted to marry into a rich family. My parents were still alive then, and when my father learned that I was seeing Rosita, he warned me to be careful. He did not forbid me to see her, for he believed a young man should sow his wild oats.

"Rosita became pregnant. She pleaded with me to marry

her, and because I was so infatuated, I actually considered it. I went to my father and told him. He was enraged and said he would disown me if I married her. I left home for a couple of days to give myself time alone to think. When I returned, I went to Rosita's home. Her mother told me that my father had given Rosita money, and that she had moved away to live with relatives. She would not tell me where I could find Rosita." He shrugged indifferently. "To be honest, I did not try all that hard to find her. I went on with my life, and filled it with more women.

"Five years after Rosita left, she returned home, penniless and with her bastard son. If I had any doubts that her child was mine, they were quickly dissolved the first moment I laid eyes on him. He was undoubtedly a Morelos. I was no longer infatuated with Rosita, but I felt a certain obligation toward the boy, and I gave her a generous allowance. She remained with her family, and they lived a life of relative ease. I never told the boy that I was his father, but eventually Rosita told him. But by then I was engaged to Adela, and she had become my whole life—she was all I lived for. I seldom gave my son a second thought. I cannot be sure, but I think when Rosita learned that I was determined to marry Adela, she gave up hope that someday I might marry her. The day after Adela and I were wed, Rosita married a man who was a stranger; not even her family knew anything about him. She took her son and moved away with her husband, but she came back one time to visit. The boy was fourteen years old. He came to the hacienda to see me. His visit was short, but civil. I never saw him again."

Cade regarded Antonio closely. "The man Rosita married—was his last name Lopez?"

"Sí," he replied.

"And yours and Rosita's son—is his name Hernando?"

He nodded his head. "Hernando Lopez, the Comancheros' leader, is my bastard son."

"And you haven't seen him since he was fourteen years old?"

"No, but I never lost track of him."

"Why are you so sure he won't kill you?"

"The day he came to my hacienda, he was very polite. I do not think he harbors hard feelings."

"All these years, he's been within your reach—why the hell didn't you get to know him? My God, he's your son!"

"I did not think you would understand. You do not know our ways, but Hernando does. An aristocrat does not claim a peasant woman's child. It simply is not done."

"How did Hernando become an outlaw?"

"I am not sure. Rosita's husband was a bandit, and I suppose he led Hernando into that kind of life."

"And you didn't do anything to stop that from happening?"

"It was not my place, nor my responsibility." Antonio held up his hands, as though warding off any further questions. "I did not tell you about Hernando to have you judge me. What's done is done."

"I don't aim to judge you. My own life isn't above scrutiny. And you don't have to worry—I'll keep this conversation confidential."

"Gracias, amigo, I know I can trust you. A little over a year ago, a vaquero who only worked for me a short time mentioned to Juan that when a man wants to contact Hernando's band of Comancheros, he builds a huge fire within sight of the mountains. In the morning, we'll ride in closer, build a fire, then wait and see what happens. By the way, I think you should put away your badge. If the Comancheros see it, they are liable to shoot you on sight."

Cade removed his badge and put it deep within his carpetbag. He again gazed at the distant mountain range, his thoughts on Jodie. Knowing she was at the mercy of outlaws had his nerves on edge. The Comancheros were reputed thieves, murderers, and rapists. He knew Mexico was filled with bandits who were labeled Comancheros, some bands more ruthless than others.

He turned to Antonio. "In your opinion, is Hernando capable of harming a woman, or letting his men harm her?"

"The boy I knew seemed sensitive and caring. But maybe the years have changed him. I am sorry, amigo. I wish I could tell you that Señorita Walker is safe, but I cannot be sure." He smiled hesitantly. "I cannot even assure you that Hernando will not kill us. But I do not think he will."

"I hope you're right," Cade replied.

After bathing and washing her hair, Jodie relaxed in the tub as the warm water eased her tired muscles. She remained immersed until the water turned tepid; then she stepped out and dried herself with a towel. Grass Woman had brought a change of clothes, and she quickly slipped into the garments. Although there was no mirror in the room, she could tell that the blouse and skirt were a good fit. The attire was comfortable, for the light-fabric blouse felt cool against her skin, and the ankle-length skirt flowed loosely about her legs. The black slippers, fortunately, were a good size.

Without a mirror, grooming her long hair seemed an impossible task. She had a brush in her carpetbag, and sitting on the edge of the bed, she ran it briskly through the damp tresses. She continued brushing until her hair was dry. She didn't need a mirror to know that it was a mass of curls. She often wished for hair that wasn't quite so unruly, but fate had given her naturally curly tresses that were as stubborn as their owner.

A knock sounded at the door.

"Yes?" Jodie called.

Grass Woman entered. "It is time for dinner. Hernando is waiting."

Jodie didn't need further encouragement, for she was terribly hungry. She followed Grass Woman down the hall and to the dining room, which, like the rest of the house, was built on a small scale.

Hernando was seated at the head of the table, but rose to his feet at Jodie's arrival. His eyes raked her from head to foot. She was indeed a fetching sight, for the white blouse tastefully defined her full breasts, and the colorful skirt emphasized her womanly hips. Such curly tresses lent her a disheveled aura that was starkly sensual, and Hernando longed to run his fingers through the brown locks that cascaded beautifully past her shoulders in long, silky ringlets. His intense scrutiny went to her face; he felt as though he could look at her for hours without tiring of the view. He found her features exquisite: eyes as intelligent as they were beautiful, a pert nose slightly turned up at the end, a mouth shaped for a man's kiss, and a strong chin that bespoke of character.

Jodie couldn't help but return Hernando's admiration, for he was undeniably very handsome. His black hair, dark eyes, and strong but lean physique were arresting. For a moment, she had an odd feeling that she had seen him before, but she knew that was impossible. She quickly decided that he must remind her of someone, but she didn't spend time wondering who it was.

Lopez pulled out the chair next to his, and waited for Jodie to occupy it. She moved across the room, went to the chair, and sat down. He returned to his place at the head of the table, and dismissed Grass Woman with a wave of his hand. Dinner, kept warm by covered dishes, was already on the table. Hernando didn't want Grass Woman serving them, for her presence would be a disruption. He wanted Jodie's undivided attention. Earlier, he had given Breed explicit orders to stay away until morning.

Jodie, considering herself a prisoner and not a guest, didn't bother with etiquette; she simply filled her plate and began eating. She didn't care if Hernando ate or not; her aim was to eat as quickly as possible, then return to her room. Keeping company with Lopez didn't appeal to her, not in the least. Handsome or not, he was still an outlaw, and was allowing Breed to hold her here against her will.

Hernando, filling their wine glasses, smiled as he indicated Jodie's filled plate with a nod of his head. "I like a woman with a healthy appetite. Most ladies I dine with pick at their food as though they are afraid if they eat they will get fat."

"I happen to be very hungry. However, I can't picture a lady dining with you of her own free will. Maybe she picks at her food because she doesn't like being your prisoner."

He chuckled. "I do not make a habit of holding women against their will. In fact, you are the first."

"Lucky me," she grumbled.

Letting his plate remain empty, he leaned back in his chair, and toyed absently with his wine glass. He watched Jodie with a steady gaze. "Tell me about yourself, señorita," he said. "How did you become a deputy?"

"How did you become an outlaw?" she retorted, concentrating on her food and ignoring his scrutiny.

"Circumstances," he murmured.

"That's how I became a deputy."

"You aren't going to be friendly, are you?"

"No, I'm not," she replied flatly.

"That is too bad," he said, desire shining blatantly in his eyes. "I had hoped you would be more cooperative. However, there are other ways to convince you to be . . . amiable."

Jodie's appetite vanished at once. She put down her fork, and with a quickness that escaped Lopez, she slid a sharp knife from the table and into her lap.

Pushing back her chair, and holding the knife hidden behind her, she bounded to her feet and glared at him with fury. "I know what you have in mind, and you'll never have my cooperation! If you dare lay a hand on me, you'd better kill me; if you don't, I'll find a way to kill you! If you take my threat lightly because I'm a woman, you'll be making a fatal mistake!" With that, she whirled around, and left the room to return to her own quarters.

Hernando stared at her departing back with admiration, as well as anger. He admired her grit and courage, yet, at the same time, her rebuff hurt his male pride.

He left the dining room, went to the parlor, and poured himself a glass of whiskey. Taking the bottle with him, he sat in a chair; he stewed inwardly and drank excessively. His thoughts remained on Jodie, and the more he drank, the more he wanted her.

The intoxicating liquor soon drove him from his chair and down the hall to Jodie's room. The door had no lock, and he quickly turned the knob and stepped inside. The room was dark, but the light from the hall cast an aureate beacon across the floor.

He took a step toward the bed, where he expected to find Jodie, but the feel of a sharp blade against his back was a persuasive deterrent.

Jodie had expected this from Lopez, and had listened for the sound of his footsteps. Hidden behind the door, she had made her move the moment he started toward the bed.

She cut a tiny slit in his shirt, and he felt the deadly tip of the blade touch his bare skin. "Get out of here," she warned softly. "Don't turn around, just move to the door and leave."

"I can take that knife away from you, señorita," he replied, sounding confident.

She nicked his flesh, drawing a few drops of blood. "You make one fast move, and this knife will be buried in your back."

"I will still live long enough to kill you."

"Given a choice between what you had in mind and death, I'll take death."

"Do you find me that unattractive?"

"Men like you just don't understand, do you? If a man dies fighting for his honor, he's a hero. But if a woman dies fighting for her honor, she's a fool."

At that moment, Grass Woman entered. She had been on her way to bed, but the door, standing ajar, had caught her attention. She unknowingly shoved the door against Jodie. Lopez reacted instantly, and as the door hit Jodie's arm, he whirled around and grabbed her wrist. He squeezed painfully and the knife fell from her hand.

Grass Woman could hardly believe her eyes—this was out of character for Hernando. She had never known him to mistreat a woman.

Hernando kicked the knife out of Jodie's reach, and it slid across the bare floor. But keeping a firm hold on her wrist, he drew her closer. His face was mere inches from hers, and she could smell whiskey on his breath. "I was not going to rape you, muchacha. I intended to seduce you. But I think maybe you are a woman who cannot be seduced. You have a mind of your own, and no man will ever change it."

She pried his fingers from her wrist, stepped back, and spat sharply, "Get out of my room!"

He favored her with a mock bow from the waist. *"Buenas noches,* señorita." He moved to the knife, bent over, picked it up, and left. His admiration for Jodie was now stronger than before.

"Are you all right?" Grass Woman asked Jodie, the moment Lopez was gone.

"Yes, I'm fine," she replied.

"I can't believe Hernando did this. I've been with him five years, and I have never known him to force himself on a woman."

"He said he came here to seduce me, not force me. For some reason, I believe him."

Grass Woman smiled. "Yes, seducing you would appeal to Hernando, for he would consider it a challenge. He is accustomed to women taking the initiative and beckoning him into their beds." She moved to the door. "Goodnight, Miss Walker."

"Goodnight, and please call me Jodie."

"Sleep well, for Hernando won't return. He is an outlaw, but he is also a gentleman."

"You think very highly of him, don't you?"

"He treats me kindly. For that, I'm grateful." She left quickly, avoiding further inquiries.

Chapter Nine

Bill Lawson had finished breakfast and was drinking a second cup of coffee when his housekeeper came into the dining room and told him that Dirk Bradley wished to see him. Bill told the woman to show him in.

Bill invited Dirk to sit at the table, poured him a cup of coffee, and asked, "What can I do for you?"

Bradley dreaded breaking such serious news to Lawson. He hoped he wouldn't hold him responsible. "I was in Villa de Lazar," Dirk began. "I was in the town's cantina when Jodie showed up."

"Jodie!" Bill butted in. "What was she doing in a cantina?" Exasperated, he brushed a hand through his hair. Jodie in a Mexican cantina? Good Lord, what would she do next?

"She was looking for the two men who killed her father." Dirk sheepishly admitted that he had ridden with Red and Breed, assuring Lawson that he didn't know they had killed the sheriff. "Jodie and I left Villa de Lazar together, but we were waylaid by Red and Breed. They took Jodie with them, but sent me here to give you a message." He quickly delivered the ransom demand.

Bill was taken aback. "How did they know about me?"

Dirk swallowed heavily. "I told them about you. But I didn't know they were going to kidnap Jodie. I swear I didn't!"

Bill rubbed his hands together, for nervous perspiration was accumulating on his palms. He believed delivering the ransom was the same as riding into certain death. Those two murderers would not let him live. Anger rose within him—damn Jodie for doing this! If she had stayed home where she belonged, this wouldn't have happened! Refusing to pay the ransom was a temptation, for Jodie had gotten herself into this situation without his help; in fact, he had practically begged her not to leave. The more he thought about it, the angrier he became; however, despite his rage, he still had feelings for Jodie. Nevertheless, he wasn't about to risk his life. This was a job for a law officer.

He pushed back his chair and got to his feet. "Let's ride into town and let Deputy Riker know what has happened."

"Red and Breed won't like you bringing the law into this."

"I don't give a damn if those murderers approve or not!"

"I don't see why you want to tell Jonas. He won't be any help; he's just a drunk."

"I understand he wasn't always a drunk. Before he lost his wife and children, he was a respected law officer. They say he was real good with a gun."

"Well, the only thing he's good at now is draining a bottle of whiskey."

"Nevertheless, I intend to speak to him about this ransom demand."

"I'll ride to town with you, but I can't stay very long. I haven't gone home yet, and I imagine Pa's worried about me."

"Yes, he is. In fact, he asked a U.S. Marshal to look for you. The man's name is Brandon; he came through town after you left."

"Jodie mentioned that she was riding with the Marshal."

"Then why wasn't he with her at the cantina?"

"She said she left him at a hacienda because he was sick."

Lawson huffed arrogantly. "Some law officer he is! He lies back and takes it easy, while Jodie takes all the risks!"

Jonas Riker had a room in the rear of the sheriff's office. He awoke with a pounding headache, and he groaned aloud as he swung his legs over the side of the bed. He silently damned his pain, wondering why after so many years he was still cursed with hangovers.

You'd think a body would grow accustomed to abuse, he thought crankily, standing and teetering slightly. He was still feeling the effects of last night's binge. He made his way to the water basin, filled it, and washed his face. He had slept in his clothes, and they were wrinkled and whiskey stained. Delving inside a chest of drawers, he found a clean shirt and a pair of trousers. He changed his clothes, then looked into a mirror that hung over the chest.

He rubbed a hand across his face; he needed a shave badly. He tried to recall the last time he had shaved—it had been at least two or three days. He ran a comb through his hair; he also needed a haircut.

Jonas Riker, despite his years of alcohol abuse, was still an attractive man. At the age of thirty-five, his physique was as tightly muscled as it had been in his youth. The planes of his face were angular, his features masculine. His thick reddish-blond hair was unruly, and a wayward curl insistently fell across his forehead, lending him a boyish charm that the years had failed to erase. His brown eyes, deeply set under prominent brows, were expressionless, as though they had never twinkled with happiness, softened with love, or teared with sorrow.

A loud rapping sounded at the front door, and Jonas left the small room, strode past two empty cells, and through the office. He admitted Lawson and Dirk, who barged inside as though time was of the essence.

Bill quickly told Riker about Jodie.

Riker liked Jodie, and learning she was kidnapped was upsetting. Cole Walker had been a good, loyal friend, and now that he was gone, Jonas felt responsible for Jodie. He should never have let her leave for Mexico, but the day she had come by the office to tell him good-bye, he had been drinking. His mind had been on whiskey, not on Jodie's welfare.

Dirk recounted the abduction for Jonas, then asked if he could leave. Although he dreaded facing his father's tirade, he was anxious to get it over with.

But Jonas wasn't ready for him to leave. "The ransom is supposed to be delivered next week. Is that right?"

"Yeah, that's right," Dirk grumbled, resenting Jonas for keeping him here. Who did he think he was? He was just a damned drunk with a badge pinned to his shirt.

"And you're supposed to take Bill to deliver the money?"

Dirk hesitated; he was dead set against making the trip, for he wouldn't put it past Red and Breed to kill him. "I don't see . . . any reason for me to go along," he stammered. "I can tell Bill where he's supposed to go. It's an easy area to find; it's only a couple miles from Villa de Lazar."

For now, Jonas was finished with Dirk, and he gave his permission to leave. Young Bradley left at once.

"I need some coffee," Jonas told Bill. His head was still pounding; he hoped coffee would help. A wood burning stove stood in the corner; he lit the fuel and put on a full pot. The coffee would take time to brew, and he motioned for Bill to have a seat. Jonas walked around the desk, and sat in his chair as Lawson took the chair facing him.

Bill cleared his throat uneasily, and toyed with the hat he held in his hands. He didn't know how to say what was on his mind without sounding like a coward. He didn't think of himself as a coward; he thought of himself as practical.

"Jonas," he began hesitantly, "I'm not sure how to say this. I don't want you to get the wrong impression. I love Jodie very much, and I'm quite willing to pay the ransom. However, I don't think I should be the one to deliver the money. It's a job for someone more . . . more experienced. I'm afraid that my inexperience might cost Jodie's life, as well as my own."

Riker saw straight through Lawson and to the yellow streak running up his back. However, he saw no reason to confront him. The man was undoubtedly a coward, but what the hell, he had no room to judge—he, himself, was nothing but a drunk!

"Do you want me to deliver the ransom?" Jonas asked.

"Would you?" he responded. "This agreement is just between the two of us, but I'll make it well worth your time. I know you aren't supposed to accept bribes, but we won't consider it a bribe. . . . will we?"

A cold grin crossed Riker's face; Lawson was not only a coward, but a pathetic manipulator as well. "Keep your bribe, Lawson. I don't want your money."

"Are you sure?" he asked, arching a brow. "It would buy a lot of whiskey."

"And my silence," he quipped.

"What exactly does that mean?"

"I'm sure you don't want me telling Jodie that you asked me to take your place. She might consider that cowardly of you."

Lawson appeared offended. "I didn't ask you to take my place; you offered. Furthermore, I only have Jodie's best interest in mind. I am not a gunman; in case of trouble, you can protect her much better than I could."

Jonas decided to let the matter rest. Moreover, he wanted Lawson to leave; he didn't like him—had never liked him. He couldn't understand why Jodie seemed so smitten with him.

"I'll deliver the ransom," Riker said. He indicated the front door. "Good day, Lawson."

That Riker had the gall to dismiss him so curtly angered Bill, but he held his temper and left the office with a flourish. He wasn't about to say anything that might alienate Jonas, for he might refuse to deliver the money—then it would be up to him, and he certainly didn't want to face two cold-blooded murderers!

Jodie's home was small, so Laura had shared a room with her mother, but the morning after Jodie left, Laura moved her things into her dead uncle's bedroom. She knew the move might upset her cousin, but that didn't stop her. Surely, once Jodie saw that she was comfortable here, she would let her remain. The room she shared with Doris was entirely too cramped; furthermore, she desired privacy.

This morning, she slept in late, took her time dressing, then went into the kitchen, where she found her mother laboring over the ironing.

Doris' smile was filled with love as she wished her daughter good morning.

Laura pulled out a chair and sat at the table. "There's nothing good about this morning," she complained.

"Laura, honey, what's wrong?"

"Oh Mother, I'm so bored! This pathetic little town is so dull! There is absolutely nothing to do."

Doris felt sorry for her daughter; she also felt badly about bringing her here. Laura had been so much happier living in St. Louis. But following her husband's death, Doris had been left almost penniless, for Laura's father had squandered his money; he also left behind gambling debts that Doris had been forced to pay. Neither Doris nor Laura knew the first thing about supporting themselves; therefore, Doris had decided to move in with her brother-in-law. She had figured it was about time for Jodie to marry, and then Cole would need a woman to take care of his home. She hoped Laura would marry too. However, there weren't very many eligible bachelors for her daughter to choose from. The most promising catch was Bill Lawson, but Jodie had already claimed him. Garth Bradley was unmarried, and although he wasn't especially handsome, his father was wealthy. Her daughter could do a lot worse, but Garth didn't seem interested in Laura, nor did she appear interested in him. The younger brother, Dirk, was out of the question, for he was entirely too irresponsible.

"Would you like some breakfast?" Doris asked Laura, going to the stove and pouring coffee.

"I'm not hungry," she mumbled.

Doris put a steaming cup of coffee before her daughter. "Drink this; it will perk you up. Things will get better, darling. Just wait and see."

Laura frowned petulantly; she wished her mother wasn't always so chipper—sometimes it drove her to distraction!

"I need to bring in some laundry," Doris said, picking up an empty basket. She went out the back door and to the clothesline.

Doris had barely stepped outside when a knock came at the front door.

Laura wondered who was calling; more than likely it was one of her mother's matronly friends. As soon as she could, she would excuse herself and go to her room, for she found Doris's companions boring.

She went to the front door, opened it, and was pleasantly surprised to find Bill Lawson.

"Good morning, Laura. May I come in?" he said, doffing his hat.

"Of course," she replied, stepping aside for him to enter. She took him to the parlor, sat on the sofa, and drew him to sit down beside her. "Your visit is such a wonderful surprise," she remarked, giving him a radiant smile.

He was flattered; Jodie never seemed this happy to see him. "Laura, you always make me feel so welcome."

"I'm always pleased to see you."

"I have news of Jodie."

"Oh?" she questioned, wishing he hadn't brought up her cousin. She didn't want to discuss Jodie.

"She's been kidnapped."

Laura was astounded. "Kidnapped?" she exclaimed.

He recounted his visit from Dirk, then told her that they had gone to see Deputy Riker. "Jonas suggested that he deliver the ransom. I finally agreed. However, I did so reluctantly."

"I think Jonas is right. Those men won't care who brings the money, just as long as they get it. This is a job for a law officer. He's paid to risk his life."

"But I feel as though I'm letting Jodie down."

"Nonsense," she replied. "Besides, Jodie got herself into this mess. You asked her not to go."

"I pleaded with her," he admitted wretchedly.

She placed a consoling hand on his. "Bill, I know I shouldn't talk against Jodie. After all, she's my kin. But she is . . . is kind of strange. I mean, she doesn't act like most women. If you marry her, I'm afraid she won't make you happy. I think you're the kind of man who wants a wife who will fully dedicate herself to you. Jodie will never do that. She's too independent, willful, and thinks only of herself."

Bill didn't stick up for Jodie, for he totally agreed with Laura. He was indeed worried that Jodie wouldn't make him happy, for her rebellion frayed his patience and roused his anger. However, his desire for her was strong—she was beautiful, sensual, and he wanted her more than he had ever wanted any woman. He had waited two years to take her to his bed, and he wasn't about to give up on that dream, not yet!

"Laura, I realize Jodie will be difficult to live with. But once she's my wife . . . ? Well, I'll just put down my foot and demand that she do as I please."

Laura responded with laughter. "Honestly, Bill! Do you really believe you can change Jodie?"

He got to his feet to leave, for their discussion wasn't to his liking. Laura's words had more truth to them than he cared to admit. Jodie would indeed be a handful, but he was determined to tame her—one way or the other!

"I must go," he said to Laura.

"Can't you stay a little longer?"

"I need to get back to my ranch."

"Maybe someday soon I can ride out to your home for a visit," she hinted. "I get so bored staying in town."

"Why don't you and Doris come for dinner?"

"When?" she asked.

"Friday at seven o'clock?"

"That will be fine."

"I'll escort you to my ranch, or send someone in my place."

She showed him to the door, and as she closed it behind him, a sly grin was on her face. She intended to have dinner alone with Lawson, for she planned to convince her mother to stay home.

Cade and Antonio stood a short distance from the blazing flames. They had built the large fire over an hour ago, but so far no Comanchero had come down from the mountain to investigate. Cade was beginning to wonder if

Antonio had been misinformed about building a fire as a signal. More than likely, they were burning kindling for nothing.

But the thought barely crossed his mind when distant riders came into view. It took a few minutes for them to arrive. Antonio stepped forward and spoke Spanish to the man who seemed to be in charge. Following a short discussion, the leader turned his horse around and headed back.

Antonio moved to Cade, and explained why the man had left. "He is taking my name to Hernando, along with the message that I wish to see him."

Cade indicated the remaining outlaws. "I take it, they're going to wait with us."

"Sí," Antonio replied.

Cade cast the Comancheros a cursory glance; the ten men were heavily armed, and appeared more hostile than a band of marauding Apaches.

"I had to give the Comanchero your name, as well as mine," Antonio continued. "If Hernando has heard of you, and knows you are a U.S. Marshal, then he might decide to kill you, and kill me for bringing you here."

"What happened to that polite son you told me about?"

Antonio smiled. "Let us pray, amigo, that he has not changed all that much."

The Comanchero delivered Antonio's message. Hernando was incredulous to learn that his father wished to see him, but was puzzled to hear that he was riding with Cade Brandon. Lopez had heard of Brandon and knew he was a U.S. Marshal. He told his man that he would see Morelos and Brandon, and that he wanted them brought to him unharmed.

He waited for his guests in the parlor, with a glass of whiskey for company. He wondered about Antonio's visit. Could it have anything to do with Señorita Walker? Did he and the Marshal know that Breed had brought her here?

As though thinking about Breed conjured up his presence, the man suddenly came into the parlor. "I came in through the back door," he explained. "Grass Woman said I would find you here." He pointed at the liquor cabinet. "Mind if I fix myself a drink?"

"Help yourself," Lopez replied. "Breed, is Marshal Brandon tailing you?"

"He might be," he said, pouring a glass of whiskey.

"I just gave one of my men permission to bring Brandon and Antonio Morelos into camp."

The men, immersed in conversation, didn't detect Jodie's soft footsteps as she left her room to go to the kitchen. She was moving past the parlor door when Breed's next words brought her steps to a sudden halt.

"Brandon is coming here?" he remarked. "That is the best news I've had in a long time." He took a long, gulping swallow of whiskey. "I think I will kill Brandon slowly."

"No!" Jodie exclaimed, darting into the room. She turned a pleading gaze to Hernando. "Please don't let Breed kill him!"

Lopez was taken aback. "You are not too proud to plead for Brandon's life, but last night you were willing to stand on pride and forfeit your own life. You are in love with Brandon, sí?"

"We're partners."

"Partners? There are many kinds of partners, señorita. But do not look so worried. Maybe I will let Brandon live." He moved quickly to her side, grasped her arm, and drew her against him. He was so close she could feel his breath on her face. "Whether or not Brandon lives might well depend on you. I told you, muchacha, there are ways to convince you to be amiable."

She thrust her hands against his chest and pushed away.

"I should have killed you last night when I had the chance!"

He laughed heartily, turned to Breed, and said, "You have captured a wildcat. Do not turn your back on her, amigo."

Breed didn't want to discuss the woman, for he felt he could handle his captive. He looked at Lopez with murder in his eyes. "Brandon will not leave this place alive! He is a U.S. Marshal, and killing a lawman gives me pleasure."

Hernando responded with a menacing smile. "I will decide who lives and who dies. Do not forget that!"

Breed feared no man, but he wasn't about to further anger his host, for he suspected Lopez would not hesitate to order his death.

Chapter Ten

Jodie left the parlor and went out the front door. A small stoop led up to the house, and she stood on the top step and watched for Cade. That he had followed her to the Comancheros' camp didn't surprise her. But she wished that he hadn't. His life was in danger, and she blamed herself.

Hernando came outside and stood beside her.

"I'm amazed that you're allowing Cade into your camp," she told him. "I thought your men would have killed a U.S. Marshal on sight."

"A U.S. Marshal is not a threat to me or my men. This is Mexico, señorita."

"I realize that," she replied impatiently. "But I heard Comancheros killed all lawmen, regardless of their jurisdiction."

"Do not believe everything you hear. But if it were only Brandon, I would not have given my permission for him to come here. Antonio Morelos is riding with him, and he is the man I wish to see."

"Antonio is with Cade?" she asked, surprised.

"You know Morelos?"

"Yes, but not very well."

"Brandon and Morelos know you are here, do they not?"

"I'm sure they do. I don't think they made this trip because they had nothing better to do!"

He chuckled. "Muchacha, I wonder what I should do with you. Should I let you leave with Brandon, keep you for myself, or give you back to Breed?"

Her eyes flashed. "You act as though I'm your property!"

"For now, señorita, you are. It would be in your best interest to remember that. Your future is in my hands. If I were you, I would not anger me."

Breed came outside, his presence an interruption.

Lopez pierced him with a steely gaze. "There is no reason for you to be here. Brandon is my guest—" his eyes twinkled as he turned to Jodie and continued, "—soon, maybe, he will be my prisoner."

Breed resented Lopez's arrogance and superiority. The man had taken over his captive, and was now ordering him to stay away from Brandon. A murderous rage simmered within him, but he kept it under control, for he knew there was nothing he could do.

"Well?" Hernando said to Breed. "I told you to leave, did I not?"

Jodie and Lopez were blocking the top stoop, and as Breed moved down the steps, his huge frame barreled between them, almost knocking them off balance.

Hernando laughed at his angry departure. "Maybe he will go on the warpath, sí?"

"You shouldn't take him so lightly," said Jodie. "He's a murderer, and he'd probably just as soon kill you as look at you."

"Let him try, señorita. Just let him try." There was no consternation in his voice; he spoke calmly, but with a threatening undertone. Jodie knew he was not afraid of Breed.

The sound of horses caught their attention, and they watched as four riders came in view. Two Comancheros were escorting Cade and Antonio to Hernando's home. However, the guides left before reaching the house, for they had disarmed their prisoners and knew they were not a threat.

The sight of Jodie eased Cade's mind. She seemed well and unharmed. But now that he knew she was all right, the anger he had suppressed resurfaced. He was still upset that she had slipped away from the hacienda to go to Villa de Lazar. It was a miracle she hadn't gotten herself killed!

Lopez stepped forward to greet the pair as they reined in and dismounted. He hadn't seen his father in thirteen years, and he stared at him as though he wasn't sure if he should shake his hand or spit on him.

Antonio returned Lopez's stare, and was somewhat impressed to find that Hernando was a younger replica of himself. He almost wished he hadn't forfeited his fatherly rights, for he and Adela had never been blessed with a son, and he longed desperately for one.

Lopez gestured toward the front door and invited his guests inside.

Cade ignored the invitation and went to Jodie. "Are you all right?" he asked.

She saw anger flicker deep within his eyes. "Yes, I'm fine. But you shouldn't have followed me here."

"Your gratitude amazes me," he replied irritably.

Antonio decided to interrupt before their tempers flared. "Let us go inside," he said, stepping to Jodie and taking her arm. He quickly led her away from Cade and into the house.

Lopez motioned for Brandon to precede him, and they followed Morelos and Jodie into the parlor. As Hernando poured whiskey for himself and his two newly arrived guests, Cade intensely watched Jodie, who was standing her ground, eyeing him with the same intensity. He had never seen her look more lovely, for the borrowed blouse and skirt softly enhanced her delicate curves. The curly tresses, held back from her face with a comb, glistened with freshly washed highlights. It was obvious to Cade that Lopez had treated her like a guest, and not like a prisoner.

Jodie knew Cade was angry, and she didn't really blame him. After all, they were partners, and she had left him behind. She wanted to make amends, and if he would show her a little civility, she'd be willing to apologize. But she had a feeling their tempers were on a collision course. She began to feel uneasy under his acute scrutiny, but it wasn't the anger in his eyes that made her uncomfortable; it was the desire his gaze was lighting inside her. His stare held her spellbound, and it seemed as though they were the only two people in the room. His piercing eyes were like two magnets drawing her heart, soul, and willpower from her body and into his. She felt defenseless against him. It was a startling revelation, but also a very disturbing one, for her temperament clashed with Cade's; any passion between them would be as turbulent as a raging sea.

"Señorita," Hernando said.

She welcomed the interruption, for it broke Brandon's hypnotic spell. She turned to Lopez to see what he wanted.

"Will you please go to the kitchen and ask Grass Woman to serve coffee?"

She was glad to comply, and promptly left the room.

Lopez asked his guests to be seated. They sat on the sofa, and their host handed them their drinks. He eased into a chair, faced them, and asked, "Why are you here?"

"We came for Señorita Walker," Antonio answered.

"She is not my prisoner. She belongs to Breed."

"Breed's prisoner?" Cade questioned. "Where's Red?"

"He is dead. On the way here, his horse threw him over the cliff."

"Why did Breed bring Jodie here?"

"He plans to collect a ransom. He thinks Señor Lawson will pay two thousand dollars for her release."

"If money is all he wants," Antonio said, "I will give him the two thousand."

Lopez smiled. "Surely, you do not believe he will let her live. He will kill her and both of you."

"He might not find it that damned easy," Cade remarked.

Lopez was familiar with Brandon's reputation. "I believe you, señor. I know you are not an easy man to kill, for too many have tried and failed."

"Hernando," Antonio pleaded, "I cannot believe you will let Breed keep the señorita. You are not like that."

Lopez seethed with resentment. "How would you know what I am like. You never knew me. And you do not know me now."

"I would like to know you."

Hernando released his resentment through laughter. "It is too late for that, dear Pápa!"

"I did not realize you were so bitter."

Jodie, returning, heard their exchange, and she was shocked to hear Hernando address Antonio as "Pápa." She now knew why Hernando had looked so familiar. She went to the spare chair and sat down, keeping her eyes averted from Cade. The amorous feelings his gaze had stirred still had her uneasy.

Hernando, changing the subject, said to Antonio, "I will tell Breed that you are willing to pay the ransom."

"You don't have to pay the ransom," Cade told Antonio. "I'll pay it."

"You are not rich, amigo. Let me do this favor for you and the señorita."

"She's my responsibility, and I'll take care of the ransom."

Jodie was piqued. "I'm not your responsibility," she

fumed, her eyes now meeting Cade's with anger instead of desire. "I never asked you to ride with me; you insisted that we work together. I don't want your charity!"

"Who said anything about charity?" he asked, a brow quirked. "I expect you to pay back that two thousand. You got yourself into this situation, and you should pay your way out. However, I'll take installments, regardless of how small."

"And you'll get every penny of it!" she snapped.

Grass Woman's entry quieted their spat. She carried a tray laden with cups and a coffee pot. She was about to put the tray on the table in front of the sofa, when she happened to glance at Cade. She exhaled sharply, as though an invisible force had knocked the air from her lungs. Her eyes grew extraordinarily wide, her face blanched, and the filled tray fell from her hands. The cups shattered as they hit the bare floor, and the pot turned over, spilling hot coffee over Cade's and Antonio's boots.

Morelos responded by leaping to his feet, but Cade, staring into Grass Woman's face, was too stunned to move. His complexion paled as though he had seen a ghost; in a way, he had!

Grass Woman whirled around awkwardly and fled the room. Cade's mobility returned, and bounding from the sofa, he called raspingly, "Alison? My God! Alison?" For a moment he stood riveted, as though glued to the floor, but then he hurried after her.

Jodie turned to Antonio and Lopez, who were totally baffled. "I think Grass Woman is Cade's sister," she told them, remembering her name was Alison. "Twelve years ago she was kidnapped by the Comanches. Cade thought she was dead." A feeling of joy rose within her, for she was happy for Cade and Grass Woman. No, not Grass Woman, she thought. Alison; her name is really Alison.

* * *

As Cade entered the kitchen, he caught a glimpse of Grass Woman slipping out the rear door. Hurrying, he reached her before she could escape. He grasped her arm and turned her so that she was facing him. For a long moment, he stared into her face; he recognized the features he had once known as well as he knew his own. She had changed. She was twelve years older, but it was more than that—in her face, he saw years of sadness, abuse, and heartbreak.

"Alison," he whispered. "I thought you were dead."

Cade looked blurry to her, for tears had flooded her eyes. Still, she could see that he was as handsome as she remembered. "Why didn't you and Pa find me?" she asked tremulously. "I waited and waited, but you never came." Her voice sounded like that of a young girl's.

"We tried to find you. But Pa fell ill; he died a year after your abduction."

A soft groan sounded in her throat, but she didn't say anything.

"I kept on looking," Cade continued. "Finding you was all I lived for, but it was as though you had vanished from the face of the earth. I finally talked to a Comanche chief who said that a white woman had died of diphtheria. He described her and I thought it was you. Nevertheless, I held onto a shred of hope and continued searching. But, finally, I gave up."

Cade still had hold of her arm, and he coaxed her to sit beside him on the porch steps. "Alison, I don't know where to begin, or what to say. I guess I'll begin here— why are you with Lopez?"

"My name is Grass Woman," she said, her voice now strong. "Alison died years ago."

Now that Cade had found his sister, he was not about

to lose her again. "Alison isn't dead," he argued. "She's very much alive, and I'm taking her home."

"Home?" she questioned sharply. "Where's that?"

"I have a ranch in Texas. Uncle Charlie's taking care of it for me."

"Uncle Charlie?" she murmured, a faint smile on her lips. "I was always so fond of him."

"He helped me look for you; sometimes we searched together and other times we split up. He'll be overjoyed to see you."

"He won't see me," she remarked firmly. "I'm not leaving with you."

"Alison, you can't mean that!"

She leapt to her feet, stood before him, and regarded him harshly. "Oh Cade, you aren't dense, so stop acting like you are! You know what happens to women who are abducted by Comanches! Do you think for one moment that I could return to the life I had before? I don't belong there anymore!"

"You sure as hell don't belong in a Comancheros' hideout!"

"Why not? They treat me with respect! Do you think I'll find respect in Texas? I remember how people treat former Comanche captives. Walter Rawlins's wife was abducted by the Comanches. You remember him; he was a friend's of Pa's. Three months later the army found his wife and brought her home. Our own people treated her as though she had the plague. Not even her husband seemed to care about her anymore. You remember what happened to her, don't you?"

Cade nodded solemnly. "She killed herself."

"Is that the same fate you want for me?"

"Of course not!" he replied. "But, Alison, I sold the old homestead and moved a long way from there. Where I live now no one knows you. They'll never know about your abduction if you don't want them to know."

"Can you guarantee that?" she demanded. "Can you promise me that no one from my past will come along and announce to everyone that I was a Comanche's slave?"

He rose to his feet, and drew her into his arms. "Alison, please don't do this to yourself and to me. You don't belong here. You belong with your family—Charlie and me. We love you."

She leaned into his embrace, cherishing the feel of his strong arms about her. She had always idolized her brother, and had come to believe that she would never see him again. But now that he was here, she wished he hadn't come. It was better that he believed her dead, for the sister he had known and loved had ceased to exist years ago. She pushed gently out of his arms, and gazed up at him through tear-filled eyes. "Cade, if only I could make you understand. The Alison you knew is dead. Please bury her memory and let her rest in peace."

"Never," he replied. "Damn it! You aren't dead! The Alison I remember was spirited, courageous, and a survivor. That girl is still somewhere deep inside you, and I intend to find her again."

"Spirited?" she questioned. "My spirit was broken by the Comanche warriors who abducted me. Courageous? I lost my courage after my first owner sold me to his cousin who used me night after night. Survivor? Losing two babies destroyed my will to survive."

"Babies?" he murmured.

"Yes. I gave birth to two children—a boy and a girl. The boy was born too soon and lived only a couple of hours. A year later, I gave birth to a daughter. She was sickly and lived only three months."

"God, Alison!" Cade groaned.

"God?" she repeated harshly. "Where was God when I needed Him? Where were you and Uncle Charlie?"

He drew her back into his arms. "Don't," he murmured.

"Don't feel this way. I swear I tried to find you. Please believe me! I would never forsake you."

"If you love me, Cade, you'll let me go. I don't want to leave with you. I want to stay here."

He stepped back so that he could see into her face. "Are you and Lopez . . . ? Do you want to stay here because you're in love with him?"

"I'm not in love with Hernando. I'm his housekeeper, and nothing more. But he has been kind to me, and I like him very much."

"How did you end up here?"

"The Comanche who owned me finally sold me to a man of mixed blood—he was white and Mexican. He thought I was part Comanche, and I never told him differently. He brought me into Mexico, but we were attacked by Apaches. The Apaches killed him but before they could do anything to me, Hernando and his men arrived. They had heard the shootout and came to investigate. The Apaches fled, and Hernando brought me here. I've been here ever since."

"Does Hernando know everything about you?"

"No. He asked about my past, and I told him I didn't want to talk about it. He never brought it up again. He only knows me as Grass Woman. I keep his house, cook his meals, and do his laundry. I don't mind his business, and he doesn't inquire into mine. It's an ideal arrangement, and I don't care to give it up."

"In other words, you want to stay here and hide from life. You're only twenty-six; you've got a full future ahead of you. Damn it, Alison! You can't quit! You can still marry and have a family."

She shook her head. "There are no feelings left inside me. The Comanches stole my life as surely as if they buried a stake in my heart."

"You do have feelings; you loved your babies."

"Back then, I was still alive. My babies gave me a reason

to live, to hope, and to pray that we would be rescued. After I lost them, I lost the will to care about anything."

"You still cared, Alison. You stayed alive, didn't you? The will to survive was still in you."

She couldn't deny his words, for her presence was a living testament. "I need time alone, Cade. I must think. This is all so unexpected. Seeing you again has me too confused."

"I'll give you time alone, Alison. But I'm not leaving here without you."

"You can't force me to leave."

He sighed heavily. "Maybe not; but I'll sure as hell try."

She stood on tiptoe and kissed his cheek. "I had forgotten what it was like to have someone care so much about me."

"Of course, I care," he replied. "You're my sister."

She managed a weak smile, before whirling around and fleeing down the porch steps. Cade watched as she headed away from the compound and toward the wild foliage that grew between the house and the mountain's high cliff.

He went back into the house and to the parlor, where he found Antonio and Hernando. "Where's Jodie?" he asked.

"In her room," Lopez replied. "She left so that Antonio and I could talk privately."

"Which room is hers?"

"The last one on the left."

Cade turned to leave, but Hernando detained him, "Señor, is Grass Woman your sister?"

"Yes, she is."

"I knew she was not part Comanche, but I did not question her."

"You have treated her well. For that, I thank you."

"She is a good woman, but she carries much grief. Maybe now she will find a way to overcome the pain that is still in her heart."

Cade was impressed by Hernando's sentiment; maybe Antonio was right about him. A compassionate outlaw seemed odd, but in this case, it might very well be true.

He left the parlor, strode down the hall, and knocked on Jodie's door.

It was opened immediately. She waved him inside, asking, "How is Grass Woman . . . I mean, Alison?"

"It's hard to say."

She closed the door. "I don't understand."

"I'm not sure if she'll leave here with me."

"Why not?"

He told her about their conversation.

"Maybe she'll change her mind about not leaving," Jodie told Cade, hoping to encourage him. "When she's had time to think about it, she'll realize her place is with you and your uncle."

"I certainly hope so."

"Did you know that Antonio was Hernando's father?"

"I didn't know until last night."

"I left the room so they could be alone."

Cade glanced at the door as though he could see through it, down the hall, and into the parlor. "I sensed a lot of bitterness in Lopez. I think Antonio's in for a rude awakening." He turned his gaze back to Jodie, and a glint of anger shone in his piercing blue eyes. "Why did you leave the hacienda?"

She braced herself for an altercation. "I wanted to capture Red and Breed before they left Villa de Lazar."

"Instead, you got yourself captured!"

She confronted him with a flash of defiant spirit, "Don't lecture me, Cade Brandon! You wanted to ride with me; I didn't ask for your help!"

"Leaving your handkerchief behind was asking for help, wasn't it?"

"That was a mistake that I soon regretted!"

He waved his arms in a gesture of exasperation. "Naturally, Jodie Walker would regret asking for help! What is it with you? Why are you so determined to do everything on your own?"

"Because I learned a long time ago that a woman shouldn't be dependent on a man!"

"What the hell does that mean?"

"I think it's self-explanatory!"

His tone softened. "Who was it, Jodie? Who hurt you so badly that you built this protective wall about yourself?"

"My father," she murmured, the answer slipping out before she could stop it.

Chapter Eleven

Seeing Antonio again stirred mixed emotions in Hernando. He wanted to accept his father graciously, yet, at the same time, he was very bitter. The man had turned his back on him and Rosita, and although he understood the reason, a part of him remained resentful. If he had a son, he felt he would never forsake him . . . regardless.

"Hernando," Antonio began hesitantly, "why did you become an outlaw?"

"Why do you ask?"

"I am curious, and I also care."

Hernando laughed tersely. "You care? Why do you want to lie to me? You do not care about me, and you did not care about my mother."

"Where is Rosita?"

"She is dead."

"I had not heard. When did she die?"

"Eight years ago. After my stepfather left her, she became a *puta*. She died from a whore's disease."

"*Madre de Dios!* Rosita a *puta*?"

"It was the only way she knew to support herself and her son."

"That day you came to my hacienda, had your stepfather already left Rosita?"

"Sí, he had been gone a long time."

"Why did you not tell me? I would have helped you and Rosita."

"It did not cross my mind to tell you that my mother was a whore. But it did cross my mind to kill you."

Antonio was stunned. "Kill me? But you were not hostile. You were very civil."

"The hate was there, señor. But it was so deep, you could not see it."

"And now?" Antonio asked intently.

Lopez laughed as though it wasn't important. "I am no longer a fourteen-year-old boy. Hate you? I have not even thought about you in years."

Morelos didn't believe him; he had a feeling that Hernando's bitterness hadn't mellowed with time, and that he still thought about the father who had deserted him.

"Why did you become an outlaw?" Antonio asked again.

"About a year after Rosita died, my stepfather found me. He asked if I wanted to ride with him and the Comancheros. I was cleaning hotel rooms; joining the Comancheros sounded more exciting and much more lucrative. Lopez soon became the leader; I stayed with him a couple of years, but then I left and several Comancheros left with me. We formed our own band, and settled in this valley."

"Why did you leave your stepfather?"

"We did not agree."

"What does that mean?"

"He enjoyed killing too much, señor."

Antonio understood. "Hernando, maybe you are too kind-hearted to be a Comanchero."

"Maybe my band and I are no longer Comancheros. Maybe we are just outlaws."

"You rob from the rich, for a price you hide bandits, and you have stolen from the Apaches."

"We only take what the Apaches steal when they pillage."

"Your rewards can not be very large. There are not many chances to rob the rich, hide bandits, or steal from the Apaches."

"We do not need a lot of money. This valley is fertile and we grow our food. We also have livestock. We are self-supporting. You and others think of us as outlaws, but we see ourselves as rebels. We do not wish to live under the government's dictatorship. You can not understand because you are an aristocrat. But for the poor, señor, Mexico is worse than living in hell."

"You think of yourselves as rebels?" Antonio questioned. "Do you not understand? It makes no difference what you call yourselves; the law calls you Comancheros. The government will not rest until all the Comancheros are exterminated. You will not be spared."

"I am not afraid to die."

"But what about the women and children in this valley? What will happen to them when their men are executed?"

Hernando bounded angrily from his chair, and glared resentfully at his father. "Do not lecture me! You do not care what happens to me and the others! All you aristocrats are alike—you only care about your own well-fed stomachs, your wealth, and your precious lands! To you, Mexico's poor are rubbish; you have to live with it, but you don't have to clean it up."

He started to leave, but Antonio got quickly to his feet and said, "Wait! What about Señorita Walker? Will you let her leave with us?"

"She is free to go."

"Will you tell Breed that Cade will pay her ransom?"

"Forget the ransom," he said impatiently. Suddenly, he wanted to be rid of his father, Brandon, and even Jodie.

He damned Breed for bringing Jodie here, which inevitably led to Antonio's and Brandon's arrival. He continued testily, "I do not want men like Breed thinking they can use my camp to hold their prisoners."

"Breed won't like you doing this."

"I am not afraid of Breed."

"Hernando," he began curiously, "did you tell Señorita Walker that you intended to set her free?"

"No, I did not tell her."

"Why not?"

"I was not sure that I would release her. She is very lovely, and I hoped . . ." He shrugged his shoulders. "However, I think she is in love with Señor Brandon." He left the parlor and went into the kitchen, looking for Grass Woman.

"Your father?" Cade asked Jodie. "He's the man who hurt you? I don't understand."

She wished she hadn't said anything about her father, but the words had slipped out before she could stop them. "I didn't mean that like it sounded," she tried to explain. "My father never intentionally hurt me. He loved me very much, and I thought the world of him."

"But something must have happened."

She lifted her chin stubbornly. "It doesn't matter. Besides, I'd rather not talk about it."

"Maybe it would help if you did."

"It would help if you'd stop pressuring me."

"Pardon me, for caring. For a moment, I forgot that Jodie Walker doesn't need a helping hand or a sympathetic ear."

"My independence really galls you, doesn't it?"

Moving with the quickness of a stalker, he suddenly had her in his clutches. He stared down into a pair of eyes that were fearless and defiant. "I admire your independence," he uttered gruffly. "It's your attitude that I find annoying.

Someday, the right man will come along, and when he does . . . ?"

"You told me that once before," she replied, his closeness sensual and disturbing. "You also said you didn't have time to awaken my passion."

He drew her closer, their bodies touching. "And you said that your passion didn't need awakening."

She leaned into his embrace, and his arm tightened about her waist, pressing her thighs intimately to his. Desire, like she had never known before, coursed through every nerve in her body. She wanted desperately to surrender, but her better judgment intervened, warning her to beware. Cade might very well steal her heart, her virtue, then disappear from her life.

Cade's passion soared, for Jodie's closeness had set his loins on fire. He was about to kiss her, when a sudden knock came at the door. Cade silently cursed the interruption; however, Jodie welcomed it—her willpower had been dangerously close to crumbling.

Antonio was the intruder; he came to let them know that Jodie was free to leave. Jodie, avoiding being alone with Cade, insisted that they go to the parlor for coffee.

Hernando stepped out the back door, and saw Grass Woman walking toward the house. He stood on the porch and waited. "I was looking for you," he said, as she drew nearer.

She paused at the bottom of the steps. "Is anything wrong?"

"No," he replied. He waved a hand toward the door, and continued, "Let us go inside."

She preceded him into the kitchen, and they sat at the table. It was a moment before Hernando broke the silence between them, "You should have told me who you were. I would have arranged for you to return to your family."

"I didn't want to go back; I still don't."

"You must leave with Señor Brandon."

"Why?" she pleaded. "Am I not a good servant?"

He smiled tenderly. "I am sending you away for your own good. You do not belong here." He reached across the table and placed a hand on hers. "Go back to your people, señorita. I do not know what happened to you when you lived with the Comanches, but I can well imagine. It has been many years; it is time for your heart to heal."

She blinked back a trace of tears. "I don't think my heart will ever heal, but it seems I have no choice but to leave with my brother. Hernando, what about Jodie? You'll help her, won't you?"

"What do you think?" he asked gently.

"Considering what happened last night, I'm not so sure."

He laughed mildly. "The señorita is a gem. I have never met a woman like her. But I was not going to harm her; I hoped to seduce her. I could very easily love a woman with her spirit and courage."

At that moment, the kitchen door opened, and Jodie came inside. "I'm sorry," she said. "I didn't mean to intrude. I was going to make a pot of coffee."

"I'll do that," Alison replied, getting up.

"If you don't mind," Hernando said to Alison, "the señorita can make the coffee. I would like to talk alone with her."

Complying, she left the kitchen.

Hernando remained seated as Jodie went to the stove and prepared the coffee. He watched her every move, for he found her fascinating—her beauty, grace, and spirit were unique. She set the pot on the stove, and he indicated the chair across from his. "Sit down, señorita, and we will talk as the coffee brews."

She was agreeable, for she had a few things to say herself. "Hernando," she began, a flash of fury in her eyes. "Why did you play cat and mouse with me? You never intended to keep me here, did you? Nor did you intend to hold Cade prisoner. It was all a game to you. Is your life so dull that you find intimidating a woman entertaining?''

He chuckled. ''You were never intimidated. I bear a small cut on my back that proves I am right. However, muchacha, I apologize for my behavior. But I could not help myself. As far as playing cat and mouse, it was not a game. Your beauty and spirit are very tempting, and keeping you here did cross my mind.''

''Men like you make me so mad!'' she seethed. ''You treat women as though God put them on this earth strictly for a man's pleasure.''

''Señorita, no harm was done. Can we not be friends?'' He smiled charmingly, and his expression reminded her of a naughty boy asking for forgiveness.

Her anger mellowed. ''I don't intend to hold a grudge.''

He pushed back his chair and got to his feet. ''I must find Breed and let him know that you are leaving. He will not be pleased.''

Jodie knew that was an understatement. ''I'm sure you have several enemies, but I think you're about to make your most dangerous one.''

Her words hung in the air like a dark premonition. A strange, nervous unease settled in the pit of Hernando's stomach. Breed was not a man to cross, and he might very well seek revenge. He supposed he could have him killed; then he wouldn't have to worry that he might try to even the score. But Lopez couldn't order a man's death under such circumstances; furthermore, Breed might chalk up the ransom as a lost venture and forget about it. He couldn't imagine Breed confronting him and his rebels; it would be suicidal.

He summoned a carefree smile for Jodie. ''I do not fear Breed.''

She watched as he turned around and left through the

back door. Jodie, however, feared Breed, for she sensed a violence in him that was blood-chilling. Nevertheless, he had killed her father, and she still intended to see that he pay for his crime.

Hernando found Breed camped at the edge of the compound. He was not a mingler; he preferred to be alone. That he and Red had ridden together had always amazed Hernando, for he knew Breed didn't make friends. But then, he and Red probably weren't friends; they had most likely teamed up because it was convenient.

Breed was sitting at the campfire, but Lopez remained standing, for he didn't intend to stay very long. "I am releasing Brandon and Morelos," he said evenly. "They will take Señorita Walker with them."

Breed bounded angrily to his feet. "The woman is mine!"

"Once you brought her into my camp, she became my property. I am giving her back."

"She is worth two thousand dollars. I will give you half."

"I do not take that kind of money."

A cold, murderous rage distorted Breed's face. "The woman has blinded you with her beauty. She has made you weak and very foolish!"

Hernando responded with a smile. "Sí, maybe you are right, amigo. But she will go free." His dark eyes suddenly hardened, and his face became deadly serious. "If you harm her, I will kill you!" With that, he turned on his heel and walked away.

Breed's gaze bore steadily into his back as he moved farther and farther into the distance. Hernando's threat created anger instead of fear, and the burning rage inside Breed consumed him. He knew only retribution would put out the flame.

* * *

Jodie took the coffee into the parlor; Alison was there with Cade and Antonio. Alison had told her brother that she would leave with him, and he now announced her decision to everyone in the room.

As Jodie placed the tray on the table, Cade continued, "I think we should leave at once."

"Now?" Alison questioned. She was sitting on the sofa beside him, and she turned to him with surprise. "But why not wait until morning?"

Antonio answered, "Cade is right. The sooner we leave this place, the better."

Jodie poured the coffee, and handed everyone a cup. Then sitting in a chair, she remarked, "Breed is safe as long as he's here, and he won't leave until we do. I agree with Cade; let's pack up and go."

"Wait a minute," Cade said. "What does Breed have to do with us leaving?"

Jodie eyed him without a waver. "He's still wanted for my father's murder. Have you forgotten the reason I left Crystal Creek?"

"What do you intend to do? Camp on the other side of the mountain and wait for Breed to ride into your camp and surrender? He could stay here for weeks, even months! Or he could slip by you in the middle of the night—and probably slit your throat in the process!"

"You have apparently given up, but I haven't."

"It's not a question of giving up. There's nothing you or I can do until he crosses the border. We can't continue looking for him in Mexico. There are too many places he can hole up where we could never find him. Pursuing him now is a waste of time."

"Maybe Hernando will hand him over," Antonio said.

"No, I will not do that," Lopez suddenly spoke up. He had entered the room undetected. "He came here because he trusted me, and I will not betray that trust." He strode farther into the parlor, turned to Jodie, and continued, "You should listen to Señor Brandon, for he is right. Mexico is no place to pursue Breed. Someday he will again cross the border. You must be patient, señorita."

Patience was not one of Jodie's stronger points; however, she had to admit that she really had no other choice. Chasing Breed across Mexico was as futile as chasing the wind.

"All right," she relented. "I'll go home."

Alison stood up. "I'll pack my things."

"Do it quickly," Cade told her. "If we leave soon, we can reach Antonio's hacienda a few hours after dark."

"I'll help you pack," Jodie said to Alison.

The moment the women were gone, Lopez warned Cade, "Be careful, señor. Breed is a formidable enemy. He might decide to kill you and the señorita before either of you can kill him."

Cade nodded. "I've thought of that. Maybe I should go to him and get this over with right now."

Ordinarily, Lopez was not opposed to a fair fight, but he already felt as though he had been disloyal to Breed. He had known the man for years; Breed had ridden with Lopez's stepfather's Comancheros. "I can not let you confront Breed," he said to Cade. "Take your fight elsewhere. As long as Breed is here, he is under my protection."

Cade understood—there was, after all, honor among thieves.

The women were soon ready to leave; the horses, along with the confiscated weapons, were brought to the house. Hernando led his guests outside. Three Comancheros, mounted and heavily armed, waited as an escort.

"When you reach the cliff," Lopez said to the others, "you will be blindfolded."

A shudder coursed through Jodie as she remembered the dangerous trek up the mountainside. It had cost Red his life!

Hernando went to Alison and hugged her fondly. "I hope you find happiness, and that your heart will find peace."

"*Gracias,* Hernando," she murmured. His tenderness touched her deeply; however, she believed happiness and peace was lost to her forever. A vision of her babies flashed across her mind; such heartbreak would never go away.

Lopez then turned to Jodie, and with a charming smile, said, "I will never forget you, señorita."

She felt the same way; despite his devilish manner, she couldn't help but like him. "Goodbye, Hernando." She went to her Appaloosa, and Cade gave her a hand-up.

Except for Antonio, who had remained on the porch, everyone was ready to leave. He shifted his weight uneasily from one foot to the other. He knew he should get on his horse and simply ride away. But a force he couldn't define held him back. After all, Hernando was his son—he should say something more than just good-bye.

Lopez sensed his thoughts, and made it easy for him. "Good-bye, Antonio. And do not feel so guilty. We are nothing to each other."

As though Hernando's words had freed him, he moved down the porch steps and mounted his horse. He took one last look at his son, and was startled by a sudden impulse to beg Hernando to come home with him. The impulse disappeared as quickly as it materialized, but that such a thought could even cross his mind left Antonio stunned.

Lopez watched as the group turned their horses about and followed their escort. His eyes were glued to his father, and the rejection he had suffered as a boy returned to haunt him again.

Chapter Twelve

It was late evening when Antonio and the others arrived at his hacienda. Lucinda, who was getting ready for bed, heard her father and his guests enter the house. She put on a robe, and hurried downstairs. She found everyone in the parlor. She hugged Antonio, then turned to Cade with a radiant smile. "I thank God that you and Pápa are alive and well! I have been so worried!" She cast Jodie an icy stare. "If they had died, it would have been your fault!"

"Lucinda!" her father admonished. "I cannot believe you said such a thing! I insist that you apologize to Señorita Walker."

"She doesn't owe me an apology," Jodie said. "She's right; it would have been my fault. The next time I pursue fugitives, I'll go alone. That way, I won't be responsible for anyone else."

A wry grin touched Cade's lips, causing his black moustache to curl on the ends; it lent him a piratical charm. "The ever independent Deputy Walker."

She lifted her chin defiantly. "It has nothing to do with

independence. I can simply do my job better if I don't have to worry about a partner.''

Antonio spoke up, ending their banter. "Lucinda, I want you to meet Alison.''

"Alison!" she exclaimed. She knew Cade had a sister named Alison, who had been abducted by the Comanches. She looked closely at the woman standing beside her father and saw a resemblance to Cade. "Are you Cade's sister?" she asked.

Alison hesitated. Lucinda probably knew about her abduction and was most likely envisioning all the horrid details. She wanted to turn and run away from the morbid curiosity she imagined in Lucinda's eyes.

"Yes," she finally answered. "I'm Cade's sister."

"Where did he find you?"

Jodie sensed Alison's discomfort, and she said to Antonio, "It's late; I'd like to retire, and I think Alison is also tired."

"Yes, I am," Alison said quickly. "Lucinda, Cade can tell you where he found me. I'm really too fatigued to talk about it."

Morelos summoned his housekeeper and told her to take the ladies to their rooms.

"Are you hungry?" Antonio asked Cade.

He shook his head.

"I could use a bite. If you will excuse me, I will go to the kitchen and see what I can find."

As he left the parlor, Lucinda slipped her hand in the crook of Cade's arm, and said, "Let's take a stroll in the garden. It is such a lovely night. I want to hear all about Alison. How wonderful that you found her!"

They went outside, and as they strode leisurely toward the flower garden at the back of the house, Cade told Lucinda about finding Alison.

An intricately-carved gazebo, surrounded by a multitude of flowers, stood majestically in the center of the colorful garden. An ornate iron bench was inside the large gazebo, and Lucinda urged Cade to sit beside her. A full moon illuminated his handsome features, and as Lucinda gazed adoringly into his face, she placed a hand atop his, and murmured seductively, "The night is very romantic, is it not?" She leaned against him, and with her lips very close to his, she asked, "Do you find me attractive?"

Her seduction came as no surprise to Cade, for he figured she had brought him out here for that reason. "Lucinda," he began firmly, "I know why you wanted us to be alone. But I didn't come here to make love; I hope to convince you to forget about me in that way."

"But why?" she cried. "Do you not find me pretty?"

She was a vision of beauty: the moon's saffron glow emphasized her delicate features, and her long black hair was like dark silk. The light fabric dressing gown gracefully defined her ample breasts, curvaceous thighs, and shapely legs.

"I find you very beautiful," Cade told her tenderly. "But I'm not in love with you, Lucinda."

Jodie's bedroom faced the garden, and Cade didn't see Jodie step out onto the terrace, but Lucinda caught a glimpse of her. Believing Jodie stood between her and Cade, she suddenly flung her arms about Cade and kissed him passionately. She knew Jodie was watching.

Freeing himself from Lucinda's aggression, Cade remarked irritably, "Damn it! Haven't you heard a word I've said? There can never be anything between us but friendship."

Lucinda stole a quick peek at the terrace; Jodie was no longer there.

Cade stood, drawing Lucinda to her feet. "Let's go back to the house." He took her arm firmly, forcing her to match his determined strides. "I'm leaving in the morning," he told her. "I don't know when I'll be back; it could be years, maybe never. I plan to retire and move to my ranch. Therefore, for your own sake, forget this fantasy you have about us and think about your fiancé. If you give yourself half a chance, you might fall in love with him."

Miguel Huerta was only a name to Lucinda—a man her father had chosen. "I do not want to think about him!" she cried desperately. "I love you—I have always loved you! If I cannot have you, then I will . . . I will run away! I will not stay here and marry Señor Huerta!"

Her childish tantrum didn't faze Cade, for he knew Antonio and Adela had spoiled their daughter. He didn't take her threat seriously, for he didn't think it would amount to anything. Lucinda always believed such behavior could get her anything she wanted.

"Run away?" he questioned. "Don't you think a threat like that is a little childish?"

She flung his hand off her arm, and with eyes blazing furiously, she spat, "You have always treated me like I am a child! Sometimes, Cade Brandon, I love you so much that I hate you! Go live on your ranch; I do not care! I hope I never see you again!" With that, she hurried away and fled into the house. She almost stopped, turned around, and went back. But anger was stronger than her desire to make amends. Furthermore, she had her pride— she would no longer humble herself! Her threat to run away had been spoken in the heat of the moment. Now, however, she began to give it considerable thought. She didn't want to marry a man her father had chosen. If she couldn't have Cade, then she would find someone of her own choosing!

Jodie, fuming, paced back and forth across her bedroom floor. She wasn't sure why the interlude in the garden was upsetting; after all, she and Cade were partners, not lovers. Moreover, she didn't even want him to court her, for she didn't care for men like him. Most of the time, he was overbearing, rude, and . . . and had almost trifled with her affections. At Hernando's house, only Antonio's interruption had prevented Cade from kissing her. Now, only moments before, he had kissed Lucinda! He was evidently a womanizer on the prowl! Well, she was one prey he would never catch!

A knock came at the door; she opened it and was startled to find Cade. "Think of the devil, and here he is!" she remarked tartly.

He was totally baffled. "What does that mean?"

"Never mind," she said tersely. "What do you want?"

"I came to see how you're doing. I don't intend to stay long."

"You aren't staying period!" she snapped.

She started to close the door, but he quickly blocked it with his arm, squeezed inside, and shut the door himself. Perplexed, he asked with a note of impatience, "What's bothering you? You're the most confounded woman I've ever met. I never know what the hell you're thinking or why you're upset."

"I'm not upset," she replied, knowing full well that she was indeed troubled. But she wasn't about to admit such a thing. "However, I don't understand why you sought my company," she continued. "Do you always move so quickly from one woman to another?"

"I don't understand," he replied.

She indicated the terrace, saying, "It overlooks the garden and the gazebo. I stepped outside for a breath of fresh air. I didn't mean to spy, but I couldn't help but see you and Lucinda in a lovers' embrace."

"I can explain . . ." he began.

"No explanation is necessary," she intervened, as though unruffled. "Your personal life is none of my business, nor do I care. But I do care when you leave Lucinda's side to make a beeline for my bedroom. This room is off limits to you, Cade Brandon, and so am I. Do I make myself clear?"

"You're a lot clearer than you think."

"What are you implying?"

"That you're jealous."

She laughed harshly. "Jealous? That's a conceited interpretation."

Cade continued as though she hadn't contradicted him. "But you have no reason to be jealous. I'm not interested in Lucinda. Furthermore, I didn't kiss her; she kissed me."

"Of course," she retorted. "Lucinda is so strong that she simply overpowered you."

"I've never known a woman so stubborn or so unreasonable," he mumbled irritably.

"Well, look on the brighter side," she said with sarcasm. "You won't know me much longer. It's time for you to turn in your badge and retire to your ranch. Our paths will probably never cross again."

"Aren't you forgetting something?"

"What's that?"

"Breed. He's still at large."

"Surely, you don't intend to find him before you leave for your ranch. That could take weeks, months, maybe years."

"You're right. And I am considering forgetting Breed and going to my ranch. But I'm worried that you'll pursue him."

"Then I'll put your mind at ease. I don't intend to spend my life looking for Breed. But if he ever shows his face in Crystal Creek, or somewhere nearby . . ."

"Jodie, don't go after him. He'll kill you."

Cade's warning hung suspended in the room, like a dark presence promising doom. Breed's formidable image flashed across Jodie's mind, and it sent fear into her heart. But she hated being afraid, for she considered it an intolerable weakness.

Brandon saw her fear; he moved to her side, and gazed caringly into her face. Her vulnerability touched him profoundly, for Jodie always appeared confident and dauntless. He knew he was seeing a side of her that she normally kept safely concealed.

"Please, Jodie," he murmured. "Forget Breed. Trying to apprehend him isn't worth your life. Your father wouldn't have wanted it this way."

His closeness was intoxicating, jumbling Jodie's thoughts and weakening her resolution. Pursuing Breed seemed unimportant—Cade's sensual proximity was all that mattered.

Desire was mirrored in her eyes, compelling Cade to draw her into his arms and kiss her. Initially, his lips caressed hers with exquisite tenderness, but as his passion took flame, he drew her tightly against him and kissed her demandingly.

Jodie surrendered, crushed in the strength of his arms and captured by the thrill of his lips. Primitive . . . exciting desire spread through her like wildfire, causing her to press every inch of her body to his.

His mouth left hers long enough to murmur, "Jodie, I need you." Then he was kissing her again, the second kiss as persuasive as the first.

This time, however, Jodie didn't surrender; instead, she pushed out of his arms. She was a little afraid of such overwhelming passion. In Cade's embrace, her willpower seemed to sprout wings and fly, leaving her unprotected and vulnerable. She didn't trust herself, nor did she trust Cade.

"What's wrong?" Cade asked gently.

She answered candidly, "I'm not ready for this."

"What does that mean?"

"I don't really know you, Cade. And when I'm in your arms, I don't seem to know myself."

He smiled knowingly. "I bet you don't feel such passion in Bill Lawson's arms."

He was right: with Bill, she was always in control.

Cade decided not to pressure her, for he knew she needed more time. He hoped he wouldn't have to wait too much longer; he wanted her with every fiber of his being—he had fallen passionately in love. He strongly suspected that he had loved her at first sight.

Jodie left his side and moved to the door leading out to the terrace. She opened it, admitting the night's gentle breeze. Desert-like terrain lay beyond the hacienda; the breeze, like a floating sea vessel, carried the warmth of a desert wind on its sails.

"Cade," Jodie began, her back turned to him. "When do you plan to leave for your ranch?"

"I don't know," he replied. "I guess that depends on you."

She turned and faced him. "Why does it depend on me?"

"I don't want to leave you. I hope I can take you with me. If we give ourselves a little more time, I think we'll fall in love." He smiled somewhat boyishly. "However, I don't think I need more time. I already know how I feel."

"Are you asking me to marry you?"

"Not if you aren't ready."

Happiness flickered in her eyes, but it was so fleeting that Cade almost missed it. But Jodie's wall of protection quickly returned, sheltering her emotions within its invisible enclosure. Cade sensed its return, for he had confronted it before.

Her chin rose willfully; Cade knew that look and it didn't please him. He felt a stir of anger.

"If I married you," Jodie began, "I suppose you'd expect me to live on your ranch."

"Of course I would."

"And be totally dependent on you?"

"What's wrong with that? You'd be my wife and the mother of my children."

"Your children?" she quipped. "Wouldn't they be ours?"

"I didn't mean that the way it sounded."

"Oh, I think you meant exactly what you said. All men feel that way. A wife and children are a man's property and his sole responsibility. If he later regrets taking on a family, he is still obligated to fulfill his duty to them. . . . regardless. And the wife? Well, she's completely dependent on her husband, isn't she?"

Jodie folded her arms over her chest, regarded Cade sternly, and continued, "That kind of dependency is not for me. I intend to stay in Crystal Creek and run for sheriff."

"You can't be serious!" he exclaimed. "You have no business running for sheriff!"

"Why not?"

"That's not a job for a woman!" He waved his arms angrily. "Furthermore, you shouldn't be a deputy! Why can't you see that?"

"Why can't you give me credit?" she returned.

"I do give you credit. I know you're competent. But you need more than competence to be a law officer—you need to be a man!"

Her patience had reached its limit. "I don't want to discuss this any longer. I want you to leave."

"Fine!" he retorted, his own patience exhausted. He whirled on his heel, went to the door, opened it, then turned back and faced her. "Maybe someday you'll feel like telling me why you're afraid to be a woman."

"I'm not afraid!" she said sharply.

"Yes, you are. You're so damned afraid that you won't even admit it to yourself." He left, shutting the door with a solid bang.

Sudden tears smarted, but Jodie held them back. She

wasn't about to cry, for she had learned a long time ago that crying didn't solve anything. However, she was a little perplexed; she wasn't sure why she even felt like weeping. She had known from the beginning that she and Cade had clashing temperaments. She was attracted to him physically, but the attraction ended there; otherwise, they had nothing in common. He was too set in his ways to see her point of view, and she would not relinquish her independence—not even for Cade Brandon!

Cade made a straight course to Antonio's parlor and to his liquor supply. He poured himself a shot of whiskey, downed it, and refilled the glass. He silently cursed his love for Jodie, for he figured it was a lost cause. He had a feeling she'd never let any man into her heart; first, he'd have to penetrate her damned wall of independence, which was probably an impossible feat!

"Mind if I join you, amigo?" Antonio asked, coming into the room and interrupting Brandon's turbulent thoughts. "I will have a brandy."

Cade downed his second drink, then poured another whiskey for himself and a brandy for his host. He took the snifter to Antonio, who was sitting on the sofa. Cade eased into a chair, but he didn't quaff his third shot. He decided to sip it.

"I have been thinking about Hernando," Morelos said. "I cannot get him out of my mind."

"That's understandable; he's your son."

Antonio sighed deeply. "I wonder, amigo, if I made a mistake. Maybe I should have married Rosita."

"But you weren't really in love with her, were you?"

"I loved her beauty. But she was not of my class. If I had married her, Hernando's life would have been different."

"Different, yes. But maybe not all that much better. Your

father would have disowned you. Hernando wouldn't have grown up here surrounded by security and wealth."

"Sí, you are right. And I certainly do not regret the years I had with Adela. I loved her very much, and I adore Lucinda. I wonder if I should tell her that she has a brother."

"I can't advise you. That has to be your decision."

"I will give it more thought. But I think maybe I will tell her. She has a right to know." He took a sip of his brandy, sighed again, and murmured, "My heart aches to see Hernando again. I am not sure why. He was born twenty-eight years ago. Why has it taken so long for me to care?"

"Maybe you always cared, but never acted on it."

"I am a father filled with guilt, amigo. I failed my one and only son, and I also failed myself. I think Hernando hates me, and I do not blame him."

Cade wished he could say something to ease his friend's guilt, but Antonio had indeed failed his son, and he was now paying the price—a price Cade felt he had brought on himself.

Hernando didn't ordinarily ride into Villa de Lazar in the middle of the week, but tonight he made an exception. Seeing his father again had left his nerves on edge, and Jodie's sensual presence had left him wanting a woman. At the cantina, he planned to calm his nerves with tequila and appease his passion with a prostitute. He was accompanied by twelve Comancheros; Lopez and his entourage practically filled the small cantina.

Deciding to have a couple of drinks before indulging his lust, Hernando got a bottle of tequila, went to a table, and sat down. His men didn't follow him, for he had told them that he wished to be alone.

His musings were on Antonio when a young woman walked up to his chair. He was staring down at his half-filled glass and didn't bother to look up. Mistaking her for a *puta*, he said tersely, "I will let you know when I am ready."

"Hello, Hernando," she said softly.

Recognizing the voice, he glanced up quickly. "Felisa! It has been a long time." He gestured toward a chair. "Please, sit."

Complying, she murmured, "Hernando, I have missed you."

His masculine gaze quickly summed up her beauty. "You are still very beautiful."

He had not seen Felisa in many years. When he left his stepfather's Comancheros, Felisa had left with him. They had been lovers, and although Hernando was very fond of her, he could not make himself fall in love. Driven by desperation, she had finally given him an ultimatum—if he didn't marry her, she would leave. He helped her pack her clothes and ordered an escort to deliver her safely back to the other Comancheros' hideout. Her father, a bandit, lived there with his wife.

"How is your father?" he asked politely.

"He is dead. My mother and I moved in with her brother and his family. Last week, my mother remarried, and we moved to Villa de Lazar. Her husband owns the restaurant down the street. He has living quarters above the restaurant, and I was looking out my bedroom window when you rode by on your way to the cantina. I just had to come here and see you again. Many times I have been tempted to come back to you, but I did not know if you would take me back."

He didn't want to begin keeping company with Felisa again. "I do not think we should become lovers again."

"I thought you would feel that way, and until I saw you again, I believed I could live without you." She reached across the table and clasped his hand. "But, Hernando, the moment I saw you riding past my window, all the old feelings returned. You are the only man I have ever loved. I do not think I will ever love anyone else."

He shifted uncomfortably in his seat; Felisa's love had always been demanding, and he had often felt smothered by it. He was feeling that way again. "It is over, Felisa," he said firmly, but not unkindly.

"It is not over," she replied. "It will never be over; not as long as our son is alive."

"Son!" he gasped. "Felisa, what are you saying?"

"We have a son, Hernando. I did not know I was pregnant when I left. I thought about coming back to you, but I had my pride. Now, my pride does not seem to matter. I never stopped loving you; I tried, believe me, I did try."

He didn't want to hear about her feelings; he wanted to know about his son. He sprang to his feet, the movement knocking his chair to the floor. "Where is the child?" he demanded.

"He is here."

He grasped her arm, pulled her to her feet, and demanded, "Take me to him!"

As he escorted Felisa through the crowded cantina and outside, his thoughts were on the father who had deserted him. Like a man who is drowning, his childhood flashed across his mind, bringing back the pain and heartache he had suffered at Antonio's rejection.

He wiped the memory from his mind, and set his jaw firmly. Now, he had a son of his own, and he would not forsake him!

Chapter Thirteen

Jonas left the sheriff's office and sat outside on the chair beside the door. He tilted the chair back so that it touched the building, balanced it on two legs, and propped his feet on the railing in front. He had been nursing a headache all day, and he grimaced as another dull pain pounded at his temples. He reached into his vest pocket, pulled out a flask, uncapped it, and took a long drink. The whiskey went down smoothly, and he swigged a second drink before capping the flask and putting it away. He hoped the whiskey would ease his headache; however, if it didn't, after a few more drinks he wouldn't know if his head hurt or not.

He patted the flask gently. Whiskey took care of everything; it was the miracle cure! Without it, life would be intolerable.

Jonas glanced down the street; three riders caught his attention, and he got quickly to his feet. He watched Jodie, astride her magnificent Appaloosa, ride closer to the sheriff's office. She was flanked by the Marshal and a woman

Jonas didn't recognize. Jodie reined in, but Brandon and the woman rode to the hotel.

"I'm sure glad to see you," Jonas said, as Jodie dismounted. "I thought you were kidnapped."

"I was," she replied. "I suppose Dirk delivered the ransom demand to Bill."

"Yes, he did."

She waved a hand toward the door. "Let's go inside." He followed her into the office.

"Has anything happened during my absence?" she asked.

"Not a thing," he said. "The town's been real peaceful. Do you mind telling me how you got away from your abductors?"

"It's a long story, Jonas."

"I don't mind." He sat in the chair that faced the desk, removed the flask, and took a generous swallow. "I've got nothing but time. Tell me how you escaped."

Riker's drinking didn't disturb Jodie; she had grown so used to it that he and his flask seemed inseparable. She moved behind the desk, sat in the sheriff's chair, and told Jonas everything that had happened. She omitted Antonio's relationship to Hernando, and she didn't mention Alison at all.

"Who's the woman with Brandon?" Jonas asked.

So much for not mentioning Alison, she thought. "The woman is Brandon's sister."

"How did you two meet up with her?"

Jodie pushed back her chair and got to her feet. "I'd rather not discuss Alison. Let's just say, her story is her own to tell."

Jonas nodded. "I understand. I didn't mean to sound nosey."

"I know you didn't." She headed toward the door, saying over her shoulder, "I need to get home. I'll see you later."

"Jodie?" he called.

She turned and looked back at him.

"You never asked if Lawson planned to deliver the ransom."

"I just assumed that he did." Her brow furrowed. "Was I wrong?"

Jonas, believing Jodie was in love with Lawson, faked a smile and replied, "No, you weren't wrong." He didn't want to hurt her feelings.

"Is there something you aren't telling me?"

"No, not a thing," he mumbled.

She opened the door and left; Jonas opened the flask and took a drink.

Jodie stabled her horse before going into the house. She entered through the back door, and found Doris sitting at the table with a cup of coffee. The woman jumped to her feet and hugged her niece tightly.

"Thank God, you're home!" she exclaimed. "How did you get away from those horrible men?"

"I'll explain later. Right now, I just want to take a bath and get out of these dusty clothes."

"But . . . But the tub . . . I mean, Laura is using the tub." The woman was evidently nervous about something.

"That's all right. I'll use it when she's through. Aunt Doris, is something bothering you?"

She clasped her hands together, wringing them as though she were about to make a startling confession. Jodie waited patiently.

"Laura moved her things into your father's bedroom. Please don't be angry with her. We were so cramped in one room, and . . . and . . . Cole's room was empty. I packed Cole's belongings and stored them in the attic."

"Laura could have asked me before making such a move."

"But, dear, you weren't here."

Actually, Jodie didn't really care that Laura was using the room. They had more serious problems than who slept in whose room—like who was going to keep a roof over their heads and food on the table. Her deputy's salary couldn't cover the rent, let alone feed three people.

"Aunt Doris, do you have any money?" she said abruptly.

The question, coming out of the clear, took Doris totally unaware. "I . . . I don't have very much. I have a little over a hundred saved."

"Is that all?" Jodie asked.

"Your Uncle John didn't provide for Laura and me."

"Well, it looks as though Laura will have to get a job. I don't make enough money to support us."

"Please don't say anything to Laura about working. I can bring in extra income. I'll take in laundry and sewing."

"I appreciate your willingness to help, but there's no reason why Laura can't do her part."

"Honey, you must realize that Laura isn't skilled. She has never had a job."

"The restaurant can always use help. I'm sure she can get a job waiting tables."

Doris exhaled sharply, as though someone had knocked the air from her lungs. "Laura waiting tables? My heavens! Why Jodie, she'll come into contact with all sorts of unsavory characters. No! No, I won't let her work in a place like that."

"Well, she'll have to work someplace," Jodie replied, her patience wavering. She headed toward her bedroom, taking her carpetbag with her.

Doris, her nerves on edge, sat at the table. Maybe she should have told Jodie that Laura had a dinner date with Bill. She hoped Jodie wouldn't be too upset.

Meanwhile, Jodie had decided not to pass her father's room. She put down her carpetbag, and knocked on the door.

"Come in, Mother," she heard Laura call.

"It's not your mother," Jodie responded, coming into the room.

Laura was in the tub. She certainly hadn't expected to see her cousin, and she gaped at her as though she were a ghost. "What . . . what are you doing home?" she stammered. "I thought you were kidnapped."

"I was," she replied, glancing about the room. The decor had changed; it was now very feminine. Lace curtains adorned the windows, and a bright pink spread covered the bed. New pictures decorated the walls, and two plush rugs were added: one beside the bed, and the other in front of the dresser, which was now laden with perfumes, toiletries, and jewelry. "Where did you get the money to decorate my father's room?" Jodie asked, her tone tinged with anger.

"I don't see why that should concern you, but if you really want to know, I got the money from Mother."

"Don't go on any more buying binges. We have to watch our money closely."

"What?" Laura questioned. "What in the world are you saying?"

"I'm saying we're almost broke."

"Broke? But you have a job."

"It doesn't pay very much, and Papa didn't leave me anything. It took all his salary just to make ends meet. Tomorrow, I want you to find a job. Try the restaurant."

"Caroline's?" she asked, as though Crystal Creek had more than one restaurant.

"I'll talk to Caroline in the morning and put in a good word for you."

"Oh, no you won't!" Laura said. Standing, she grabbed a towel, wrapped it around her, and stepped out of the tub. "I'm not going to work in a restaurant. Good Lord! Sometimes, Jodie, I can't believe you!"

"You'll either get a job, or get out!" she retorted.

A hateful grin curled Laura's lips. "Finally, your jealousy

has come to this. You're going to throw me into the streets. You know, Jodie, you wouldn't have to be so jealous of another woman if you started thinking and acting like a woman yourself." The more she ranted, the angrier she became. "Well, you have a right to be jealous of me. Who do you suppose has invited me to his house for dinner?" She didn't give her time to answer, "Bill, that's who."

Jodie couldn't have cared less. She went to the door, opened it, looked back, and remarked, "I meant what I said—get a job or get out." She closed the door with a solid bang.

Cade came into Alison's hotel room and placed a package on the bed. "I hope this will do," he said. "I'm not very good at shopping for a woman."

"I'm sure you did fine," Alison replied. She opened the package and held up a blue gingham dress. It looked like a perfect fit. The attire she had on was a mixture of Comanche and Mexican; it was the only style she owned. The style was common among the women at Lopez's camp, but it looked out of place in Crystal Creek. She didn't want to draw attention to herself, and she had asked Cade to buy her a simple but stylish dress.

"I'll wait for you in the lobby," Cade said; he was taking Alison to dinner.

He turned to leave, but she detained him. "You look very dashing," she said.

Cade had visited the barbershop for a shave, as well as a bath. He had stopped at his room to change clothes before delivering Alison's package. Dark trousers that fit like a glove, a black vest, and a shirt as blue as his eyes enhanced his masculinity and his swarthy good looks. His gun, ensconced in its holster, was strapped to his hip, the leather thong tied securely about his leg.

"Dashing, am I?" he asked with a wry smile.

"Maybe handsome is a better word."

He opened the door, glanced back, and said, "Your dashing brother will dash downstairs and wait for you."

She laughed easily.

The sound of her laughter lifted Cade's spirits. He was hopeful that Alison would put the past behind her and start anew. He went downstairs to the lobby and was about to sit down when Mayor Wrightman came through the door. He spotted Cade immediately.

"I heard you were back," Wrightman said, shaking Brandon's hand. "Shall we sit?" he asked, indicating the lobby sofa, which had two matching chairs.

Cade eased into one of the chairs. The mayor sat on the sofa, but he was poised on the very edge of the cushion, as though he expected to take flight at any moment.

"Marshal," Wrightman began, clearing his throat. "I have a favor to ask."

Cade's expression grew curious.

"I could wire the governor and ask him to intervene on the town's behalf, but I'm sure that won't be necessary. You and I can work this out, gentleman to gentleman."

"Work out what?"

"Crystal Creek is without a sheriff . . . and its deputies are . . . Well, one is a drunk the other one is a woman. This town needs federal help. I'm asking you to stay until a sheriff can be appointed. After all, you are a U.S. Marshal and protecting this town is part of your job."

"When do you expect to appoint a sheriff?"

He answered reluctantly, "To be perfectly honest, Mr. Brandon, I don't know. No one seems interested in the job."

"Why don't you appoint Jodie? She plans to run for sheriff anyhow."

"Good Lord!" he huffed. "That's utter nonsense. She'll not win a vote."

"What if no one runs against her?"

"Marshal, I'd run for sheriff myself before I'd let that happen. Whoever heard of a woman running for office? Heavens! Women aren't even allowed to vote! Cole should never have sworn her in as his deputy. Believe me, he angered several citizens. Cole knew Jodie was skilled, of course, but that wasn't why he hired her—his main objective was to cause trouble between her and Bill Lawson."

"Are you sure?"

"Cole told me so himself."

"Does Jodie know?"

"I don't think so. I certainly haven't told her, and I'm sure Cole didn't."

"Sheriff Walker was a little extreme, wasn't he?"

"I don't think he saw it that way. Crystal Creek is not a lawless town, and he didn't think Jodie was in any real danger."

"Apparently, his ploy didn't work. She and Lawson are still together."

"Yes, they are," he murmured. "Marshal, will you consider staying here until I can appoint a new sheriff?"

"Why don't you appoint Deputy Riker?"

"The man is a drunk."

"He can still be a sheriff until one is elected."

"I thought of that, and I asked him. He refused to be sworn in."

"I'll stay a few days," Cade said. "But you'd better start looking for a sheriff. I don't intend to hang around too long."

"Well, I guess a few days are better than nothing at all. At least the town is protected for awhile."

"What makes you think Jodie can't protect this town?"

He got to his feet. "She might be skilled, but she's still a woman. Against a man, she is physically limited—and she can blame God for that! However, I don't guess she'll be a deputy much longer. Now that Cole is gone, the townspeople want her resignation. I have to break the news to her." He wiped a hand across his brow. "She's not going to like it."

Cade knew that was an understatement. He caught sight of Alison and went to meet her.

"You look very lovely," he said, holding her hands, his eyes sweeping her from head to foot. Her hair was unbound, and the dark tresses fell past her shoulders in waves as black as a raven's wings. The gown gracefully defined her full breasts and small waist. Long lashes accentuated green eyes that had once reflected vitality, but her eyes were now dull, as though life had negated all her dreams and destroyed her soul.

Wrightman had followed, and Cade made introductions. "Alison," he began, "this is Mayor Wrightman. Mayor, I'd like to you to meet Miss Brandon—my sister."

"How do you do, Miss Brandon," the mayor said warmly. He wondered why Brandon's sister was traveling with him, but was too polite to ask.

Cade finished the amenities quickly, then ushered Alison outside. He knew the mayor made her uncomfortable, for she feared probing questions.

"Before we go to dinner," Cade began, "do you mind if we stop at the sheriff's office?"

"I don't mind. Are you hoping to find Jodie?"

"No, I want to meet Deputy Riker. I saw him once but that was only for a minute or so. Also, I have something to tell him." He let Alison know that Wrightman had asked him to stay.

Crossing the street, they walked to the sheriff's office and went inside without knocking. Riker was sitting behind the desk, a bottle of whiskey within his reach.

"What can I do for you, Marshal?" he asked. His eyes flitted to Alison, then back to Cade.

"Wrightman asked me to stay until he can appoint a sheriff. Until then, I'll be in charge."

Riker smiled dryly. "Are you about to fire me, boss?"

"No, I don't intend to let you off that easily."

"Oh hell, Brandon," he said, as though indifferent. "I don't like preachin', and I don't like lectures, so don't come here and start that kind of crap with me." He looked at Alison. "Pardon my language, ma'am."

"I'll be back in the morning," Cade said, and his expression wasn't very amiable. "Just for the record, I don't preach and I don't lecture."

Riker picked up the bottle of whiskey, took a drink, and replied, "I'll see you in the morning, Marshal."

The moment they were outside, Alison asked, "Is Mr. Riker a heavy drinker?"

"He's a drunk," Cade replied.

"Why does he drink? Do you know?"

"He lost his wife and children in a house fire. He consoles himself with whiskey."

"I feel very sorry for him."

He took her hand and squeezed it gently. "You and Riker have had more than your share of heartache. Maybe you can help him."

"No," she said at once. "I can't help him. There is no cure for the pain he suffers; believe me, I know."

They reached the restaurant and went inside.

Bill Lawson arrived in his buggy; he intended to escort Laura and Doris to his house for dinner, for he was not about to allow two ladies to travel alone after dark.

Doris answered his knock at the door.

"Are you and Laura ready?" he asked.

"I'm not coming," she replied, showing him into the parlor. Laura had insisted that she not go; finally, Doris had given in. She suspected Laura of being romantically interested in Bill, and she didn't really blame her. After all, he was handsome, suave, and wealthy. But Bill was evidently in love with Jodie; however, Doris wasn't so sure that Jodie felt the same way.

"I'm sorry you don't plan to join us," Bill said.

"I'm not so sure Laura will join you either. You might decide to cancel dinner when you hear my news." She smiled widely. "Jodie is back."

"Jodie!" he exclaimed. "Where is she?"

"In her room. I'll tell her you're here."

"That won't be necessary," Jodie suddenly said, entering the parlor.

Bill's eyes raked her with desire. Her hair, freshly washed, was still damp, and curly ringlets framed her face. She had changed into a white dress; its beauty lay in its simplicity.

Lawson took her into his arms and hugged her gently. "Jodie, thank God you're safe. Did you escape your kidnappers?"

"No, not exactly," she replied. "It's a complicated story. I'll tell you about it when you have time."

"I have time now," he was quick to say.

Laura, stepping into the parlor, heard what Bill said. "Does this mean you've canceled our dinner?"

"There's no reason to change our plans. Jodie can have dinner with us."

"Thanks," Jodie said. "But I have work to do."

"Work?" Bill questioned.

"Yes, I need to talk to Jonas. I want him to act as temporary sheriff until I can get elected."

Lawson staggered backwards, as though Jodie's words had impacted him physically. "My God!" he choked. "You can't be serious!"

"I'm serious, all right."

"No man will vote for a woman!"

"You don't know that."

"And you don't know what people say behind your back."

"What does that mean?"

"Why don't you ask Jonas?"

"I will!" she remarked, anger emerging. She went out the door and headed toward the sheriff's office. She walked swiftly and got there within five minutes. She found Jonas sitting at the desk.

"Anything wrong?" he asked. He could see that she was disturbed.

"What are people saying behind my back?"

Jonas wasn't sure he understood. "About what?"

"About my job, apparently."

He grimaced; like Wrightman, he was aware that several people wanted her resignation. "They want you to turn in your badge," he answered candidly, for he saw no reason to lie.

"But why?"

"Because you're a woman. Jodie, if Cole hadn't been your father, the people in this town would not have tolerated a woman deputy."

"Papa knew I was capable; why can't the people see that?"

He decided it was time for her to learn the whole truth. "Cole didn't make you a deputy because he wanted you to have the job. He hoped it would come between you and Lawson. He figured Lawson would give you an ultimatum—him or your job. He figured you'd choose your job. But Lawson was too smart for Cole."

Jonas paused, then continued gently, "Jodie, Cole never intended for you to remain a deputy. When he realized his scheme wasn't going to work, he decided to take away your badge. The night he was killed, he told me that he was going to talk to you the following morning. He intended to dismiss you."

Jodie looked as though she were about to cry. "Then it was nothing but a travesty. Papa never really believed that I was capable of handling the job."

"That's right," Jonas murmured, albeit reluctantly.

"Cole admired your skills and independence, but he wasn't about to risk your safety."

Turning, she fled outside, where she almost collided with Lawson, who had followed her to the sheriff's office.

With tears brimming, she said with as much dignity as she could muster, "You once said that Papa made me his deputy hoping it would come between us. You were right." She brushed past him, but he caught her arm.

"Where are you going?" he asked.

"Home," she said.

"I'll walk with you."

He took her arm and they strode down the street. Jodie didn't say anything, and Bill didn't try to draw her into a conversation. He knew she needed to sort out her thoughts.

Jodie had been dealt a tremendous blow; earning her father's full support had meant everything to her. But, apparently, she had never earned it; he had used her, lied to her, and made her believe she was something she wasn't. In the final analysis, he had seen her as helpless, dependent, and too naive to pick a husband.

Chapter Fourteen

Lawson located one of his wranglers at the Silver Dollar and sent him home to let his family know he would not be home for dinner. Although Doris didn't have much advanced notice, she managed to prepare a delicious meal. Jodie had no appetite and merely picked at her food. Bill's appetite, however, was hearty, for his spirits were soaring. He believed Jodie would turn in her badge and marry him. He had waited two years to make her his wife, and he could barely contain his joy. He had never desired a woman so fervently.

Like Jodie, Laura simply toyed with her dinner. She was too upset to eat. She bitterly resented her cousin's return. If only those kidnappers had kept her a little longer. She was certain with more time she could have persuaded Bill to marry her.

Following dinner, Bill invited Jodie onto the front porch, saying he needed to talk to her. She preferred to go to her room and be alone with her thoughts, but she accompanied Bill outside. He had been very attentive and kind during dinner, and she didn't want to be rude.

Full night had descended, but the moon, resplendent in a clear sky, cloaked the porch in a golden hue. Bill drew Jodie gently into his arms, and murmured, "You're so lovely, and I adore you very much. Jodie, darling, why don't you turn in your badge and marry me?"

His proposal didn't surprise her; she had been expecting it. "I'm not ready for marriage," she said softly.

Her response tried his patience. How much longer did she expect him to wait? He was tempted to press her body flush to his and kiss her into submission. However, he controlled the urge, for he wasn't sure if Jodie could be subdued.

"My patience is wearing thin," he said. "I love you, Jodie. However, I'm tired of waiting for you to make up your mind."

She didn't blame him. "Maybe you should find someone else. I don't think we can make each other happy. But I do hope we'll remain friends." She felt she should have uttered these words a long time ago, and she experienced a pang of guilt—she shouldn't have left Bill dangling this way. But she hadn't really been sure of her feelings until now.

Her words had a finality that rocked Lawson. Night after night, he had lain in bed imagining her naked body beneath his. The dream was like an obsession, and he wasn't sure if he could relinquish it.

"I don't want to find someone else," he finally said, straining to keep his voice disciplined.

"Bill," she began gently, wishing she didn't have to hurt his feelings. "I'm not in love with you."

"Have you found another man?" he asked, sudden jealousy emerging. "Did you lay with him?"

Jodie didn't take his accusation calmly. "How dare you

say such a thing to me! Who do you think you are?" Her eyes flashed fiercely.

"I'm sorry," he was quick to apologize. He could hardly believe that he had spoken so impulsively.

"I think you should leave," she demanded.

"Please say you'll forgive me."

Her anger dissipated; she simply wanted him to go away. She had too much on her mind to deal with his jealousy. "You're forgiven," she said unemotionally. "Now will you please leave?"

He lifted her hand to his lips and kissed it lightly. "Goodnight, Jodie. And I am truly sorry."

"Goodnight, Bill." Her tone was as expressionless as her face.

His standing with Jodie was dubious—he couldn't tell if he had irreparably damaged their relationship or not. He decided to leave, but come back tomorrow and make amends. He refused to believe that it was over between them and that she didn't love him. He would return bearing a gift—presents always soothed a lady's ruffled feathers.

Jodie watched as he went to his buggy and climbed inside. He offered her a friendly wave before slapping the reins against the matched pair of palominos.

Jodie decided not to go back in the house; she preferred not to see Doris or Laura, for she didn't feel like making conversation. She chose to go to the stable. As she left the porch, she didn't see Cade walking down the street. But he caught a quick glimpse of her as she darted behind the house.

She went inside the stable and lit a lantern. Moving to the Appaloosa's stall, she hung the lantern on a hook. The Appaloosa nudged its nose against her hand, looking for a cube of sugar. A burlap bag was stored beside the stall; she reached inside, got a sweet tidbit, and gave it to the horse.

A trace of tears moistened her eyes, but her dispirited

mood was not related to Bill's jealous accusation. It was not even on her mind. Her thoughts were fully on her father. That he had deputized her under false pretenses was almost more than she could bear. From the time she was a young girl, she had tried so hard to earn Cole's respect and admiration. His pride and approval had meant everything to her. But all her efforts had been in vain— he had still thought of her as a helpless female in need of a man's guidance and care.

She blinked back her tears, for she refused to give in to despair. Crying wouldn't make the hurt go away, or undo the injustice done to her by her father.

"Jodie?" Cade's voice sounded softly.

Startled, she whirled around. Brandon was standing in the open doorway. "What are you doing here?" she asked, saying the first words that came to mind.

"Looking for you," he answered. He moved to her side.

"How did you know I was out here?"

"I saw you go behind the house, and I followed." He gazed thoughtfully into her face. "You seem troubled. Is something wrong? I couldn't help but see Lawson leave. Did you two have a lovers' quarrel?"

"If only it were that simple," she murmured.

"Do you want to talk about it?"

"I'd rather not."

Cade didn't press her; furthermore, he hadn't really expected her to open up to him—not the ever independent Jodie Walker! He decided to discuss the reason behind his visit. "I came here to tell you that Mayor Wrightman asked me to stay on until he can appoint a sheriff."

"Did you agree to stay?"

"For awhile. But if you'd rather I didn't . . ."

"By all means, stay. Apparently, Wrightman doesn't think Jonas and I are capable of maintaining law and order." She suddenly shrugged indifferently. "It doesn't matter. I don't care what he thinks, nor do I care what the people of this town think. I'm tired of fighting a losing battle. My badge is in the house. I'll come to the sheriff's office in the morning and give it to you."

"Why are you resigning?"

"What difference does it make?" she mumbled bitterly.

"Did Wrightman talk to you this evening?"

"No," she replied.

"But somebody must have said something."

She regarded him closely. "You know, don't you? Wrightman told you that the town doesn't want me as their deputy."

"Yes, he told me."

"Did he also tell you why my father made me his deputy?"

"He told me that too. But where did you hear it?"

"I confronted Jonas, and he told me everything."

He placed his hands gently on her shoulders. "I'm sorry, Jodie. I know this has been a terrible blow for you."

She stepped back out of arms' reach. "Don't feel sorry for me. I don't want pity." Her chin was raised stubbornly.

"Jodie, I don't know why you're so damned determined to be strong, but I do know it has something to do with your father. You trusted him, and learning that he misused that trust has got to be staggering. For once in your life, why don't you lean on someone besides yourself?"

"Someone like you?" she asked.

"Why not me?"

Silence fell between them, and Cade waited patiently, hoping she would confide in him. He didn't know if he could help, but he wanted the chance to try. She appeared very vulnerable as a trace of tears came to her eyes, her expression suddenly wistful. He longed to take her in his arms and hold her protectively.

But Jodie's emotions didn't remain unguarded for very long, and she said with a defiant flair, "I don't need to lean on anyone, least of all you!" She didn't mean to say that exactly, but the words had slipped out before she could stop them. She knew, however, that in a way they were true. She certainly didn't want to leave herself vulnerable to Cade; he was too much like her father.

"I was right about you all along," Cade mumbled irritably. "You're about as friendly as a riled bobcat." He stepped forward, grabbed her shoulders, and pulled her against him. "Sheathe your claws, Miss Walker; I'm not a threat. I know you consider all men a threat to your independence, but it's not your independence that I want."

His masculine body pressed tightly to hers was physically exciting—she could feel the beating of his heart against her breasts. "What do you want from me?" she asked, a slight tremble in her voice.

"This," he said, bending his head and kissing her aggressively.

Her arms went about his neck, as she responded with a fervor equal to his. Somewhere in the back of her mind, her better judgment cried out a warning, but she willed it to go away. She didn't want to be practical—she wanted to lose herself in the throes of passion.

"Sweetheart," Cade murmured, planting taunting little kisses along one cheek, then the other. "I want you . . . I want you with all my heart."

Again, his lips were on hers, the urgent contact sweeping all reasoning from Jodie's mind. She was conscious only of his nearness, and the power of his kiss.

"Marry me," he whispered in her ear. "Let me take care of you."

His words, like a cold gust of wind, cooled Jodie's desire and brought back her senses. "Take care of me?" she snapped, pushing out of his embrace. "Do you think I'm looking for a man to take care of me? I am perfectly capable of doing that myself!"

"I don't believe you!" he retorted testily. "Everything

comes back to your damned independence. You can't go through life, Jodie, without needing someone."

"Needing someone and being dependent on him is not the same thing."

"In your warped reasoning, it is!"

He incurred her temper. "Get out!" she ordered, pointing at the open doorway.

"Not a chance!" he mumbled. "This is one time you aren't sending me away!" Turning, he strode quickly to the open stable door and closed it with a resounding bang. He started back toward Jodie, who was heading for her bullwhip. It was hanging close to the Appaloosa's stall, but Cade quickly moved between her and the whip. Her path blocked, she stopped and glared fiercely at him.

"Did you intend to use that whip on me?" he asked, his blue eyes smoldering.

"If necessary," she replied.

He laughed, but there was no humor in it. "Surely, you didn't think I was going to force myself on you."

She was suddenly embarrassed, and her cheeks reddened noticeably.

In two quick strides, Cade had her back in his arms. "I'd never hurt you, Jodie. I only want to love you, but you won't let me."

"Oh Cade!" she cried, sounding sweetly vulnerable. "I'm so confused. And . . . and I'm afraid."

"Afraid?" he questioned gently. "Afraid of what?"

She longed to tell him what was in her heart, and to confess the fear she carried deep within, but the words wouldn't come.

"Tell me, Jodie," he persisted. "What happened between you and your father? Why are you afraid?"

She couldn't bring herself to talk about it; not now—maybe later. The shock of her father's betrayal was still too new, and if she started talking about the past—that, coupled with her recent disappointment, would be more than she could bear without breaking down and crying like a baby. Tears were a weakness she was determined to avoid.

Pushing out of his arms, she looked into his face and said firmly, "I don't intend to talk about it. I appreciate your concern, but this is something I have to handle on my own."

Cade's patience snapped. "You hold onto your independence like it's your lover! Does your damned independence keep you warm at night? Does it make you feel loved and desired? Does it appease your passion?" He brought her roughly back into his arms. "You need a man, Jodie Walker!"

She eyed him defiantly. "You told me that before. You also said that you aren't that man."

"I was wrong," he uttered, before pressing his lips to hers in a kiss so demanding that Jodie's knees weakened, sending her leaning against his sinewy frame.

He swept her up into his arms, carried her to an empty stall, and placed her gently on a stack of hay. He lay beside her, drew her against him, and placed a pinning leg over hers. His mouth was suddenly on hers, and his thrilling kiss compelled her to shift closer to him, her thighs touching his intimately. She knew this was wrong and that she should resist, but Cade's kiss was playing havoc with her reasoning.

"I love you, Jodie," he whispered.

Gone was her better judgment; she was lost in a maze of passion, and she felt she never wanted to escape. Placing a hand at the nape of his neck, she urged his lips to hers, her tongue boldly thrusting against his.

Cade's arms tightened about her, as he pressed his thighs even closer to hers. She was aware of his arousal, and she instinctively thrust against him, loving the feel of his hardness. A sweet ache built within her, and a yearning like she had never imagined coursed through her powerfully.

Cade, dangerously close to the point of no return, sat up unexpectedly, gazed down into Jodie's passion-glazed eyes, and murmured, "If you want me to leave; I will. But heed my warning, darlin', if I remain, I'll make love to you. My self-control is limited."

She stared at him as though she didn't understand, but she fully comprehended his warning; it was her own emotions that confused her. Was she putting her heart at risk? He said that he loved her and wanted to marry her, so why was she so afraid? Why couldn't she trust him? Like she had trusted her father, she suddenly mused. Yes, she had trusted him, and he had failed her miserably.

The stable door suddenly opened, and Jodie was actually grateful, for she had been very close to putting her heart on the line and surrendering totally to Cade.

Cade, on the other hand, silently damned the interruption. He stood quickly, took Jodie's hand, and drew her to her feet. Moving out of the stall, they found Laura staring at them.

She smiled cattily, looked at Jodie, and said, "I didn't mean to intrude, but Mother sent me to look for you. I noticed a light in the stable, and I figured I'd find you here. However, I thought I'd find you alone."

Jodie was flushed; she couldn't help it. Clumps of hay clung to her skirt, and she brushed them to the floor. "Laura . . ." she stammered, "this is Marshal Brandon." She turned to Cade. "Laura is my cousin."

"Pleasure to meet you, ma'am," Cade murmured; he, too, was uncomfortable with the situation.

Laura looked Brandon over admiringly; she didn't really blame Jodie for rolling in the hay with him. He was incredibly sensual. She was, however, flabbergasted, for she never imagined that Jodie was capable of this kind of behavior. Apparently, her cousin was not only indiscreet, but unfaithful as well. She could hardly wait to tell Bill about this.

Cade removed blades of hay from Jodie's hair, then smiled at her tenderly, and said, "I'll see you tomorrow."

"Goodnight, Cade," she replied.

As he walked past Laura, he mumbled, " 'Night, ma'am."

The moment Cade was gone, Laura remarked, "You'd better be glad I came looking for you instead of Mother. She would've been shocked. Honestly, Jodie! Rolling in the hay! I thought you were above such conduct."

"We weren't rolling in the hay!" she spat.

"Oh? What do you call it?"

"I call it none of your business!" she replied, brushing past her cousin. "Extinguish the lantern before you leave," she said over her shoulder, before darting outside.

Laura was left more astonished than ever—Jodie didn't plead with her not to tell Bill. Could this mean that she had chosen Brandon? She certainly hoped so!

Alison awoke from a recurring nightmare that had haunted her for years. In the dream, she was again living with the Comanches, suffering mistreatment and enduring relentless heartache.

She swung her legs over the edge of the mattress and lit the beside lamp. The soft glow illuminated the small hotel room, and she sighed aloud, as though she had expected to find herself in a Comanche village. She was trembling, her brow was damp with perspiration, and her cheeks were wet from the tears she had shed in her sleep.

She left the bed, went to the wardrobe, and took out her old clothes. She dressed hastily, then braided her long hair. She quickly packed her carpetbag, and went out the door.

She felt she couldn't stay in this town any longer, and she planned to return to Lopez's hideout. He would let her stay; she was certain of that. At first, he'd try to talk her into living with her own people, but he would eventually give her permission to remain.

She hurried out of the hotel and started down the street toward the livery. Her Comanche apparel, which was mixed with a Mexican style, caused some people to look at her curiously, but she ignored their stares and kept on walking.

She had to cross the street to reach the livery, which took her past the sheriff's office. She was passing the door when Jonas suddenly opened it and stepped outside. Alison had to stop abruptly to avoid a collision and nearly lost her balance.

He grasped her arms in a supportive hold. "Whoa there!" he said. "Where are you going in such a hurry?" Her clothes, braids, and carpetbag caught his attention, as well as his curiosity.

"I'm going to the livery," she replied. "If you'll kindly let go of my arms, I'll be on my way."

He released her. "I'm sorry—Miss Brandon is it? Or are you married?"

"It's Miss Brandon."

"Are you leaving town?" he asked.

"Yes, I am."

"I don't think that's a wise move."

"I didn't ask for your advice."

"Does Brandon know you're leaving?" he asked, stepping in her path, his body barring her way.

"Mr. Riker, will you please step aside?"

"No, I won't."

"Then I'll simply walk around you."

She moved to do just that, but he was again in front of her, obstructing her path.

"Ma'am," he began, "I'm not about to let you leave town at night without your brother's permission."

"What makes you think I don't have his permission?"

A small smile curled his lips, and she was suddenly aware that this man was extremely attractive. That she even saw him in that way was shocking; she hadn't felt that way toward a man since the day the Comanches had abducted her. For a moment, her emotions fluttered, as though they were trying to wake from a dormant state.

"Let's not play games, ma'am," Jonas continued. "You're running away, aren't you?"

"What if I am?"

"Why would you want to do something like that?"

"Please let me by."

"I'm afraid I can't do that. I guess I'll have to lock you up for your own good. Then I'll find Brandon and tell him to come get you."

"Locking up my sister won't be necessary," Cade suddenly spoke up. He had walked up to them too quietly for detection. Having left Jodie's house, he was on his way to the hotel when he saw Alison and Jonas. He reached out and took his sister's carpetbag. Turning to Jonas, he said, "Thanks for detaining her." He then clutched Alison's arm with his free hand and ushered her across the street.

"What the hell is wrong with you?" he asked gruffly. "You can't run off in the middle of the night! Where in the hell were you going?"

"Back to Hernando's."

"Why, for God's sake?"

"I don't belong here."

"You sure as hell don't belong in a Comancheros' hideout!"

She sighed heavily. "Oh Cade, I don't belong anywhere! Not really!"

"You belong with me, and with Uncle Charlie."

They reached the hotel, and Cade brought their steps to a halt. He gazed tenderly down into his sister's face. "Alison, promise me you won't try this again. You haven't even given yourself time to adjust."

"Adjust to what, Cade? Gossip and whispers?"

"Did somebody say something to you?"

"No, not yet. But it will happen. It's only a matter of time before the truth is known."

"You don't know that. Furthermore, to hell with what people think or say! Damn it, Alison! You've got to be strong!"

"Like Jodie?" she asked. "Cade, believe me, I do wish I had her strength and courage. But you don't understand. You don't know what it was like for me."

"I know what it was like for me. Finding you was all I lived for. God, Alison, do you think losing you didn't tear me to pieces, that I didn't grieve? Do you think I could stand losing you a second time?"

His anguish pulled at her heartstrings; she knew she couldn't cause him more grief. Standing on tiptoe, she kissed his cheek, and murmured, "I won't try to run away again. I promise." She indicated the door. "Are you going to your room?"

"Later. First, I think I'll go to the saloon and have a few drinks." He hoped to find a corner table, sit alone, nurse his drinks, and try to make some sense out of his situation with Jodie.

Alison bid him goodnight, took her carpetbag, and went inside. As she climbed the stairs, her thoughts drifted to Jonas. There was something about him that awakened her emotions. She wasn't sure why; he was entirely too bold, and was also a heavy drinker. But maybe her attraction went much deeper than that—like her, he was a lost soul.

Chapter Fifteen

Jonas was sitting at the desk when Cade arrived. The deputy waved a hand toward the stove where a pot of coffee was simmering.

Cade filled a cup, and took the chair facing Riker. He studied Jonas across the span of the desktop. Riker was freshly shaved, and although his hair still needed a trim, it was combed and clean. His eyes were clear, and he appeared well-rested. It was evident that Riker hadn't spent the night nursing a bottle of whiskey.

Jonas sensed Cade's thoughts, and he said with a wry smile, "I wanted to be sober this morning."

"Why is that?"

"I figured I should be in full control of my faculties when I turn in my badge."

"Why do you want to quit?"

"It's better then being fired."

"What makes you think I'm going to fire you? Furthermore, I don't have that authority. I'm not the sheriff."

"Wrightman has the authority, and if you want me gone, he'll send me packing."

Cade took a drink of his coffee, placed the cup on the desk, and regarded Jonas intently. "I don't intend to dismiss you. You see, I don't give a damn if you're a deputy or not. This isn't my town; therefore, I don't intend to get involved. My stay here is temporary. But for the short time you'll be working with me, I'll expect you to be sober. When you aren't on duty, you can drink yourself into oblivion for all I care. But if I find you drinking while on duty, then you're going to wish that I had fired you."

Riker smiled dryly. "That sounds like a threat."

At that moment, the door opened and Jodie came inside. Cade pushed back his chair and got to his feet. He looked at her admiringly. She was wearing a light summer gown that softly enhanced her delicate frame, and her curly tresses were pulled back from her face and secured with a blue ribbon that matched the color of her dress. Although she was still in mourning, she preferred not to wear traditional black.

"You look very lovely," Cade told her.

"Thank you," she replied. She handed him her badge. "I said I'd turn this in this morning."

"You don't have to do this, you know."

"Oh yes, I do!" she said firmly. "The people in this town don't want me as their deputy. Besides, I either resign or Mayor Wrightman will dismiss me. At least this way, I leave with my pride intact."

Jonas propped his feet on the desktop, leaned back in his chair, and said evenly, "Let her go, Marshal. Like you said, this isn't your town and there's no reason for you to get involved. Jodie knows what she's doing."

"Do you?" Cade asked Jodie. "Are you sure this is what you want?"

"It's not a question of what I want, but what the town

wants." With that, she whirled around, opened the door, and left.

"Jodie, wait," Cade said, following a couple of seconds later.

She was about to cross the street, but turned back to face him.

He grasped her hand tightly. "Jodie, marry me."

His proposal, coming out of the clear, was so startling that she gasped aloud.

"This town doesn't want you, but I do."

"I . . . I don't know what to say," she stammered. "I can't give you an answer right now." Did she want to marry him? Yes, a part of her longed desperately to be his wife, but that other part of her demanded that she tread cautiously. I don't want to end up like my mother! she thought suddenly.

Cade squeezed her hand gently. "I don't expect an answer this minute. Will you have dinner with me tonight? Following a romantic dinner, maybe I can convince you to marry me."

"Yes, I'll have dinner with you. I'll meet you at Caroline's at six o'clock."

"I'll come to your house and escort you to the restaurant."

"Honestly, Cade! I'll be perfectly safe walking from my house to Caroline's."

"Nevertheless . . ." he replied, a warm twinkle in his eyes.

She gave in. "Very well, Cade. Have it your way."

"Now that wasn't so difficult, was it?" he asked, grinning disarmingly.

"What does that mean?"

"Conceding," he replied. "Giving up your independence long enough for me to escort you to a restaurant."

She eyed him with sudden defiance. "If I marry you, I suppose you'll expect me to give up my independence entirely. Well, that will never happen, Cade Brandon! I'll never be a burden to you or any other man!"

"You could never be a burden," he replied quickly. Her fiery response didn't surprise him, for he was familiar with her mood swings. But he did wonder why she thought a man would find her a burden.

"I'll see you tonight," she said tersely, ending the discussion. She turned to cross the street, but Cade detained her.

"Where are you going?" he asked.

"To Caroline's. I intend to ask her for a job. I have three people living in my home, and we can't very well survive without income."

"If you'd marry me, you wouldn't have to work in a restaurant. I'd take care of you."

"Thank you, but I can take care of myself," she replied, a willful tilt to her chin.

Cade watched as she walked across the street and toward the restaurant. He noticed how proudly she moved; her back ramrod straight and her head held high. That she could think of herself as a burden was amazing, when she carried her own burdens so well.

He turned around and went back into the sheriff's office. He was looking forward to dinner, for he had a feeling that Jodie would agree to marry him.

On her way to the restaurant, Jodie walked in front of the stage depot, which also served as a post office. The door opened, and the man in charge stepped outside.

"Good morning, Miss Jodie," he said, tipping his hat with his free hand, for the other one carried mail, along with wanted posters.

"Good morning, Mr. Daniels," she replied warmly, for she was quite fond of the man. She had known him all her life, and he had been a good friend of her father's.

HERE'S A SPECIAL INVITATION TO ENJOY TODAY'S FINEST HISTORICAL ROMANCES— ABSOLUTELY FREE! *(a $19.96 value)*

Now you can enjoy the latest Zebra Lovegram Historical Romances without even leaving your home with our convenient Zebra Home Subscription Service. Zebra Home Subscription Service offers you the following benefits that you don't want to miss:

- 4 BRAND NEW bestselling Zebra Lovegram Historical Romances delivered to your doorstep each month (usually before they're available in the bookstores!)

- 20% off each title or a savings of almost $4.00 each month

- FREE home delivery

- A FREE monthly newsletter, *Zebra/Pinnacle Romance News* that features author profiles, contests, special member benefits, book previews and more

- No risks or obligations...in other words you can cancel whenever you wish with no questions asked

So join hundreds of thousands of readers who already belong to Zebra Home Subscription Service and enjoy the very best Historical Romances That Burn With The Fire of History!

And remember....there is no minimum purchase required. After you've enjoyed your initial FREE package of 4 books, you'll begin to receive monthly shipments of new Zebra titles. Each shipment will be yours to examine for 10 days and then if you decide to keep the books, you'll pay the preferred subscriber's price of just $4.00 per title. That's $16 for all 4 books with FREE home delivery! And if you want us to stop sending books, just say the word....it's that simple.

It's a no-lose proposition, so send for your 4 FREE books today!

4 FREE BOOKS

These books worth almost $20, are yours without cost or obligation
when you fill out and mail this certificate.
*(If the certificate is missing below, write to: Zebra Home Subscription Service, Inc.,
120 Brighton Road, P.O. Box 5214, Clifton, New Jersey 07015-5214)*

Complete and mail this card to receive 4 Free books!

YES! Please send me 4 Zebra Lovegram Historical Romances without cost or obligation. I understand that each month thereafter I will be able to preview 4 new Zebra Lovegram Historical Romances FREE for 10 days. Then if I decide to keep them, I will pay the money-saving preferred publisher's price of just $4.00 each...a total of $16. That's almost $4 less than the regular publisher's price, and there is never any additional charge for shipping and handling. I may return any shipment within 10 days and owe nothing, and I may cancel this subscription at any time. The 4 FREE books will be mine to keep in any case.

Name _____

Address _____ Apt. _____

City _____ State _____ Zip _____

Telephone ( ) _____

Signature _____ LF0597
(If under 18, parent or guardian must sign.)

Terms, offer and prices subject to change without notice. Subscription subject to acceptance by Zebra Home Subscription Service, Inc.. Zebra Home Subscription Service, Inc. reserves the right to reject any order or cancel any subscription.

4 BOOKS FREE!

A $19.96
value....
absolutely
FREE
with no
obligation to
buy anything,
ever!

AFFIX
STAMP
HERE

ZEBRA HOME SUBSCRIPTION SERVICE, INC.

120 BRIGHTON ROAD

P.O. BOX 5214

CLIFTON, NEW JERSEY 07015-5214

He had gray hair, a long beard, and was so thin that her father often said a strong gust of wind would blow him away.

"I was just on my way to the sheriff's office to make a delivery," Daniels told Jodie.

"Anything important?" she asked, before remembering she no longer worked at the sheriff's office.

"These wanted posters are kinda important." There were six identical copies stacked neatly together; they were no bigger than a a regular sheet of paper, and he handed one to Jodie. "I recognized that face," Daniels said. "The man was in town a couple of days ago. I saw him at the Silver Dollar. I even talked to him. He said he was goin' to Mexico."

Jodie looked closely at the poster. The man was wanted in Abilene, and a thousand dollar bounty had been placed on his head, dead or alive. *A thousand dollars!* she thought. She would have to work at Caroline's for years on end to make that much money.

"This came with the poster," Daniels said, giving Jodie an envelope.

She knew she had no right to open it, but she didn't let that deter her. She unfolded the paper and perused it quickly. "Good Lord!" she gasped.

"What is it?" Daniels asked.

"The man's name is Jason Edwards. He raped a woman, then killed her and her twelve-year-old son. The woman's husband is paying the bounty."

"The husband must be mighty rich," Daniels remarked.

"Do you think Edwards was telling you the truth when he said he was going to Mexico?"

"I think so. Anyway, I didn't get the feelin' that he was lyin'."

"Are you sure he was the same man in this poster?"

Daniels looked at the top poster in his hand. The artist

had captured the man's features flawlessly. "Yep, it's him all right."

Jodie returned the letter to the envelope and handed it to Daniels. However, she kept the poster. "Here, you'd better deliver this letter to the Marshal."

"I heard he was goin' to stay around for awhile. How do you like workin' for a U.S. Marshal?"

"I don't work for him. I turned in my badge."

Daniels shook his head, as though admonishing her. "Miss Jodie, if you're no longer a deputy, then you shouldn't have read that letter."

"Old habits are hard to break," she replied with a smile.

"I reckon no harm was done," he drawled. "Have a good day, Miss Jodie." He walked away, forgetting the poster in Jodie's possession.

Jodie didn't resume her course to the restaurant; instead, she headed toward her home. Hurrying, she reached the house within minutes and went straight to her bedroom. She began to pace back and forth as thoughts skimmed the surface of her mind like a thrown pebble skipping across a body of water. A thousand dollars! The bounty loomed temptingly. If she married Cade, the money would guarantee her independence, for she would always have it to fall back on. If she didn't marry him—the money would keep a roof over her head and food on the table.

Her pacing stopped abruptly; her nerves tensed and her heart began to beat a little faster. Did she truly have the courage and grit to pursue a wanted killer?

Why not? she asked herself. She hadn't hesitated to go after her father's murderers, so why waver now? This man had murdered a woman and a child, and he should be brought to justice.

Her thoughts turned to Cade. If he knew she was even considering chasing after Edwards, he would undoubtedly be enraged. He'd certainly do everything within his power to stop her. She decided telling Cade was not an option, for she preferred to avoid the altercation that would arise between them.

She went to the dresser, peered into the mirror, and asked her reflection, "Do I really want to do this? Maybe I should forget the thousand dollars, go to Caroline's, and ask her for a job." She squared her shoulders, and raised her chin dauntlessly. "I think not! I have something to prove to myself, as well as to this town."

She whirled away from the mirror, and as her thoughts went to her father, a streak of pain zigzagged through her heart like a bolt of lightning. She knew it was illogical, but she felt she had a statement to make to her father as well. The wound he had inflicted on her would take a long time to heal.

Her mind made up, she quickly changed into her riding clothes and packed a carpetbag.

She got her rifle and ammunition from the gun cabinet, then entered the kitchen. Doris and Laura were sitting at the table. Laura, an habitual late riser, was finishing breakfast.

"Where are you going?" Doris asked Jodie, waving a hand toward her carpetbag. She eyed the Winchester uneasily.

"I'm leaving town for a few days," she replied. "It's business."

"What kind of business?"

Jodie began packing food. "I've decided on a new line of work."

"Jodie, will you please stop beating around the bush, and tell us what you're up to?"

"There's a thousand dollar bounty on a man named Jason Edwards. He left for Mexico, and I'm going after him. I'll probably find him in Villa de Lazar."

"Jodie, no!" Doris exclaimed, bounding from her chair. "I won't let you do this!"

Laura waved an impatient hand. "Sit down, Mother. Do you really think you can stop Jodie?"

"Laura's right," Jodie said. "My mind is made up."

Doris sank back into her chair. "But a bounty hunter? Jodie, you can't be serious!"

"Why not? It's a lucrative profession. Besides, Edwards killed a woman and her young son. He should hang from the end of a rope!" Finished packing food, she picked up her carpetbag and started toward the back door. "I don't know when I'll be back. Look for me when you see me coming."

"But Jodie!" Doris called. "What should I tell Bill?"

"My life is no longer his concern."

"You mean, he's no longer your beau?"

"Yes, that's exactly what I mean."

Laura smiled happily; Bill was now hers for the taking. "Jodie," she began, a sly grin on her face. "Does Marshal Brandon know you're leaving?"

"No," she replied.

"Do you intend to tell him?"

Jodie knew she owed Cade an explanation, but she didn't want to face him with her decision. She turned to her aunt, and asked, "Would you mind telling Marshal Brandon that I've left town?"

"No, I don't mind."

She wanted to get a head start on Cade in case he decided to follow her. "Give me a few hours start before you see him."

"Very well, dear, if that's what you want."

"Thank you," Jodie murmured. She went out the door, and closed it soundly behind her. She hastened to the stable, saddled her Appaloosa, got her bullwhip, and rode out of town without a backward glance.

She tried not to dwell on Cade, but the effort was futile, for she couldn't rout him out of her mind. She knew he would be furious, and would probably come after her. She lifted her chin defiantly; let him follow, she didn't care. She had to make a living, and her adventurous nature was more attuned to this kind of work than waiting tables in a restaurant.

Doris left the house to visit a friend, and Laura was there alone when Lawson knocked on the door. He carried a small box in his hand. It was gift-wrapped.

"Is Jodie home?" he asked Laura.

"She isn't here," Laura replied, showing him inside and to the parlor.

"Do you know where she is?"

Laura smiled inwardly. "I'd better fix you a strong drink before I tell you what Jodie's up to now." She went to the liquor cabinet and poured Lawson a glass of brandy. Taking it to him, she asked him to sit on the sofa. She promptly sat beside him.

Placing the box on the table, he asked, "What's going on?"

She gestured toward the box. "A gift for Jodie?"

"Yes. It's a locket."

"That's not an appropriate gift for Jodie. A Colt .45 would be more fitting, or perhaps a new rifle."

"Where is Jodie?" he asked, losing patience with Laura's hedging.

"She has embarked on a new career. She's now a bounty hunter."

"Good God!"

"She left a short time ago for Mexico. She's looking for a man named Jason Edwards. He's wanted for murder. There's a thousand dollar bounty on him, and Jodie intends to collect it."

Lawson took a big swig of his brandy, put the glass down none too gently, and bounded to his feet. Waving his arms angrily, he ranted, "This is the last straw! I don't think I can take any more!"

"Oh there's more," Laura informed him. "That is, if you're still interested."

"What is it?" he asked.

"Last night, I caught Jodie in the stable with Marshal Brandon. They were . . . they were in a lovers' embrace. Or at least, I assume they were. They were together in an empty stall. I couldn't actually see them because they were lying down."

Lawson's temper exploded. "Why that cheating little tramp! How could I have been so wrong about her? Despite her rebellion and foolish notions, I thought she was a lady! But apparently I was wrong!"

Laura stood and placed a calming hand on Bill's arm. "Just be thankful that you found out what's she really like before you married her."

"I wouldn't marry her now if she got down on her knees and begged me!"

Laura's fingers caressed his arm, and she leaned so close to him that her breasts rested against his chest. "Forget about Jodie," she said softly. "She doesn't deserve one minute of your thoughts."

Bill was suddenly aware of Laura's gentle caress, and the feel of her breasts pressed against him. He pushed Jodie to the far recesses of his mind, slipped an arm about Laura's waist, and drew her closer. "You're very beautiful," he whispered, sensual hunger suddenly in his eyes.

Delight flowed through Laura, for his desire was obvious. However, she was not about to submit quite this easily. "I find you very attractive, Bill. I also think the world of you, and I always wished you weren't courting Jodie."

"I'm not anymore," he said, his lips nearing hers.

She drew back.

"What's wrong?" he asked.

"I don't want to be a second choice. Until you are completely over Jodie, I think we should just remain friends."

Certain he could seduce her, he smiled confidently. "Let's be very close friends, shall we?" His arm was still about her waist; he brought her body flush to his, bent his head, and kissed her with passion.

She responded fervently, but did not surrender. Leaving his embrace, she stepped back and said a little tremulously, "This is happening too quickly. My emotions are swirling, and my heart is beating like a drum. I've desired you for so long, and now I suddenly find myself in your arms. Bill, please give me time to calm my emotions and take control of my heart."

He was flattered that his kiss had affected her so ardently. If only Jodie had responded this way. He was suddenly annoyed with himself for letting Jodie back into his thoughts. He forcefully thrust her from his mind, offered Laura a tender smile, and asked, "Will you have dinner with me tonight?"

"I'd love to."

"I'll pick you up at six, and we'll have dinner at my ranch. This time, it won't be canceled." He picked up his glass and finished his brandy. He gestured tersely toward the wrapped box. "You can have that if you want it, or you can throw it away. I really don't care."

Laura walked to the door with him, and he bid her good day with a chaste kiss on the lips. She was feeling victorious as she went back into the parlor, for she was certain Bill would soon ask her to marry him. A worried frown furrowed her brow—he probably expected her to be a virgin. She hadn't been a virgin since she was eighteen. She shrugged the problem aside, deciding she'd deal with it when the time came. She sat on the sofa and picked up Jodie's present. She ripped off the paper, opened the box, and was impressed with the locket inside, for it was an elegant piece of jewelry. It wasn't all that expensive, but she liked it; therefore, she decided to keep it.

She absently toyed with the locket as she debated if she should give in to Bill's seduction tonight or make him wait a little longer. That she might hold him off until he married her wasn't an option, for she intended to seduce him into marrying her. She had every confidence in her womanly charms, and once she made love to Bill, she was certain he'd want no other woman. She was skilled in the art of pleasing a man, and Bill Lawson would soon be like putty in her hands.

Chapter Sixteen

Cade was alone in the sheriff's office when Doris arrived. He was sitting at the desk looking over the mail that Daniels had delivered earlier. Having other things to take care of, he had allowed the mail to lie on the desk unopened. He was just now getting around to perusing it.

The lady's presence brought him to his feet. "What can I do for you, ma'am?"

"Marshal, my name is Mrs. Talbert. I'm Jodie's aunt."

"Pleasure to meet you, Mrs. Talbert."

"Jodie left town, and she asked me to let you know."

Cade was taken aback. "Left town? Where did she go?"

Doris answered a little hesitantly, for she had a feeling the Marshal was going to be upset. "She's headed for Mexico."

Cade was more than upset; he was irate. "Why the hell did she leave for Mexico?"

"Somehow, she learned there's a thousand dollar bounty on a man named Jason Edwards. She thinks he went to Villa de Lazar, and she's going after him. Now that she's no longer a deputy, she has decided to become a bounty hunter.'' Doris's expression deepened with worry. ''I wish I could have stopped her, but once Jodie's mind is made up, no one can change it.''

''How long has she been gone?''

''She left about four hours ago.''

''Why did you wait so long to tell me?''

''It's what Jodie wanted. I suppose I should have come to you immediately, but I did as she asked.'' She silently berated her own weakness, which always bowed to others' demands. Although she often disapproved of her niece's rebellious ways and independence, she was sometimes envious and wished she and Laura were more like Jodie.

Cade remembered seeing the wanted poster on Jason Edwards, but he hadn't yet read the letter that accompanied it. He now did so quickly. Then he balled the paper in his hand, his fingers squeezing it like it was a threatening life form that had to be destroyed. He suddenly dropped the wadded letter on the desk as one would drop something so repulsive that he couldn't wait to get rid of it.

Doris, watching Brandon's face harden with anger, took a couple of steps backwards, as though she wanted to put more space between herself and the Marshal's rage.

''Damn!'' Cade raved. ''I can't believe Jodie did this! What the hell drives that woman to such lengths?'' His gaze met Doris's. ''Why is she like this? Do you know?''

''She said a bounty hunter's profession is lucrative.''

''That's not what I mean!'' he said testily. ''What the hell goes on in Jodie's mind? What compulsion drives her?''

Doris shook her head. ''I don't know. From the time she was a child, she was a tomboy. I think she tried to make up for the son her father never had.''

''Jodie's problems go deeper than that.'' A look of determination flashed in his piercing blue eyes. ''I'm going after her, and when I find her . . . !'' He left the sentence hanging, but his patience with Jodie had reached its limit.

The door opened, admitting Jonas. Doris grasped the opportunity to brush past him and leave while the door was still ajar. The Marshal's anger was unnerving to her, and she gladly made a hasty exit.

"Is something bothering Mrs. Talbert?" Riker asked Cade.

Brandon smoothed out the letter he had wadded into a ball, and gave it and a wanted poster to the deputy.

Riker looked at the poster, then read the letter.

"Jodie's gone after Edwards," Cade told him.

"Good God!" Jonas exclaimed.

"Riker, you're coming with me to the mayor's home so that he can swear you in as sheriff. You should be the one in charge. It's your obligation, not mine. The people who live in this jurisdiction pay your salary, and it's about time you started earning it.''

"What makes you think I want to be sheriff?"

"You have a responsibility. I'm going after Jodie, and it'll be up to you to maintain law and order in Crystal Creek. As I said before, this isn't my town and I don't intend to become involved. But it's your town, Riker.''

He smiled, but the smile never quite reached his eyes. "All right, Brandon. I'll let Wrightman swear me in as sheriff. But it's only temporary. As soon as a sheriff is elected, I'm leaving here for good.'' He suddenly felt he should have made the decision to leave a long time ago. Why had he stayed when this town held so many painful memories for him?

"One more thing," Cade said.

"What's that?"

"While I'm gone, will you keep an eye on my sister? I don't think she'll try to leave town again, but she might.''

"I'll do my best to keep an eye on her. I don't suppose you'd want to tell me why she would leave?"

Cade shook his head. "It's private."

Riker indicated the door. "Let's get to the mayor's house. The sooner you go after Jodie, the sooner you'll catch her." He paused, then added in a worried tone, "I hope you find her before she finds Edwards. He's already killed one woman; I doubt if he'd hesitate to kill another."

Wrightman swore Riker in as sheriff. However, he wasn't overly pleased about it, for he considered Jonas a drunk and seriously doubted his ability to handle the job. He wanted Cade to stay on as acting sheriff, but it was evident to Wrightman that Brandon was determined to pursue Jodie. That Jodie had left town to go after a wanted killer for the bounty shocked the mayor. He decided that Cole had failed miserably as a father. He should never have taught Jodie skills a father normally teaches to a son.

Jonas went to the sheriff's office, as Cade hurried to the hotel to see Alison. He knocked on the door and was admitted almost at once.

She was wearing the gown he had bought her, and her long black hair was flowing loosely about her shoulders. He studied her for a moment; she would be beautiful if it weren't for the haunted look in her eyes, and the sorrow etched deeply in her face.

"I'm glad to see you," she said. "I get so bored cooped up in this room. I wish I had something to do to keep me busy."

Cade agreed; she did need to stay occupied. "I noticed that the sheriff's office needs a good cleaning. But if you'd rather not . . . I mean, that kind of work is strenuous and tiring."

"That's exactly what I need," she said. "I'm not used to so much leisure. I'll change clothes and start cleaning right away."

"Alison, I have to leave town."

"Leave town? But why, and for how long?"

He told her about Jodie's pursuit. "I don't know when I'll be back, but I should be gone only a few days."

"I can't imagine Jodie doing something so reckless."

"At first, I couldn't believe it myself. But I guess I shouldn't have been so surprised. Nothing she does should shock me!"

"You're very angry, aren't you?"

"Why shouldn't I be?"

"Cade, are you in love with Jodie?"

He sighed heavily. "Yes, I am. I asked her to marry me."

"What did she say?"

"She hasn't given me an answer yet."

"Do you think she loves you?"

He gave her question serious thought. "I really don't know. Sometimes I think she does, then other times I'm not so sure. Jodie's a very complicated young lady. In fact, I've never known a woman like her." He stepped to his sister, and placed a light kiss on her cheek. "Alison, promise me you'll be here when I get back."

"I promise I won't leave." It was a promise she hoped to keep.

Cade kissed her cheek a second time, then left in a hurry. Jodie was hours ahead of him, and he had no more time to waste.

Cade had been gone over an hour before Alison decided to change clothes and go to the sheriff's office. She had spent the hour debating whether or not she should clean the office. The work was not a burden, for she wanted to keep busy. Jonas Riker was the deterrent; she wasn't sure if she wanted to be in his company. He stirred emotions within her that she thought had died years ago. Without them, she had achieved peace of mind. It was a stoical kind of peace, but was better than none at all. At one time, she had thought she was on the verge of losing her mind, but Lopez's intervention and kindness had saved her sanity. She then wrapped herself in a stoical cloak, letting it protect her from the agonizing memories of the years she had lived with the Comanches. Only in her sleep did the cloak lose its power to hold the memories at bay. She could live with the nightmares, but she wasn't sure if she could survive resurrecting the emotions she had tried so hard to bury. Along with feelings came heartache, pain, and a flood of memories too horrible to bear. Somehow, she must not let Jonas Riker bring back the emotions she had believed were gone forever.

Remaining in her room and away from Riker was indeed a temptation, but she could no longer tolerate staying cooped up. Moreover, all this leisure was not to her liking. She needed something to do. She was used to work and felt lost without chores to keep her busy. Therefore, given a choice between avoiding Jonas or staying in her room, she chose to clean the office.

She left her room, wearing a Mexican skirt and blouse. The colorful attire, along with her long ebony hair flowing about her shoulders, lent her a vivacious flare that was quite arresting. She hurried down the stairs, and as she moved quickly through the populated lobby, she was oblivious to the people who turned to stare at her.

She went outside and started across the street to the sheriff's office. Riker was sitting outside beside the front door. He watched her from the moment she came out of the hotel, taking special note of her graceful gait and the gentle sway of her hips. That he found her attractive didn't surprise him, for he hadn't remained celibate since his wife's death. He often paid a prostitute for her favors. Although he had ceased caring about his own self-respect, his drive was as active as ever.

He stood at Alison's arrival, and murmured, "Good afternoon, ma'am."

"Good afternoon, Mr. Riker. Before Cade left, he mentioned that your office needs a cleaning. If you'll show me where I can find what I'll need, I'll get started immediately."

That she had come here to clean took Jonas by surprise. Cade had said nothing to him about it. "I appreciate your offer, Miss Brandon, but cleaning my office is a lot of work. Jodie always kept it neat and tidy, but since she's been gone, I haven't done a thing except mess it up."

"I don't mind the work, Mr. Riker. It's better than staying cooped up in my room with nothing but leisure time on my hands."

"Well, if you really want the job, I guess it's all right. I'll pay you, of course."

"That isn't necessary."

"Yes, it is," he said adamantly. "I won't have it any other way."

"Very well," she replied, trying not to look at him too closely. Nevertheless, she was fully aware of his presence. Clean-shaven, a wayward curl falling over his brow, he emitted a boyish charm that was irresistible, yet, there was a rugged, masculine aura about him that was overwhelming. She found herself gazing into his brown eyes, and saw a hopelessness in them that reminded her of her own. A house fire had taken his family, destroyed his happiness, and negated all his dreams. She empathized with his pain, for she knew all too well what it was like to die inside. She quickly lowered her eyes from his; despite her resolution, emotions were trying to surface.

Jonas opened the door to the office, and stepped aside for her to precede him. Following her inside, he said, "There's a small storage room off the bedroom in back. You'll find everything you need in there."

"Thank you, Mr. Riker."

"Jonas," he said.

She smiled somewhat hesitantly. "I'm Alison."

"Were you living in Mexico?" he asked.

"Why do you think that?"

"Well, that's where Brandon and Jodie were when they came across you." His eyes swept briefly over her attire. "Your clothes are apparently Mexican."

"Yes," she said softly. "I was living in Mexico."

"Whatever prompted you to move there?"

"I'd rather not talk about it."

"Sorry, ma'am," he apologized. "I didn't mean to pry. I was just trying to be friendly."

"I understand," she replied. "Now, if you'll excuse me, I need to start cleaning."

"I'll be outside if you need me."

He stepped to his desk, grabbed his flask, and left. Returning to his chair, he rested it on its back legs, then propped his feet on the railing. He uncapped the flask, and took a generous swallow of whiskey. He hadn't had a drink since yesterday, and he welcomed the liquor's soothing effect. He was tempted to keep guzzling until the effect went from soothing to numbness, but he controlled the urge and recapped the flask. He was the only law officer in town, and drinking himself into oblivion could have serious consequences.

His musings turned to Alison, as he wondered why she had been living in Mexico. She wasn't married, so she didn't move there to live with a husband. A perplexed frown wrinkled his brow. Alison Brandon was indeed a mystery; she was also quite attractive. In fact, she was almost beautiful. But there was something about her that defied beauty. He wasn't sure what it was; maybe it was the emptiness in her eyes. As he conjured up a picture of Alison in his mind, he knew it was more than just her eyes; her face had the haunted look of a person who had suffered tremendous pain. He knew that look, for he saw it every time he looked into a mirror.

Such thoughts encouraged him to open the flask and

take another swig. He didn't stop at one, but took two more gulping swallows before securing the cap and putting the small container beside his chair, within easy reach. Whiskey was his salvation, and he always kept it close by.

Jonas dozed off and was asleep in his chair when Alison came outside. She had been cleaning for over two hours. A lawman's instincts still survived within Riker, and Alison's presence brought him awake with a start.

He rose quickly, asking, "Are you finished?"

"Yes, I am. There's a lot of dust in this town; your office should be cleaned at least twice a week and dusted at least every other day."

"I'll keep that in mind," he replied, knowing full well that he'd never get around to cleaning. "I have some cash in the office. If you'll wait, I'll get your pay."

"You can pay me later."

"All right, ma'am."

She bid him a quick good day and started across the street. She had reached the other side before catching a glimpse of two men walking her way. She recognized one of the men, and his dreaded presence brought her steps to a brusque halt. Sudden perspiration beaded up on her brow, and her heart began to beat erratically. She felt sick to her stomach, and every nerve in her body tightened.

The man looked her way, it took a moment for recognition to set in. But when it did, it placed a cruel smile on his moustached lips. Nudging his companion, and motioning for him to follow, he moved swiftly to Alison.

"Well, I'll be damned!" he said loudly, ogling Alison from head to foot. "I remember you. Hell, how could I ever forget you? I still got a scar on my cheek where you slashed me with a knife." He leaned closer to her, his face mere inches from hers. Touching the scar with his finger, he said, "See what you did."

The mark was so faded that it was barely noticeable.

He spoke to his friend, "This gal used to live with the Comanches. I visited their village once. I had some business with 'em. Took care of some business with the Indian-lovin' whore too."

The man was speaking so loudly that passers-by stopped and listened curiously.

He laughed harshly. "This damned white squaw put up one hell of a fight, but it didn't matter, I still got what I wanted!" He turned away from his companion to leer at Alison. "Didn't I, you white-Comanche whore?"

Anger robbed her of her fear. "I wish I had cut your throat instead of your cheek!"

The gathering crowd grew larger, all of them hanging on to every word.

"Don't get uppity with me! Any decent woman would've killed herself before lettin' Comanche warriors take her! Hell, you enjoyed matin' with 'em, didn't you?"

Her fear returned, and the need to run to her room and away from this nightmare became overpowering. She tried to brush past the man, but he blocked her way. "Let me by!" she demanded, a quaver in her voice exposing her fear.

Suddenly, she felt a hand on her shoulder. Reacting impulsively, she threw off the hand, whirled around, and came face to face with Jonas.

His calm demeanor was in stark contrast to his words. "Do you want me to permanently disable this son of a bitch?" he asked Alison.

She gasped sharply, for she had a feeling that he meant what he said. "No," she cried softly. "Don't fight with him. Just make him go away."

Meanwhile, the man in question blurted out angrily to Riker, "I'd just like to see you try to fight me! If you get the hell out of here right now, I just might let you live."

Jonas pushed aside his vest, revealing his sheriff's badge.

"You're the one who's leaving. You have one minute to get out of my town, or I'll lock you up, and leave you in the cell until you rot."

The man wasn't about to tangle with the law. He and his companion were on their way to Villa de Lazar, where they hoped to find Jason Edwards. They had only stopped in Crystal Creek for dinner and provisions. The man waved a terse hand at his friend. "Come on; let's get the hell out this two-bit town."

"Just a moment," Jonas said. "You owe the lady an apology."

"No!" Alison cried, grasping Riker's arm so tightly that her fingernails dug through his sleeve and into his flesh. "Please just let them leave!"

Jonas looked at the two men. "You heard the lady."

Their horses were tied at the hitching rail in front of the general store. Jonas kept his eyes on them until they were mounted and headed out of town. He then dismissed the bystanders testily with an angry sweep of his arm.

Taking Alison by the hand, he led her into the lobby of the hotel and to the sofa. He sat beside her, and asked tenderly, "Are you all right?"

"I think so," she murmured shakily. "How much did you overhear?"

"Enough," he replied.

"I didn't live with the Comanches willingly. I was abducted when I was only fourteen. I was never one of them—I was always a slave."

"Will you have dinner with me?" he blurted out, and realized, embarrassed, that such a request was probably too sudden.

His invitation was so unexpected that Alison gaped at him with astonishment.

He hid his embarrassment with a wry grin. "I can be a charming dinner companion—honestly."

"Why would you want to have dinner with someone like me?"

"Why not? You're very attractive and very likable."

She suddenly stiffened. "Is it really dinner that you want me to share with you?"

"I know exactly what you're implying. And I find it insulting that you'd even make such an accusation, and I'm angry that you think so little of yourself. Your company at dinner is all I'm asking for. I'll meet you here in the lobby in one hour. That should give you plenty of time to freshen up."

He got up to leave, but she placed a deterring hand on his arm. "Jonas, why haven't you asked me about . . . about my life with the Comanches?"

He patted her hand gently. "I don't figure it's any of my business."

Admiration was in her eyes as she watched him leave. For a moment, a feeling of happiness rose inside her, but it died very suddenly as she remembered the bystanders. They had heard every word between her and the man from her past. Soon the whole town would know that she had lived with the Comanches. Now, she'd have to endure vicious whispers and looks of contempt from every person she passed on the streets or came into contact with. She wasn't sure if she was strong enough to bear it.

Chapter Seventeen

The man who had accosted Alison threw his bedroll on the ground as though it were a living thing that had incurred his wrath. He was steaming inside, for he was still irate that the sheriff in Crystal Creek had run him out of town. He despised all lawmen; they always hid behind their tin stars, threatening jail time instead of meeting their opponents face to face, gun to gun, and bullet to bullet.

There was no need for a campfire, for the man and his companion had already eaten, and the evening was warm. They had considered crossing the border before stopping for the night, but they were extremely fatigued and stopped to catch a couple of hours' sleep before continuing on to Villa de Lazar.

They chose an area that was partially enclosed by trees and shrubbery. Sitting on his bedroll, the man rolled a cigarette, lit it, then inhaled the smoke deeply into his lungs. He glanced at his companion, who was sitting on his own bedroll, cramming a wad of chewing tobacco into his mouth. The man's name was Louie, and like his comrade, he was in his middle thirties, moustached, and somewhat unkempt. But their likeness didn't end there—they were both thieves, as well as murderers.

"Whatcha thinkin' 'bout, Rafe?" Louie asked, for his friend seemed deep in thought.

"Nothin' in particular," he mumbled.

"It'll be good to see Jason again, won't it?"

Rafe nodded. "Yeah, I ain't seen my brother in months."

"You sure he'll be holed up in Villa de Lazar?"

"There ain't no way I can be a hundred percent sure. But considerin' there's a bounty on 'im, I imagine he headed across the border." Rafe frowned harshly before continuing, "He sure as hell screwed up when he killed that rich bitch and her kid. A thousand dollar reward is gonna send every bounty hunter in the West a-lookin' for 'im."

It was simply by chance that Rafe and Louie had spotted a wanted poster on Edwards. They had been in San Antonio, where the posters had been nailed all over town. A thousand dollar bounty was almost unheard of, causing the posters to draw more attention than a shootout in the saloon that had occurred only moments after the bounty had been posted.

"My little brother," Rafe began, for Jason was five years younger, "has got a serious problem. He's always horny. I told him time and time again that someday dippin' his pecker was gonna put a rope around his neck. I swear to God, most of the time his brain is hangin' between his legs." Rafe suddenly laughed heartily. "He walks around with a permanent erection! Hell, I reckon I kinda envy 'im. Thirty seconds inside a woman, and my prick goes off like a half-cocked pistol."

Louie laughed. "Kinda fast on the trigger, huh?"

Rafe's hand shot upwards, a signal for silence. "Quiet," he whispered. "I hear someone comin'."

Louie, listening, heard the unmistakable sound of horses

approaching. He grabbed his rifle, and along with Rafe, leapt to his feet. They hid behind a tree, and peeked around its wide trunk. A buggy, drawn by a pair of magnificent palominos, rolled out of the shadows and into the moonlight, illuminating the two occupants inside. The woman interested Rafe, and within seconds his evil mind conjured up special plans for her. He gently nudged Louie with his elbow, muttering softly, "Let's take 'em."

"What for?" he asked.

"I want the woman."

Louie smiled. "Does your half-cocked prick need firin'?"

"The woman ain't for me; she's for Jason. He's gonna have to hole up in the mountains 'til them wanted posters shrivel up and turn to dust. There ain't no way that horny rascal's gonna stay hidden unless he's got a woman with 'im."

Louie agreed. "If we're gonna take the woman, we'd best do it now 'fore they ride past us."

Rafe dropped his cigarette, grinding it into the dirt with the toe of his boot. He handed Louie his rifle, removed his pistol, then unbuckled his holster and put it on the ground. Reaching behind him, he stuck the pistol into his belt and out of sight.

"Stay here," he said to Louie. Their horses were unsaddled; he hastened to his saddle, and swung it over his shoulder.

He moved into the open, and the moonlight silhouetted his brawny frame. "Hello in the buggy!" he called in a friendly voice.

The stranger, seemingly coming out of nowhere, took Lawson by surprise. He wasn't sure if he should stop or slap the reins against the horses and run from possible trouble. His instincts, which were ruled by a lack of courage more than a sense of caution, demanded that he send the palominos fleeing, as though the devil himself were in pursuit. However, he found himself drawing back on the reins, for he was worried that Laura, who was sitting at his side, would think him a coward. She would certainly tell her mother; and Doris Talbert, a known gossip, would spread the news to her friends. Soon the whole town would be talking and laughing behind his back. Lawson had spent his life avoiding dangerous confrontations; he had also successfully avoided anyone knowing about it.

Now, faced with a dilemma he couldn't avoid, he slowly brought the horses to a halt. He drew his pistol with a trembling hand; he had never shot anyone, and beads of nervous perspiration popped out on his brow as he watched the stranger nearing the buggy. He quickly noticed that the man was unarmed, and he sighed inwardly with relief.

"Evenin' folks," Rafe said, keeping a furtive eye on the pistol in Bill's hand. "My horse fell a couple of miles back. It broke its leg, and I had to put it down. That's why I'm afoot."

"Do you always travel unarmed?" Lawson asked.

"Don't believe in firearms," Rafe replied. "I'm a Mormon."

"What are you doing in these parts?"

"Just passin' through. Anyway, I don't reckon you could give me a lift?"

"As you can see, this buggy holds only two people."

Rafe cast Laura a cursory glance, and was pleased to find that she was pretty—Jason would certainly like his present.

"I have a ranch close by," Bill continued. "I'll send one of my wranglers to take you to town."

"Thank you, sir. And God bless you."

"My man should be here within the hour."

Bill then foolishly holstered his pistol, leaving Rafe free

to draw his gun from behind his back. Pointing it at Lawson, he ordered gruffly, "Get down from that buggy!"

Fear shot through Bill, and slapping the reins against the palominos flitted through his mind. With luck, he might get away before this man could shoot him. But he knew the odds were not in his favor; he had a feeling the pistol would go off the moment he lifted the reins. He winced, as though he could actually feel the bullet slamming into his chest and sending him into a early grave. Suspecting the man was after money, he decided evading robbery was not worth risking his life. He glanced at Laura, whose face was deathly pale—he didn't want to put her life at risk either.

He patted her hand soothingly. "It'll be all right, my dear. Once I give him money, I'm sure he'll let us go."

"I ain't gonna tell you again to get down from that buggy!" Rafe demanded.

Bill complied; his knees were trembling, and he staggered as though he were slightly intoxicated.

"Unbuckle your holster, and put it on the ground real slow-like."

Bill released his holster with a shaky hand, and carefully laid it at his feet.

"Now, kick it over this way," Rafe said.

He did as he was told.

Rafe, keeping his eyes on Lawson, said to Laura, "Now you get down, little lady!"

Laura was too scared to move.

"Do it!" Rafe shouted harshly.

Tears filled her eyes, and her heart thumped against her rib cage so powerfully that she could barely catch her breath. She tried to rise, but waves of grayness passed over her; her head was as light as a feather, and dizziness sent her falling back on the seat.

Louie, emerging from the dark shadows, joined his comrade, who told him to help the woman down from the carriage. He went to Laura, reached an arm about her waist, and lifted her from the seat and onto the ground. She was too weak to stand alone, and needed her captor's support.

Rafe sneered, for he had no patience with this kind of fear, even from a woman. "Hell, let her fall!" he said to Louie. "She might as well get used to bein' on her back, 'cause once Jason gets her, she'll be on her back all the time." He laughed.

Laura's fear increased. Were these men planning on kidnapping her and taking her to someone named Jason? The name suddenly struck a bell. Jason! The criminal Jodie had left to find was named Jason Edwards. Could this possibly be the same Jason?

Rafe ordered Louie to check Lawson's pockets; he hoped the man was carrying a good sum of money.

Louie took Lawson's wallet and was pleased to find bills inside.

Rafe wondered if he should kill the man or be merciful and let him live. He decided to kill him; he didn't want to leave a witness behind. In a flash, he cocked his pistol and fired.

It happened so quickly that Bill didn't have time to plead for his life. One second he was standing and facing his opponent; the next second he was on the ground, engulfed in blackness.

Laura let out a guttural cry of terror; the scream seemed eternal as it carried shrilly over the quiet plains. The palominos trembled nervously in their harnesses, and an owl flew from a nearby tree, its wings flapping like a sheet blowing in the wind.

"Shut her up!" Rafe told Louie.

He took a step toward Laura to silence her, but it wasn't necessary, for the scream died in her throat, and she sank to the ground in a dead faint.

Rafe stayed with Laura as Louie rolled up their bedrolls

and saddled their horses. It took him a good fifteen minutes; still, Laura remained unconscious. Rafe slung her limp body over his shoulder, then placed her across his saddle like a slaughtered deer.

They rode quickly away from the area, leaving Lawson's body where it lay.

Jonas was in the lobby when Alison came downstairs. He had changed clothes and was freshly shaved. She caught a pleasant whiff of cologne.

"You're very lovely," he said, his eyes sweeping over her blue gingham gown. Her dark hair was unbound, and the raven tresses cascaded gracefully past her shoulders.

She thanked him demurely, then stepped back as though she wanted to keep an unnecessary distance between them.

"Is anything wrong?" he asked.

"Jonas," she began somewhat hesitantly. "I . . . I don't think I should join you for dinner."

"Why not?"

"The restaurant . . . there will be people there. News travels fast in small towns. By now, several people will know that I lived with the Comanches. I don't think I can bear their stares and their whispers."

He moved quickly to her side, grasped her hand, and squeezed it encouragingly. "You can't hide from gossip, Alison. Besides, who cares what other people think?"

"I care," she whispered.

"You know, it might not be as bad as you think. Sure, a few heartless snobs will turn up their noses, but most people are kind and understanding."

"I'm afraid," she said softly.

Her vulnerability touched a chord deep inside Jonas, arousing feelings he hadn't experienced since he lost his family. He suddenly felt more alive than he had felt in years.

"I don't know about you," he said with an easy smile. "But I'm famished. Let's have dinner, shall we?"

She slipped her hand into the crook of his arm. "Stay close, Jonas. I think I can make it through the evening if I have you near me."

"You have me—for as long as you need me."

That she needed someone the way she needed Jonas came as a complete surprise to Alison. The revelation was sudden. Although it took her by surprise, it didn't rock her composure or send her emotions swirling. Needing Jonas seemed the most natural thing in the world.

They left the hotel and crossed the street to Caroline's. The establishment wasn't overly crowded, but more than half of the tables were occupied. Mayor Wrightman, his wife, and the three Bradleys were having dinner together. Riker acknowledged their presence with a slight nod of his head. Knowing Alison would prefer to sit apart from the other diners, he escorted her to a corner table.

A waitress came to their table. Riker often ordered Caroline's pot roast and knew it was delicious. He said as much to Alison, and they ordered that for dinner, along with a bottle of wine.

Jonas talked about nothing in particular as they waited for their wine. He kept jumping from one trivial topic to another, hoping to keep Alison's mind on him and away from the other patrons. But he could see that he was failing, for her eyes kept wandering about the room to see if people were staring at her, or whispering behind her back.

"Stop it," he said firmly.

Her eyes turned from the diners and to his face. "Pardon?"

"Stop trying to see if people are looking at you. To hell with them." He reached across the table and gently caressed her hand. "Besides, we're the only two people in the room."

She smiled gratefully. "Jonas, you always know the right thing to say. I've never known a man so kind and considerate."

"There are many who would differ with you. The people around here don't think too highly of me."

"But you can remedy that. They are only opposed to your drinking."

"I might as well give up breathing. Liquor is the only thing that keeps me alive. Without it, the memories are too painful to live with."

"I think I understand," she replied. "I also have painful memories."

"How do you deal with them?"

"One day at a time," she murmured.

The waitress brought their wine, opened it, and filled their glasses. When they were alone again, Jonas gazed deeply into Alison's dark eyes, and asked, "Do your memories become more bearable with time?"

"Yes, I suppose. Do yours?"

"I'm not sure. I seldom stay sober long enough to find out."

"When did you lose your wife and children?"

"Four years ago."

"How many children?"

"Two."

"What were their ages?"

"I had a four-year-old boy, and girl nine months old."

"Oh, Jonas!" she moaned. "How does a parent ever recover from losing children?"

"You sound as though you're talking from experience."

"I lost two babies. I also had a boy and a girl. They had a Comanche father."

Jonas took a drink of his wine. "It seems we have both been to hell and back."

"I don't think we came back. I think we are still in hell."

Riker swigged the remainder of his wine and refilled his

glass. "You're right. We're still living in our own private hells."

The waitress returned with their dinner. The food smelled delicious, and Alison suddenly became aware that she was quite hungry. In fact, she couldn't recall the last time she had such a ravenous appetite. It must be the company, she thought. *Jonas makes me feel as though I want to live again!* She wondered if, together, they could escape the walls of their private hells.

Dinner passed pleasantly, for they didn't dwell on their troubled pasts, but discussed books, music, and history. Alison was amazed to find that Riker was so knowledgeable. Upon questioning, he admitted that he had attended college back East. To please his father he had planned to be a lawyer, but had forfeited his education to travel West. His father had been sorely disappointed, but Riker had never regretted his decision to leave.

"I was halfway through law school," he said to Alison, "before I realized that I didn't want to be a lawyer. I was always fascinated with the West, and I somehow knew this was where I belonged. But enough about me—how did you become so well-informed? Didn't you say you were only fourteen when you were abducted?"

"Yes. I lived with the Comanches for seven years. I was then sold to a man who was half mexican and half white. I was with him a short time before I ended up living with Hernando Lopez and his band of rebels. Hernando knew I was thirsty for knowledge, and he brought me books to read. I'm not sure how he acquired them, but I always had an ample supply."

"How did you end up with Lopez?"

She was finished eating, and she pushed her plate aside. Leaning back in her chair, she told Jonas about the apaches killing her new owner, that Hernando had arrived in time to save her, and had then offered her employment in his home as his housekeeper.

"That's where Cade found me," she completed. "In Hernando's home."

They were interrupted by a sudden commotion. A wrangler who worked for Lawson had barged into the restaurant, shouting for Riker.

Jonas quickly got to his feet. "I'm over here!" he called.

The man hastened to Riker. "My boss has been shot!" he exclaimed. His excited voice could be heard by everyone in the room. Wrightman rushed over, followed by Emmett Bradley.

"Exactly what happened?" Jonas asked the wrangler.

"Mr. Lawson came to town to escort Miss Talbert to the Double-L for dinner. Me and two other wranglers were on our way here when we came across the boss's buggy. He lay beside it, shot in the chest. He was still alive, thank God. We took him to Doctor Blackburn's house, then I came lookin' for you."

"Was he shot after picking up Miss Talbert?" Jonas asked.

"I reckon; the buggy was headed toward the ranch."

"Miss Talbert was nowhere around?"

"Not a sign of her. We couldn't ask the boss 'cause he was unconscious. But I think he was tryin' to come to when we got to the doctor's house."

"I certainly hope so. I need to question him." Jonas turned to Wrightman. "Will you take Miss Brandon to the hotel?"

"I think I'd better go with you."

"I'll have one of my boys escort her," Emmett spoke up.

Riker offered Alison a warm smile. "I'll talk to you later." He reached into his pocket, placed enough money on the table to cover their meals, then hurried out of the restaurant with the wrangler and Wrightman following close behind.

Emmett lifted a hand, getting Dirk's attention. Dirk left the table and moved to his father. He wondered what he wanted with him.

"Dirk, I want you to escort the lady to the hotel."

Alison pushed back her chair, stood, and said, "That isn't necessary. The hotel is only across the street."

"I don't mind," Dirk was quick to say.

Alison didn't want to draw more attention to herself, so she conceded. The hotel was only a minute's walk; she'd soon be closed in her room and away from so many staring eyes.

She left the restaurant with Dirk at her side. As they started across the street, he took her arm; there was something about the contact that sent an inexplicable chill up her spine.

"I know who you are," he said.

"What do you mean?" she asked, drawing away from his touch.

"You're the woman who lived with the Comanches. People all over town are talkin' about it."

She hastened her steps, but Dirk caught her arm. "What's your hurry? You don't have to run away from me. I don't care how many warriors you slept with; their stink don't rub off. I know some men won't bed a woman who has been with an Indian, but hell, it doesn't matter to me. You're a good-lookin' woman, and I bet those warriors taught you to be a real savage in bed. How about it, huh? You wanna invite me up to your room? We'll pretend we're on the warpath, and I'll impale you with my spear." He laughed heartily, for he thought his joke hilarious.

Alison jerked free, and with Dirk's cruel laughter echoing in her ears, she fled to the hotel. She ran blindly up the stairs, retrieved her key from her skirt pocket, and dashed inside. She slammed the door and pushed in the bolt.

She fell across the bed. Tears gushed from her eyes, and her whole body shook with rasping sobs. That the pleasant evening with Jonas had ended on such an ugly note made the pain all that more excruciating.

Chapter Eighteen

Alison had her tears under control and was washing her face when a knock came at the door. She tensed. "Who's there?"

"Jonas," came the reply.

She hastened to let him in.

He could see that she had been crying. "What's wrong?" he asked.

"Nothing," she murmured.

"Alison," he began gently. "So far, our friendship has been based on honesty; let's keep it that way. Now, why have you been crying?"

"Is it that obvious?" she asked.

"Yes. Your eyes are red and swollen."

"The gentleman—I don't know his name—had one of his sons walk me to the hotel. The young man insulted me."

"What did he say?"

She looked away from Jonas. "It doesn't matter."

He placed a finger beneath her chin, and turned her face back to his. "It matters to me."

She found it embarrassing to repeat Dirk's proposition, and her cheeks blushed scarlet as she recounted the scene.

Jonas was fierce, but for Alison's sake, he held his rage in check. He didn't need to ask which son had insulted her; Garth Bradley was above such crude behavior. He knew Dirk was the guilty party, and his hands balled into fists as he envisioned plowing them into young Bradley's face.

"Jonas," Alison began, "I don't think I can stay in this town."

"Don't let a creep like Bradley run you out. Sooner or later, you've got to make a stand. You can't keep running for the rest of your life." He placed his hands on her shoulders, drew her close, and gazed down into her eyes. "Alison, the time has come to stop running."

"I suppose you're right," she murmured. "I'll try to stay."

"Good for you." He kissed her cheek, then stepped back away from her. "I just came from Doctor Blackburn's house. Lawson will live. He said that two men robbed him. They apparently took Miss Talbert with them. He described the men and they sound like the two who gave you trouble earlier today. Do you know their names?"

"I know the one who did all the talking. His name is Rafe. I don't know his last name. About six years ago, he came to the Comanche village where I was living. He sold whiskey to the Comanches. The warrior who owned me became intoxicated. Rafe used his drunken state to his advantage and waylaid me in the woods. I had gone alone to a nearby creek. Rafe became very angry when I refused to respond to him. He hit me several times. I managed to grab his knife, and I cut his cheek before he got the knife away from me. After that, he nearly knocked me unconscious." She paused, and with a heavy sigh, added, "He had his way with me. He left that night, and I never saw him again until today.''

Jonas's face was inscrutable, but inside he was badly shaken. His heart ached for Alison; she had suffered tremendous atrocities. He suddenly had the urge to draw her into his arms and protect her from further cruelty. But he repressed the urge, for he was too unsure of himself. He couldn't quite picture himself in the role of protector; half the time he couldn't take care of himself, let alone someone else.

"I'm sorry, Alison," he finally murmured. He was disappointed in himself, for his response sounded pathetic. But how, he wondered, do you express sympathy to a woman who has endured such acts of brutality? Words were certainly inept. He changed the subject. "I'm going to ride out to where Lawson was shot and see if I can pick up a trail. I'm sure the men are headed for the border."

"Do you intend to chase them across the border?"

"Legally, I can't do that. But considering they have Miss Talbert with them, I won't let a law like that stop me. The mayor will temporarily swear in Garth Bradley as deputy until I return."

"Garth Bradley?" she questioned.

"Yes. Emmett Bradley is his father. He's the man who had his son walk you to the hotel."

"Which son is Garth?" she asked.

"I'm sure he isn't the one who insulted you. He's the older brother. He has a moustache and dark hair."

"No, he isn't the one."

"I don't know how long I'll be gone, but I do hope you'll be here when I get back."

She smiled timorously. "I'll be here."

He told her good-bye, hurried down the stairs and outside. He went straight to the Silver Dollar, where he expected to find Dirk. He wasn't disappointed; young Bradley was standing at the bar alongside his brother and father.

Jonas stalked to Dirk, grabbed his arm, and swung him around. "I oughta beat the hell out of you!" he seethed.

"Hold on!" Emmett said, puffing arrogantly. How dare Riker threaten his son!

"Stay out of this!" Jonas warned him. "Dirk's got a beatin' comin', and I'm the man to do it!"

"What did I do?" Dirk asked, a whine in his voice. He wasn't a fighter, and was afraid of Riker.

"You insulted Miss Brandon. If you ever bother her again, I'll make you wish you were dead! Do you understand?"

"All right, all right, I understand," he answered at once. Thinking Riker was going to let him off with only a warning, he sighed with relief.

But Jonas was not about to be so lenient. His fist struck invisibly fast, his knuckles smashing against Dirk's jaw. The strong blow sent young Bradley stumbling backward.

Emmett stepped forward to stop Riker, but Garth caught his father's arm. "Stay out of it, Pa. Dirk's got it coming."

Jonas delivered a second blow, and his fist plowed into Dirk's nose. Blood spewed copiously down Dirk's shirt and onto the floor.

"Fight back, you damned coward!" Riker shouted.

Emmett felt he had to intervene. He stepped in front of his battered son, shielding his offspring with his own body. "Enough, Riker!" he said strongly. "You've made your point. Dirk will stay away from Miss Brandon. If it pleases you, I'll have him apologize to her."

"I don't want him that close to her!"

"All right; have it your way. Now, don't you have more important matters to take care of? You are not paid to brawl, but to enforce the law. Correct me if I'm wrong, but wasn't Bill Lawson ambushed, and wasn't Miss Talbert kidnapped? Why aren't you doing something about it?"

"You're a pompous ass, Bradley!" Jonas replied angrily. Garth decided to become involved. He despised his brother and had enjoyed watching the sheriff beat up on him, but he was not about to stand by and allow his father to be insulted. "Your conduct is totally uncalled for!" he said to Jonas.

Riker didn't want to argue with Garth. Not that he especially liked him; he didn't have any use for any of the Bradleys. But he disliked Garth less than the other two. The man was as arrogant as his father, but he possessed a certain fairness that was lacking in Emmett. Time, however, was the dissuading factor preventing Jonas from taking on all three of the Bradleys.

"I don't have time to argue with you," he told Garth. "Just keep your brother away from Miss Brandon!" With that, he wheeled around and left the saloon.

Garth handed his brother a handkerchief. "You're a bloody mess!" he muttered. He was totally disgusted with his younger sibling.

Emmett, frowning thoughtfully, murmured, "Did you notice that Riker appeared sober? I don't think I've seen him completely dry in years."

Garth picked up a whiskey bottle, filled his glass, and downed the liquor in one swallow. He turned to his father, and said with conviction, "Sober, Riker's a man to reckon with—he'll make one hell of sheriff."

Emmett concurred, but he doubted Riker's ability to remain sober. "He'll be swigging whiskey again before you know it."

Garth shrugged indifferently. "You're probably right."

Jodie stopped to rest in an area partially protected by mesquite trees and sparse shrubbery. She had crossed the Rio Grande hours ago, but despite her fatigue, she had kept plodding onward. Knowing Cade was surely behind her, she wanted to keep as much distance between them as possible. He would undoubtedly insist that she return to Crystal Creek. If she refused, he'd probably try using force. She preferred to avoid such a confrontation.

She didn't intend to stop for very long; a couple of hours' rest was all she needed. A fire was out of the question, for it might be seen by bandits or Apaches. She tended to the Appaloosa, then, taking her rifle with her, she spread a blanket, sat down, and ate a cold supper. Night had fallen quite some time ago, but a bright moon kept pitch darkness at bay. The desert-like terrain was softly lighted with a golden tint, and the cloudless sky was dotted with sparkling stars. The serene tapestry had a soothing effect on Jodie, relaxing her tired muscles and lulling her into a slumberous state. Her eyelids soon grew heavy, and she was unable to stifle a yawn. She knew she couldn't go on without a couple hours of sleep. But sleep would leave her vulnerable, and she wished there was some way she could avoid it. That, of course, was impractical. Without sleep, she wouldn't be very alert, nor would her skills be in top form.

She lay back on the blanket and stared idly up at the thousands of stars lighting the vast heavens. She considered Cade's marriage proposal. Just thinking about being his wife sent her pulse racing, and her heart beating faster than normal. She had never admitted to herself that she was in love with him; but, now, as she lay alone, surrounded by the mystic night, she found she could no longer escape her feelings. She loved Cade with all her heart, and wanted to marry him.

What if my marriage ends up like my parents'? she suddenly wondered. That Cade might someday feel sorry for her in the same way her father had pitied her mother was more than she could calmly consider. It set her nerves on edge, and strengthened her resolve to hold on to her independence. The thousand dollar bounty became all important; if she married Cade the money would stand between her and dependency.

Again, her eyelids grew heavy, and within moments, she had surrendered to sleep.

An hour or so later, she was awakened by the Appaloosa's soft whinny. She sat up, grabbed her Winchester, and listened closely. She heard nothing. The horse whinnied a second time, and Jodie bounded to her feet, cocked her rifle, and slipped behind a tree. A few minutes later a rider came into view. The man was dressed in dark clothing, and she couldn't really make him out, but she assumed it was Cade.

Mistakes were uncommon for Jodie, but this time she made a huge one. She lowered her rifle and moved out from behind the tree. "Darn it, Cade!" she said crankily. "How did you find me so soon? Aunt Doris must've run to your office right after I left."

As the rider drew closer, she looked away to lay her rifle on the blanket. When she looked up again, the man was in clear sight; so was the pistol in his hand. Her eyes widened, and a sharp gasp emanated from deep within her throat.

"Evenin', ma'am," he drawled, ogling her hungrily. "My name ain't Cade, and I sure as hell don't know Aunt Doris."

Jodie, recognizing the intruder, could hardly believe that she was actually face to face with Jason Edwards. A shiver teased her spine—the predator was now the prey!

Edwards dismounted slowly, keeping his pistol pointed at Jodie. Meanwhile, she cautiously edged closer to her horse. The coiled bullwhip escaped Jason's detection, and he said with a cold smile, "Goin' for your horse won't do you any good. You mount that beast, and I'll shoot it right out from under you."

She had reached the Appaloosa, and pretending hysteria, she turned toward the horse and faked heaving sobs. At the same time, her hand stealthily crept upwards until her fingers encircled the whip's handle.

"There's no reason to cry, sugar babe. If you cooperate,

I won't have to kill you.'' Edwards was astounded at finding a beautiful woman alone in the Mexican desert. He silently blessed his good luck.

But his luck had run out. At that moment, Jodie whirled around, and taking Jason by surprise, she sent the whip's lash against the gun in his hand. The pistol flew into the air as though it had magically sprouted wings. Jason turned swiftly to dash for the rifle on his horse, but Jodie was faster; the lightning quick lash curled about his legs like a snake, tripping him to the ground.

She rushed to the blanket and picked up her Winchester. By the time Jason got back on his feet, she had the gun aimed at him. ''Make one wrong move,'' she warned, ''and I'll kill you. The bounty on you is dead or alive. I don't care if I deliver you sitting up in your saddle or flung across it.''

He eyed her incredulously. ''Bounty? I don't believe my own ears! Hell, you're a woman!''

''It's only right that a woman should bring you to justice, for you killed a woman! You also killed a twelve-year-old boy! It's too bad the law can't hang you twice!''

His lips curled into a sneer. ''Are you plannin' on takin' me all the way to Abilene? That's a long ride. A lot can happen between here and there.''

''I don't intend to take you any farther than Crystal Creek. Abilene will be notified to come get you.'' She told him to move aside. She then went to his horse, got his rifle, and pitched it into the shrubbery. ''Mount up,'' she said. ''We're leaving.''

She waited until he was on his horse before retrieving her whip and mounting the Appaloosa. ''Ride in front of me,'' she told him.

He took the lead, and she kept her horse close behind his. ''By the way,'' she began, ''don't make any sudden moves. I won't hesitate to shoot. If I were you, I wouldn't even flinch from a mosquito bite.''

Laura had been conscious for quite some time; nevertheless, Rafe kept her slung over his horse like so much bag-
gage. The position was terribly uncomfortable; her
stomach was painfully pressed against the saddle, her arms
and legs were numb, and her head pounded as though
the blood vessels were about to burst.

"Please let me up," she pleaded to Rafe, for at least the
tenth time.

Rafe liked seeing women in pain; it was arousing. However, he decided to stop and allow the woman to sit up.
After all, she was a present for his brother, and he should
take better care of her.

He reined in, causing Louie to do likewise. Rafe slid off
his horse, reached up, and lifted Laura from the saddle.
Holding her body pressed to his, he slowly lowered her
feet to the ground. He kept her pinned against him, as
his aroused manhood thrust between her thighs. He came
very close to raping her, but knowing Apaches could be
nearby, he decided poking a woman was not worth the
risk. In this territory, a man had to stay alert; otherwise,
he might find himself surrounded by Apaches.

Laura squirmed weakly against Rafe's hold, her heart
pounding, her stomach queasy. The stench from his
unwashed body was overwhelming. His hardness pressed
against her thighs was more frightening than any nightmare she could have encountered.

When Rafe suddenly released her, and told her to get
on the horse, she was more astonished than relieved. Afraid
he might change his mind, she hiked up her cumbersome
skirt and mounted quickly. Rafe swung up behind her.

They continued onward, and with moonbeams lighting
their way, they maintained a steady course toward Villa de
Lazar.

Cade stopped to rest. He ate a cold meal, then stretched out on a spread blanket. Over an hour passed before he was able to fall asleep. He awoke forty-five minutes later, refreshed, and ready to go.

He held the stallion at an easy pace; he was in dangerous territory, and an exhausted horse could cost him his life.

A bright sunrise was igniting the sky as Cade approached a hill laden with cottonwoods and mesquites. He ascended the rise, but the confronting sight on the other side caused him to rein in sharply.

"Well, I'll be damned!" he said with a grin.

His smile expanded as he watched Jodie bring in her prisoner at gunpoint. That she had already captured Edwards was stunning; he wondered how the hell she had managed it. He wouldn't be surprised to learn that she had carried it off with relative ease. He thought his admiration for Jodie could go no higher, but he found himself admiring her even more. No wonder he loved her so much.

He guided his horse behind a tree and out of sight. He didn't want to infringe on Jodie's success. However, her life could be threatened at any moment; therefore, he intended to keep an eye on her, but from a safe distance. She wouldn't know she had an extra gun close behind, not unless trouble erupted.

He rode farther back into the trees, and remained hidden as Jodie and her prisoner covered the hill and descended the other side. He then left his place of concealment and followed stealthily behind.

Vegetation grew thicker as Jodie and Edwards traveled closer to the border. A grove of trees, nestled among prickly bushes and colorful wild flowers, lay up ahead. Jodie recognized the verdant area, and knew the Rio Grande was not too far away. The thought was uplifting, for she was anxious to reach Crystal Creek before dusk. She glanced up at the sky; it was mid-morning. A lot of miles still stretched before her.

She wondered why she hadn't come across Cade. She had taken for granted that he would try to find her. Had she misjudged him? Did his absence mean that he no longer cared? Learning she had traded in her badge, only to turn bounty hunter, might very well have destroyed his love.

As they rode into the tree-shaded region, Jodie forcefully pushed Cade to a far corner of her mind. It was imperative that she keep her concentration sharp and centered on her prisoner. The sun's rays had been uncomfortably warm, and Jodie welcomed the drop in temperature. She was tempted to rein in and rest for a few minutes, but decided against it—this was no place to stop, for the trees would hide an approaching enemy.

As indeed they did! A distance ahead, two such enemies sat astride their horses, safely concealed by the thick vegetation and full-branched trees.

Louie had his pistol drawn, but Rafe's hand was over Laura's mouth, smothering any attempt to scream. Earlier, they had almost cleared the area before spotting Edwards and Jodie. They had quickly backtracked and were now considering their next move.

Rafe clamped his hand even tighter, bent his head, and whispered in Laura's ear, "If you cry out, I'll kill you. Do you understand me, gal?"

She managed to nod her head.

He cautiously removed his sweaty palm. Laura could taste his foul smelling sweat; she came close to throwing up.

"Do you know the woman with Jason?" Rafe asked her.

"Yes. She's my cousin."

"How come a woman's got my brother at gunpoint?"

"Jodie used to be a deputy; she's now a bounty hunter."

Rafe, as well as Louie, were dumbfounded.

"Well, I'll be a donkey's ass!" Rafe exclaimed softly. "I've heard everything now." He suddenly turned to Louie. There was no time to dwell on such shocking news; he had to move and move quickly. "Since these gals are cousins, I'll offer to trade prisoners." He intended to recapture his prisoner, along with her cousin, but he wasn't about to say this in front of Laura. It wasn't necessary, for Louie knew what he was thinking.

"Get down," Rafe told Laura. "I want you on Louie's horse."

It was half a dismount, and half a shove from Rafe that sent Laura falling from the horse and onto the ground. She got up shakily, accepted Louie's outstretched hand, and swung up in front of him.

"Follow a short distance behind me," Rafe ordered Louie. "And keep your gun unholstered."

Laura was afraid, but she was also hopeful that her horrible ordeal was coming to an end. Jodie would undoubtedly make the trade, and she would soon be home! Her thoughts jumped suddenly to Lawson. She believed him dead; a trace of tears wet her eyes, for her dreams of wealth and luxury had died with him.

Chapter Nineteen

Jodie heard the sounds of advancing horses before the riders came into view. She cocked her Winchester, and was ready to fire at a moment's notice. Rafe's gun was holstered, and he held up his hands in a don't-shoot pose. He cautiously rode closer to Edwards and Jodie. Meanwhile, Louie reined in. He and Laura waited close by.

Jodie was shocked to see Laura with these two men. She wondered why her cousin was with them.

Rafe brought his horse to a stop; he was only a few feet away from Jodie and Edwards. He acknowledged his brother with a slight nod of his head, then turned his full attention to Jodie. "Howdy, ma'am," he said, as though they were sharing a pleasant encounter.

Jason smiled largely; he could hardly believe that Rafe and Louie had materialized out of nowhere. It seemed he could always depend on his big brother.

"I got your cousin," Rafe said to Jodie. He waved a hand toward Louie and Laura. "As you can see, my partner's got a gun pointed at her. You try anything, and he'll splatter her brains all over the ground."

"What do you want?" Jodie asked.

"I thought maybe we could make a trade—your cousin for my brother." He smiled complacently. "If you need a moment to think it over . . ."

Jodie didn't need to think it over; she wasn't about to sacrifice Laura to collect a bounty. The trade was not in question—carrying it out was the problem. She had to find a way to exchange prisoners, and at the same time guarantee that she and Laura would be safe. Once the trade was completed, these men would undoubtedly come after them.

"I do need time to think it over," she finally said to Rafe.

Laura, listening, was flabbergasted. She was also enraged. How dare Jodie place a bounty above her life! She had always known that Jodie didn't like her, but she had never imagined that she hated her. But she apparently did; otherwise, why would she need to think over the man's proposal?

"You think about it, little lady," Rafe drawled, as though he had all the time in the world.

Jodie considered opening fire, but quickly ruled out the option; the act would probably result in Laura's death. She didn't see any choice but to trade prisoners; therefore, she concentrated on minimizing the danger to herself and Laura.

Meanwhile, the birds inhabiting the trees did not react to the lone rider who was furtively circling the wooded area. He and his horse, perfectly attuned to each other, moved so quietly that the birds stayed perched on their limbs or snug in their nests. A loud flapping of wings, followed by a sudden flight, was a warning Rafe would certainly have heeded, but it was not to be.

Cade had barely entered the wooded region before realizing that something was amiss. He had reined in and dismounted, and advancing on foot had spotted Jodie and the others. He had quickly returned to his horse.

Now, as he circled around the group, he drew his pistol, and slipped up behind Louie and Laura. He saw that the man's gun was not aimed directly at Laura; he was certain he could shoot him before he could turn the gun on his prisoner. The man confronting Jodie had his weapon holstered; however, Jodie's Winchester was ready to fire. Cade knew Jodie was not in danger; if the man was foolish enough to draw his gun, he didn't doubt that she'd shoot him.

"Drop your weapon," Cade said to Louie, taking the man totally by surprise.

Louie made a fatal mistake; he swung around with his gun in hand. Cade fired, and the bullet struck its victim in the chest. As Louie fell from his horse, his hands clutched wildly at Laura, sending her falling to the ground beside him. Louie's death coincided with Laura's blood-curdling scream.

In the meantime, Rafe did foolishly draw his pistol, for he underestimated Jodie. Because she was a woman, he thought she would hesitate to shoot. He thought wrong; Jodie fired her rifle, and Rafe was hurled from his horse as though a powerful wind had picked him up and slammed him to the ground.

Dismounting, Jodie warned Jason not to make a move. She went to Rafe, knelt, and checked to see if he was alive. He was dead. She stood up slowly; her stomach was queasy, and she felt a little light-headed. She took a couple of deep, calming breaths; it seemed to help.

Cade came to her side. "Are you all right?"

"Yes," she replied, a slight quaver in her voice. She gestured toward Louie. "Is he dead?"

"Just as dead as that one," Cade replied, pointing a finger at Rafe's body.

"Oh, Cade!" she exclaimed softly. "Everything happened so fast; my mind is swirling."

He could see that she was badly shaken, but before he could say anything, Laura intervened.

"I don't believe you!" she said to Jodie, her eyes blazing. "You were going to let those men have me, weren't you? The bounty meant more to you than my life!"

Laura's tirade had a positive effect on Jodie, for her cousin's outrage overshadowed Rafe's death. Jodie was quickly back in control. "What makes you think something like that?" she asked testily.

"Well, you had to think it over, didn't you?"

"I was trying to think of a way for us to get out of this alive! I never intended not to make the trade."

Laura wasn't sure if she believed her or not.

"How did you end up with those men?" Jodie asked.

Laura explained what had happened, announcing tearfully that Lawson was dead.

Bill's death hit Jodie with a staggering force. "My God!" she gasped.

Cade watched Jodie closely, looking for signs of a woman who had lost the man she loved. He saw sincere sorrow in Jodie's eyes, but no outward display of overwhelming grief. It didn't surprise him; he had suspected for a long time that she wasn't in love with Lawson.

Cade decided to take charge; he draped Rafe's and Louie's bodies over their saddles, securing them with ropes looped beneath the horses' bellies. Laura mounted behind Jodie, and they moved onward.

Jason Edwards still a prisoner. Losing his brother was a tremendous blow to Jason. Rafe had always been there when he needed him. A hangman's noose awaited him in Abilene, and any hope of escape had died along with his brother.

Shortly after the group rode away, a man moved into the area where Louie and Rafe had died. He was leading his horse, for earlier he had been crouched in the surrounding foliage, watching what had taken place. He had arrived right after the shootings. It wasn't by chance that he had come upon the scene; he had spied Jodie and her prisoner hours ago. He was also aware that Brandon was trailing her. He had planned to ambush the Marshal, kill him, then pursue Jodie, but his plans had changed. Now that the two were riding together, the odds were no longer in his favor.

He mounted his horse, and rode slowly through the wooded area, for he was in no hurry. Patience was one of Breed's stronger points, and he was willing to wait for a better opportunity to kill Jodie and Brandon.

Early afternoon shadows were slanting across the landscape when Cade and the others caught sight of Riker riding in their direction. They reined in and waited for him.

Jonas was relieved to find Laura safe and unharmed. The two bodies draped across the horses painted a violent picture. A shootout had evidently occurred.

They decided to stop and rest for a spell. Two large cottonwoods shaded the nearby area, and they stood beneath one of the trees, welcoming the cooler temperature. Canteens were opened, and everyone drank water. Cade then told Riker exactly what had taken place.

Jodie moved away, went to the other cottonwood, stood alone, and stared vacantly into the distance. That she had actually taken a man's life was difficult for her to deal with. She didn't know that Lawson had survived, and believing he was dead added to her depression. Tears welled up in her eyes.

She heard approaching footsteps, but didn't bother to turn around. She knew it was Cade, and she didn't want him to see her tears.

"Jodie?" he murmured.

She didn't reply.

He placed his hands on her shoulders, and firmly turned her so that she was facing him. Her eyes were downcast, and he said gently, "Look at me, Jodie."

She blinked back her tears, then raised her gaze to his.

"Taking a life is never easy," he said, his tone understanding, as well as tender. "But it comes with the job. Whether you're a law officer, or a bounty hunter, killing someone is inevitable. For some it gets easier with time, but for others it never does. That's why I intend to turn in my badge; it never got easier for me."

"Oh, Cade!" she cried. "I never really thought what it would be like to kill someone. I always knew I could kill in self-defense, but I . . . I never . . . never . . ."

He drew her into his arms, and held her close. "Don't, Jodie," he whispered. "Don't let what happened tear you to pieces inside. It was your life or his. The bastard asked for it."

She clung tightly. "I'll make it through this, Cade. I know I will."

At that moment, Laura's happy squeal interrupted their embrace. "Bill's alive!" she yelled to Jodie and Cade. "He's alive!" She suddenly threw her arms about Riker and hugged him as though the bearer of the good news was somehow responsible.

Jonas quickly unwrapped her arms; he needed to keep a sharp eye on their prisoner.

Jodie smiled happily at Cade. "Thank God, Bill's alive."

"You aren't in love with him, are you?" he asked.

The question took her by surprise. "Why . . . why do you ask that?"

"If I have a rival, I'd like to know about it."

She smiled again; it was a lovely, warming smile. "No, I'm not in love with Bill."

He arched a brow, and a wry grin lifted the corners of his black moustache. "Are you in love with someone else?"

Her eyes twinkled flirtatiously. "I might be."

"Anybody I know?"

"Oh yes, you know him very well. One might say, you know him as well as you know yourself."

"He's a handsome devil, I bet."

"Strikingly handsome," she played along.

"Smart, considerate, and one hell of a nice guy."

"Also, conceited and hard-headed."

"Then it can't be me."

She laughed; it was music to Cade's ears. He knew she was going to come through her ordeal with no permanent scars.

Jonas called out to them, suggesting that they move on. He wanted to reach Crystal Creek before dark.

They agreed, and walked back to their horses, hand in hand.

Doris happened to be looking out the window as her daughter and the others entered Crystal Creek. Jodie's home was at the edge of town, and they had to ride by it to reach the sheriff's office. Laura and Jodie had already decided to stop at the house; Riker and Brandon could take Edwards to the jail and the outlaws' bodies to the undertaker.

Doris flung open the front door and rushed outside. The instant Laura dismounted, she had her in her arms, hugging her with an amazing strength.

"Laura, darling!" she cried. "I was so worried, and so frightened! I thought I might never see you again!" Releasing her, she stepped back so that she could look her over. "Are you all right? Those men didn't hurt you, did they?"

"No, not really. I'm fine, Mother."

As Jodie dismounted, Cade said that he would see her

later. Then he and Riker continued on to the jail with their prisoner.

Doris caught a glimpse of the two bodies, and she asked Laura, "Were those the men who kidnapped you?"

She said that they were.

"What happened? How did they die?"

"The Marshal shot one of them; Jodie shot the other one."

Doris's mouth dropped open, and staring wide-eyed at Jodie, she gasped. "Heavens above! You actually killed a man?"

"He left me no other choice. It was his life or mine."

"Oh, Jodie!" She sighed, as though her patience could take no more. "Just look where your outlandish behavior had gotten you. Your dear mother, God rest her soul, must be rolling over in her grave."

Jodie ignored her aunt's scolding, and taking the Appaloosa's reins, she said, "I'll be in later. I need to tend to my horse." She headed for the stable out back.

Doris turned to Laura; she was again smiling cheerfully. "I can hardly believe you're home! I thank God that you're alive and unharmed!"

"It is a miracle!" Laura agreed.

It didn't dawn on either lady to also thank Jodie and Brandon.

Doris wrapped an arm about her daughter's waist. "Let's go inside, and while I prepare you a bath, you can tell me exactly what happened."

"Mother, how's Bill?" Laura asked, as they started toward the front door.

"He's doing exceptionally well. Fortunately, the bullet didn't penetrate any vital organs. Doctor Blackburn said he'll make a complete recovery. Bill, of course, is very worried about you."

"After I bathe and have something to eat, I'll visit him. Is he at the doctor's house?"

"Yes, he'll be there another day or two."

Laura's mood was chipper as they entered the house. Her dreams of riches, now resurrected, were as strong as ever.

Laura's mood took a downward plunge when, later that evening, Jodie offered to accompany her to the doctor's house. She didn't want Jodie along; she was afraid that her cousin would monopolize Bill's attention. Although Bill had claimed he wouldn't marry Jodie if she got down on her knees and begged him, Laura suspected he had been speaking more from anger than conviction. But she had no plausible reason to refuse Jodie's company; therefore, the cousins left the house together to visit Lawson.

The ladies, dressed in summer gowns, their tresses freshly washed and glittering with shiny highlights, made a fetching sight. Several eyes turned and looked their way as they strode through the heart of town and to the doctor's home. The two-story house was located three doors down from Caroline's. A side entrance led into the physician's office, but at this time of night it was closed. The cousins knocked on the front door.

It was opened by the doctor; an elderly widower, he had a housekeeper, but she was busy in the kitchen. As he admitted his callers, his masculine gaze was complimentary. The sight of such beauty made him wish he were thirty years younger.

He led them upstairs and to Lawson's room. Bill had learned of Laura's rescue, and her presence didn't surprise him; nor was he especially surprised to see Jodie. He had figured she would stop by for a visit. As the ladies came to his bed, one standing on each side, his eyes flitted back and forth from one cousin to the other. He compared them with a silent scrutiny; they were both very lovely, but Jodie's appeal was more tantalizing. He still desired her, and losing her was the disappointment of a lifetime. He turned his gaze to Laura, and let it remain there. She was indeed attractive, but she was still second choice.

Jodie only stayed a few minutes, and Laura was glad to see her leave. Surprisingly, her cousin hadn't monopolized Bill's attention, but her presence had prevented Laura from weaving her inveigling web.

Leaving the doctor's house, Jodie found Cade waiting for her by the front stoop.

"Your aunt said I'd find you here," he told her. "How's Lawson?"

"He's seems to be doing quite well."

He slipped her hand in the crook of his arm, and they started down the wooden sidewalk.

"Have you had dinner?" he asked.

"Not yet."

"You owe me a dinner. If I remember correctly, you stood me up."

She smiled. "I didn't exactly stand you up. I sent Aunt Doris to you with a message."

"I think we should avoid discussing your most recent escapade. It's still a touchy subject with me."

"Why is that?"

He waved an exasperated arm. "Learning that the woman you love left town to chase down a cold-blooded killer is not exactly calming news."

"I'm sorry, Cade. But it was something I had to do."

"Did you really want the bounty that badly?"

"Yes, I did." She didn't bother to explain its importance.

"I sent a wire to the sheriff in Abilene. His response came quickly. He and a deputy will be here in a few days to pick up Edwards. He'll bring your money with him."

She didn't say anything.

They reached the restaurant, and Cade brought their steps to a halt. "What do you intend to do with a thousand dollars?"

"It depends," she replied.

"On what?"

"On whether or not I marry you."

His brow furrowed dubiously. "Am I supposed to understand what the hell you're talking about? Did I miss the point somewhere along the way? Or are you just being your usual confusing self?"

She laughed lightly. "Do you really find me confusing?"

"Among other things?"

"For instance?"

"I also find you beautiful, vivacious, charming, and admirable. On the other hand, you're unreasonably stubborn and recklessly independent."

She laughed again. "You wouldn't want a woman who's submissive and helpless, would you?"

"No, but I do want a woman who isn't always putting her life in jeopardy."

"I don't think you have to worry about that. I am no longer a deputy, and I don't intend to become a bounty hunter."

Oblivious to the people walking past them, Cade drew her into his arms, gazed down into her face, and asked softly, "Now that you're no longer a deputy or a bounty hunter, what do you intend to do next?"

"I have a wonderful occupation in mind."

The adoration mirrored in her eyes sent Cade's expectations soaring. "What occupation is that?"

"I'd like to become Mrs. Cade Brandon."

"That can be arranged," he replied; then, as passers-by looked on, he drew her closer and sealed their commitment with a lingering kiss.

Jonas sat at his desk, staring at a half-filled whiskey bottle. The moment Cade had left the office, he had opened the bottle, telling himself he'd only have a couple of drinks.

A couple had grown into several swigs. He had remained relatively sober for two days. Emotionally it hadn't been all that difficult, for his friendship with Alison had brightened his life. But he was physically addicted to liquor. He needed whiskey; his entire body cried out for it. He tilted the bottle to his mouth, and quaffed the liquor like it was water.

He was intoxicated, but by now he didn't care. That he was sheriff no longer mattered; he was a slave to the bottle.

Sober, Jonas would have heard the front door creak open, but his faculties were clouded with whiskey.

Riker's back was facing the intruder, who moved furtively, raised his pistol, and sent it crashing against his victim's head. Jonas, rendered unconscious, slumped over in his chair, and his face smashed against the desktop. The impact sent blood spewing from his nose and onto a stack of papers. The whiskey bottle lay on the floor at his feet.

Edwards had watched the scene from his cell. Now, as the intruder grabbed the keys and came his way, he asked, "Who the hell are you?"

"Your goddamned saviour!" he mumbled with a demonic grin. The cell door was quickly unlocked. "Our horses are out back." He had stolen Edwards's horse from the livery; the owner had caught him, and the man now lay dead with a stab wound through his heart.

"Why are you breaking me out?" Edwards asked; too stunned to leave his cell.

"I know what happened in Mexico. I saw Brandon and his woman kill the men who were trying to help you."

"The woman killed my brother."

"Then you probably want revenge, don't you?"

"You're damned right I do!"

"I broke you out because I might need help killing Brandon and the woman. Do you want to ride with me or not? I can lock this door as easy as I unlocked it."

Edwards sensed an evil force in the man that gave him

reason to pause. He felt as though he were looking into the eyes of a demon. But he didn't hesitate for very long; given a choice between a hangman's noose or leaving with the stranger, he decided to leave.

He hurried out of the cell, found his gun, and strapped it on. "I'm ready; let's get the hell out of here. By the way, my name's Jason Edwards."

"You can call me Breed," the stranger replied.

Chapter Twenty

Cade and Jodie enjoyed a delicious meal, but left room for a slice of Caroline's famous apple pie. Now, over dessert and coffee, Cade decided to use Jodie's amiable mood to his advantage—he hoped she would confide in him. Something disturbing had happened between her and her father; it was so compelling that it caused Jodie to protect her feelings behind a wall of defiance and independence.

Cade finished his pie, leaned back in his chair, and regarded Jodie intently. "Do you want to tell me about your father?"

"My father?" she questioned, somewhat confused. "He was a lot like you, if that's what you want to know."

"How are we alike?"

"Like you, my father wore a badge, he was fast with a gun, he exuded a strong presence, and he was very self-confident."

Cade grinned mildly. "Lately, I've been questioning my confidence."

"Why is that?"

"From the moment I met you, my confidence has been on shaky ground. Half the time you've got me running around in circles. I love you, Jodie Walker, but I'll be damned if I really know you. Do you want to tell me about yourself?"

"What do you want to know?"

"What happened between you and Cole?"

Cade could see that his inquiry made her uncomfortable. She toyed with her napkin, her face was somewhat flushed, and her eyes refused to meet his.

"Tell me, Jodie," he persisted gently.

"It doesn't matter," she murmured, evading the issue. She didn't want to talk about it—not now. Why ruin a lovely evening?

Cade gritted his teeth to keep from losing his patience. He silently damned Jodie's impenetrable wall. "Whatever happened, it's still driving you," he said firmly. "If you become my wife, how can I help you if I don't know what makes you do the things you do?"

She frowned petulantly. "Don't try to change me, Cade Brandon!"

"Change you?" he asked. "I'm trying to understand you!"

"I don't think I'm that complex!"

"The hell you aren't!" he retorted, his patience frayed.

Before their tempers could fully collide, they were interrupted by Mayor Wrightman, who had barged into the restaurant. He was out of breath and was puffing heavily as he hurried to their table.

"What's wrong?" Cade asked, pushing back his chair and standing.

"I just came from the sheriff's office. Someone knocked Riker unconscious and broke Edwards out of jail. Riker was coming to when I got there. I was about to leave and search for you when Mrs. Anderson showed up. When her husband didn't come home from the livery, she went looking for him. She found him at the livery; dead—he had been stabbed.''

"Good Heavens!" Jodie exclaimed, leaping to her feet.

Cade dropped money on the table. "Let's get out of here."

They hastened outside; Cade and Jodie headed toward the sheriff's office, but Wrightman went home to send his wife to Mrs. Anderson. The woman was alone in her grief, for her grown children lived elsewhere.

Riker was coming out of the back room when Cade and Jodie arrived. He had washed his face. His nose had stopped bleeding, but it was still a little sensitive. He also had a lump at the back of his head, and his temples were pounding as though he were recovering from a terrific hangover. That his headache was partly due to whiskey was a possibility he had considered. But even if he hadn't had a drop of liquor, he doubted if his head would hurt any less. The culprit who broke Edwards out of jail had delivered a tremendous blow; he had been knocked out cold for quite some time.

Cade moved closer to Riker; the smell of whiskey was overwhelming. "You drunken fool!" Cade uttered. "I warned you not to drink on duty!" Moving with incredible speed, he smashed his fist across Jonas's jaw.

Riker reeled under the punch. "You want a fight?" he shouted angrily. "Then come on; let's do it!" He doubled his hands into fists.

Jodie quickly stepped between them. "Stop it!" she demanded. "This is no time for you two to be at each other's throats!"

Cade's temper cooled. "I shouldn't have hit you, Riker."

Jonas's own anger had dissipated. "Forget it, Brandon. Besides, I had it coming. If I hadn't been drinking, Edwards would still be in his cell. This is my fault."

Cade concurred; therefore, he didn't try to make Riker feel any better about the situation. He went to the desk, opened a drawer, and took out a box of ammunition. "If I leave now, I might be able to pick up a trail."

"I'll hurry home, change clothes, and saddle my horse," Jodie told Cade. "Stop by the house; I'll be ready."

"Wait a minute," Cade replied. "I'm not taking you with me."

"Edwards is my prisoner, and I'm going after him. With or without you!"

"If I find Edwards, the bounty will still be yours. There's no reason for you to come along."

She placed her hands on her hips, and eyed him fiercely. "I'm going, and that's that!"

He threw the box of ammunition on the desk, moved to Jodie, and grasped her arms. His eyes met hers in a battle of wills. "Twice you have left town to chase down killers," he said irritably. "You were damned lucky you didn't get yourself killed. Sooner or later, Jodie, your luck's bound to run out."

"Luck?" she snapped. "I hardly think so! Luck had nothing to do with it!" She tried to free herself, but he merely tightened his hold. "Let me go!" she cried angrily. "By now you should know that I do as I damned well please!"

"Not this time!" he muttered, swooping her up into his arms. He carried her, fighting and squirming, to an empty cell, where he deposited her onto the cot. Before she could get to her feet, he walked out of the cell, picked up the key Breed had pitched to the floor, and locked the *cell* door.

Jodie clutched the bars so tightly that her knuckles turned white. "Let me out of here!" she demanded. "Damn you, Cade! I'll never forgive you for this!"

"I'm doing this for your own good, Jodie."

She turned a pleading gaze to Riker. "Jonas, will you please unlock this door?"

He shook his head. "I'm sorry, Jodie. But I agree with Brandon. It's about time you stopped risking your life."

Jodie was so enraged that she stamped her foot, as though she were a child trying to get her own way. She also shook the bars, even though she knew such an act was futile.

A wry grin touched Cade's lips. "A temper tantrum won't help, Jodie." He spoke to Jonas. "Let her out in the morning. By then it'll be too late for her to come after me or Edwards."

"Cade!" Jodie raved. "Don't you dare leave without unlocking this door!"

"I'm sorry, darlin'. But I love you, and I intend to keep you alive. If you weren't so unreasonable, this wouldn't have been necessary."

"If you weren't so set in your ways, you'd admit you need my help!"

"I need you, all right. But not to hunt down killers." With that, he retrieved his ammunition and walked out the door.

Cade had been gone about thirty minutes when Alison arrived. Jonas wasn't expecting her, and her presence made him uneasy. She had undoubtedly heard that Edwards had escaped because he'd been drinking on duty. He was almost ashamed to face her.

"Cade sent me here," Alison explained. "He thought I should be here for Jodie." The sight of Jodie locked in a cell made her angry, even though she understood why Cade had done such a thing. In a way, she agreed with her brother: Jodie must stop risking her life. On the other hand, she admired Jodie's courage, and wondered if Cade had gone too far. The fury she saw in Jodie's eyes told her that he had indeed overstepped his boundaries. She knew her brother had met his match.

"Unlock Jodie's door," Alison told Jonas. "I'll stay in the cell with her. There's no reason for her to be locked in there alone like some kind of criminal."

Riker was glad to comply; Alison's company would be good for Jodie. He hoped that if Jodie had someone to talk to it would cool her temper.

He got the key, stepped to the cell, and unlocked the door. Jodie was standing at the bars, and the moment the key turned, she swung the door against Jonas, sending him stumbling backward.

She headed for the front door, but Jonas moved quickly and caught her arm.

She swung around and kicked him sharply in the shin. "Don't you dare try to stop me!"

"Ouch!" he complained, hobbling on his uninjured leg as though Jodie's kick was crippling. "Damn it, Jodie! That hurt!"

"That's nothing compared to what I'll do next if you don't let me leave!"

"Jodie, I can't do that." He took a determined step toward her.

"Oh yes, you can," Alison intervened, moving to Jonas and placing a restraining hand on his arm. She looked at Jodie. "Leave, but please be careful."

"I will," she replied. "Thanks, Alison."

The moment Jodie darted outside, Alison murmured gravely, "If anything happens to her, I'll never forgive myself."

"Then why did you insist that I let her leave?"

"If she wants to risk her life, I believe she has that right."

"Brandon's in love with her, you know. He'll never forgive either of us if she's injured or killed."

"I know," she whispered; the thought was too depressing to dwell on, and she quickly changed the subject. "Jonas, why were you drinking on duty?"

He turned away from Alison, and sat in the chair behind

the desk. It was quite some time before he offered a reply, "I had the shakes."

She quickly sat across from him. "The shakes? I'm not sure I understand."

"My hands were trembling, and my stomach felt as though it were on fire. I needed a drink. Hell, I had to have a drink!"

"You're addicted," she said.

He heaved a surrendering sigh. "I guess I'm doomed to be a drunk until I die."

"Nonsense!" she declared. "You can break your dependency on liquor. It won't be easy, but it can be done. But you have to want to stop."

He smiled off-handedly. "Maybe that's my problem. Maybe I don't really want to stop."

"Why not?"

"Why should I?" he came back, his voice tinged with bitterness. "My life ended the night I lost my family." The whiskey bottle was still on the floor; he reached down and picked it up. Some of the contents had spilled, but there was still plenty left. He tilted the bottle to his mouth and took a big swig. He sat silently for a minute or so, then turned his gaze back to Alison. A lamp sat on the desk, and its golden glow illuminated the pain in his eyes. "When I got home that night," he began softly, "the house was still burning. The flames were so intense that I couldn't get inside. I stood by helplessly and heard my wife's last dying scream as she and my children perished. Her scream lasted only a second or so, but it seemed like an eternity. Later, I removed their charred bodies from the smoldering ruins." He helped himself to another swig. "Why should I quit drinking? It's my only salvation."

"It's not a salvation, Jonas. You use liquor to numb your feelings. You're afraid to love again. You're even afraid to care about anyone. I know, because I'm just as dead inside as you are. I almost believed that we could help each other, but I now know I was wrong. First, we would have to come alive, but we are both so deeply embedded in our emotionless graves that we'll never dig our way out.'' She got to her feet, looked kindly at Jonas, and said, ''With you, I came so close to believing that I could find the courage to start over.''

She left the office. As the door closed behind her, Jonas was bringing the bottle up to his mouth. However, his arm stopped halfway to his mouth. He slowly lowered the bottle, grabbed it by the neck, and sent it flying across the room. It smashed against the far wall, and shattered into tiny fragments.

Jodie was still fuming as she rummaged through her wardrobe and withdrew a set of riding clothes. Her aunt, watching her, sighed with exasperation. She had followed her niece into the room, spouting reasons why she shouldn't pursue a dangerous fugitive. Her words had made no impact on Jodie.

Doris decided to try again. ''Don't you realize you could be killed? Why must you continually risk your life?''

Jodie removed her dress and pitched it on the bed. ''Aunt Doris, I'm in no mood for a lecture.''

''I feel that I must speak in place of your mother. My sister never intended for you to act this way. If she were alive . . .''

''Well, she isn't!'' Jodie interrupted sharply. But she was immediately apologetic. ''I'm sorry, Aunt Doris. I have no right to snap at you. But my life is mine to do with as I please.''

''You're thinking only of yourself.'' Jodie had told her that Cade had locked her in a cell, and Doris continued, ''Considering Marshal Brandon went to such lengths to keep you here, I venture to say that he's in love with you. If something were to happen to you, what do you think that would do to him? Why don't you put his feelings before your own?''

This time, her words got through to Jodie. She hesitated, but only for a moment. She was too enraged to forgive Cade; how dare he lock her in a jail cell! She put on her riding skirt and blouse, sat on the bed, and slipped into her boots.

"Jodie?" Doris murmured tentatively. "Did you hear what I said?"

"I heard," she replied. Leaving the bed, she grabbed her hat from a hook beside the dresser. "Cade didn't consider my feelings when he put me in that cell."

"He took a firm hand with you, which is something Cole should have done a long time ago."

"Aunt Doris," she began patiently. "I could never make you understand why I must do this." She walked through the open doorway, saying over her shoulder, "I don't know when I'll be back."

Hurrying to the parlor, she got her Winchester from the gun cabinet, along with extra ammunition. She went out the back door, entered the stable, and quickly saddled the Appaloosa. She slipped the bullwhip over the saddle horn, mounted, and rode out of town.

She wasn't sure which direction Cade had taken, but she guessed that he had headed south. Edwards and his companion were probably hell-bent for Mexico.

Jodie traveled the most commonly used trail between Crystal Creek and the border. Cade had about an hour's head start; therefore, she kept the Appaloosa at a well-paced gallop. She had every intention of catching up to him. She was anxious to tell him exactly what she thought of him, but more importantly, two fugitives were at large— she could use Cade's help.

It was well past midnight before Jodie caught up to Cade. She did so without any warning. She was riding past a thick patch of foliage when, suddenly, he rode out of the shadows and into her path. He had known someone was close behind; he wasn't surprised to find it was Jodie.

Jodie reined in so sharply that the Appaloosa reared up on its hind legs. It took all her effort to stay in the saddle.

"I see you convinced Riker to unlock the cell," Brandon said calmly.

There were no clouds to block the moon's rays, and they could see each other clearly. She met his eyes with a furious gaze. "Actually, it was Alison who convinced Jonas."

"Betrayed by my own sister," he remarked with a cynical grin.

"You have no right to talk about betrayal!"

He gestured toward the surrounding foliage. "Let's get off the main trail. We need to talk."

She agreed; they rode into the thicket, found a small clearing, and dismounted.

"I should be surprised to see you," Cade began. "But I'm not. I think I'm finally beyond that point."

Jodie turned on him with pent-up fury. "How dare you lock me in a cell! Who do you think you are? Don't you ever do anything like that to me again!"

"Do what?" he returned. "Try to keep you alive?"

"I can take care of myself! Why can't you get that through your thick skull?"

"Why can't you admit you're a woman?"

"It always comes down to this, doesn't it? I'm a woman; therefore, I should be totally helpless!"

"I never said you were helpless. But, damn it, sometimes you go too far!"

"And so do you!" she retorted, stepping forward and drawing back an arm to slap his face.

But he caught her wrist, twisted it behind her back, and drew her body flush to his. "There's no reason to resort to violence."

"You deserved to be lashed!" she cried angrily.

"You're probably itching to attack me with that bullwhip of yours." He tightened his hold on her wrist. "You fiery little wildcat. I oughta . . ."

"You ought to what?" she asked; then, taking him off guard, she brought up her knee powerfully against his groin. He loosened his hold; she broke free, and hurried to the Appaloosa. Removing the whip, she whirled around, snapped the lash, then sent it hurling. It struck Cade's hat, dispatching it into the air as though it were caught in a windstorm.

"I can flick a fly off a horse's ear," she said. "I suggest you remember that!" She recoiled the whip and returned it to the saddle.

Leaving his hat where it lay, Cade sauntered leisurely to Jodie; his casual demeanor was merely a ploy. Jodie was unsuspecting, and when he suddenly lifted her into his arms, she was taken totally by surprise. He went to a fallen log, sat down, and slung her over his knees. "You've had this coming for a long time," he uttered.

"Don't you dare!" she demanded, squirming to no avail.

He smiled, and his eyes twinkled. "This is going to hurt me more than it hurts you."

"Don't hand me that old line! It won't hurt you at all!"

"I'll forget the spanking if you make me a promise."

She stopped squirming. "What kind of promise?"

"I want your promise that for the remainder of this night, you'll forget your whip, your Winchester, and your damned independence."

"Why should I do that?"

"So we can do this," he replied, turning her over in his lap. He bent his head and kissed her without warning.

Her pride demanded that she not respond, but love was a much stronger emotion. She accepted Cade's kiss with breathless abandonment.

"Do I have that promise?" he whispered in her ear.

She smiled timorously, her passion awakened. "I haven't decided yet. I think I need more persuasion."

He removed her hat, dropped it on the ground, and kissed her again. His mouth claimed hers with a demanding force. In response, her hand swept to the back of his neck, and her lips opened fully beneath his.

"Persuaded yet?" he murmured huskily.

"No, not yet," she whispered, nibbling at his earlobe.

"You teasing little vixen," he muttered, swooping her into his arms, and standing. He carried her to a bed of grass, and laid her down with care. He stretched out beside her, took her into his embrace, and asked softly, "How much more persuasion do you need?"

"A lot more," she murmured. She slid her arms about his neck and kissed him passionately.

Chapter Twenty-One

Cade went to his horse, removed a rolled blanket, and spread it on the ground. He then lifted Jodie from the grass and onto the blanket. He lay beside her, brought her into his arms, and kissed her with deep devotion.

"I love you," he murmured, the whisper of his breath on her cheek.

She pressed against him, molding every curve of her body to his. "I love you too, Cade. I truly do." She urged his lips to hers, surrendering breathlessly and urgently. She marveled at the strength in his embrace, and the feel of his masculine frame flush against hers. Passion more powerful than a raging sea washed over her in rapturous waves. Her father's betrayal, pursuing Jason Edwards, and her need for total independence were left behind in the real world; she had soared to a utopian paradise, where only she and Cade existed.

Cade's hand moved to her breasts, softly caressing one and then the other. Jodie gasped softly, for no man had ever touched her this way before. She tensed, as though she were about to push his hand away. But his intimate caresses soon evoked a sensuous response, and she arched toward his touch, her nipples hardening beneath his skillful fingers.

"Jodie," he said, his tone raspy with passion. "I want you. Darlin', I wonder if you really know how much I want you. If we go any further with this, I won't want to stop. Do you understand what I'm saying?"

Her smile was filled with love. "Yes, I understand. I'm not that naive. I want you too, Cade. And who said anything about stopping?"

A grin touched his lips. "Stopping? Never heard of the word. What does it mean?"

"It means you talk too much," she whispered, pressing her lips to his.

He drew her tightly against him, turning their kiss into one of unbridled passion. Currents of unanswered desire coursed through them, their hunger ravenous and all-consuming.

Jodie's untutored sensuality had been fully awakened. Still, somewhere in the back of her mind, a voice told her this was wrong—she wasn't married to Cade. But whispered endearments, shared caresses, and stormy kisses were more powerful than her conscience. She craved love's fulfillment with every beat of her heart—an ecstasy she somehow knew only Cade could make her reach. She banished the voice of reason to the recesses of her mind, and responded fully to the man she loved.

Cade sat up, and removed her boots. He then unbuttoned her blouse, and she watched his face as he performed the simple task. She studied his features by the light of the moon; he was so strikingly handsome that just looking at him sent her pulse racing. A gentle breeze ruffled his black hair, causing a stray lock to fall across his brow. She brushed it back in place with loving fingers.

Although Cade was eager to see her silken flesh, he

removed her blouse slowly and carefully laid it aside. A lace chemise concealed her breasts from his sultry gaze. He silently damned the undergarment as he unlaced the tiny ribbons. He removed it with a flourish, for he was growing more anxious by the minute.

As the night air caressed her bare breasts, Jodie instinctively crossed her arms over her chest. She suddenly felt modest, and exposed.

Cade smiled tenderly. "Don't hide yourself from me, darlin'. Let me look at you; you're so beautiful." He gently uncrossed her arms, his eyes admiring her perfectly formed breasts. He bent his head, and his mouth teased the taut nipples.

Shivers scurried along her spine, and an unspeakable pleasure pulsed through every nerve in her body. She tangled her fingers in his dark hair, pressing his mouth ever closer to her breasts.

His hand moved down to her skirt, and his fingers fumbled for a button at the waist. The garment fastened in the back, and Jodie gently pushed his hand aside.

"I'll do it," she said, sitting up. She reached behind her and undid the button, then she quickly slipped the skirt past her hips and down her legs. She picked it up and placed it beside the other discarded clothing.

Cade knelt beside her and removed the final undergarment. She now lay before him in full surrender. His hungry eyes raked every inch of her naked flesh, and he found her more beautiful than words.

He drew her back into his arms, kissing her time and time again, each kiss deeper and more voracious than the one before. Jodie felt as though she were lost in a maze of mindless ecstasy; her breathing was rapid, and her head was spinning.

Cade caressed her breasts, then with a feather-like touch, his fingers traveled past her stomach and below. She welcomed his intimate caress, for she knew only his touch could soothe the sweet ache between her thighs. A soft moan of passion escaped her lips as she arched toward his probing finger, ecstasy flowing through her as she accepted his sensual assault.

Cade's passion was now burning beyond control, and he could wait no longer to claim his lovely prize. He quickly took off his boots, unbuckled his holster, and placed it within easy reach. Getting to his feet, he stripped away his clothes as though they were on fire and his life depended on speed.

As his manly physique was revealed to Jodie's intense scrutiny, her eyes measured him boldly. A mass of dark, curly hair covered his strong chest; his stomach was flat, and his legs were long and muscular. His erect maleness sparked Jodie's desire into a leaping flame, and she beckoned him with open arms.

He moved over her, and kissed her passionately as his hands grasped her hips, bringing her thighs to his. He stole her virginity slowly, carefully, for he hoped to ease her pain.

Jodie trembled beneath him.

He kissed her lips tenderly. "There will be no more pain," he murmured. He moved inside her with measured strokes, and her hips instinctively matched his erotic rhythm. His hardness totally filled her, and she clung to him tightly, accepting each deep thrust with a fervor equal to his.

Cade's strokes grew more demanding; no woman had ever ignited his passion so fiercely. It took all his effort to control himself, for he knew he shouldn't rush Jodie. He wanted her to reach love's complete rapture. But his need was too powerful to be denied for very long. His mouth suddenly swooped down on hers, and lifting her legs, he wrapped them about his waist.

His hardness, now even further inside her, sent her desire spiraling to even greater heights. Engulfed in the wonder of their love, they came together with total abandonment, giving and receiving unspeakable pleasure. Ecstasy soon crested, taking them to that place of utter rapture; where they were both totally fulfilled.

Cade kissed her softly, lay beside her, and took her into his arms. He searched for words to describe his elation. There didn't seem to be any way to adequately depict how he felt; his feelings had soared beyond words.

"Jodie," he murmured. "I never knew it was possible to love a woman the way I love you. Sweetheart, you mean everything to me."

She snuggled intimately. "I know what you mean. I feel the same way. You're my life, my heart, and my very reason for existing."

He leaned over her, kissed her deeply, then said with reluctance, "Although I'd love to keep you in my arms just the way you are, we'd better get dressed. We aren't that far away from the main road. Some unlucky hombre might come across us."

"Why would he be unlucky?"

"I'd have to shoot him after he saw you this way. Your beautiful body is for my eyes only."

Laughing, she sat up and reached for her clothes. "In that case, I'd better hurry. I wouldn't want to be responsible for someone's murder."

"Wait a minute," Cade said, getting up and going to his horse. He reached into his saddlebag, withdrew a bandanna, and wet it with water from his canteen.

Jodie watched him intently, admiring his naked flesh, which was illuminated by moonbeams. A flash of warmth spread through her. Cade Brandon was her man, and she loved him completely.

He brought her the bandanna. "You can use this," he said.

She thanked him, washed between her thighs, then hurried into her clothes. Cade, fully dressed, strapped on his holster.

"Should we stay here for the rest of the night?" Jodie asked. "Or do you think we should move on? We probably should keep going; we don't want Edwards to get too far ahead."

"We're going back to Crystal Creek," he replied.

She eyed him impatiently, then grew angry. "Darn it, Cade! Don't start this with me again! Edwards is my prisoner, and I'm the one to bring him in! I'm heading for Mexico with or without you!"

"You won't find Edwards in Mexico."

"Wh . . . what? Are you sure?"

"If he was heading for Mexico, somewhere between here and Crystal Creek I'd have found recent tracks. I was on my way back to town when I came across you." He smiled obliquely. "Best thing that ever happened to me."

"Yes, we should meet like this more often." Her eyes twinkled saucily.

"Although I have nothing against the great outdoors, the next time we make love we'll be in bed."

"Oh?" she questioned. "Whose bed did you have in mind?"

"Our marriage bed." He brought her into his arms, held her close, and said, "Let's get married as soon as possible—tomorrow."

"Tomorrow!" she exclaimed, stepping back so that she could see his face.

"Why should we wait?"

Now that her passion was sated, her uncertainties returned, sending her mind swirling. She wanted to marry him, but without the thousand dollars, she had no security, no way to protect herself. She would be wholly dependent on Cade. If he should stop loving her, she would become a burden, a responsibility, and an obligation. She would be like her mother!

"Cade . . ." she began haltingly. "I . . . I want to marry you, but I think I should look for Edwards first."

He flinched, as though her words were a slap in the face. "Are you saying a thousand dollars means more to you than our marriage?"

"Of course not. But this is something I have to do. I can't explain why."

"I didn't expect an explanation. You never explain why you do the things you do."

"Cade, please don't be angry."

He took her arm, urging her toward the Appaloosa. "It's late; let's start back to town." He helped her mount, then he retrieved both hats, handing Jodie hers.

She watched Cade roll up the blanket, place it on his horse, and swing into the saddle. That she had hurt him tore painfully into her heart. If only . . . if only she could free her mind of the past.

"Jodie," he began evenly, "you can't just ride out and find Edwards. He could be headed most anywhere. To find him, you'd have to stop in town after town and ask questions. You'd spend most of your time traveling across the countryside. Along the way, you'd encounter all kinds of characters; some of them will be murderers, thieves, and rapists. Whether you like it or not, a woman has no business placing herself in that kind of jeopardy. A thousand dollar bounty is not worth that kind of risk. But if you really want the money that badly, I'll go after Edwards myself. It could take a long time; I might not be back for weeks, maybe even months. But, damn it, I'll be back, and I'll have your thousand dollars with me!"

"We'll go together," she decided.

Cade's patience snapped. "Didn't you hear a word I said?"

"Of course I did. But you should know by now that I can't be dissuaded through scare tactics."

Before Cade could reply, pounding hooves carried from

the main road. "Sounds like a lot of riders," he said. "We'd better check it out."

They rode through the foliage, but stopped at the edge. Concealed by trees and shrubbery, they watched a large group of horsemen come their way. Cade recognized the man in front. "It's Antonio!" he exclaimed.

He and Jodie rode onto the main road, their presence bringing the riders to a sudden halt.

"Amigo!" Antonio remarked. He could hardly believe that Brandon and the señorita had appeared out of nowhere. "I was just on my way to see you."

"Has something happened?"

"Sí," he replied. "I was hoping Lucinda was in Crystal Creek with you, but since you are here, I guess she is not with you."

"Why would Lucinda be with me?"

"She has run away from home. I know, amigo, that she is infatuated with you. That is why I thought she might come to you."

"How long has she been missing?"

"Since last night."

"Did you tell her about your relationship to Hernando?"

"Sí, I did."

"Maybe she went to him."

Antonio seemed surprised. "I had not considered that. I told her everything about Hernando; I even told her how to contact him and his Comancheros. I will ride to the mountains and build a fire. I am sure Hernando will agree to see me."

Cade felt somewhat responsible; that night at the gazebo Lucinda had threatened to run away. He should have handled the situation better. But he hadn't taken her seriously.

"This is partly my fault," Cade told Antonio. "Lucinda told me she was going to run away, but I didn't believe her. I should have told you."

"Do not blame yourself. I should have seen it coming.

She is determined not to marry Miguel Huerto. He arrived this morning; that is why she ran away last night.'' He motioned to one of the riders, and he came forward.

The young man, majestically handsome, was dressed in black trousers and a white shirt. He was riding a magnificent palomino.

Antonio introduced Jodie and Cade to Miguel Huerto.

Jodie was quite impressed with Huerto's good looks and bearing. Antonio had chosen well for his daughter. She wondered if Lucinda would have run away if she had seen Miguel first. She didn't think so.

"Antonio," Cade began, "I'll ride along. You might need my help."

"You are more than welcome."

Cade turned to Jodie. "I want you to come with us." He needed to keep her with him; otherwise, she might get it in her head to chase after Edwards.

She knew what he was thinking, but she was willing to be agreeable. Besides, finding Lucinda was more pressing than finding Edwards. "I'll ride with you," she said; then, casting him a light-hearted smile, she added, "After all, we're partners, aren't we?"

"I sometimes wonder," he uttered crankily. It wasn't the response she had hoped for. Apparently, he was still upset with her.

Riding steadily, they crossed the Rio Grande and entered Mexico at mid-morning. They traveled a few more miles before stopping to eat and rest their horses. From here, Antonio planned to send his vaqueros back to the hacienda, for Hernando and his followers would certainly find this many riders a threat. Juan and Miguel would remain.

Following a cold meal and a couple hours of rest, the group went their separate ways: the vaqueros toward the hacienda, the others headed in the direction of Lopez's hideout.

The sun was slanting westward when they came upon Apache tracks. Cade estimated more than twenty ponies had passed this way. The signs were not very old; therefore, Cade decided to ride ahead. His rifle drawn and placed across his saddle, he spurred his horse into a gallop, putting a safe distance between himself and the others.

Jodie rode beside Antonio, with Juan and Miguel directly behind. Knowing renegade Apaches were in the area had their nerves on edge. Jodie was not only tense, but she was also frightened for Cade. He was out there alone. If the Apaches spotted him, he would have no chance against twenty or more warriors.

Hours went by; they passed interminably slowly for Jodie. Her eyes actually hurt from straining to look into the distance, hoping to see Cade riding back. That he might have been killed was more than she could bear. He would come back to her! She refused to think otherwise.

Dusk had painted the distant mountains in a purple mist before Cade finally rode into sight. Jodie sighed a long exhalation of relief. Thank God, he was alive and well!

They reined in and waited for Cade to reach them.

Cade slowed his stallion from a fast gallop to an easy canter. He dreaded facing Antonio, for he had terrible news to deliver. A nerve twitched at his temples, and despite the coolness of a desert wind, his brow was layered with perspiration.

He brought his horse to a stop alongside Antonio's. He spoke slowly, wishing there was some way to soften the blow. "The Apaches are camped about a mile ahead. I managed to sneak in close enough to observe them. They have Lucinda. I don't think she's hurt. But the Apaches have whiskey; once they get some liquor in them . . ."

He didn't need to say more; Antonio understood only too well. His shoulders bowed, and a rasping moan sounded deep in his throat. That his daughter was at the mercy of Apaches caused an icy snake of fear to coil in his stomach, despite the warm temperature, he felt a sudden chill that shook his entire body.

"Antonio?" Cade asked. "Are you all right?"

Morelos's inner strength prevailed, and he regained his composure. "Sí, amigo, I am all right. But how can we save Lucinda? There are so many Apaches, and only five of us."

"I have a plan, but it's a long shot."

"Tell me, amigo."

"You are well known in these parts; even the Apaches have heard of you, and they know that you're wealthy and own many horses. You and I will ride into their camp, hope they don't shoot us on sight, and hope at least one of them will know who you are. I can understand enough Apache to communicate in case none of them speaks English. We'll ask them to trade Lucinda for horses. In the meantime, Juan, Miguel, and Jodie can ride to the hacienda and tell the vaqueros to round up twelve prime horses, then deliver them to the Apaches' camp."

"Once the horses are delivered, do you think the Apaches will let us live?"

"Your vaqueros will be armed. The Apaches might prefer to avoid a fight."

"Sí, my vaqueros carry weapons, but they are not gunslingers. I think I should tell you, my friend, that they might not be able to protect us."

"Then I guess we'll have to find a way to protect ourselves. It's the only plan I can come up with. If you have a better idea . . ."

"I am not opposed to your plan, amigo. I know it is Lucinda's only chance. But maybe I should ride alone into their camp. There is no reason for you to risk your life."

"You're my friend, Antonio. You've always been there for me, and I'm not going to let you do this alone."

Jodie had to bite into her bottom lip to keep from asking Cade to change his mind. He was taking a terrible risk, and she was afraid the Apaches would kill him.

"I'll take all of you to their camp," Cade said, but he was speaking directly to Antonio. "That way, the others will know where to bring the horses."

They moved onward, Cade leading the way. Jodie rode beside Antonio, but she longed to urge the Appaloosa forward and join Cade. She restrained herself from doing so, for she knew fear would compel her to try to talk Cade into staying with her and the others. She also knew he wouldn't agree, and she would only despise herself for asking him to put his life before Lucinda's. Cade's compassion and courage were among the reasons why she loved him. She didn't want to change him; she only wanted him to stay alive!

Full darkness had descended by the time they reached their destination. The Apaches were camped in an area protected by small boulders, shrubbery, and sparsely spaced trees.

The riders reined in a safe distance away, dismounted, and slipped stealthily through the shrubbery. They carefully scaled a boulder, and looked down upon the Indians' campsite.

The area was lighted by a blazing fire. Lucinda, nude, her hands and feet tied, was lying in the middle of the encampment. The warriors sat around her, bottles of whiskey passing among them.

Jodie's heart ached for Lucinda, for only another woman could fully understand such degradation; stripping away her clothes had stripped away her last shred of dignity.

Antonio was outraged, but he was also filled with despair for his daughter. He moved down the boulder and crept quietly back to the horses. Jodie and Juan followed, but Cade remained, for Miguel appeared lost in thought.

Cade nudged him gently with his elbow, and the gesture got through to him. He climbed down the boulder alongside Brandon, and they joined the others.

Miguel spoke to Antonio, "I will ride into the camp with you and Señor Brandon."

Morelos was stunned. "Why do you want to do that? Do you not realize how dangerous it is?"

The young aristocrat wasn't sure how to explain himself. He considered speaking in Spanish, for English was sometimes difficult for him. However, he felt Señor Brandon and the señorita should not be left out of the conversation. "Antonio," he began, "seeing Lucinda"—he placed a hand over his chest—"touched me deeply in my heart. I want to honor the agreement made between you and my father. I hope very much to marry your daughter. She is very beautiful. But I could not marry her if I did not try to save her life. I would not deserve her, and I would not be a man. She has been promised to me in holy matrimony, and I will ride into that camp and claim my future bride."

Jodie was impressed. Apparently, Antonio felt the same way, for he gave Miguel permission to accompany him and Cade.

Taking Jodie's arm, Cade led her a short distance from the others. "It's a long ride from here to Antonio's hacienda. You and Juan can't push your horses too hard. If you do, they'll die of exhaustion. You must maintain a steady but untiring pace."

"I realize that," she replied. "But it won't be easy. Time may be of the essence. I don't think Apaches are known for their patience."

He drew her into his arms. "I love you, darlin'. Remember you're in dangerous territory. Please be careful; I don't want anything to happen to you."

She clung tightly to him. "I love you too. And don't you dare let anything happen to yourself."

When he bent his head, she met his lips halfway. Tears filled her eyes, and began to trickle down her cheeks; the taste of salt mingled with the sweetness of their kiss.

Cade reluctantly broke their embrace, and brushed a tear with his fingertip. Summoning a smile, he said, "I'll keep this tear until we're together again."

She braved a smile in return. "We'll be together again; nothing can keep us apart."

Antonio was reluctant to interrupt, but he was anxious for Juan and Jodie to be on their way. "Amigo," he said to Cade, walking up to them. "Juan and the señorita must leave."

Cade agreed. He took Jodie to the Appaloosa and helped her into the saddle. Juan mounted quickly, and coaxed his horse into a canter. Jodie, following close behind, glanced over her shoulder and took one last look at Cade. Pain shot through her heart as she wondered if she would ever see him again—alive!

She caught up to Juan, and they held their steeds to a steady but easy pace. Clouds had rolled in from the west, grappling with the moon for dominance of the night sky. Dark shadows, blanketing the landscape, cloaked the barren knoll that lay ahead. Juan and Jodie didn't see the three mounted Apaches crest the rise until it was too late. They reached for their sheathed weapons, but one warrior already had his rifle in hand. He took aim, and fired a bullet into Juan's chest, hurling him from his horse and onto the ground. The gunshot ricocheted off the nearby boulders, sending the riderless horse into a panic; it bolted like a streak of lightning.

Jodie's hand hovered above her encased Winchester, but she didn't draw her gun. She knew it would mean certain death. Putting both hands on the reins, she drew in sharply. Before she could dismount to check on Juan, the three Apaches appeared alongside her.

At that moment, the moon peeked out from beneath a cloud, and Jodie looked into the face of the Apache who had shot Juan. She saw an expression in his eyes that she couldn't define. She started to speak to him, but he held up a silencing hand.

He then reached over, took her Winchester and bull-whip, and handed them to one of his men. Grabbing the reins to her horse, and taking his captive with him, he and the others headed back in the direction Jodie and Juan had just come from.

Jodie knew where they were going; she would see Cade a lot sooner than she had expected.

Chapter Twenty-Two

The Apaches were too involved in drinking whiskey to place guards at the edge of camp. Cade and the others rode freely into the area, and were nearing the campfire before the warriors knew they were there. The Indians had their weapons alongside them; they grabbed their rifles and leapt to their feet. That these men had the nerve to ride into their camp rendered them temporarily stunned; their shock gave the visitors time to ride into the center of camp. They reined in, and although they had left their guns behind, they raised their arms—a non-threatening sign in any man's language.

Lucinda was circled by the Apaches, and she saw them as they jumped to their feet. She also saw their shocked expressions. Because she was lying on the ground, she couldn't see what had happened. She tried to sit up, but her tied hands and ankles made the simple maneuver difficult. After two failed attempts, she finally succeeded. The Apaches had broken the circle, leaving an open space between her and the three intruders. Her eyes widened incredulously as she saw Antonio, along with Cade and a man she didn't know. Their presence sent her hopes skyrocketing. Surely, her father and Cade would find a way to save her! She suddenly remembered her nudity. Her hands were tied behind her, and she couldn't even cross her arms over her breasts. Naked to the Apaches' scrutiny was degrading enough, but for some reason, it seemed more degrading to be exposed this way to her father, Cade, and the man riding with them. She lay on her side, and drew her knees up to her chest. Curling up was the only protection she had.

Antonio's gaze lingered on his daughter's body; his heart ached so severely that he felt as though it were being ripped out of his chest.

"Do any of you speak English?" Cade asked the Apaches.

"I speak your tongue," a warrior said, stepping forward.

"Have you heard of Antonio Morelos?"

"He is a rich Mexican."

Cade indicated Antonio. "This is Morelos. We are here to trade horses for your captive. His vaqueros will bring them here, but it will take time. Are you willing to wait?"

"How many horses?" the Apache asked. He was interested.

"Twelve," Cade replied. He then counted fingers in case the warrior didn't fully understand.

The Apache spoke to the other warriors in their own language. A short discussion ensued, then, turning back to Cade, he said, "We will wait for Alchise."

"Alchise? Where is he?"

"Hunting. He will be back soon." He again spoke to his men. Five warriors hurried over, and motioned for the visitors to dismount. They were frisked for hidden weapons, then taken to where Lucinda still lay curled in a tight ball. The five warriors practically shoved them to the ground.

Miguel, moving faster than Antonio, removed his shirt and placed it over Lucinda.

She dared to look into his face. "Who are you?"

"Miguel Huerto," he replied, his gaze filled with kindness.

Despite the present danger, she was impressed with Huerto. She had never imagined that he would be so handsome.

Antonio moved to her side, and drew her into his arms. Tied, she could only lean helplessly against him.

Her father's presence brought bottled up tears to the surface. "Oh Pápa!" she cried. "I should not have run away! I am so sorry!"

He kissed her brow. "Do not cry, little one. It is my fault. I was wrong to insist that you marry a man you do not know. Where were you going? Did you hope to contact Hernando?"

"Sí, Pápa," she murmured, sobbing softly.

Cade called out to the warrior who spoke English, asking him if Lucinda could be untied.

The Apache was agreeable; he had lost interest in the woman. Horses now filled his mind.

Antonio undid the ropes, then helped his daughter slip into Miguel's shirt.

Now that she was decently covered, a semblance of dignity returned. She looked at Cade, and said, "I cannot believe you and Pápa are here. It must be a dream." She turned to Miguel. "Señor Huerto, your presence is even more shocking. Why have you risked your life for a woman you don't know?"

A warm smile curled his lips, emphasizing his good looks. "I could not ask you to marry me if I was too cowardly to try to save your life."

"You mean . . . after what has happened . . . you would still consider marriage?"

"Sí, if you would have me. I plan a long visit at your father's hacienda. We will have plenty of time to get acquainted."

The sounds of arriving horses drew everyone's attention. They looked on as three warriors, along with their captive, rode into camp. The sight of Jodie sent Cade and the others bounding to their feet.

As a demonstrative discussion erupted among the Apaches, Jodie looked about the camp. She quickly found Cade, and managed a brave smile.

Her captor suddenly dismounted, moved to the Appaloosa, and lifted Jodie from the saddle. Clutching her arm, he led her to the other captives, and left her there.

She was immediately in Cade's embrace. He held her tightly for a moment, then, holding her at arms' length, he asked, "What happened?"

"Juan and I were taken off guard."

"Where is Juan?" Antonio asked.

"He was shot."

"Is he . . . dead?"

"I don't know. I didn't have a chance to check him."

Cade sighed heavily. "It won't take long for those Apaches to figure out that Jodie and Juan were on their way to the hacienda to get the horses."

He had barely said the words when the warrior who spoke English approached. Jodie's captor was with him. Cade wondered if he was the one called Alchise.

The English-speaking warrior asked Cade, "Were the woman and the man riding with her going after the horses?"

"Yes, they were. Why don't you turn the women loose and let them go to the hacienda? They can send vaqueros back with the horses."

The warrior was willing to think it over, but the Apache with him was strongly opposed. A verbal confrontation resulted. It wasn't necessary to understand their language to know that they were arguing, for they were shouting and waving their arms angrily.

Jodie's captor evidently won the argument, for the other

warrior, sulking, moved away, sat down, and returned to drinking whiskey.

The victor turned his attention to the prisoners. "I am called Alchise," he said, speaking English without hesitation. "There will be no trade. You will die at sunrise." Then, moving rapidly, he grabbed Jodie's arm, jerked her to his side, and forced her to leave with him.

Cade was about to go after them, but Antonio's arms were quickly about his chest, holding him back. "No, amigo," he said firmly. "If you follow, you will be killed." Alchise had not taken Jodie very far; they were in clear sight. "Wait and see what happens," Antonio told Cade. "I do not think the Apache plans to harm her."

Cade agreed, and Antonio released him.

Lucinda moved into her father's arms. "I wonder why he took Jodie?" she murmured.

Cade, his eyes glued to Alchise and Jodie, was wondering the same thing.

Alchise stared into Jodie's face; his expression more thoughtful than hostile. She soon grew uneasy under his intense scrutiny. "What do you want with me?" she dared to ask.

"You ride the Appaloosa, you carry a whip, and your hair is full of curls. My brother told me these things. You are the woman who saved his life."

Jodie was at a loss. "I don't understand."

"My brother, myself, and other warriors steal your Appaloosa and a roan stallion. You and your man steal back your horses. My brother went after you. Do you now remember?"

"Yes, I do. I shot your brother."

"But the shot did not kill him. My brother told me that many Mexicans arrived, and their leader wanted my brother dead. You would not let him be killed. You saved my brother's life, and he is in your debt. Now, I save your life. You and my brother are even. He is no longer indebted to a white woman."

"Is your brother here?"

"No. He is still too ill to travel. I will tell him that I took care of his debt. This one time, I spare your life. Do not try for a second time."

Jodie's eyes swept over the warrior, as though she were measuring him as a possible opponent. He wasn't very tall, and his frame was stocky. He wore a long-sleeved, embroidered shirt, white pants, and brown boots. His black hair, parted in the middle, was shoulder-length. A turquoise necklace hung about his neck. His dark skin was leathery from so many hours in the hot Mexican sun. He was intimidating, and Jodie didn't find him even remotely handsome.

He suddenly grabbed her arm, and ushered her toward the Appaloosa. "You are free to leave."

She broke his hold. "Please let the others go with me."

"No more talk!" he ordered, lifting her into his arms and putting her on the Appaloosa. Her Winchester and bullwhip were returned.

Jodie's first impulse was to dismount and demand that he let her stay with Cade and the others. She felt she'd rather die alongside Cade than live without him. But her better judgment wisely intervened—dying with Cade was not the solution; she had to find a way to save him. A plan suddenly came to mind.

"Leave!" Alchise shouted testily. He slapped a hand against the Appaloosa's flank, sending it into a startled gallop.

As she rode out of camp, Jodie glanced back at Cade, wishing she could tell him that she'd be back. She hoped he didn't think she was deserting him and the others.

Quite the contrary, as Cade watched her leave, he was overwhelmed with relief. Alchise had apparently decided to spare her. The reason why didn't matter; Jodie's life was all that mattered.

Jodie returned to the area where she and Juan had encountered the Apaches. Although time was pressing, she had to ride back in case the vaquero was still alive. His body lay where it had fallen. His horse had wandered back and was grazing nearby.

She dismounted, and knelt beside Juan. He was dead, his eyes staring sightlessly. She gently closed his eyelids; then she managed to drag his body and place it between two huge rocks. She got a blanket from the vaquero's horse and spread it over the body. She quickly unsaddled the horse and removed its bridle. It was free to stay, go home, or return to the wild.

She mounted the Appaloosa and headed toward the distant mountain range. She traveled at a strenuous pace, for time was of the essence. She hated pushing the Appaloosa this way, but lives were depending on them. She had to contact Lopez as soon as possible.

The Appaloosa's endurance was innate, and the powerful steed maintained the arduous speed for miles before it began to tire. It broke Jodie's heart to force the animal to continue, for she knew its stamina was fading. Its mouth lathered, and its body was layered with sweat; still, Jodie spurred it onward.

Finally, the mountain range loomed before her like a great fortress. It was a heavenly sight to Jodie. She reined in, and the Appaloosa trembled beneath her as she dismounted. She wished she could tend to the steed without delay, but there was something else she had to do first. She patted its neck, which was dripping with sweat. The Appaloosa hung its head, and the pitiful gesture brought tears to Jodie's eyes. She forced herself to move away from the horse and gather kindling. Working quickly, she collected anything that would burn and stacked it into a large pile. She got matches from her saddlebags and started a fire. As it burned, she added more fuel until the flames were shooting upward as though they were trying to light the dark heavens.

She then went to the exhausted Appaloosa and unsaddled it. Taking a blanket, she used it to rub down the horse. When its labored breathing gradually slowed to normal, she uncapped her canteen, poured water into her hat, and offered it a drink.

The fire had ebbed, and she added more kindling before walking the Appaloosa so the strained muscles in its legs wouldn't tighten up. She knew the Appaloosa would be all right, and for that she was grateful. She removed its bridle and returned to the fire.

She threw in the last of the kindling she had gathered, and sat down to wait, for there was nothing else she could do. She was tired, yet every nerve in her body was tightly strung. Her stomach was empty, but the thought of food was nauseating. Too tense to remain seated, she got up and began pacing back and forth. She knew she should reserve her strength, but how could she rest knowing Cade and the others were supposed to die at sunrise? If only she could hold back the dawn!

She suddenly heard the sound of horses. She looked into the distance, and could barely make out a group of riders. As they drew closer, she could see them better; there were five horsemen.

They rode up to the fire and reined in. She recognized them, for they were the same men who had answered Breed's fire when she had been his captive.

"Do any of you speak English?" she asked.

"Sí, señorita," one of them answered. He dismounted and came to stand before her. He exuded a threatening appearance, for he was strongly built and heavily armed.

His bearded face was barely distinguishable beneath his wide-brimmed sombrero.

"Do you remember me?" Jodie asked him.

He smiled. "How could I forget a señorita so lovely?"

"You must take a message to Hernando. Tell him Antonio Morelos, Cade Brandon, and two others have been captured by the Apaches. One of the captives is a woman. They need his help."

"Where are these Apaches?"

"About ten miles from here."

"How many Apaches?"

"About twenty. They plan to kill their prisoners at sunrise. We don't have much time. Please take my message to Hernando!"

"You do not want to take him the message yourself?"

"My horse is too tired to go any farther."

"I will do as you ask."

He returned to his horse, mounted, and left with the others. Jodie watched them until they were swallowed up by the night.

She sat back down and stared vacantly at the fire that was now burning much lower. She wondered about the time, but she didn't have a pocket watch. How many more hours until sunrise?

Minutes dragged into an hour as Jodie waited for Hernando. Her heartbeat was like an inner clock, each beat taking Cade closer and closer to his time of death.

At last, the distant pounding of hooves—carried across the countryside. She bounded to her feet, and watched as Hernando and his rebels came into sight. She was pleased by their great number; there had to be at least fifty or more.

The group came to an abrupt stop, and their horses' hooves stirred up loose dirt. The raining particles smothered the dying fire.

Hernando dismounted, went to Jodie, and favored her

with one of his devilish smiles. *"Buenas noches,* señorita. I did not think I would ever see you again. Tell me, muchacha, why are you always in trouble? Do you not know that women are supposed to stay home and out of harm's way?"

"Hernando, we don't have time to waste words," she said testily. "Cade and Antonio will die at sunrise if we don't save them. So will Miguel Huerto and your sister."

"My sister?" he questioned.

"Surely, you know Antonio has a daughter."

"Sí, I know. But I never really thought of her as a sister."

"Are you going to help or not?"

"I am here, am I not? I even brought you a fresh horse. Alberto said that yours is fatigued." He ordered Jodie's mount brought to her.

Lopez offered her a handup, mounted his own horse, and rode to her side. "Lead the way, señorita," he said with a wave of his hand.

Jodie took a quick glance at the Appaloosa, hoping it would be there when she returned.

She set a steady tempo, but not an exhausting one, for over fifty horses had to survive the journey. Hernando was riding at her side, and she asked him, "Do you have a plan in mind?"

"Sí, we will charge the camp and kill the Apaches."

"You make it sound so simple."

"It is simple. That is the only way to deal with the Apaches."

"But if we charge their camp, they might kill their prisoners."

"They will be too busy defending themselves. Trust me, señorita, a surprise attack is our best chance."

Jodie prayed that Hernando was right.

* * *

Antonio left his daughter's side to talk to Cade, who was sitting across from them. Miguel took advantage of the opportunity, and moved closer to Lucinda.

"I wish I could have saved you," Miguel murmured. "I guess I am not a knight in shining armor."

"But you are," she replied. "I have never known a man more courageous. That you risked your life to save mine amazes me."

He took her hand into his. "I am sorry you found our marriage so repulsive that it drove you to run away."

"I did not find it repulsive. I only wanted to choose my own husband."

"I understand," he said. He started to let go of her hand, but she tightened her grip.

"I should not have run away. I was foolish not to wait and meet you. Now, all of us will die, and it is my fault." Captivity had matured Lucinda.

Meanwhile, Antonio, watching his daughter and Miguel, said to Cade, "I think, amigo, if we survive, there will be a wedding. Miguel is a fine young man, and I think maybe Lucinda will fall in love with him."

"I hope she does. I like Huerto too. But odds are we won't live past sunrise."

Antonio glanced at the Apaches; they were all drinking whiskey. "Why do you suppose they want to wait until morning? Why not kill us now?"

Cade shrugged. "I'm not sure; maybe they want to be sober."

"I wonder why Alchise released Jodie."

"I don't know. Whatever his reason, he didn't bother to tell me."

"Do you think Jodie went for help?"

"I'm sure she did."

"But it is such a long way to my hacienda. She cannot possibly get there and back before sunrise."

"I doubt if she headed for your hacienda."

"Then where did she go?"

"Lopez," he replied.

"Hernando?" He gasped. "Sí, his hideout is much closer. But there still may not be enough time." He paused to sigh deeply before continuing, "Maybe, amigo, Hernando will refuse to help. He harbors much bitterness. I know he resents me."

"It's ironic that your life may well depend on the son you deserted. Let's hope he doesn't desert you in return."

"Sí," Antonio murmured. "If he does, we will all die."

Chapter
Twenty-Three

The sun was cresting the horizon as Jodie and her band of outlaws neared the Apaches' camp. They stopped a short distance away. Hernando turned to Jodie and said in a commanding tone, "Señorita, you will stay here. I will tell Alberto to stay with you."

She wasn't sure if she wanted to stay behind or not. A part of her longed to charge the camp alongside Lopez and his men, yet another part of her preferred to avoid any more killing. She had already been forced to take a man's life; she didn't want to kill again.

Hernando sensed her inner conflict. "You will obey my orders, señorita. I am not as compromising as Señor Brandon. I do not fight alongside women."

She accepted his decision. Mainly because there wasn't enough time to discuss it, for the sun was climbing steadily higher. "I'll stay here," she replied.

His smile was undeniably charming. "You have done your part, muchacha; now my men and I will finish the job." He reached over and patted her hand. The tender gesture meant a lot to Jodie.

Lopez ordered Alberto to remain with Jodie, then he and his rebels rode toward the Indians' campsite. They split into three groups so they could charge from more than one direction.

Jodie's heart was beating rapidly as she watched them leave. Her nerves were taut, and her stomach roiled. She drew a calming breath. God, she prayed, please keep Cade and the others safe!

As the morning sun obliterated the last shred of darkness, the captives sat huddled together; and like the darkness, their last shred of hope was quickly fading. They were certain to die if help didn't arrive soon.

Cade didn't doubt that Jodie had gone to Lopez, but more than ten miles lay between here and the mountain range. It would take time for her to contact Hernando, ask for his help, then cover the miles back. Every minute was precious, and Cade wasn't sure if there were enough minutes for Jodie to accomplish so much.

The Apaches were breaking camp; they planned to kill their prisoners as soon as they were finished.

Lucinda's eyes were glued to the warriors, as though if she looked away an unknown assailant would decide to kill her. She wanted to look away, for an unexpected death was better than staring her prospective killer in the eyes. However, she continued to watch the Apaches.

Antonio, sitting beside her, had an arm draped about her shoulders. He drew her closer, searching for words to bolster her courage and to make death easier for her to face. But there were no words that could work such magic. A sob caught in his throat, and tears watered his eyes. His own life didn't matter; he grieved for his daughter's. As he watched the Apaches through a teary blur, he prayed that Lucinda's death would be fast and painless.

Miguel Huerto wasn't watching the warriors; his gaze was centered on Lucinda. That he was about to die filled his mind, but it was Lucinda who filled his heart. He wished he could have saved her; she was too young and too lovely to die. A sigh escaped his lips—they were both too young to die. They had their whole lives ahead of them.

A small flock of birds were perched in a nearby tree. Their sudden flight escaped everyone's notice, except for Cade's. The Apaches were too busy breaking camp to heed the birds' warning, and the captives were too involved in their private thoughts.

Cade said quietly to his fellow captives, "Lie as close as you can to the ground." He then spoke directly to Antonio. "Cover Lucinda the best you can."

Morelos didn't ask questions. He urged his daughter to the ground, and shielded her body with his. Meanwhile, Cade and Miguel lay flat, keeping their heads down.

At that same moment, the pounding of hooves vibrated the earth as though a freight train was approaching. The vibration was quickly accompanied by multiple gunshots.

Lopez and his men charged the campsite with a vengeance. The Comancheros were excellent shots, and ten Apaches fell dead before the remaining threw down their weapons and surrendered. Two Comancheros were slightly wounded.

Lopez dismounted and hurried to the captives. They were getting to their feet. "Is anyone hurt?" he asked.

"We're fine," Cade told him. "Thanks to you and your men."

Hernando's gaze went to Lucinda. She was decently covered in Miguel's shirt, but the hem barely fell past her hips. "Where are your clothes?" he asked her.

"I am not sure."

He quickly ordered one of his men to find them.

"Hernando," Antonio began a little hesitantly, "I am very grateful. I was afraid your bitterness toward me would stop you from helping us."

"I do not like Apaches. Killing them is a good way to start the morning. Do not think, señor, that I care whether you live or die. You are nothing to me."

Hernando's cold response surprised Lucinda. She hadn't imagined that he despised her father so intensely. Running away to contact her brother had been a tremendous mistake, for his resentment probably included her. After all, she had been loved and raised by the father who had deserted him.

Lucinda's clothes were found and returned to her. She went behind a boulder to dress.

Jodie and Alberto rode into camp. They had been close enough to hear the battle; they started out the moment the gunshots ceased.

Cade hastened to Jodie, and had her in his arms the moment she dismounted. They held tightly to each other, their bodies flush, their hearts beating as one.

"Never again," Cade murmured.

"Never again, what?" she asked, gazing into his eyes with love.

"Never again will we be separated. I'm going to marry you and take you to my ranch if I have to hog-tie you to get you there."

She laughed lightly. "Is that a proposal or a threat?"

"I'm through proposing," he said, a twinkle in his eyes. "I've already proposed on two or three different occasions. It's time for threats."

Her expression saucy, she replied, "Will you please threaten to make love to me at the first opportunity?"

"That's not a threat, darlin'. But a promise."

"I intend to hold you to that."

"You'll find I'm a man of my word."

Lucinda had returned, and with Lopez leading the way, she and the others approached Jodie and Cade.

"It is time to leave," Hernando said.

Jodie looked about the campsite. She spotted Alchise. He was shot in the shoulder; it didn't look too serious. "What do you intend to do with the survivors?" she asked Lopez.

"I will leave some of my men here. Once we are gone, they will carry out the executions."

"There's no reason for you to order their deaths!" Jodie exclaimed. "Take their weapons and let them go free."

"Do you not understand, señorita, that the Apaches are Mexico's enemies?"

"As far as the Mexican government is concerned, you and your men are enemies. You should feel a certain empathy toward these Apaches. You are both despised and hunted by the Mexican soldiers."

"But these Apaches you long to save were about to kill your friends and the man you love. Do you not seek revenge?"

She waved a terse hand toward the dead Apaches. "How much revenge is needed?"

Cade intruded, "Lopez, you might as well concede. Take my word for it; you can't win an argument with Jodie. Furthermore, she's right. There's no reason for more killing."

Hernando yielded with an insouciant shrug. "The Apaches will live. We will take their weapons but leave their horses." He started to move away, but paused brusquely. He seldom spoke impulsively, but words spilled out of his mouth as though they had a will of their own. "I would like all of you to come to my home and stay the night. You can leave in the morning." He looked directly at Antonio. "There are two people there I want you to meet."

"I appreciate the invitation. But I am anxious to take

Lucinda home, and I am sure Cade and Jodie are anxious to return to Crystal Creek.''

''I should think, señor, that you would do me this little favor. After I saved your life, it is the least you can do.''

Antonio gave in. He didn't see any other choice. Furthermore, it would give him more time with Hernando; maybe if they spent some time together, Hernando's bitterness would start to mellow.

''Very well,'' he replied. ''We will visit your home. But we must leave tomorrow morning.''

Lopez turned to Cade and Jodie. ''You will come too, sí?''

It was Jodie who answered. ''I have to go back that way anyhow to get my horse.'' She hoped it was still there. ''So I don't see any reason why Cade and I can't accept your invitation.'' She looked at Brandon for affirmation.

He was agreeable.

As Lopez walked away to talk to his men, a puzzled frown furrowed Antonio's brow. ''Hernando said he wants me to meet two people. I wonder who they could be?''

No one ventured a guess, but then, Antonio wasn't expecting one.

With Jodie leading the way, they rode to where she had hidden Juan's body between two large rocks. The vaquero had no family; therefore, Antonio decided to bury him here. Juan's horse was still nearby; it was bridled, saddled, and led away with the group.

The distance to the mountain range was covered in a steady but untiring pace. Although everyone was anxious to reach Hernando's hideaway, where they could rest and have something to eat, pushing the horses was out of the question. The steep climb up the mountainside still lie ahead, and it was imperative that their mounts not be overly tired.

Jodie was glad to find her Appaloosa where she had left it. It was now rested, and with Cade's help, it was quickly saddled. She preferred to ride her own horse; the sheer, winding path that had taken Red's life still unnerved her. She trusted her Appaloosa to remain surefooted and in control.

The visitors were blindfolded, with Comancheros holding the reins to their horses. Again, Jodie hated the pitch blackness behind the blindfold. She wondered how well the others were holding up. Considering Cade and Antonio had gone through this before, she figured they were seasoned. However, it had to be unsettling for Lucinda and Miguel.

The treacherous climb was completed slowly, carefully, and with no mishaps. Jodie wondered if she could find this path if she had to. Probably not; the massive mountain was most likely filled with winding trails.

When they had descended the other side and were in the hidden valley, the blindfolds were removed. They rode straight to Hernando's home. Leaving their horses in the care of Lopez's men, the visitors followed their host inside. He asked them to wait in the parlor.

A few minutes later, Hernando returned. He was accompanied by a lovely young lady, who was holding a baby. Although Hernando's announcement was meant for everyone, he looked directly at Antonio. "This is my wife, Felisa. The child is my son. His name is Ricardo, and he is four months old."

Antonio and the others were too stunned to reply. It was Jodie who first responded. "Congratulations, Hernando." She turned to Felisa. "Do you speak English?"

"Sí, I do."

"You have a beautiful son. May I hold him?"

Felisa handed the baby to Jodie. He was indeed a beautiful child; he had big brown eyes, rosy cheeks, and thick black curls.

Cade, watching Jodie with the infant, imagined the day when she would hold and nurture a child of theirs. It was a good feeling, and it warmed his heart.

Lopez introduced his guests to his wife. Felisa knew Antonio Morelos was Hernando's father; she also knew that Hernando harbored a lot of bitterness toward him.

Antonio moved to Jodie and the child. He gently brushed his fingers through Ricardo's dark curls. Love was born instantly. He had failed his son; he was determined not fail his grandson! Turning to Hernando, he asked, "May we talk alone?"

He was agreeable. The house had two spare bedrooms; Felisa showed the women to one room and the men to the other. Antonio remained in the parlor with Hernando.

Lopez poured two snifters of brandy. Antonio was sitting on the sofa; Hernando handed him his drink, then took the chair facing him.

"Why did you want to see me alone?" he asked.

"First, let me ask you why you wanted me to meet your wife and son?"

The question stumped Hernando, for he wasn't sure why. He had made the request on the spur of the moment. He answered candidly, "I am not sure."

"Well, I think I know why. You are reaching out to me, Hernando."

"That is ridiculous!"

"I think not," Antonio argued. "You do not want this kind of life for your son. Deep down in your heart, you are hoping I will ask you to come live with me. You want Ricardo raised as an aristocrat. You want him to have all the advantages you were denied. I can not undo the injustice done to you, but I will not make the same mistake twice. I failed you, but if you will let me, I will not fail my grandson. Hernando, you and your family are welcome in my home. You are more than welcome; you are needed."

Hernando frowned harshly. "Do you really think you and I could live together as father and son?"

"Sí, in time."

Lopez helped himself to a long and thoughtful drink of brandy. Antonio's speculation had gotten to him. He had not invited Morelos here hoping he would ask him to move to his hacienda, or had he? Hernando's thoughts turned to his son. He could remain here and raise Ricardo as a rebel, move somewhere and try to scrap out a living, or take Antonio up on his offer and give Ricardo a secure and wealthy future. Given the alternatives, there was no choice. He was now a father and wanted the best for his son.

"I will do as you ask," he told Antonio.

Morelos was grateful, as well as overjoyed. "You will not regret this. You have made the right decision." He took a sip of brandy, then said, "Learning you have a wife and son was very surprising."

Hernando told him about his relationship with Felisa and that she had come to him at the cantina in Villa de Lazar. "I married her the next day," he explained.

"Do you love her?"

He sighed heavily. "I married her because it was the right thing to do."

Antonio flinched slightly. "Sí, you are a better man than I was. I should have married your mother."

"I hope in time I will learn to love Felisa."

"Will you leave with us tomorrow morning?"

"That is very sudden, but it can be arranged. Alberto is second in command. The people will not be left without a leader. But I am wanted by the law. Once I move to your hacienda, I might be arrested."

Antonio smiled confidently. "Do not worry about that, Hernando. I will take care of the law."

"Sí, I suppose you will. You have much political power."

"I have power, money, and influence. As my son, you

will possess the same. Use your new authority to help the people you care about. You can do more for the poor as Hernando Morelos than you could ever do as Hernando Lopez."

"You want me to change my name?"

"Morelos is your name; it is also Ricardo's name. It is a birthright you were denied; do not deny it to your son."

Antonio leaned forward, and his eyes bore intensely into Hernando's. "Take back your birthright, Hernando. It is a privilege granted to you by virtue of your birth." He held out a hand. "It has taken me twenty-eight years, but I now grant it to you, my son."

He accepted his father's hand. Antonio's hold tightened, and, following a moment's hesitation, Hernando responded with a grip just as firm.

Hernando's guests slept for four hours, then were awakened for dinner. Everyone was famished, and they did justice to the meal. Antonio happily announced that Hernando and his family were moving to his hacienda. Lucinda found the news highly suspect. Lopez despised her father. She could not imagine him moving to the hacienda without an ulterior motive. Following dinner, she asked to speak alone to Hernando. She intended to get to the truth.

They went outside and stood on the porch. Night had descended, but the moon bathed the land in a soft glow. Hernando could see Lucinda clearly, and he read the suspicion in her eyes.

She didn't mince words, but got right to the point. "Why are you moving to the hacienda? Are you after Pápa's money?"

"I am making this change for my son's sake. He is a Morelos, is he not?"

"But you hate Pápa! I cannot imagine you living with him. You will probably kill him as he sleeps!"

"If you think that, then you do not know me at all."

"I know your kind!" she snapped.

"If you think so badly of me, why did you run away to find me?"

She was startled.

"Antonio told me why you were captured by the Apaches."

"I am not sure why I wanted to find you."

"I think I know why. You wanted to hurt your father, and you thought you could accomplish that by coming to me. You are the one who hates your Pápa, not me. I have always been honest with him."

"I do not hate Pápa!" she cried angrily.

"Neither do I," he replied. "I thought I hated him, but I now know those feelings do not exist. I hope Antonio and I can become friends." He placed his hands on her shoulders, and met her eyes without a waver. "I understand your concern. I swear before God that I harbor no ill will toward our father."

"Our father?" she repeated.

He was taken off guard. "That is the first time I ever really thought of him in that way."

"Perhaps it will be easier for you if you continue that line of thought."

He smiled warmly. "Does this mean that you trust me?"

"Sí, I think I do. I somehow sense there is no evil in you."

"I wish we could have known each other. I grew up without any brothers or sisters."

"So did I," she replied. "But we are brother and sister."

"Maybe we can learn to care about each other in that way."

The front door opened, and Cade stepped outside. "I'm sorry," he said. "I didn't know you two were here. I figured you probably went for a walk."

Lucinda asked Hernando, "Do you mind leaving us alone? I need to talk to Cade."

Complying, he went back into the house.

Brandon lit a cheroot. He hoped Lucinda was over her infatuation with him. He dreaded another scene like the one at the gazebo.

"Cade," she began, "I am sorry that I threw myself at your feet. I behaved very foolishly. I know you do not love me and that you never will. You are in love with Jodie, are you not?"

"Yes, I am. We're going to be married."

She smiled brightly. "I am happy for you. Believe me, I truly am. What do you think of Miguel Huerto?"

"I like him."

"So do I," she said. "I think maybe I will fall in love with him. He is so handsome, charming, and very brave."

"In that case, you shouldn't waste your time with me. Why don't you go to Miguel? He's in the parlor, and keeps looking toward the front door, waiting for your return."

Flattered, as well as pleased, she hurried inside.

Cade sat down on the top stoop, and as he smoked his cheroot, his thoughts ran deeply. Jason Edwards was still at large, and he wondered if Jodie was still determined to go after him. He hoped not, for he was eager to marry her and return to his ranch. However, he wasn't very hopeful; he was too familiar with Jodie's stubborn nature.

A frown creased his brow—instead of heading for the marriage altar, he and Jodie would most likely head across the countryside in pursuit of Jason Edwards!

Chapter
Twenty-Four

Lawson sent two ranch hands to escort Laura to his home. He didn't want her making the trip alone after dark. He was still bedridden, but he planned to have dinner with her in his room.

She arrived a little after six o'clock. The housekeeper led her upstairs and to Bill's room. Wearing a silk robe and pajamas, he was lying in bed with the covers at his feet. Pillows were propped against the oak headboard so that he could sit up. His eyes raked Laura appreciatively as she came into the room. She had donned her most revealing gown; it was cut daringly low. Her auburn tresses cascaded past her bare shoulders in silky waves that glowed with reddish highlights.

She moved to the bedside, smiled radiantly at Bill, and said, "You're looking much better. You'll soon be as good as new."

His eyes were drawn to the deep cleavage between her ample breasts. He felt a stirring in his loins. "I am much better," he replied with an imperceptible grimace, for his desire was rising uncomfortably. He hadn't made love to a woman in a long time, for he refused to pay a prostitute for her favors. Harlots repulsed him. Last year, he had indulged in an affair with the woman who owned the dress shop in town. Marriage was never discussed; their relationship was purely physical. Crystal Creek was merely a stopover for her. She didn't intend to spend her life in a small town; her goal was to reach San Francisco. At that time, Bill was determined to marry Jodie. Therefore, when his paramour sold her shop and left for California, he told her good-bye with only one regret—he now had no one to appease his lust. Although he was not averse to a licentious affair, he would never marry a promiscuous woman. His bride must be virtuous and above reproach. He had believed Jodie was that special person, but he had misjudged her. She was undoubtedly making love with Brandon. He had placed her on a pedestal, and she had made a fool of him. He desired revenge and hoped that Brandon would take what he wanted from her, then ride out of her life. It would serve her right!

Dinner was served. Bill's meal was brought to him on a tray. A small table had been set for Laura and placed beside the bed so that she and her host could enjoy their food and conversation in close proximity.

Following dinner, the housekeeper arrived with brandy for Lawson and a glass of sherry for Laura. The dishes were removed, and the couple was left alone with their drinks.

As Laura nursed her sherry, she debated whether or not to seduce Bill. He was still convalescing, but there were ways to please a man without having him exert himself. He would receive all the pleasure, true, but experiencing her expertise would surely persuade him to marry her. She laughed inwardly—persuade? Why, he would beg her to be his wife!

Her mind made up, she put down her glass and

approached Lawson like a black widow about to trap an unsuspecting mate. She sat on the edge of the bed, and gazed into his eyes with adoration. "Bill, may I make a confession?"

"By all means," he replied, his eyes dipping to her cleavage.

"I love you, Bill. I have loved you since the first moment I saw you. If you hadn't been courting Jodie . . ."

"But Jodie and I are no longer courting." He drew her gently against him, and the feel of her breasts pressed to his chest kindled his passion.

Taking the initiative, Laura kissed him provocatively, her tongue darting into his mouth and entwining with his.

Her boldness startled Bill. He had believed she was inexperienced, but it took a lot of practice to kiss a man the way she was kissing him. Evidently, Laura Talbert was not the virtuous lady he had judged her to be. He was disappointed, but only for a moment, for his erect member became all important. A passionate moan sounded deep in his throat; he needed a woman badly.

But he was too ill, and he reluctantly drew his mouth away from hers. "Laura, what are you trying to do to me? You know I'm in no condition to respond to such a kiss."

She smiled enticingly. "Darling, there's no reason for you to exert yourself. Let me give you pleasure. When you're fully recovered, you can do the same for me."

He didn't know what to say. Her harlot's ways still had him somewhat in shock. Nevertheless, he wasn't about to refuse her provocative offer.

She kissed him again, her tongue moving into his mouth with urgent passion. Responding, his returned her sensual assault, as his hand slid up the bodice of her gown to touch a bare breast.

She reached behind her, undid the tiny buttons at the back of her gown, then drew the fabric down to her waist.

She then unlaced her chemise and drew it aside, revealing her full-shaped bosom to Bill's hungry scrutiny.

His fingers kneaded her breasts with lust-driven exploration before he gently drew a taut nipple into his mouth. Her hand swept to the back of his neck, pressing his face closer. His lips circled one erect nipple then the other, which fueled their passion.

Laura's body moved over his, and she could feel his hardness between her thighs. She was glad to find that he was so thoroughly aroused and so responsive to her seduction. She lay beside him, and untied the sash holding his robe together. She then reached down and slipped her fingers under his nightshirt. Her searching hand caressed his throbbing member. Bill writhed and moaned fervently, his injury forgotten.

Slowly, Laura moved down the bed until her head was even with Bill's hips. She was well-schooled in the art of giving pleasure, and taking him into her mouth, she used her expertise to spiral him to a shuddering climax.

Afterward, she kissed him on the lips, then snuggled against him, placing her head on his shoulder.

Although Lawson was sated, he was somewhat aghast at Laura's behavior. A high-paid prostitute could not have been more erotic. He questioned Laura's past.

Meanwhile, Laura was waiting for a marriage proposal. Now that Bill knew she was no prude in bed, she figured he'd certainly want to marry her. He was probably dreaming of all the nights that lie ahead, nights of wondrous rapture.

Bill, tugging at the bodice of her dress, said, "You'd better straighten your clothes. My housekeeper might return. We didn't lock the door, remember?"

Leaving the bed, she laced her chemise and buttoned her gown. She went to the dresser, picked up a brush and ran it briskly through her hair. Returning to her chair, she retrieved her glass of sherry, tipped it to her mouth, and drank it neatly. She looked at Bill; he was staring back at her. She couldn't interpret his expression, and she asked, "What are you thinking about?"

"You," he replied.

She naturally assumed that he was thinking about her. But she wanted to know exactly where his thoughts were taking him. "I hope your thoughts are kind," she said, smiling coquettishly. "You do love me, don't you?"

He cleared his throat uneasily, and despite his injury, he moved so that he was sitting on the edge of the bed. "Laura," he began, his tone hesitant, "I never said that I was in love with you."

She tensed, and her eyes widened with surprise.

Before she could say anything, he held up a hand of silence. "Please let me continue. I am quite fond of you, and I have a proposition. If you'll become my mistress, I'll make it well worth your time. But there is a stipulation—when it's over, it's over. Someday I hope to marry and have a family. When that day comes, I will not tolerate an interfering mistress."

Laura bounded angrily from her chair. She glowered at Bill and her eyes burned with rage. "Your mistress?" she screeched. "How dare you insult me this way after what just happened?"

He laughed shortly. "Insult you? I hardly think so. Come now, Laura. Do you think I am a complete fool? You are evidently a very experienced woman."

"I might have some experience, but that doesn't make me a harlot! Four years ago I was involved with an older man. He took advantage of my innocence. I thought he was going to marry me. When I learned he was already married, I broke off our affair." She spoke the truth; however, she didn't bother to mention all the lovers who had followed. She did, however, bury her face in her hands and pretend to be visibly upset. Her shoulders shook, and hard sobs sounded in her throat. "Oh Bill, I was such a fool!" she cried. "But I was only eighteen! Must I pay for that one mistake for the rest of my life?"

"Don't cry, Laura," he said.

She thought she detected kindness in his voice, and she gave the impression that she was pulling herself together.

"I don't think you have told me the complete truth," Bill said. "Actions speak louder than words, and your actions are proof that you've had a lot of experience. However, it doesn't matter. Marriage is not even debatable. The woman I marry must be a virgin. Nothing you can say or do will change my mind. I do not like whores; therefore, I will not marry one."

"I am not a whore!" she shouted.

"But you are the next thing to a whore. You are promiscuous and conniving." A crazed fury suddenly flared in his eyes. "Do you think for one moment that I'd let a woman like you be the mother of my children? I had a mother like that! After my father died, she became a whore. I was raised in a house of ill-repute, where I was surrounded by harlots. When I reached puberty, they teased me unmercifully. One of the whores finally took me to her bed, and when I failed to please her, she laughed at me. She told the others, and they all had a good laugh at my expense. When I turned sixteen, I ran away and never returned. But the aroma of cheap perfume, the smell of unwashed sheets, and the stench of whores are still with me."

Laura knew she was defeated, and she sank back into her chair. Bill was not about to marry her, and no amount of inveigling or pleading was going to change his mind.

"My offer still holds," he told her. "Do you want to be my mistress?"

She sat stiffly, her face blank, as though she hadn't heard a word that he said. After a minute or so, she slowly got to her feet. She didn't want to become a mistress. Her ambition was still as strong as ever; she intended to marry a rich man.

She looked Bill in the eyes, and said with as much dignity as she could summon, "Go to hell!" With that, she whirled around and walked out of the room.

Doris was sitting in the parlor with Mr. Daniels when her daughter came home. Laura wasn't all that surprised to find him with her mother; the man had been around a lot lately. She supposed he was interested in Doris. She viewed romance at their age dull and not worth a moment of her thoughts.

Daniels considerately excused himself and left.

"Mother," Laura said tediously, "you aren't considering marrying that boring widower, are you?"

"He isn't boring. I like Mr. Daniels very much. As far as marriage, we're just good friends."

"He isn't hanging around here for his health. It's only a matter of time before he starts courting you."

Doris blushed becomingly. "He did suggest we go on a picnic Sunday."

Her happiness deepened Laura's depression. She was miserable and wanted her mother's sympathy. But Doris was too infatuated with Mr. Daniels to see that her daughter was troubled. Laura had always been the center of her mother's life, and she resented losing that place to someone else.

"Mother," she began. "Aren't you going to ask me why I'm home so soon?"

"Of course, dear. Did something happen? Was Bill feeling poorly?"

"I'm not going to see him again. It's over between us."

"What happened?"

"He's pompous and overbearing. I could never fall in love with someone like him."

"That's too bad," Doris answered absently, for her mind was still on Sunday's picnic.

It was obvious to Laura that she wasn't going to receive any sympathy. She wheeled about to leave, but Doris suddenly detained her.

"Laura?"

She turned back and faced her. "Yes, Mother?"

"Jodie mentioned that you might find work at Caroline's. At the time, I was against the idea. But I'm sure Jodie will marry Marshal Brandon, which means we won't have her income."

Laura inhaled sharply. "Are you implying that I should work as a waitress?"

"Yes, I'm afraid I am. I can help by taking in laundry and sewing."

Tears flooded Laura's eyes. She fled from the parlor and to her room, where she threw herself across the bed. She cried hysterically, for she felt very sorry for herself—Bill had rejected her—her mother was preoccupied with Mr. Daniels—and she had to get a job!

Jonas left the sheriff's office, locking the door behind him. There were no prisoners inside, but there were plenty of guns to tempt a burglar. He crossed the street and headed toward the hotel. He intended to visit Alison; he hoped he'd be welcomed.

He moved through the lobby, climbed the stairs to Alison's room, and knocked on the door.

"Who's there?" she called.

"Jonas," he replied.

A moment later, she released the bolt and opened the door.

"May I come in?" he asked.

She stepped aside, and closed the door behind him.

"I had dinner at the restaurant tonight," Jonas began. "Caroline told me that you have your meals delivered here to your room."

"Is there anything wrong with that?" she asked, obviously defensive.

"Why do you want to cloister yourself in a hotel room?"

"Did you come here to preach to me? Honestly, Jonas! You have no right to find fault with someone else."

"I'm not here to preach," he replied. She was dressed in clothes she had brought from Lopez's hideout. Her hair was braided, and the expression in her eyes was empty. She had looked this way the first time he saw her. But the night they had dinner at Caroline's, her eyes had come alive. She had smiled often, and a spark of vitality had been reborn. He wondered if he was the cause behind her now obvious decline. He removed his hat, his hands nervously toying with the brim. "Alison," he began haltingly, for he wasn't sure how to express himself. "I hope . . . I hope I didn't do or say anything . . . Are you staying in this room because of me? Are you trying to avoid me?"

She moved to the window, drew aside the curtain, and gazed down vacantly at the main thoroughfare. She kept her back turned to Jonas. "I'm not comfortable with people," she said evenly. "That's why I prefer to stay in my room. It has nothing to do with you."

But Jonas felt that it did. He placed his hat on a chair, went to her, and put his hands on her shoulders. He gently turned her so that she was facing him. "I haven't had a drink in over twenty-four hours," he said, as though they had been discussing his problem. "I haven't had so much as one swallow. I swear it's the truth."

"I'm happy for you, Jonas. But your life is really none of my concern. You must stop drinking for yourself, not for me."

"Maybe I want to stop drinking for us."

She was taken by surprise. "Us?" she questioned. "What does that mean?"

He looked away, for he was suddenly very unsure of himself. "I don't know why I said that," he admitted, facing her again. "It just slipped out. Maybe somewhere deep down inside, I don't want to lose you. I can't be sure of my feelings, for I haven't had feelings in years. I've forgotten what it's like to care."

Alison understood only too well. "I wish I could help you, Jonas. But my emotions are just as dead as yours."

"Are they?" he asked, his hands suddenly gripping her arms. "Are our emotions really dead? Let's find out, shall we?"

She was stunned by the smoldering passion in his eyes. "Find out?" she stammered. "But . . . But how?"

"Like this," he uttered, his mouth seizing hers aggressively.

Responding, she shifted closer to him. She hadn't kissed a man since she was fourteen years old. She'd had a beau back then, and she had allowed him one kiss. Comanche warriors didn't practice the custom, and the night Rafe had raped her, he hadn't bothered to try and kiss her; it was a small blessing. At Lopez's hideout, a few Comancheros had made overtures, but she had firmly thwarted their advances.

Now, the touch of Jonas's lips on hers felt strange, but certainly not unpleasant. Quite the contrary, it was breathlessly exciting. The woman in her started to come alive.

Jonas embraced her, holding her as though he never intended to let her go. "Alison," he murmured. "I need you. We need each other."

She stayed in his arms, relishing his nearness, his strength, and the wonder of the moment. A tremble rocked his body; she suspected it was not brought on by passion. She moved out of his embrace, and looked into his face. Perspiration was beading up on his brow, and he appeared to be in pain.

"Jonas, what's wrong?"

His hands had started shaking, and he clasped them

together tightly. "I get this way sometimes when I need a drink," he moaned. "It's just a spell; it'll pass."

She didn't think it would pass too quickly.

"I'd better leave," Jonas said. "I don't want you to see me like this."

She clutched his arm. "Don't leave. Let me help you through this."

"It can get pretty ugly."

"A minute ago, you said that we need each other. If you truly meant it, you won't turn away from me."

A stomach cramp hit without warning, doubling him over. He stumbled to the bed and sat on the edge. "God, I need a drink!" he groaned.

"No, you need me," Alison said, hurrying to sit beside him. She placed an arm about his shoulders and held him close.

"If I can only make it through this night . . ." Another cramp hit, but this one was more severe. Jonas felt panic rising inside him—he wanted a drink so desperately that he could almost taste it. He grabbed Alison's hand so tightly that she winced. "Don't let me leave!" he pleaded. "If I walk out of this room, I'll head straight for the Silver Dollar. I don't have enough willpower; I need yours."

"I have a lot of willpower," she replied. "I can give you all you'll need. Stay with me. I'll take care of you."

"Yes," he moaned. "I'll stay. If I leave, I may be lost forever."

They both knew it was going to be a long night.

As the first light of dawn infiltrated Alison's room, it fell across the bed, where she and Jonas lay entwined. They were fully dressed, for their embrace was not one of passion, but one of fatigue. Through the long, gruelling hours before dawn, Jonas had suffered physical as well as mental pain. Years of heavy drinking had taken its toll. He needed liquor just as he needed air to breathe. Withdrawing from such an addiction had nearly driven him over the edge. Only Alison's firm support had prevented him from leaving the room, getting a bottle of whiskey, and drinking himself into oblivion.

About an hour ago, they had drifted into a restful sleep.

Now, as Jonas slowly came awake, his mind was muddled. For a moment, he was confused to find that he wasn't in his own bed. But everything came back to him in a sudden rush. He grimaced as he recalled the long hours of pain and torture. But he knew the worst was over. That thought bolstered his spirits; considering he made it through last night, he could overcome any discomfort that lie ahead. He knew, though, that he couldn't have survived the night without Alison.

Moving carefully so that he wouldn't awaken her, he gazed down into her face. She was beautiful in repose, for her heartache and suffering were masked in sleep. Awake, her beauty was marred by haunted memories and years of abuse.

Her eyes suddenly opened, and when she saw that he was watching her, she smiled—it was lovely, heart-warming, and somehow intimate.

"Good morning," he murmured.

"How do you feel?" she asked.

"Hungry as a bear."

"In that case, we'd better go to Caroline's."

"The restaurant's not open yet. It's barely past dawn."

"I guess you'll have to wait."

She moved to stretch her cramped muscles, inadvertently pressing a hip against his loins. The touch was electric, and Jonas quickly forgot about breakfast. He bent his head and kissed her lips softly. The contact was tender, yet more persuasive than a passionate exchange.

She laced her arms about his neck, and turned her body to his. Passion, henceforth unknown to Alison, had been awakened. She was a grown woman, and although she had never experienced such desire, she fully understood its implication. She needed Jonas's love, and he needed hers. In each other's arms, they would come alive, each giving the other the strength and courage to bury the past and start anew.

"Make love to me," Alison murmured. "Oh Jonas, I want to live again!"

"I know," he whispered. "I feel the same way. Marry me, Alison. Be my wife and the mother of my children."

"Children?" she repeated, as though he had asked the impossible. "Do we dare? We know what it's like to lose them. Do we dare risk our hearts again?"

"Life's a risk, sweetheart. Let's not be afraid. We've spent years running from life because we lost the courage to face it."

A warm shiver ran up her spine as she imagined having a baby to love and raise. "Yes, Jonas, let's dream the same dreams of young lovers."

"Young lovers?" he asked with a sensual grin. "My dear, we are just now hitting our stride. Young lovers have nothing on us. We're way ahead of them."

Her smile was inviting. "Show me what you mean."

"The pleasure's all mine," he whispered, before capturing her lips in a demanding exchange.

Chapter Twenty-Five

Dirk Bradley rode toward town, and away from his father's ranch. This morning, he had received another lecture from Emmett; chastising him for his gambling debts. Garth had stood by smugly, inserting his own comments whenever Emmett paused to catch his breath, which wasn't very often. This time, his father's tirade had not only been lengthy but practically nonstop. It had ended with an ultimatum—Dirk had to change his ways or get out!

He wasn't about to get out, for he had no place to go. Furthermore, he wasn't about to relinquish his inheritance. But changing his ways wouldn't be easy; in fact, Dirk didn't think it was possible. His father expected him to quit gambling, drinking, and spending the rest of the time in some prostitute's bed. He also insisted that he start doing his share of work at the ranch. Emmett expected him to work alongside the wranglers as though he were one of them. But Dirk hated ranching and everything it entailed. When his father died—he hoped it would be soon—he planned to sell his half of the business to his brother. Then he would leave for San Francisco and never come back!

Now, as Dirk galloped toward Crystal Creek, this morning's tirade was very much on his mind. His father, along with Garth, had left the house to oversee a day's work. He was supposed to remain home and think over everything Emmett said. However, the moment his father and brother rode away, he saddled his horse and left for town. He would do his thinking at the Silver Dollar.

Dirk caught sight of two men riding his way. He slowed his horse to a slow canter. At first, he thought he was about to encounter Emmett and Garth, but as the riders drew closer, he realized he was mistaken. He suddenly recognized one of the men. It was Breed. Although he preferred to turn around and race for home, he reined in and waited. His nerves were on edge, and his heart pounded. Breed was a crazed murderer, and he wanted no part of him. However, he wasn't about to run for fear that such an act would anger Breed. He would probably chase him down and shoot him just for the hell of it!

Dirk forced a smile as Breed and his companion brought their horses to a stop alongside his. "Good morning, Breed," he said, a slight quaver in his voice. "I sure didn't expect to see you. You're taking a big risk being in these parts. Marshal Brandon's still hanging around."

"I know," Breed replied. "That is why I'm here."

"I'm not sure I understand."

"Then I will make it clear. I am here to kill the Marshal and the woman deputy."

"You plan to kill Brandon and Jodie?" he exclaimed. "Hell, Breed! Why don't you just hightail it out of here before you get yourself killed or end up with a noose around your neck?"

"I did not find you to listen to your advice."

"Find me?" he questioned. "You mean, this meetin' isn't accidental?"

"I know you lied to Red and me when you told us you were a drover. I know your father is a wealthy rancher and that we are on his land. But that does not matter. I have waited two days to catch you alone. I need your help."

"My help?" he asked, gulping deeply. "Wh . . . what's in it for me?"

"What do you want?"

"I don't know. I guess that depends."

Breed waved a hand toward his companion. "This is Jason Edwards."

"So you're the one who broke Edwards out of jail!" Dirk said to Breed. "I haven't been in town for the last couple of days, but one of our wranglers mentioned there was a jail break." He paused for a moment, then asked gingerly, "Exactly what do you want from me?"

"I want you to go to the sheriff's office and unlock the back door. Edwards and I will sneak into town and hide in the alley at the back of the jail."

"Why do you want to break into the sheriff's office?"

"That is where I will find the Marshal and the woman."

Because Dirk had been at the ranch for two days, he didn't know that Cade and Jodie had left town to look for Edwards. "I don't know about this," he said hesitantly. "I could get in a lot of trouble."

"Find an excuse to use the back door. I will make it look as though you were taken by surprise."

"Jodie and Brandon might not even be there. Hell, Jodie ain't even deputy any longer."

"If they aren't there, then I will find a way to get them there."

Dirk didn't want to get involved, but he was scared that Breed would kill him if he refused.

Breed sensed his fear; he also knew that Dirk needed a good reason to carry this through without bungling it.

There had to be something in it for him. "You do me this favor," Breed began, "and I will do you a favor in return." He eyed Dirk intensely. "Your father is very rich. When he dies, you will receive a large inheritance. But that could be years and years away. Would you like me to erase all those years?"

"Good God!" Dirk exclaimed. "Do you think I want my father dead?"

Breed shrugged indifferently. "It was only an idea. Maybe I was wrong to come to you. I will find another way to capture the Marshal and the woman." He gave the impression that he was about to turn his horse around.

"No! Wait!" Dirk said strongly.

Breed smiled inwardly—the seed he planted had taken root.

"Wh . . . when would you kill my father?" he stammered.

"First, I will take care of the Marshal and the woman. Then I will kill your father. After that, I will leave for Mexico."

Dirk felt as though someone else's voice had taken over his body as he continued, "Do you think you could kill my brother too? I'll make it well worth your time, for Pa keeps a lot of money in his safe. You shouldn't have any trouble getting rid of them at the same time. They're always together." Dirk swallowed nervously—the voice was his all right; it was merely spilling a desire that had been in the back of his mind for a long time.

Breed smiled coldly. "For a thousand dollars, I will kill both of them."

"You've got a deal," Dirk replied without a moment's hesitation. A large grin spread across his face; he'd sell the ranch and go to San Francisco a very rich man!

Alison and Jonas had breakfast at Caroline's before going to the sheriff's office. Alison planned to spend the day with Jonas, for she didn't want to stay cooped up in her hotel room. At noon, they would leave the office and enjoy a leisurely picnic. Jonas knew an ideal location where they wouldn't be disturbed, and they promised themselves a very romantic afternoon.

They had been inside the office only a few minutes when Dirk arrived. He was disappointed to find that Brandon and Jodie weren't there. Jonas was sitting at the desk, and Alison was sweeping the floor.

"What do you want, Dirk?" Riker asked, his tone unfriendly. He hadn't forgotten about Bradley insulting Alison.

Dirk's calculating mind quickly formed a plan. Pretending remorse, he turned to Alison, and apologized. "I'm sorry, ma'am, about the way I treated you. My behavior was uncalled for." He glanced down at his feet, as though he were too ashamed to face her.

"Let's just forget it, shall we?" Alison murmured.

He lifted his gaze. "Thanks, ma'am. You're a real kind lady."

"Now that you've apologized," Jonas remarked, "get the hell out of here!"

"Do you mind if I use the back door?"

"Why do you want to do that?"

"I think Pa's in town, and I don't want him to see me. I'm supposed to be at home, but I wanted to come here and apologize to Miss Brandon."

Jonas waved an impatient hand toward the rear entrance. "Go ahead." He started to get up.

"You don't have to show me out," Dirk said quickly.

"Kick you out is more like it! Show you out, hell! My intent is to lock the door behind you."

"I'll do that," Alison said. She motioned for Dirk to come with her.

As Dirk followed Alison through the back room and toward the rear entrance, his nerves grew taut. He wasn't having second thoughts, for he was willing to carry out his part of the deal. After all, his part was small compared to what he would get in return. But he couldn't help but be nervous; what if something went wrong?

The moment Alison released the bolt, the door swung open from the outside. Before she could scream, Breed's large hand was clamped over her mouth. He remembered Alison as Grass Woman. He wasn't surprised to find her here, for Hernando had told him that she was Brandon's sister.

"Wh . . . what's going on?" Dirk exclaimed, playing innocent.

Jason pointed his pistol at young Bradley, and ordered him not to make a sound.

Breed, his hand still preventing Alison from crying out, forced her with him through the back room and toward the office. Bradley and Edwards followed close behind.

Jonas, looking over the morning mail, glanced up as they came through the doorway. Edwards turned his pistol from Dirk and pointed it at Riker. At the same time, Breed drew his gun, and held the barrel to Alison's head.

"Try anything," Breed said to Jonas, "and this bitch's brains will be all over the floor. Now, stand up real slow and unbuckle your holster."

Jonas cooperated.

"Put the holster on the desk, then step away and put your hands at the back of your head."

Again, Jonas did as he was told. He was not about to take a chance with Alison's life.

"Get his holster," Breed told Edwards. "Then put a pair of cuffs on him."

Jason quickly carried out Breed's instructions.

"Listen to me, bitch!" Breed said to Alison. "I'm going to take my hand off your mouth, but if you scream, I'll kill you and the sheriff. Do you understand?"

She nodded stiffly.

He removed his hand cautiously, but she had no intention of screaming. "I'm looking for Brandon and his woman," he said to Alison. "I want you to find them, and bring them here. If you tell anyone else, I'll kill the sheriff." He gestured toward Dirk, adding, "I'll kill him too."

Dirk gulped; he hoped Breed was simply drawing suspicion away from him.

Breed continued, "You tell Brandon and the woman if they don't want to be responsible for two deaths, they'd better come alone." He shoved her in the direction of the front door. "Go on; get out of here and do as I told you!"

Alison turned away from the door and faced Breed. "Cade and Jodie aren't in town."

"Don't lie to me, bitch!"

"I'm not lying! They left town to look for Jason Edwards."

"Well, I'll be damned!" Jason remarked. "They're out lookin' for me, and I'm right here in their office. If that don't beat hell!"

Breed was furious with himself. He should have known those two would go after Edwards! For a moment he considered releasing his rage through killing the woman, the sheriff, and even Dirk. But he was too prudent to act so impulsively. The mission was not an entire failure; it could still be used to his advantage. He turned to Dirk, who was watching him warily.

"Brandon and the woman probably headed for Mexico," he said to Bradley. "When they don't find any fresh tracks, they'll come back to Crystal Creek. I got a message for you to deliver. You tell them that I'm at the way station that used to belong to a man named Graham, holding the sheriff and the woman."

"Used to?" Dirk questioned.

"I passed by it a few days ago. It was abandoned. The Army probably ordered it closed because of the Apaches. I can see a long way from that way station, and I'll know if Brandon and the woman aren't alone. You tell them if they bring any help, I'll kill the hostages."

Moving unexpectedly, he went to Bradley, clutched his arm, and jerked him forward. He spoke too quietly to be overheard. "I have to make this look real." He then took a step back, and raised his voice, "I don't want you warning anyone about this! You keep your mouth shut until Brandon and the woman show up. If a posse comes after us, I'll kill this bitch and the sheriff. Then I'll come after you!" He slammed the butt of his pistol against Dirk's temple, hitting him hard enough to knock him off his feet, but the blow was too light to render him unconscious. He lay perfectly still and pretended he was out cold.

Breed stepped quickly to Jonas, raised his gun, and sent it crashing against Riker's head. This time, his victim really was knocked unconscious. He hefted Jonas's limp body over his shoulder, and motioned for Jason to grab Alison and follow.

They hurried out the back door and into the deserted alley. Breed slung Jonas over his saddle, then mounted behind him. Meanwhile, Edwards had put Alison on his horse. Her back was pressed against his chest, and she was trapped in the circle of his arms.

They guided their horses down the alley, which led to a back road that was not commonly used. It was empty, making it possible for them to leave town without detection.

Jodie and Cade left the Comancheros' hideout along with Antonio and the others. The treacherous trek over the mountain was completed with no accidents—Jodie hoped this trip was her last. Scaling the sheer bluffs behind a blindfold was too unnerving. Although Felisa's eyes were not covered, Hernando insisted on holding the baby, for he had made the climb so many times that he knew every twist and turn.

The group traveled together until it was time for Jodie and Cade to veer north. Warm good-byes were exchanged, then the riders took their separate courses.

Jodie and Cade, holding their horses to an easy pace, covered several miles before the first signs of dusk fell across the countryside. They found a good place to camp for the night, for trees and vegetation afforded a protective wall about the small area. Because the Apache situation was perilous, they decided against a fire.

Following a cold supper, they unrolled their blankets and placed them side by side. They sat close together; Jodie kept her Winchester close, and Cade didn't remove his holster. His rifle, like Jodie's, was within arm's reach.

Dusk gave way to night, and the tableau was bathed in golden moonbeams. A coyote's howl sounded in the distance; a moment later it was answered by a chorus of howls. The canine music drifted on a desert wind, which blew gently over the vast region.

Jodie's head was resting on Cade's shoulder; she was so still that he wondered if she was asleep. He moved her carefully, and she looked into his face.

"Are you sleepy?" he asked.

"A little," she murmured.

"Why don't you get some rest? I'll take the first watch."

"Later," she said. "I'm really not that tired yet."

"In that case," Cade began. "There's something we need to discuss."

"What's that?"

"Pursuing Jason Edwards. Do you still intend to go after him?"

"He murdered a woman and a child; he should be brought to justice."

"That's not the issue here, Jodie. Besides, it's not justice that's driving you; it's the thousand dollars."

She lifted her chin stubbornly. "Edwards was my prisoner, and it's my job to catch him."

"It's not your job!" Cade argued. "Why don't you leave him to the law?"

"You're the law," she replied. "Aren't you coming with me?"

"I sure as hell don't intend to let you go alone. But, Jodie, it could take months to find Edwards. Maybe I'm a selfish ass, but marrying you and taking you to my ranch means more to me than chasing after Edwards. I want to turn in my badge, love my wife, raise a family, and build a prosperous ranch. I've spent years pursuing fugitives. Hell, I've done my part to civilize the West. I've earned my retirement."

Jodie understood and was sympathetic. "I agree with you, Cade. You should return to your ranch. You deserve that kind of life. I'll look for Edwards myself. After I find him, and turn him over to the law, I'll come to your ranch. Then we can be married."

Cade's temper blew. "Look for him yourself! Damn it, Jodie! Why must you be so hard-headed?"

He bounded to his feet, reached down, grasped her shoulders and drew her upright. His piercing blue eyes bore into hers with an intensity. "My patience has had it! Jodie, you're going to tell me why that thousand dollars means so much to you—or else!"

"Or else, what?" she asked, her expression defiant.

"Without trust and honesty, I don't see how our love can survive."

She felt a moment of panic—she couldn't lose Cade; she just couldn't! She loved him too much. But he was right; she owed him the truth. If only . . . if only the truth weren't so painful. She turned away from his intense gaze to stare vacantly into the distance. She opened her mind to the past, and allowed the memories to return. An ache caught in her throat, and a trace of tears wet her eyes. She swallowed deeply; the ache went away. She then blinked back the tears and faced Cade. "I idolized my father," she said, as though he had been the center of their discussion. "Even after I learned the bitter truth, I loved him with all my heart."

"What happened between you and Cole?"

"Nothing," she murmured.

"Don't do that, Jodie! Don't shut me out!"

"But it's true. Nothing happened. I never told Papa that I knew how he really felt. He stayed with Mother and me because he considered us a responsibility—an obligation! We were a heavy burden for Papa to carry, for we cost him the woman he truly loved."

Jodie returned to the blanket, and Cade sat beside her, taking her hand into his.

"Emmett Bradley bought his ranch from a woman named Ruth Jennings," Jodie began. "She was a widow; her husband had died a few years before. But she successfully operated her ranch; a man couldn't have done any better. Ruth was independent, willful, and could take care of herself. I liked her a lot, and I used to visit her every other day or so. When I grew up, I wanted to be just like her. One day, when I was twelve years old, I went to her home. Her housekeeper told me she wasn't there but that she expected her back very soon. I decided to wait in the parlor. There was a long sofa in front of the hearth, and its high back faced the center of the room. It was a little chilly that day, and I sat on the sofa to warm myself by the fire. I grew sleepy, and I stretched out on the sofa and fell asleep. Later, I was awakened by voices. I started to sit up and make my presence known, but when I realized one of the voices was my father's, I hesitated. That moment's hesitation turned into a nightmare.

"My father and Ruth were discussing how deeply they loved each other. She wanted him to run away with her to Montana. There, they could buy land and build a ranch.

I can still hear the heartache in Papa's voice when he told her that he couldn't leave his family. I never heard Papa sound so sad, or so filled with despair. It was apparent that he loved Ruth very much. Nevertheless, he put his obligation to his family first. He told Ruth that Mother was too helpless and dependent on him to survive on her own. Even if he sent her money every month, she wouldn't be able to make it. He was right—Mother was a clinging vine. She couldn't get through a day without depending on Papa for something. Mostly, it was something as minor as repairing the clothesline, or chopping extra wood. Papa used to encourage her to become more independent, but such encouragement always resulted in Mother breaking into tears and claiming that he didn't love her anymore. He finally stopped trying to change her.

"Ruth was the complete opposite of Mother. Even at the tender age of twelve, I knew Ruth was Papa's soul mate—they were so much alike. No wonder they fell in love.

"I remained hidden on the sofa. By now, I felt too guilty to make my presence known. I knew eavesdropping was wrong. But I was riveted to that sofa; I don't think I could have moved if I had wanted to. Papa told Ruth good-bye that day. It wasn't necessary to see them to know that they were in each other's arms. Ruth cried, and Papa cried with her. Hearing my father weep like that was shocking. I mean, he was always so strong and such a powerful figure.

"I should have despised Papa for cheating on Mother, but I didn't. In a way, I felt sorry for him. He and Mother were so wrong for each other that I can't imagine why they married. I suppose opposites do sometimes attract. But the shock and pain of learning that Papa didn't really want to share his life with Mother and me was heartbreaking and traumatic.

"When Papa left, Ruth went upstairs, and I slipped outside. I hurried to the stable, got my horse, and rode away as quickly as possible. If the housekeeper told Ruth I was there, then I assume Ruth figured I left before she and Papa arrived. Otherwise, I'm sure she or Papa would have said something to me.

"Ruth moved away soon after that. Papa was never again quite the same. He did his job, took care of his family, and enjoyed his friends. But I often found him sitting alone, forlorn, his mind lost in memories that refused to go away. He never stopped loving Ruth. When Mother died, he tried to find her. Ruth had a sister who lived in Albuquerque, and Papa wrote her a letter. She sent back a wire. Mr. Daniels gave it to one of Papa's wranglers who was in town, and he delivered it to the house. Papa read it, wadded it up, and threw it into the fireplace. He then stormed out of the house. The flames hadn't reached the wire; I fished it out and read it. Ruth had died on her journey to Montana. I waited up for Papa, but he didn't come home that night. He stayed away for three days.

"I will always wonder if he blamed himself for Ruth's death. If he had been traveling with her maybe she wouldn't have died. I also wonder if he held Mother and me responsible for his unhappiness. I suppose in a way, he did."

Cade was still holding Jodie's hand, and her fingers gripped his tightly, as she continued, "I made a vow to myself that I would never be like my mother. My husband will never see me as a responsibility or as a burden."

Determination shone in her eyes, and that impenetrable wall returned to protect her emotions.

"I can take care of myself," she said defiantly. "That thousand dollar reward will keep me financially independent, for then I can pack up and leave at a moment's notice."

Chapter Twenty-Six

Cade wasn't sure if he should chastise Jodie for making such a comment, or take her into his arms and kiss her. He decided on the latter. He drew her close, and his lips caressed hers tenderly.

"Darlin'," he murmured. "You'll never need that thousand dollars. I'll always love you."

"I'm sure Papa believed he would always love Mother."

"There are no guarantees, Jodie. But considering how different your parents were, it's easy to understand why Cole turned to another woman. But you and I aren't opposites. We have a lot in common, and everything going for us. That is, everything except your faith."

"My faith?"

"You apparently have no faith in our love. You're determined to start our marriage with escape money in your pocket. Darlin', I could sit here all night and profess my undying love over and over again, but unless you believe in us, nothing I say will matter."

"I do believe in our love," she replied. "But . . . but I'm

so afraid that someday . . . Oh Cade, I couldn't bear it if our marriage ended up like my parents'."

"I might be a lot like Cole, but you aren't anything like your mother. So how the hell could our marriage be anything like theirs?"

She gazed deeply into Cade's eyes. "I need time. I've lived with Papa's secret for eleven years. Talking about what happened has helped, but I can't erase all my doubts and insecurities overnight."

"Of course, you can," he replied, drawing her into his embrace. "Just let them go, for they have nothing to do with us. Our love is destined to last forever. You're everything to me, Jodie. I'll never stop loving you." He eased her back onto the blanket, murmuring soothingly, "Surrender your heart to me, darlin'. I'll handle it with the utmost care."

A tiny smile touched her lips. "Promise?"

"From the depth of my soul."

"Do I have your heart, Cade?"

"Yes, you do. I never imagined I could love a woman the way I love you. I love everything about you, even your fiery temper. In my eyes, you are perfect, and I wouldn't change a thing about you."

"Not even my independence?"

"There's nothing wrong with a woman being independent. I don't want to enslave you; I want us to share our lives as equal partners."

Her eyes twinkled saucily. "Equal? Does this mean we'll take turns having babies?"

"Sorry, darlin'. I can't help you with that." He smiled mischievously. "But I can make babies."

"Not without my help."

"All the more reason why I need you so much," he murmured, bending his head and capturing her lips in a hungry exchange.

Jodie laced her arms about his neck, and responded

without hesitation. Gone were her inhibitions, for Cade's love had sent her doubts and insecurities fleeing. Allowing her parent's failed marriage to come between her and Cade had been a terrible mistake.

"You do have my heart," Jodie whispered. "Cade, I promise I will never again doubt our love."

"We'll be in Crystal Creek tomorrow afternoon. Will you marry me tomorrow night?"

"I thought you said you were through proposing, and that it was time for threats."

"You're right. You'll either marry me tomorrow night or I'll take you over my knees and give you a much deserved spanking."

"Deserved?" she questioned playfully.

"Yes. For all those times you've put your life at risk. You know, loving you could make me gray-haired before my time."

"Don't fret, darling. Your hair won't prematurely turn gray. The days of putting my life at risk are over. From this moment on, I simply want to be your wife, the mother of your children, and your partner in life."

"And my lover," he put in.

Her smile was inviting. "That reminds me of a bargain we made recently. You promised to make love to me at the first opportunity." She pressed her thighs to his in a suggestive manner. "Are you a man of your word, my darling?"

"Always," he replied, his mouth swooping down on hers.

Jodie's love, now stronger than ever, drove away the shadows of yesterday and welcomed the dreams of tomorrow. As she responded fully to Cade, the real world slipped into oblivion. Only their hidden paradise existed. A desert wind, soughing through the treetops, was like a whispered melody of love. Above, a star-studded canopy, surrounding a golden moon, bathed the lovers in a romantic glow. They made love passionately, their hearts beating as one. Their pleasures alternated between giving and receiving, and their union was filled with wondrous sensations. The tide of ecstasy gradually crested; it was fathomless and utterly consuming, leaving Cade and Jodie marvelously fulfilled, and totally secure in their love.

Alison viewed the deserted way station with mixed emotions. She was anxious to sever such close proximity with Edwards, for his hands kept roaming to her breasts. Each time she had pushed his hands away only to have him laugh at her, then fondle her again. She could hardly wait to dismount and get as far away from him as possible. However, she wasn't sure if the way station would help or worsen her situation. It might merely afford Edwards the opportunity to fully carry out his manhandling. Therefore, as they approached the way station, Alison was plagued with fear and uncertainty.

Breed, the first to dismount, reached up and drew Riker to the ground. Although Jonas had regained consciousness hours ago, Breed had left him slung over his saddle. His hands were still cuffed behind him, and when Breed shoved him toward the front stoop, he tottered precariously before getting his balance.

Edwards got down from his horse, put his hands on Alison's waist, and lifted her from the saddle. He held her body pressed to his as he slowly lowered her to her feet. Thrusting her hands against his chest, she pushed away, and quickly followed Breed and Jonas into the way station. Chuckling, for he was thoroughly enjoying himself, Jason followed close on her heels.

Breed found a kerosene lamp, lit it, and turned the wick up as far as it would go. It was evident that the Grahams had left in a hurry, for the pantry door, standing open, revealed shelves lined with canned food, as well as bags of dry goods. Searching through the cabinets, which mostly held dishes, Breed found two bottles of whiskey. He grabbed one, opened it, and helped himself to a large swig. He then ordered Edwards to put the sheriff in a corner, and told Alison to fix something to eat.

Looking through the kitchen supplies, Alison found coffee, potatoes, and a slab of cured ham. She prepared the meal without complaint, for she knew Edwards wouldn't bother her while she was working. She could feel his eyes watching her every move, and his intense scrutiny was unnerving. She knew what was on his mind and wondered when he would act upon it. She had suffered unspeakable abuse for years and had somehow survived such degradation. But this time was different; Jonas's love had cleansed her soul and had washed away the ugly memories that scarred her mind. Her self-respect had been restored, but Edward's possible assault threatened to take that away from her. She felt she would rather die than submit. Loving Jonas had resurrected her pride, courage, and spirit, and she would not surrender them to Jason Edwards. She stealthily slipped a kitchen knife into her skirt pocket; if Edwards laid a hand on her, she would kill him! Breed would surely kill her in return, but she was willing to forfeit her life.

She could see Jonas from the kitchen area, and she cast him a cursory glance. He was sitting on the floor in a corner of the room, his back propped against the wall. He wasn't looking her way; he was staring down at his lap. She wondered what was going through his mind—was he thinking about her?

He was indeed thinking about Alison; he was also cursing himself for letting her fall into such peril. He had seen the way Edwards was ogling her. He didn't doubt that the man planned to rape her. He struggled against the cuffs binding him, but the effort merely chafed his wrists. He stopped; continuing would only make his wrists raw and bloody. There was no escaping handcuffs!

He was suddenly overwhelmed with self-loathing. He was a failure. He had failed his wife and children—if he had been home that night instead of helping Cole chase down cattle rustlers—he could have saved his family. Now, he had failed Alison, and like his wife and children, she would probably pay with her life.

He raised his head and looked at Breed. He was sitting at the table, swigging whiskey as though he were trying to polish off the bottle in record time. Jonas, still watching, could almost taste the whiskey Breed was greedily consuming. He needed a drink—he craved it as a man dying of thirst craves water. His self-loathing increased; he was not only a failure, but a hopeless drunk! Instead of thinking of a way to escape, he was thinking about whiskey! Willpower! God, he needed willpower!

As Jonas's eyes drifted toward the kitchen, Alison happened to look his way. Their gazes met, and the love in Alison's eyes was all the willpower Jonas needed. He forgot about whiskey, and summoned an encouraging smile for Alison. She responded with a brave smile that reached clear to his heart. Jonas was not a praying man, but he now turned to God and asked Him to spare Alison's life, and to keep her safe from Jason Edwards.

Alison put supper on the table for Breed and Edwards; she then fixed plates for Jonas and herself. She carried the food to Riker and sat beside him. She placed her plate aside to eat later. First, she had to feed Jonas.

He accepted a forkful of potatoes. "I feel like a helpless invalid," he complained.

"It's important that you keep up your strength," she said, this time offering him ham.

He chewed the food, swallowed, and mumbled, "Why should I keep up my strength? I can't do anything with my hands in cuffs. Hell, I can't even feed myself."

"All the same, I want you to stay strong. We might find a way to escape, or maybe Cade and Jodie will find a way."

She continued feeding him, and he accepted a few bites before refusing to take any more. "Now you eat," he told her. His gaze went to Jason, who was still at the table, washing down his food with gulps of coffee. Rage flickered in Riker's eyes, and his cuffed hands balled into fists.

The rage in his stare didn't escape Alison. "He's not going to rape me," she whispered.

Jonas was startled. "Why do you say that?"

"I will never again suffer a man's abuse. Jonas, your love healed my heart and restored my pride. Jason Edwards will not take that away from me." She didn't tell him about the knife in her pocket, for she figured he would try to talk her out of using it. If she killed Jason, Breed would certainly take her life. But it was a sacrifice she was willing to make; however, she knew Jonas wouldn't feel that way.

At that moment, Edwards pushed back his chair and rose to his feet. A closed door led off the main room; he gestured toward it tersely, and said to Breed, "That's gotta be a bedroom. If you don't need me for anything, I think I'll take the woman and have a little fun."

Breed, finished eating, picked up the whiskey bottle and leaned back in his chair. He took a big drink, belched, then muttered, "I don't give a damn what you do. But leave your gun with me. The woman's liable to take it away from you. I know your kind; your brain's in your pecker." Breed didn't like Edwards, but he might need his help killing Brandon and the woman. Once that was taken care of, he intended to kill Edwards simply because the man irritated him.

Jason handed over his pistol; Breed stuck it in his waistband. Jason then went to Alison, grabbed her arm, and jerked her to her feet. "Come with me sweetie; we're gonna have some fun."

Riker attempted to stand, but with his hands cuffed behind him, such a feat was difficult. He was halfway up when Edwards kicked him in the chin, and the solid blow slammed him against the wall.

"You son of a bitch!" Riker seethed. Jason's boot had cut Riker's skin, and blood trickled down his chin and onto his shirt.

Laughing, Edwards ushered Alison toward the closed door. She went with him submissively, for she saw no reason to put up a struggle. This man was not going to harm her; quite the contrary, he was the one in danger!

He took her into the Grahams' bedroom, and keeping a firm grip on her arm, he located the lamp, lit it, then slammed the door shut. Moving quickly, he drew her into his arms, holding her body flush to his. "Are you ready to play?" he asked, grinning lewdly.

She pretended to be afraid. "You won't hurt me, will you? I'll do anything you want if you promise not to hurt me."

He chuckled. "Why, sweetie, a little pain only makes it better for the woman."

She grew limp, in his arms, as though she were too fearful to stand without his support. Responding to her ploy, his hands moved to her shoulders in a supportive hold. She took a deep breath, furtively drew the knife from her pocket, and thrust the blade into his chest with vicious force.

Jason staggered backwards, shock frozen on his face. He stared down at the embedded knife as though he couldn't quite believe it. A pool of blood oozed from around the inserted blade, ran down his chest, and formed a small puddle at his feet.

Alison watched Jason without emotion, as though they were actors on a stage and none of this were real.

"You bitch!" he managed to grumble. "You goddamned bitch!"

He reached for her throat, but she sidestepped his attack, opened the door, and fled into the other room.

As Jason stumbled after her, the knife still lodged in his chest, Breed leapt to his feet. "Edwards, you idiot!" he shouted angrily.

"That bitch has done killed me!" he groaned, dropping to his knees.

Breed hurried over, and eased him down onto the floor. He gripped the knife firmly and pulled it out. Blood gushed from the gaping hole. "You won't die," Breed told Jason, then turned to Alison and ordered, "Bring me that bottle of whiskey."

She brought it to him.

It was almost empty and he poured what was left over Jason's wound. The whiskey burned his injured flesh so severely that he screamed with pain.

Breed picked up the bloody knife, stood, and looked at Alison. His dark eyes were hard and pitiless. "You caused this mess; now you clean it up. You can start by bandaging Edwards. Then find a mop and get rid of all this blood."

He moved away brusquely, went to the kitchen, and searched for sharp knives. He wrapped them in a dishcloth, then placed the bundle in the stove.

Riker was proud of Alison. He was also greatly relieved that Breed didn't kill her. Apparently, Jason's life wasn't very important to him. A smile teased his lips—Edwards was no longer a threat to Alison; she had seen to that!

Alison tended to Jason, found a mop, and cleaned the floor. Finished, she went to Riker and sat beside him. Using a wet cloth, she wiped the dried blood from his chin.

He kissed her lips softly. "I'm so proud of you. But you could've been killed, you know."

"I'd rather die than submit to Jason Edwards. But I am disappointed in myself."

"Why is that?"

"I meant to kill him!"

As the morning sun peeked over the horizon, it cast a golden radiance across a clear, turquoise sky. Dawn's light fell across the Mexican plains, imposing its glare upon the secluded paradise where Jodie and Cade had perfected their love. They had spent the night talking, making love, and taking turns standing vigil as the other one slept, but never for very long, for their passion had raged until dawn.

They ate a cold breakfast, saddled their horses, and headed toward the Rio Grande. As the sun climbed higher in the cloudless sky, the temperature grew uncomfortably warm. The desert-like terrain fairly baked under the sun's scorching rays.

When they finally reached the river, it was a welcoming sight. They stopped, watered their horses, then sat in the water fully dressed and playfully splashed each other. Their mood was chipper and their spirits were soaring. In a few hours, they planned to become husband and wife, leave Crystal Creek behind, and embark on their new life.

They left the cool river reluctantly, and began the last lap of their journey. They traveled nonstop and reached Crystal Creek late in the afternoon.

Mayor Wrightman, leaving the sheriff's office, caught sight of Cade and Jodie entering town. He hurried into the street, and waved his arms to get their attention. His effort was successful; they rode past Jodie's home and to the mayor.

"Riker's missing!" Wrightman grumbled. "I was opposed to making him sheriff. I knew he couldn't be trusted. He's probably holed up somewhere with a case of whiskey."

"How long has he been gone?" Cade asked, dismounting.

"No one has seen him since yesterday morning."

"What about my sister? Did you question her? She and Riker are friends."

"No, I didn't think about it. Actually, I didn't know they were friends. She probably doesn't know where he is anyhow. Riker's a drunk, and he's undoubtedly on a binge."

Cade turned to Jodie, who was still astride the Appaloosa. "Why don't you go home and get some rest? I'll talk to Alison. Maybe she knows something."

Jodie was willing to cooperate, for she was indeed tired. A bath and a couple of hours' rest sounded heavenly. After all, tonight she had very important plans.

"After I talk to Alison," Cade continued, "I'll pay a visit to Reverend Smith. I hope he can marry us on such short notice."

"I'm sure he can," Jodie replied. "Come to the house and let me know what you learn."

He said that he would, and she turned the Appaloosa around and started back down the street.

"I guess congratulations are in order," Wrightman said, offering Cade his hand.

He shook the mayor's hand firmly.

"Do you and Jodie plan to stay here?"

"No. I have a ranch in Texas. We'll be leaving as soon as possible. If you'll excuse me, I need to see my sister."

"But if you leave, who will take care of this town? It's obvious that Riker can't do his job."

"I suggest you start looking for a new sheriff. In the meantime, wire the governor; he can send you a law officer."

"But you're a law officer, and you're already here."

"I plan to send a wire myself—announcing my retirement." He tipped his hat, bid the mayor a good day, and went to the hotel.

He climbed the stairs, hastened to his sister's room, and

knocked eagerly on the door. He was anxious to share his good news. Last night, he and Jodie had discussed Alison. Jodie was in favor of Alison living with them. In fact, she would have it no other way.

He knocked again, louder this time. Still, there was no answer. He turned the knob and found that the door was unlocked. He went inside, looked about, and was relieved to find that Alison's belongings were still there. For a moment, he had feared that she had run away to the Comancheros' hideout.

He left the room, hurried down the stairs, and went to the front desk.

"Can I help you, Marshal?" the proprietor asked.

"I'm looking for Miss Brandon. Have you seen her?"

"Not since yesterday. Isn't she is her room?"

"No, she isn't there."

The hotel maid was dusting the lobby, and the proprietor called to her. "Have you seen Miss Brandon?" he asked, as she came over to see what he wanted.

The young Mexican woman replied, "No, señor."

"Did she order any meals today?"

"No, señor."

The proprietor turned to Cade and explained, "Miss Brandon has her meals in her room." He indicated the maid with a wave of his hand. "Maria takes Miss Brandon's order to the restaurant, then delivers the meal to her room."

"Señorita Brandon has not sent for me in two days," Maria said. "I fixed up her bed yesterday morning, but this morning it was already made. Maybe she did not sleep in her bed last night."

"She must be with Riker," Cade mused aloud. "If she comes back to her room, tell her to stay there." He whirled around and left the hotel.

Cade was plagued with mixed feelings as he went to his horse and mounted. He didn't know if he should be upset with Alison and Riker, or be worried about them. More than likely, Riker had gone on a drinking binge and Alison was trying to help him. He had to look for them, but he didn't know where to start.

He guided his horse toward Jodie's house. His expression, though troubled, was also angry. It could take hours to find Riker and Alison!

"So much for getting married tonight!" he grumbled.

Chapter
Twenty-Seven

Jodie was in the parlor with her aunt when Cade arrived. He asked if he could see her alone on the front porch.

"What is it?" she asked, as they stepped outside.

"I think Alison is with Riker. No one at the hotel has seen her, and the maid said her bed wasn't slept in last night. Do you have any idea where Riker might have taken her?"

"No, I don't," she replied. "Unless . . ."

"Unless, what?"

"Maybe they went to Jonas's home. There's nothing left but a charred chimney, but I know Jonas rides out there often. He always has a bottle with him. I guess he stares at the ruins, drinks, and remembers."

"Where is his place?"

"Due west. His land borders Bradley's spread. I can ride with you and show you where it is."

"I think I can find it. Why don't you stay home and get some rest?" He reached for her and she went into his arms. "I guess we'll have to cancel getting married tonight. How about tomorrow night?"

She smiled. "I'll have to check my social calendar, but I think I'm free."

"In that case, you wanna get married?"

She pretended to think it over. "Why not? I don't have anything better to do."

He kissed her tenderly. "I love you, darlin'."

She placed a hand at the nape of his neck, urging him to kiss her again.

He released her reluctantly. "If I don't find Riker and Alison at the ruins, I'll keep on looking. They've got to be around here somewhere."

"But what if they aren't?"

"I don't know. I'll face that decision when I come to it."

"We'll face it together," she said. "I know you, Cade Brandon. You'll search this countryside from one end to the other looking for Alison, and I intend to ride with you."

"I'd have it no other way," he murmured, drawing her close.

As he bent his head, she met his lips halfway, and kissed him with passion.

"Don't wait up for me," he said. "I might not be back until dawn or later."

"But I will see you in the morning, won't I?"

"Of course. I'll take you to Caroline's for breakfast."

He moved quickly down the porch steps. His horse's reins were looped about the hitching rail; he drew them free, then swung into the saddle.

"Be careful," Jodie called to him as he turned his horse around and started out of town. She remained on the porch and watched until Cade rode out of sight. Riker's and Alison's disappearance was mystifying, and she was somewhat troubled as she went back into the house; she hadn't ruled out foul play. Although Cade hadn't said anything, she knew it was on his mind too.

Doris was waiting for her in the parlor. "Is anything wrong?" she asked Jodie.

"Cade's sister is missing, and so is Jonas. Cade's looking for them."

"I haven't lived in Crystal Creek all that long, but I do know it's not rare for Jonas to disappear for a day or two."

Jodie agreed; Riker was most likely on a drinking binge, and somehow Alison had gotten involved.

A becoming blush colored Doris's cheeks. "Jodie," she began, "I have something to tell you. Mr. Daniels had called her a couple of times. I expect him later this evening. We are taking a buggy ride."

Jodie was pleasantly surprised. "You and Mr. Daniels? That's marvelous. Does Laura know?"

"Yes, she knows. But Laura's too unhappy to think about Mr. Daniels and me."

"Why is she unhappy?"

"Well, things didn't work out between her and Bill. I'm not sure what happened, but she said Bill was too overbearing and pompous. Also, I took your advice and told Laura she should ask Caroline for a job."

"Where is Laura?"

"In her room. She's been there all day."

"She's just feeling sorry for herself, Aunt Doris. She'll get over it. I think I'll take a bath before dinner."

Doris leapt to her feet. "Dinner! I almost forgot—I have a roast in the oven."

Laura refused to join her mother and Jodie for dinner. She did, however, allow Doris to bring a filled tray to her room.

Dinner was over, and the dishes were washed and put

away when Mr. Daniels called. He and Doris left for their buggy ride.

Jodie was considering talking to Laura and trying to lift her spirits when a knock sounded on the door. She was surprised to find Dirk. He had been drinking heavily, and he stumbled through the doorway.

"I gotta talk to you," he said drunkenly.

"What do you want, Dirk?" she asked, her tone testy.

"I ain't been home since yesterday," he began. "I've been with Lilly."

Jodie knew Lilly worked at the Silver Dollar.

"I told Lilly to tell me . . . to tell me when . . . you and Brandon got back." Dirk began to slur his words. "Ever since . . . it happened . . . I've been in Lilly's room . . . drinkin' and . . . and you know what else. How long you been back?"

"A few hours," she said, her patience wearing thin.

"Damn that Lilly! I told her . . . to let me know the moment you got back to town."

"Dirk, what did you come here to tell me?"

"I came to tell . . . to tell you 'bout Breed and Edwards."

Jodie tensed. "What about them?"

"They broke into the sheriff's office and took Riker . . . and Miss Brandon. I just . . . happened to be there. I swear I didn't have anything to do with it. Breed's got them at the Grahams' way station. He said if you and Brandon don't show up, he'll kill them both."

"Why haven't you told anyone about this?"

"Breed said if I told anyone except you and Brandon, he'd come back here and kill me."

She eyed him sharply. "I doubt your innocence in this, Dirk!" She shoved him back through the open doorway. "Go home, and stay there! I'll tend to you later!" With that, she slammed the door in his face.

She moved down the hall to Laura's room. She knocked;

when there was no reply, she barged inside. Her cousin was in bed, but she hadn't extinguished the lamp.

Jodie's intrusion sent Laura sitting upright. "How dare you come in here uninvited!"

"I knocked!" she replied.

"Jodie, when I didn't answer that meant I didn't want to be disturbed."

Jodie controlled a sudden urge to slap her cousin across the face. "I'm leaving town," she began crisply. "Breed and Edwards are holding Jonas and Alison at the Grahams' way station. Cade is out looking for Alison and Jonas, but I don't have time to try to find him. I'm afraid Breed will grow impatient and kill his hostages. Cade will be here in the morning. I want you to tell him that I decided to go to the way station. Tell him I was afraid if one of us didn't show up soon, Jonas and Alison would die."

"Honestly, Jodie! You're such a fool! Don't you realize Breed will kill you, as well as the hostages?"

"Not if I kill him first!" With that, she whirled around and went to her room, where she changed into riding clothes. She got her rifle, extra ammunition, and hastened to the stable out back. As she saddled her Appaloosa, she wondered if she should wait for Cade, or else look for him. But finding him could take hours, hours that might cost Jonas and Alison their lives. She decided enough time had been wasted—thanks to Dirk!

She rode out of town and headed south. She knew she was heading into territory frequented by raiding Apaches. Breed was not the only danger; renegade warriors could very well pose an even bigger threat.

Breed, sitting at the table, opened the second bottle of whiskey, tilted it to his mouth, and took a big drink. He had consumed enough liquor to be drunk, but Breed could drink twice as much as the average man. He was still in control of his faculties, for whiskey rarely affected him.

Edwards was lying on a pallet and was sound asleep. The man irritated Breed, and he wished he hadn't teamed up with him. Well, he didn't intend to be saddled with him much longer!

Breed's gaze went to the hostages. They were still sitting in the corner, the woman's head resting on the sheriff's shoulder. A grin curled his lips as he begrudgingly gave the woman credit for defending herself against Edwards. The horny bastard got what he deserved!

Breed helped himself to another drink, leaned back in his chair, and propped his feet on the table. His thoughts drifted to Jodie. He couldn't help but hold her in high esteem; she was courageous, and Breed admired courage. He was anxious to kill Brandon and then find a way to even the score with Lopez, but for some reason that he couldn't define, killing Jodie was somehow unsettling. She was beautiful, true, and Breed found her desirable. But he knew these feelings she provoked in him were deeper than physical. Breed was a loner; he had no real friends. He had never met a person he admired enough to call him a friend. But he admired Jodie; when she was his prisoner, she had handled herself exceptionally well—there were no tears and no hysteria. Later, she had captured Edwards as easily as a wolf captures a rabbit. Hidden in the shrubbery, he had watched the shootout that ensued; as the Marshal eliminated one man, Jodie had shot the other one without a moment's hesitation.

He took another drink, and the liquor had a soothing effect as it traveled through his body, relaxing his muscles and lulling his mind. He planned to ride to the hideout of the Comancheros that were led by Hernando's stepfather. Unlike Hernando's men, this band of outlaws was more to his liking, for they were vicious and lived by their own rules; only the fittest survived. A vision of Jodie flashed

across his mind—maybe he'd kill the Marshal but keep
the woman. He could take her to the Comancheros' hideout, leave her there, then come back and kill the Bradleys.
He wanted the thousand dollars Dirk had promised. Afterward, he'd return to the hideout and claim the woman
deputy. That such a plan even crossed his mind gave him
quite a start. He wasn't like Red and Edwards; he thought
with his brain, not with his pecker! But just thinking about
Jodie caused a stirring in his loins. Women were not
important in Breed's life; their only purpose was to satisfy
his lust—a night with a prostitute took care of that. But
he knew the woman deputy was different; he wanted to
fully possess her.

He put the bottle to his mouth and guzzled two huge
drinks. Admitting to himself that a woman had gotten to
him was hard.

Across the room, Alison, her head still on Riker's shoulder, was watching Breed. She could tell that he was
engrossed in his thoughts. "I wonder what's going through
Breed's mind," she whispered.

"He's probably thinking about killing us," Jonas replied.

"No, I don't think so. He . . . he almost looks like a man
dreaming about the woman he loves."

Riker laughed shortly. "Men like him don't fall in love."

"Nobody is immune to love. Not even Breed."

"I didn't know you were such a romantic."

She smiled lamely. "I suppose I am being foolish."

"Why don't you make yourself a pallet and get some
sleep?"

She agreed, and getting to her feet, she asked Breed if
she could spread blankets for herself and Jonas. He gave
his permission. He then escorted Alison outside, and told
her she could use the outhouse out back. Returning, he
had her lie on the blanket, and he tied her hands and
feet. He also took Riker outside, and upon their return,

he bound the sheriff's feet. Binding his hands wasn't necessary, for they were still cuffed.

Breed sat at the table, picked up the bottle, took a drink, then capped it. Now that the hostages were secured, he felt free to lean back in his chair and close his eyes. He dozed off and on through the night, but he never slept soundly; his Comanche instincts remained vigilant.

At dawn, Breed awoke Edwards and told him to watch the prisoners.

Jason's wound ached considerably, and as he sat up with a grimace, he asked, "Where are you goin'?"

"I will ride out and see if I can spot Brandon and the woman."

"How long will you be gone? I'm hurting real bad, and I don't know how long I can keep an eye on the hostages."

"I'll be back soon," he grumbled. However, if things turned out the way Breed was hoping they would, he wouldn't be back at all. He hoped to come across Brandon and Jodie, kill the Marshal, and take Jodie with him to the Comancheros' hideaway. He still wasn't sure why the woman held such power over him, but once she was his for the taking, the puzzle would surely be solved.

As he walked outside, the possible fate of those he was leaving behind didn't worry him in the least. He would have enjoyed killing Edwards, and the possibility that he might give up that pleasure was disappointing. He supposed if he didn't return, Edwards would kill the prisoners and leave.

He went to the stables and saddled his horse. He considered going back inside and packing provisions, but decided not to. It would only cause Edwards to start asking a bunch of questions. If things worked out the way he hoped, then he and the woman could survive off the land on their journey to the mountains that sheltered the Comancheros.

Breed mounted his horse and galloped away from the way station. The morning sun had cleared the horizon. Its rays were already uncomfortably warm, and Breed knew the day was going to be scorchingly hot.

Cade halted his horse in front of Jodie's home. He dismounted wearily, for he was extremely tired. He had spent the entire night searching for Alison and Riker. His mind was troubled as he climbed the porch steps and knocked on the door. It was as though Alison and Riker had disappeared from the face of the earth.

Doris answered his knock, and she invited him into the parlor.

"I need to see Jodie," he said.

Doris had returned home late last night. She had peeked in on Laura, who was asleep, then she had gone straight to her room. She had assumed that Jodie was in bed.

"I'll get her for you," Doris told Cade. She turned to leave the parlor, but Laura's sudden appearance gave her reason to pause.

"You won't find Jodie in her room," Laura announced. She looked at Cade; he was indeed a handsome devil! Suddenly she was even more jealous and resentful of Jodie.

"Where is she?" Cade asked.

Laura was glad she had donned one of her prettiest robes; she had left the sash untied, and as she moved farther into the room, the robe parted, revealing the sheer gown beneath. She gazed into Cade's face, wondering if he was enjoying the seductive view. She was disappointed to find his expression impatient instead of admiring.

"She came to my room last night," Laura began. She relished the news she was about to disclose; surely Brandon would be so enraged that he'd leave Jodie for good. Because she was miserable, she wanted everyone else to be miserable—especially Jodie!

"She told me Dirk came here to see her," Laura continued. "He told her that he was at the sheriff's office when Breed and Edwards broke in. They took your sister and the sheriff to a way station. I think Jodie said it was owned by someone named Graham. I assume they intend to trade the hostages for you and Jodie. Anyway, that's the impression I got. Jodie wasn't very informative. She simply told me she was leaving for the way station."

Cade was upset. "Damn! Why didn't she wait for me?"

Laura knew why; Jodie had made that point quite clear— she was afraid Breed and Edwards would kill the hostages if one of them didn't show up soon. But she didn't bother to pass that information on to Cade; instead, she said, "I'm sure you know how badly Jodie wants that thousand dollar reward. Believe me, there was no stopping her."

Cade left at once and headed toward the livery for a fresh horse. His stallion was too fatigued to make it to the way station. He also intended to rent two horses for Alison and Riker in case the animals were needed. He wished Jodie had waited, or else had come looking for him. What chance did she think she had alone against Breed and Edwards? Laura's words raced across his mind—did the thousand dollar bounty still mean that much to Jodie? Was she still afraid to marry him without money to fall back on? He had believed she had gotten past her insecurities and had complete faith in their love. He wondered if he could have been mistaken. The possibility piqued his impatience, as well as his anger.

He thrust such thoughts aside. Lives were in danger, and he must concentrate on finding a way to save everyone. He would deal with Jodie later. That is, if they were still alive after confronting Breed. Cade knew the half-breed was a formidable enemy, and the odds that everyone would come out of this unharmed were extremely low.

* * *

Following an hour of her mother's prodding, Laura dressed and went to the restaurant to ask for a job. In her opinion such menial work was degrading. Also, she was lazy and hated any kind of work. It was her nature to be rich and pampered; she had come so close to fulfilling that dream with Lawson. If the man weren't such a prude . . . She wrote him off as a lost venture, for she wasn't about to dwell on what she could not change.

She entered the restaurant reluctantly. She had never looked for a job in her life, and could hardly believe that she had stooped so low.

The establishment wasn't very crowded; only a few patrons were having breakfast. She saw Dirk; he was sitting alone. His clothes were wrinkled, as though he had slept in them. He needed a shave, and his eyes were bloodshot. Laura wondered if he was suffering a hangover. She paused to study him, her calculating mind quickly forming a plan. Dirk's father was wealthy, and if she were to marry Dirk, she would be a part of all that wealth. She would prefer to marry Emmett Bradley, for he controlled the money. However, trapping an older and more experienced man might be too difficult; therefore, she decided to inveigle the son. She had heard rumors that Dirk wasn't too intelligent, which should make her task even easier. Marriage to Dirk might be a delightful adventure, for he was young, handsome, and no doubt easily controlled.

Plastering a smile on her face, she went to his table. "Good morning, Dirk."

"Miss . . . Miss Talbert," he stammered, getting to his feet. That she had come to his table surprised him. He had admired her from the day she moved to Crystal Creek, but she had never shown him any interest.

"May I join you?" she asked.

"Yes, of course," he said, pulling out a chair.

"You seemed very deep in thought. Are you worried about Mr. Riker and Miss Brandon?"

He returned to his chair. "I guess Jodie told you what happened."

"Yes, she did. I hope you aren't blaming yourself."

"It wasn't my fault," he was quick to reply.

"I'm sure no one thinks that."

"Did you come here for breakfast?" Dirk asked.

Laura forced tears, and her chin quivered. "Oh, Dirk!" She sighed pensively. "I'm here to ask for employment. My poor mother isn't well, and I must find a means to take care of her."

"That's very admirable of you."

She reached across the table and placed a hand on his. "You know, I have a marvelous idea. Asking for a job can wait—why don't we take a buggy ride? I do need to get away from this town, if only for an hour or so. Will you please do me this favor?"

Dirk was flattered; he was also pleasantly taken aback, for ladies like Miss Talbert never had anything to do with him. Laura's sudden interest in him was indeed an unexpected surprise. She was beautiful, classy, and a real lady; he had always believed a woman like her was beyond his reach. He didn't bother to question her motives, for Dirk's thoughts never delved below the surface, which made him the perfect candidate for Laura's selfish ploy.

"Miss Talbert, I'd be pleased to rent a buggy and take you for a ride."

"Please call me Laura." Her smile was radiant, seductive, and as sly as the proverbial cat who had just swallowed an unsuspecting canary.

Chapter Twenty-Eight

The weather was unbearably hot, and Jodie reined in, dismounted, and reached for her canteen. She took a drink, then poured some water into her hat and offered it to the Appaloosa.

She was still four hours away from the way station. With a weary sigh, she wiped an arm across her perspiring brow. She wished clouds would roll in, but it didn't seem likely; the sun was alone in the cerulean sky. Boulders were at her back, and she was tempted to sit in their shade and rest for a few minutes. But time was essential, and she decided to keep moving. She was about to mount when a shot rang out; it came from behind one of the boulders. The bullet struck at her feet, sending dirt swirling about her ankles.

The shot startled the Appaloosa, and it pranced nervously as Jodie reached for her rifle. She couldn't unsheathe it, for the horse refused to stand still. She grabbed hold of its reins with one hand, and tried again to draw the Winchester. But it was too late.

"Touch that rifle, and I'll kill you!" a man's voice warned her.

She backed away from the weapon and whirled around. Breed, his rifle in hand, rode out from behind a boulder. He guided his horse to the Appaloosa, drew Jodie's Winchester, and removed the bullets. He then slipped it back into its leather case. Going through her saddlebags, he found extra ammunition and transferred it to his own supply. The bullwhip didn't escape his notice, and he took that too. He then turned his full attention to Jodie, who was watching him. For a moment, he studied her as a man studies a woman—she was dressed in trousers, but the manly attire didn't take away from her femininity. Quite the opposite; the trousers emphasized her womanly hips and shapely legs. Her blouse, wet from perspiration, hugged her full breasts—the effect was enticing. Chestnut curls cascaded from beneath her wide-brimmed hat, the silky ringlets framing a face Breed had found unforgettable.

Jodie saw the desire in his eyes, and it gave her quite a start. When she had been Breed's prisoner, he had never looked at her this way. Red, yes! But certainly not Breed!

"Get on your horse," he told her.

"Are the hostages all right?" she asked, mounting.

"They are unharmed. Why isn't the Marshal with you?"

"I left without him. He was away searching for the sheriff and his sister. When he learns what has happened, he'll come to the way station."

"To try to save you?"

"Yes, as well as the others."

"He will be disappointed to find that you are not there."

"What do you mean?" she asked.

"We are not going to the way station."

"But I thought—"

"My plans have changed," he butted in. "I have decided that you and I will ride to the Comancheros' hideout."

"I don't understand why you want to go there. Hernando is no longer a Comanchero; even if he was, he wouldn't help you."

"Where is Hernando?"

"He's living with Antonio Morelos. Antonio is his father."

Breed sneered. "So Hernando is now an aristocrat." He shrugged his massive shoulders. "It doesn't matter. We are not going to Hernando's hideout. We will ride to Federico Lopez's camp. He is Hernando's stepfather."

"Why are you taking me there?"

"Why do you think?" The message in his eyes was starkly lustful.

A shiver ran up her spine. "I thought you weren't like that."

"Why not? I am a man. Killing a woman like you is a waste. But do not misunderstand me—if you force my hand, I will not hesitate to kill you. You are probably thinking the Marshal will save you, but he won't. I will leave you with the Comancheros, return, and kill the Marshal and the Bradleys."

"The Bradleys?" she asked.

"The father and the oldest son. Dirk will pay me a thousand dollars to kill them."

"Dirk actually hired you to kill Emmett and Garth? I've always known Dirk was shiftless, but I never imagined he could do something like this."

"I will kill the Bradleys and take the thousand dollars. With that much money, I can pay Federico to let us stay with him for a long time."

Determination flashed in her eyes. "I'll find a way to escape, if I have to kill you!"

"You give yourself too much credit. You are a good shot, and you are very brave. But you can't get away from me. Don't even try, for it will anger me. You do not want to see me angry." Although he spoke calmly, there was a threatening undertone to his words that Jodie didn't take lightly.

Breed waved a terse hand. "Let's go. We have a long way to travel. We must ride far into the mountains."

They galloped away from the area, and Breed rode along-side his captive. Jodie was somewhat in shock, for she had never expected this type of abduction from Breed, which made it all the more terrifying. She hoped to escape, but she knew such a feat was unlikely. Breed wasn't the kind who made mistakes, and only through his negligence would she find an opportunity to get away.

Her thoughts went to Cade. He would come looking for her and Breed. She hoped he would find them before they reached the foothills, for tracking them in the mountains was very risky—it was Comanchero land! Jodie doubted Federico was anything like Hernando. Federico would cer-tainly kill a U.S. Marshal.

The sun rose higher and higher in the cloudless sky; the land baked beneath its scorching rays. Breed was forced to decrease their pace to a slow walk, for it was too hot to exert the horses.

Laura and Dirk sat on a blanket in the shade of a tree, and streaks of sunlight lanced through the small gaps in the full-leaf branches. Although the temperature was high, it remained fairly cool beneath the tree's green umbrella.

Dirk was enjoying himself, for he found Laura a pleasant and beautiful companion. He was totally mesmerized, and fawned over her as though he were grateful to be in her presence.

His adoration pleased Laura, for she was certain cajoling him into marriage would not be a problem. In fact, having Dirk for a husband might be delightful—he would surely idolize her and give her anything her heart desired. This time, however, she would change her tactics; she had tried seduction with Lawson and had failed miserably—she would trap Dirk with sweetness and vulnerability.

Now, as she gazed demurely into his eyes, she murmured, "I want to thank you, Dirk, for spending this time with me. But I suppose we should return to town. I need to talk to Caroline. I do hope she'll give me employment."

"I can't imagine you waiting tables. I mean, all kinds of characters eat at Caroline's. Why, there's no telling who you'll come into contact with."

"It can't be that bad," she said, pretending a brave smile.

"It just isn't the place for someone like you. Furthermore, a delicate lady like yourself shouldn't have to work at all."

She sighed heavily. "My father didn't leave much of an inheritance. I'm afraid finding employment is necessary. I must keep food on the table and take care of my mother."

He dared to hold her hand. "It's a shame you don't have a man to take care of you."

She lowered her eyes, as though she was suddenly embarrassed. "I suppose you think I'm a . . . a spinster."

"No, I don't," he answered quickly. "I didn't mean to imply something like that. You're so beautiful that I'm sure you've had a lot of marriage proposals."

She raised her gaze, smiled timidly, and murmured, "A few gentlemen have asked me to marry them, but none of them was the right man for me."

"What kind of man are you looking for?"

He still held her hand, and she tightened her fingers about his. "I want a man who will love me more than anything else."

"I could love you that way," he said, the words spilling forth. He hoped she wouldn't think him too forward; after all, ladies like Miss Talbert were very sensitive.

She smiled inwardly. "Could you really love me like that?"

"Yes, I could, without a doubt."

Forcing a blush, she dropped her gaze modestly. "Dirk, I do hope you aren't trifling with me."

"I wouldn't do that," he swore.

She decided the game had gone far enough for now. "I think we should leave," she said. "We've been gone for quite some time. Mother is probably looking for me."

As Dirk stood and helped her to her feet, she pretended to trip on the blanket they had been sitting on. She fell gracefully into his arms.

Having Laura so close was a temptation Dirk couldn't resist. He drew her against him, bent his head, and kissed her deeply. Her response sent his hopes soaring. He had never dreamed that someday he might marry a lady like Miss Talbert. More amazing, she truly cared about him; after Breed killed Emmett and Garth, there would be lots of women in his life, all of them after his money. But not Laura—she was evidently sincere.

They went to the buggy and started back to town. Dirk sat quietly, for his thoughts were elsewhere. He hadn't been home since he had let Breed and Edwards into the jail. His father was undoubtedly enraged—he might even send him packing. A terrifying thought struck—what if Emmett disinherited him before Breed had a chance to strike? Dirk quickly decided to try to make amends with his father. Laura could probably help. If his father knew he was courting a well-bred lady, he'd certainly believe his son was ready to settle down and change his ways.

He turned to Laura. "Will you come to my home tonight for dinner? I'll pick you up at five o'clock."

"Thank you, Dirk. I'd be pleased."

He placed a hand on hers. "Laura, why don't you wait a few more days before asking Caroline for a job?"

"Why should I do that?"

He grew bold. "Maybe someone will ask you to marry him."

She smiled sweetly. "Why, Dirk Bradley, are you saying what I think you are?"

"Would you be offended?"

"Offended? I hardly think so! I would be honored and deeply flattered." She moved closer, slipped her hand in the crook of his arm, and rested her head on his shoulder. "I can't believe we have known each other all this time, and never realized how right we are for each other."

He agreed; their sudden romance was indeed unexpected. But he was too mesmerized and too infatuated to be suspicious. Laura had him right where she wanted him—totally hoodwinked!

Edwards, his pistol in his lap, sat at the table. His wound ached painfully, and he took a drink from the whiskey bottle Breed had left behind. He hoped the liquor would numb the pain. Also, he was growing more worried by the minute, for Breed had been gone for hours. He began to wonder if something had happened to him. Maybe Brandon killed him, or he could have been killed by a band of renegade Apaches. Either possibility was terrifying to Edwards. If the Marshal killed Breed, then he would be coming after him next. If Apaches were the culprits, they might very well come to the way station, and he wouldn't stand a chance against a band of warriors. Saddling his horse and leaving began gnawing at his mind. But what should he do about the hostages? He thought it over and decided he'd kill the sheriff but take the woman with him. If Brandon trailed him, he'd need the woman for bargaining power.

Breed's failure to return was also preying on Jonas's and Alison's minds. That he might be dead had also entered their thoughts. What that would mean to them, they weren't quite sure. Alison was hopeful that Edwards would set them free, but Jonas didn't think so, for he knew Edwards was a cold-blooded killer.

Alison was sitting close to Jonas, and he whispered too softly for Jason to overhear, "Edwards isn't going to wait here much longer. We've got to do something soon."

"But what?" she asked quietly.

Alison's hands were bound, and he said, "Ask Edwards to untie you. Tell him you want to make a pot of coffee."

"Then what?"

"You must find a way to get his gun."

She tensed and her nerves fluttered. She wasn't sure she could manage such a feat. She wished she were more like Jodie, for she would undoubtedly get the better of Edwards. She drew a deep breath, calmed her nerves, and told herself she could fend him off. Jason's wound was proof of that!

"Mr. Edwards," she called. "Will you please untie me? I'd like to make a pot of coffee."

He swigged another drink of whiskey, then capped the bottle. Although the liquor eased his discomfort, getting drunk could be a fatal mistake. It was imperative that he stay alert. Coffee would certainly help. Pushing back his chair, he went to the hostages, drew Alison to her feet, and untied her hands. He then gave her an abrupt shove toward the kitchen.

As she prepared the coffee, Edwards returned to his chair. He again placed the gun on his lap. Sweat beaded up on his brow as he eyed the whiskey bottle. Surely, one more drink wouldn't matter. His wound burned as though a branding iron were searing his flesh. He reached for the whiskey, but his hand was clumsy and he knocked over the bottle.

Suddenly, Alison's hand appeared, placing the bottle upright. He looked on as she poured whiskey into a cup.

"Are you plannin' on gettin' me drunk?" he asked suspiciously.

"No," she replied. "I'm sure you're too smart to fall for such an obvious ploy. I poured you a drink because I feel responsible for your condition. I shouldn't have stabbed you. I know you're in pain, but your wound isn't life-threatening. You'll make a complete recovery."

"Oh yeah? Well, that doesn't make the pain any easier to bear."

She pulled up a chair and sat beside him. "I am truly sorry, but you see I lived with the Comanches for years, and sometimes I can be almost uncivilized. A Comanche woman would never submit to rape. However, she will submit to a man's dominance."

"What does that mean?"

"First, a man catches her interest through his virility. Then he wins her with his prowess."

Edwards still wasn't sure what she meant, but he liked the sound of it. Prowess? He felt he had a lot of that.

Alison placed a hand on his arm. "I think deep inside you are very virile. Maybe Breed's dominance overshadowed your manhood."

He was instantly offended. "Nobody overshadows my manhood!"

Her fingers caressed his arm. "Then why did you try to rape me? Why didn't you make me want you because you're such a powerful man?"

"You think like a damned Comanche squaw!"

"Have you ever bedded a Comanche woman?"

"Hell, no!"

She laughed as though she knew something he didn't.

"What's so damned funny?" he grumbled.

"Comanche women don't make love like white women. Didn't you know that?"

"Really. What do they do that's different?" The conversation was causing excitement to mount within him. Lust was all important to Edwards.

Alison played on this weakness. "I suppose savage is the

best way to describe sleeping with a Comanche woman. Although I dress like a white woman, don't let this disguise fool you. Underneath, I'm still a Comanche."

"How come you're sayin' these things to me?"

"Because I don't think Breed is coming back. I don't want to return to Crystal Creek. I hate living there. I want you to take me with you."

He gestured toward Riker. "What about him?"

She cast Jonas a look of disgust. "He is not a man! If he were, we wouldn't be your prisoners. A Comanche warrior would not have let this happen to me."

"I ain't no Comanche warrior. So how come you want to leave with me?"

"I want to return to my people. But until we go our separate ways, I'll do anything you want." She leaned closer and whispered in his ear, "You haven't lived until you've made love to a woman who responds with a savage force."

Edwards was beyond rational thought—he was now controlled by the stirring in his loins. He grew hard, and his manhood strained against his tightly fitting trousers.

His erection was apparent, and Alison slid her hand down to his thigh. "If you want, I can please you right now." She smiled cunningly. "Let me do it right here in front of Jonas. It'll serve the bastard right for letting me get captured."

"Please me?" he stammered. "Please me . . . how?"

"Put your gun on the table, and I'll show you."

He was more than willing to cooperate. Taking the pistol from his lap, he placed it on the table.

Alison's hand went immediately to his erection, and she caressed him through his trousers.

He moaned aloud with pleasure.

Meanwhile, Riker was extremely upset. When he asked Alison to try to get Jason's gun, he hadn't meant for her to do something like this. He shouted angrily for her to stop, but his outburst had no affect on her or Edwards. It was as though he wasn't even in the room.

Alison had indeed heard Riker's angry shout, but she was determined to go through with her ploy. Her life and Riker's depended on her success. As her fingers fumbled with the buttons confining Jason's erection, she leaned even closer and pressed her lips to his. His arms went about her at once, drawing her tightly against him. She kissed him passionately as her free hand inched its way to the pistol on the table. Grabbing it, she pushed out of his arms strongly, leapt to her feet, and aimed the gun at him. "Try anything, and I'll kill you!" she snapped harshly.

Edwards was enraged that he had let a woman dupe him so easily. Sex had always been his downfall, and had been the driving factor behind all his crimes.

Breed had left the key to Riker's handcuffs hanging on the peg beside the front door. Alison, keeping a sharp eye on Edwards, was about to make her way to the key when, suddenly, a rifle shot sounded, sending the front door off its hinges and making it hang obliquely.

Alison turned the gun toward the door and was poised to shoot the intruder.

The door was roughly pushed aside, and Alison sighed happily as Cade darted inside, his rifle ready to fire. He stood still for a moment as his eyes swept over the room.

"Where are Jodie and Breed?" he asked.

"I don't know," Alison replied. She got the key, hurried to Riker, and removed his cuffs.

Cade took the handcuffs and put them on Edwards. Clutching his arm, he drew him away from the table, and shoved him down onto the pallet where Edwards had spent the night.

Alison quickly poured coffee, and the three of them sat at the table. Cade was told that Breed had left early that morning and hadn't returned.

"He said he was going to look for you and Jodie," Alison explained.

A creeping uneasiness settled in the pit of Cade's stomach. "Breed must have found Jodie. But where in the hell are they? Why didn't he bring her back here?"

No one ventured a reply, for Alison and Jonas were just as confused as Cade.

Brandon finished his coffee, stood, and said to Riker, "Take Alison back to Crystal Creek." He indicated Edwards with a jerk of his head. "Take that piece of scum with you. The sheriff from Abilene should arrive soon to pick him up. I'm going to look for Jodie and Breed."

Alison got to her feet, and placed a hand on her brother's arm. "I'll pray for you and Jodie."

He embraced her warmly. "I guess I should have said this sooner, but I'm glad you're unharmed."

"Please be careful," she pleaded.

"I brought extra horses," Cade said. "I left them in the stable out back." He kissed Alison's cheek, offered her a loving smile, then left as abruptly as he had arrived.

"I'll get the horses," Jonas mumbled, not quite meeting Alison's eyes. "We need to leave as quickly as possible."

She sensed his reserve. "Jonas, is something wrong?"

"Of course not," he replied, heading for the open doorway.

She followed him outside and onto the stoop. "I know something is bothering you," she insisted.

"You'd better get inside and keep an eye on Edwards." With that, he hurried down the steps and started toward the stables.

Alison went back into the way station. She had a feeling she knew what was bothering Jonas. He was probably resentful that she had inveigled Edwards. That he would hold that against her cut into her heart like an invisible dagger. She was deeply hurt, but she was also angry.

Chapter
Twenty-Nine

Following the ride with Laura, Dirk had ridden straight home, and was standing in the doorway when his father and Garth returned from working the spread.

That Dirk had the gall to actually meet him at the front door piqued Emmett's temper. His patience had reached its limit. Time after time he had forgiven his wayward son; each time Dirk had only disappointed him again.

"Pa," Dirk said anxiously. "I need to talk to you."

"We'll go to my study," Emmett replied, waving a hand in that direction. As he followed his son down the hallway and to the study, he had every intention of sending him packing.

They entered the room, and Emmett went to the liquor cabinet and poured himself a drink; he didn't bother to ask Dirk if he wanted one.

"Pa," Dirk began lamely, "I know you're mad at me, and I don't blame you. I shouldn't have stayed in town. I was at the Silver Dollar with Lilly. Well, I can promise you that nothing like that will ever happen again."

Emmett raised a dubious brow. "Why do you say that?"

" 'Cause something wonderful has happened—something so fantastic that it has changed my life. Bedding prostitutes, drinking, and gambling don't matter to me anymore. You know, the only reason I did those things was because I had such a poor opinion of myself." He smiled widely. "But I no longer feel that way. I feel real good about myself."

"And what caused this miraculous change?" Emmett asked, questioning his son's sincerity.

"Laura Talbert," he replied. "Pa, we spent the day together. I'm still kinda shocked that a lady like Miss Talbert would want my company. But Pa, she was real sweet to me, and she really enjoyed being with me. I asked her if she'd come here tonight for dinner, and she said that she would. I'm supposed to pick her up at five o'clock. It's all right with you, isn't it? I already told the cook we were having company."

"I certainly don't object to having Miss Talbert for dinner," Emmett replied. That Laura Talbert had spent the day with Dirk came as quite a surprise to Emmett, but it was a pleasant surprise. A lady like Miss Talbert would be a good influence on Dirk, and her interest in him might make him become a better man. Emmett was hopeful, for in spite of Dirk's shiftless ways, he still cared about him.

He returned to the liquor cabinet, poured a brandy for Dirk, and handed it to him. "I had every intention of sending you packing, but I've decided to give you one more chance. Your friendship with Miss Talbert pleases me. In time, maybe you two will fall in love."

"I don't need more time to fall in love with Laura. I'm already in love. And . . . and I think she feels the same way."

"I'm not sure love can happen that quickly."

"It can happen, Pa. Believe me!"

Emmett chuckled good-naturedly. "Come to think of it,

I loved your mother at first sight. However, I courted her for a year before we married."

"I hope I don't have to wait that long before I marry Laura."

Emmett placed an affectionate hand on his son's shoulder. "I can see you are very smitten. I can't say that I blame you. Miss Talbert is a beautiful young lady." He finished his drink, then said, "Since we're having company for dinner, I need to go upstairs, bathe, and change clothes." He glanced at his watch. "If you're going to pick her up at five o'clock, you should leave soon."

"I will, as soon as I finish my brandy." Dirk had already bathed and changed clothes.

Emmett left, and the moment the door closed behind him, Dirk's mouth lifted in a cold grin. He hadn't thought it would be so easy to get back into his father's good graces. Now, his inheritance was secure, and after Breed killed Emmett and Garth, this ranch and his father's money would be his—his and Laura's! He could hardly wait!

Shadows of dusk cloaked the Mexican plains, and in the far distance, twilight clad the mountain range with a purple mist. The land lay barren except for a few widely-spaced trees. Sunlight had faded; creatures of the day were burrowing into their dens or returning to their nests—nocturnal life was beginning to stir.

Jodie's Appaloosa plodded along slowly beside Breed's horse. The animals were as fatigued as their riders. The day had been extremely hot, and hours of travel beneath the sun's scorching rays had been almost unbearable. Jodie hoped Breed would decide to stop soon, for she was so tired she could barely stay in the saddle. But, more importantly, she knew her Appaloosa needed rest. Jodie wondered how much longer Breed intended to push the tired animals.

She was about to bring up the subject, but was stopped by the sight of a lone figure in the distance. The person was on foot, and was walking at a brisk pace.

Breed drew his pistol. "Looks like we got company," he told Jodie. "Stay abreast of me, or I'll put a bullet in that Appaloosa's head."

"Whoever that is, he isn't a threat to you. Why don't you just let him be?"

"Can't you see that's a damned Apache?"

Jodie looked closer at the distant figure. "So what if he is an Apache? He still isn't bothering you."

"You just keep up with me, or I'll kill your horse and you can travel the rest of the way on foot." He forced his tired mount into a gallop, and Jodie urged the Appaloosa to stay abreast.

Within minutes, they reached the lone traveler. He was unarmed, and as they reined in, he held up his arms in a don't-shoot pose. The Apache was only a boy; he couldn't be more than twelve or thirteen. His eyes were wide with fright, and his arms, over his head, trembled slightly.

"He's only a child," Jodie told Breed. "For God's sake, leave him alone!"

Breed paid her no mind; instead, he spoke to the boy in his own language. Although Breed's grasp of the language was limited, the boy understood enough of what he said to answer back.

Breed suddenly threw back his head and roared with laughter. His laugh was cruel and somehow evil; it sent a chill up Jodie's spine.

Breed's mirth stopped abruptly, as though it had been controlled by an inner switch that was suddenly turned off. "The kid was thrown from his pony," he said to Jodie. "Can you imagine that? An Apache bucked off his horse! Apparently, the pony bolted and took off like a shot out of hell. When this kid returns to his village, his peers will tease him, and the older warriors will berate him. The poor kid will be shame-faced and embarrassed for days, weeks, maybe even years. Maybe I should spare him such humiliation."

"No!" Jodie cried. "Breed, please don't hurt him! My God, you're part Indian yourself! Don't you feel any empathy for this boy at all?"

"I am part Comanche! This boy is Apache!" He spit to the ground, accentuating his disgust. "Apaches are filth; they hunt like dogs, kill like dogs, and should die like dogs!" With one quick flick of his wrist, he pointed his pistol at the boy and fired. His aim was perfect, and the young Apache fell to the ground, drew a final rasping breath, and died.

Breed inflicted his violence so quickly that the boy was already dead before Jodie's mind could fully grasp what had happened. She turned on Breed furiously. "You murderer! How could you? Dear God, how could you kill that child?"

He held up a silencing hand. "That's enough! Apaches are dogs! Any Apache who crosses my path will die." He gestured tersely toward the dead child. "That is one Apache who will not grow into a warrior! Nor will he sire any more Apaches!"

Breed slapped the reins against his horse, and motioned for Jodie to ride at his side. Holding their mounts to a steady canter, they continued onward. The tableau was soon blanketed by full darkness. The temperature dropped drastically, and a cool desert wind caressed the night air. The refreshing reprieve rejuvenated the tired horses, making it possible for them to maintain the brisk pace Breed had set.

Emmett, along with Garth, walked onto the front porch with Dirk and Laura. The evening had been pleasant, and Emmett had enjoyed having a lady at the dinner table.

Laura had effortlessly charmed the three Bradleys, and they found her beautiful, witty, and personable.

Taking her hand, Emmett kissed it lightly. "Thank you for gracing my home."

She smiled sweetly. "It is I who should thank you for such a pleasant evening."

"I am honored, my dear. I hope you'll visit again soon."

"I'd love to," she replied.

Dirk slipped her hand into the crook of his arm, and escorted her down the steps and to the buggy.

As Dirk was helping Laura, Emmett said softly to Garth, "For the first time in years, I dare hope that Dirk will become the man I want him to be. Miss Talbert will surely change him for the better, for it's quite obvious that she's very taken with him."

Garth agreed. "Dirk just had to sow his wild oats; that's all. He's finally ready to grow up and take on responsibility."

"Yes, a woman like Miss Talbert will do that to a man. Your mother certainly tamed me."

Dirk flipped the reins against the pair of horses, and as the buggy rolled away from the house, Laura turned and waved good-bye to Emmett and Garth. She then sat close to Dirk, and said with a happy sigh, "I had so much fun this evening. Your father and brother are very charming." She put a hand on his arm, squeezed gently, and continued, "But you are more charming. You're also very handsome."

He was flattered. "Do you really think I'm handsome?"

"Yes, I certainly do. If another woman even talks to you, I'll probably be besieged with jealousy."

He laughed lightly. "I'm the one who will be jealous. Laura, you're so beautiful that just looking at you takes my breath away."

She put a hand on his. "Darling, stop the buggy."

He pulled back on the reins. "Is something wrong?"

"No, nothing's wrong. I wanted you to stop so that you can kiss me."

He was eager to cooperate, and taking her into his arms, he pressed his lips to hers. She laced her hands about his neck, and returned his ardor fervently.

"Sweetheart," he murmured in her ear, "I don't think we should kiss like this."

"Why not?" she asked, pretending innocence.

"Well ... you see, kissing a beautiful woman like you does things to a man."

"Dirk, I'm terribly confused. Are you saying you don't want to kiss me?"

"No, of course not. I want to kiss you very much. But passionate kisses will have to wait until our wedding night."

Her hands flew to her face, as though she were hiding her embarrassment. "Oh Dirk! I am such an innocent fool! Please forgive me."

He brought her back into his arms. "You're innocent, my darling. But you aren't a fool."

As she buried her face in his shoulder, and clung to him tightly, she wondered how difficult it would be on their wedding night to make him think she was a virgin. She quickly decided faking it wouldn't pose a problem; after all, Dirk wasn't very smart.

"Dirk, darling, why must we torture ourselves when it isn't necessary? There's no reason for us to deny ourselves kisses or ... or anything else. We are both adults, and we know how we feel. Why should we wait? Let's get married as soon as possible. No, on second thought, let's elope!"

He sat back, stung. "Elope?"

"Yes, why not?" she asked, her eyes bright with glee. "I don't know about your father, but Mother will insist on a lengthy engagement and a large wedding. Why, we'll be lucky if we're married by this time next year. After all, we have to live our own lives. It's not my mother's or your father's life! We should do as we please." She kissed his lips softly. "And I would be most pleased to marry you without a moment's delay."

"I want the same thing," he uttered, his mouth seizing hers aggressively. His hand moved to touch her breasts; for only a moment, she allowed him the pleasure.

Then, pushing out of his arms, she murmured breathlessly, "Darling, please don't trifle with my affections. I do love you madly. But I can't let you touch me . . . touch me like that until I'm your wife. You do understand, don't you? Please say that you do!"

"Of course, I understand. And I love you all the more because you are a lady."

She smiled inwardly; inveigling Dirk was so easy that she almost laughed aloud. "Pick me up at dawn," she said. "We can leave notes for our parents telling them we have eloped. We can go to Santa Rita; it's only a few hours away. We can get married there, then come back day after tomorrow. Emmett and Mother will probably be a little upset, but I'm sure they'll get over it very quickly. We'll ask them to give us a reception. That should soothe their ruffled feathers."

Dirk wasn't especially worried about Emmett's ruffled feathers. Furthermore, if things went the way he had planned, Emmett would soon be dead, along with Garth. He hoped Breed still intended to carry out his part of their bargain. Surely, the thousand dollar payoff would keep Breed from changing his mind.

"I'll pick you up at dawn," Dirk told Laura. Tomorrow night loomed in his mind—he could hardly wait to bed his lovely bride! A large, satisfied smile curled his lips; everything was working out splendidly—he'd soon be the sole heir to his father's fortune, and Laura was the icing on his cake!

* * *

Alison's nerves were tightly strung as she and Jonas, along with their prisoner, rode into Crystal Creek. The journey back had been filled with tension, for Jonas had remained somewhat aloof. Alison had been tempted to confront his feelings, but she didn't want to say anything in front of Edwards. This problem between Jonas and her was personal.

As they approached the jail, Jonas told her, "Why don't you leave your horse here? Later, I'll take all three horses to the livery."

They reined in and dismounted. As Riker took Edwards's arm to escort him to the jail, Alison said, "Jonas, I'm going to the hotel. Will you stop by later?"

"Yes, if I can find someone to stay with Edwards."

"See that you do. We need to talk." With that, she turned around and headed across the street to the hotel. She entered the lobby and hurried up the stairs to her room. She sat on the bed, gave into her feelings, and cried softly. That Jonas could treat her this way hurt deeply.

She controlled her tears. Crying wouldn't change anything. She went to the dresser, poured water into a basin, and washed her face. Taking a brush she ran it briskly through her dark, silky tresses, which cascaded in black waves around her shoulders.

As she waited for Jonas, she began to pace back and forth. Surely, he would come to her. If he didn't, then she would go to him and demand that he speak his mind. The jail was one room and Edwards would certainly overhear their conversation, but she was quickly getting to the point where she no longer cared.

Alison had been in her room about thirty minutes when a knock sounded at the door. It was Jonas, and she let him in.

"I asked Mr. Daniels to stay with Edwards," Riker said. "I told him I wouldn't be gone long. What did you want to talk to me about?"

She placed her hands on her hips, and eyed him sternly. "Don't play dumb, Jonas! You know why I wanted to talk to you. I want you to tell my why you've been so cold and so . . . so rude!"

"I haven't been rude."

"But you do admit you've been cold."

"Yes, I suppose I have been. Alison, when I asked you to get Edwards's gun, I never meant for you to seduce him!"

"How else was I to get his gun? Did you expect me to overpower him physically?"

"No, but I didn't expect you to kiss him and to . . . to touch him!" Riker's eyes were shining angrily.

She met his anger head on. "Heaven forbid that I should actually kiss the man and soil my lips—touch him and soil my lily white hands! Don't treat me as though I've been sheltered all my life. I lived with the Comanches for years! Kissing Edwards and touching him is nothing compared to what the Comanche warriors forced me to do! Don't you dare pass judgment on me! I saved our lives the only way I knew how!"

"You don't understand. I'm angry because I'm jealous, and because I failed you."

"Jealous?"

"How do you think it made me feel to see you kiss and fondle another man?"

"But it meant nothing to me!"

"I realize that! But I still had to see it! I should have died before letting you do such a thing."

"But you didn't know what I had in mind."

He waved his arms angrily. "But I should have known! I failed you! I wanted to love you and protect you. You've been through so much, and have suffered abuse time and time again. Instead of me taking care of you, you took care of me. How do you think that makes me feel? I'm a failure; I've been a failure all my life!"

She moved to him and placed her hands on his arms. "Jonas, don't start blaming yourself. You blamed yourself when your family died, and it drove you to drinking. You are not a failure. You think you didn't save me, but you did." She took his hand and placed it on her chest. "You saved me here, deep inside—you saved my heart, my soul, and gave me life. Forget what happened at the way station. It doesn't matter. All that matters is that we're together, and that we have our whole lives ahead of us."

He drew her into his embrace. "I love you, Alison! God, how much I love you!"

"Then kiss me, my darling."

His lips caressed hers in a deep emotional commitment. "Will you marry me, Alison?"

"Yes, of course I will."

"How about next Sunday? Is that too soon?"

She gazed up into his face, and her expression was troubled. "Let's not set a definite date until Cade and Jodie return. I want my wedding day to be the happiest day in my life, and I couldn't be completely happy not knowing if Cade and Jodie are all right."

He agreed. "I understand. We'll wait."

She went back into his arms, and held him tightly. "God, I pray they will soon be home!"

Breed, finding a area protected by shrubbery, decided to stop for the night. By now, Jodie was so fatigued that she could barely dismount. She took a rolled blanket from her horse, spread it on the ground, and sat down. The dead Apache was very much on her mind, and she was still somewhat in shock. Not because Breed could kill unmercifully; it was the quickness that had shocked her. One second the boy had been alive, his arms held in surrender; the next second he was on the ground, dead.

She watched as Breed got a rope from his horse. He

unsheathed his knife and cut a strip. She figured he intended to keep her tied through the night. She wasn't surprised; she had been expecting it.

As he came toward her, the moonlight illuminated a strange gleam in his eyes; she couldn't quite define it, but it was somehow terrifying. Her body grew taut, and her heart pounded.

She was sitting in front of a sturdy bush. Breed, moving incredibly fast, shoved her down onto the blanket, grabbed her arms, put them over her head, wrapped the strip of rope about her wrists, and tied the end to the bush.

Jodie fought wildly, but to no avail, for her strength was no match against his.

He forcefully parted her legs and knelt between them. His hands fumbled at the buttons on her trousers, but she struggled so strongly that he couldn't get them undone. His patience snapped, and drawing back his arm, he struck her soundly across the face.

The blow was potent, and Jodie's head erupted in blinding white pain. She came close to passing out, but somehow found the strength to continue fighting back. She brought up a leg and tried vainly to knee him in the groin, but he was too quick for her.

He leered down into her face. "Stop squirming! It won't do you any good, and will only make me hit you again. Relax, and let me have my way with you. Once I am inside you, maybe I will understand this power you hold over me." He suddenly grinned. "Maybe you will enjoy having me deep inside you."

Her response was to spit in his face.

He wiped away the spittle; his rage was now beyond control. He slowly doubled his huge hand into a fist, held it above her face threateningly, and said, "You bitch, I will beat you into submission!"

Chapter Thirty

"You'll never beat me into submission!" Jodie cried angrily, her eyes meeting Breed's without a flinch. "I hate you! You killed my father! I'd rather die than submit! So if you're going to beat me, then you might as well beat me to death. If you don't, I swear to God, I'll find a way to kill you!"

"I admire your spirit," Breed said calmly, as though their discussion was casual. "You are like a rebellious filly that must be broken to its owner's will. You will learn to do as I say."

"Never!" Jodie said furiously.

Breed drew back his fist, for he did indeed intend to beat his captive into submission. However, before he could strike, the horses suddenly whinnied nervously. Breed heeded their warning, and forgetting about Jodie, he leapt to his feet. As his hand reached for the pistol strapped to his hip, more than a dozen Apache warriors, astride their ponies, broke through the surrounding shrubbery. Breed moved his hand away from his pistol, for the Apaches were heavily armed.

The warrior in charge spoke to his men; then he and two others dismounted. As his two comrades went to Breed and disarmed him, the leader knelt beside Jodie.

She gasped softly as she looked into a face she recognized.

"We meet again," the warrior remarked softly.

"Alchise," she murmured.

The swollen flesh above Jodie's left eye reflected the brutality she had suffered before Alchise and his warriors arrived. Alchise felt a pang of sympathy for the white woman. He unsheathed his knife and cut the rope binding her hands.

Sitting up, and rubbing her chafed wrists, Jodie noticed a bandage on Alchise's shoulder. When Lopez and his men attacked the Apaches' camp, Alchise had been wounded.

He fingered the bandage, as though her gaze had touched him physically. "I spare your life, remember? In return, you bring back Comancheros to kill me and my warriors."

"What did you expect me to do? You intended to kill my friends and the man I plan to marry."

Sudden admiration flickered in the warrior's eyes, but it was so fleeting that it went unnoticed by Jodie. He stood, motioning for Jodie to stand also.

She got to her feet. Her heart was pounding, and fear, like a boa constrictor, squeezed her chest so tightly that she could barely breathe; however, she exuded an outward calm. She was not about to let Alchise see that she was afraid.

The warrior admired the white woman's courage. But he made no mention of this, nor did his demeanor betray his feelings. "Why you with this man?" Alchise asked Jodie, his expression inscrutable.

"He abducted me," she replied.

"You alone when he take you?"

"Yes."

"Where he find you?"

"Close to the border."

"Why white woman ride alone?"

"It's a long story."

He figured it was not only a long story, but also an interesting one. This white woman stirred his curiosity. However, he didn't have time to dwell on it; he had something more important to take care of. Waving an angry hand at Breed, he asked Jodie, "Why he kill Apache boy?"

The question took her by surprise. "How . . . how did you know?"

"We find boy, then we follow tracks. Answer! Why he kill boy?"

"I don't know. Why don't you ask him?"

Alchise responded with a grin that puzzled her.

"How do you know I wasn't involved?"

"You are not the kind to kill boy. You save my brother. When Comancheros attack camp, you ask for my life and my warriors'. Tell me, white woman, you wish to see this man die? If we not get here, he rape you. You must hate him."

"Yes, I hate him. But not because he tried to rape me. He killed my father."

Alchise ended their discussion abruptly, and speaking in his own language, he told the rest of his men to dismount. Then, moving unexpectedly, he grabbed Jodie's arm, took her to one of his warriors, spoke to him, then handed Jodie over into his care. The warrior, who was much younger than the others, indicated that she was to sit down. He then sat beside her.

Jodie watched in horror as two Apaches ripped Breed's shirt from his body, then shoved him to the ground so that he was kneeling. Drawing a knife, one Apache cut a deep gash across Breed's chest, sending blood flowing copiously. The half-breed bit into his bottom lip to keep from crying out. Again, the Apache slashed his victim's flesh, bringing on even more blood. This time, a soft moan sounded deep in Breed's throat.

"Why is he torturing him?" Jodie cried out; she didn't really expect an answer.

"The warrior is called Zele," her young guard answered. "It was his son who was killed."

Jodie was surprised to find that her companion spoke English. "You speak my language very well."

"I learn your language before leaving reservation."

"How long will Zele torture Breed before he kills him?"

"A long time."

"Well, I don't intend to watch!" Jodie said, bounding quickly to her feet.

The young warrior leapt up to stop her. She alertly evaded his groping hand, and when he reached for her a second time, she avoided him again.

Alchise saw what was happening, and he hurried over. His eyes bore questioningly into Jodie's.

Although she was still afraid, she didn't show it. "I'm leaving!" she told Alchise, as though she were simply his guest.

To her amazement, he reacted amicably. "Why you want to leave?"

Zele delayed administering further pain to turn and watch Alchise and the white woman.

"I won't stay here and watch this kind of torture!" Jodie told Alchise.

"This man kill your father. You stay and watch him die." Alchise had thought she would enjoy watching the man die. "Apache woman not too weak to watch."

"I'm not an Apache woman. And this has nothing to do with weakness."

He believed her; this white woman was not weak.

"If I'm not your prisoner," she remarked, "then I want to leave, and I want to leave now!"

For a moment, Alchise was hesitant to let her go, and keeping her crossed his mind fleetingly. But she was too strong-willed to adapt to his way of life; she would never be his mate but would always be his prisoner. Holding Jodie against her will did not appeal to him; furthermore, she was white and he considered all whites his enemies.

He motioned for her to follow him. She walked behind, and as they passed Breed, she cast him a cursory glance. She caught a look of fear in his eyes, but she also saw resignation. He knew he was going to die, and he also knew his death would be slow and painful.

Alchise took her to the Appaloosa. "You leave," he told her.

She stepped quickly to Breed's horse, got her bullwhip and ammunition, then mounted the Appaloosa. She looked down at Alchise. "I thank you for sparing my life."

"Now we even," he replied. He slapped the Appaloosa's flank, sending her on her way. As Jodie rode through the thick shrubbery, Alchise returned to Zele, who was eager to resume his torture.

Jodie had almost cleared the foliage when Breed's scream of agony carried through the quiet night. She dared not imagine what Zele had done to bring on such a howl of pain. She coaxed the Appaloosa into a faster canter, for she was anxious to ride out of hearing range. But two more screams reached her ears before she was finally far enough away.

She reined in, loaded her Winchester, then headed north, toward the way station. She wondered if Edwards was still holding Alison and Jonas there as hostages, or had he left when Breed didn't return? That he might have killed Alison and Jonas was a possibility she had to consider. But then maybe Cade got there in time to save them. She prayed that she would not reach the way station only to find that Edwards had killed his hostages.

Jodie tried not to think about Breed as she rode through the peaceful night, its tranquility in stark contrast to the horrifying scene she had left behind. She wondered if Breed was dead by now; she hoped so, but she had a sickening feeling that he was still alive. The Apaches knew how to torture their victims for hours before death finally released them from their unbearable pain. A shiver rippled up her spine, and her stomach roiled. No man deserved such torture, not even Breed. But he would die the way he had lived—violently and unmercifully.

She spurred the Appaloosa into a brisk run, leaving Breed and the Apaches for behind, physically as well as mentally.

The first rays of dawn were falling across the plains when Jodie spotted a lone rider in the distance. She reined in and drew her Winchester. She watched warily as the figure rode in closer. Within minutes he was close enough for her to recognize him. It was Cade. She put away her rifle, dismounted, and awaited his arrival anxiously.

Cade spurred his steed into a faster gallop. When he reached Jodie, he brought his horse to an abrupt stop, leapt from the saddle, and caught Jodie as she flung herself into his arms.

He held her tightly, thankful, as well as amazed, to find her alone and unharmed. He kissed her forehead and was about to claim her lips when he noticed the ugly bruise above her eye. "My God!" he groaned. "Did Breed hit you?"

"Yes; I wouldn't cooperate."

Fury burned in Cade's dark eyes. "I'll kill him! I swear to God, I will!"

"By now, Breed's dead."

"By now? What does that mean?"

She told him about Breed killing the Apache boy and that Alchise and his warriors had followed their trail. She let Cade know that Alchise had saved her from Breed's assault. A slight quiver crept into her voice as she recounted Zele's intention to kill Breed painfully and unmercifully.

"Thank God, Alchise let me leave," Jodie finished. "I don't think I could have stood watching Breed die like that."

"Alchise must think a lot of you," Cade said.

"He spared my life because I asked Hernando to spare him and his warriors."

"I think his feelings go deeper than that."

Jodie's expression revealed that the possibility had not occurred to her.

Brandon smiled warmly. "You don't know, do you? You have no idea how you affect men. They not only find you physically attractive, but that independent spirit of yours is totally fascinating. Apparently, Alchise is no exception."

Jodie didn't think so; furthermore, she had learned from experience that most men balked at her independence. She laced her arms about Cade's neck, pressed her body flush to his, and murmured, "I only care about my effect on one man, and that man is you. How do I affect you, my darling?" She rubbed her thighs against his in a suggestive manner.

Grimacing, he said with a groan, "Hard. You have a very hard effect on me. You're also a teasing little vixen."

She stood on tiptoe, placed a hand at the nape of his neck, and urged his lips down to hers. Their kiss was passionate and filled with love.

As Alison and Jonas came to mind, she left his arms with a startling suddenness. "The way station!" she exclaimed. "Did you find Jonas and Alison?"

"Yes, I did. They're fine. I sent them back to Crystal Creek."

"And Edwards?"

"They took him with him." He regarded her intently. "Your thousand dollar reward is secure."

The intimation in his words escaped Jodie, because her mind was overflowing with too much happiness, for she and Cade were now free to marry and begin their life together.

"Let's head for Crystal Creek," she said. "I'm anxious to get home."

"We should reach town by late afternoon. That means, we can get married tonight."

She smiled brightly. "I can hardly wait."

Jonas and Alison planned to have dinner together, and were about to enter the restaurant when they caught sight of Jodie and Cade entering town. Waving, they got their attention.

Stopping in front of the restaurant, Cade and Jodie dismounted. Alison embraced her brother and Jodie enthusiastically. Jodie's discolored bruise stood out blatantly.

"Who hit you?" Alison asked.

"Breed," Jodie replied. "I'll tell you about it later."

"We were about to have dinner," Riker said. "Why don't you two join us?"

Cade looked questioningly at Jodie. "I am hungry. How about you?"

"Well, I have an important engagement tonight, but I think I have time to squeeze in dinner."

Brandon leaned close and whispered in her ear, "Order a nourishing meal, my dear, for you'll need your strength to make it through the night ahead."

She eyed him saucily. "Be careful what you say; I might hold you to it. Don't boast unless you can live up to it."

"I never boast, darlin'," he said, his voice now clear and

strong. "Believe me, you'll need your strength because I'm going to make love to you all night."

Jodie, blushing, turned to Alison and Jonas, and explained, "We're getting married this evening."

Following congratulations, Riker announced that he and Alison would get married Sunday. Again, good wishes were exchanged. Cade was happy for his sister, and he whole-heartedly approved of Riker.

Over a delicious meal and bottle of wine, Jonas told Cade and Jodie that Mayor Wrightman had paid him a visit earlier and asked him to stay on as sheriff. He said that he would, and starting tomorrow, he intended to look for a deputy. He hoped to find someone soon. Alison also had news to disclose. As the mayor was visiting Jonas, Mrs. Wrightman, along with a committee of ladies, had come to Alison's hotel room to officially welcome her to Crystal Creek. That she had once lived with the Comanches was not mentioned, and none of the ladies displayed any signs of passing judgment. They had been warm and very respectful.

"I realize not everyone in this town will be so kind," Alison continued. "But it doesn't matter. Let them think what they want. Their malicious whispers and dirty looks can't hurt me. I have Jonas and I now have friends. I know I'm going to be very happy living in Crystal Creek." Jonas was sitting beside her; she reached over and took his hand. Her eyes glowed with love as she gazed into his face. "I've waited a long time for happiness; we both have."

Riker kissed her lips softly. "We have only one problem," he said, turning to Cade and Jodie. "Finding a house. I could build a home where my old one stood, but I prefer that Alison and I live in town. For the time being, we'll have to use the back room at the jail and eat at the restaurant." He shrugged his shoulders heavily. "Even if a house comes up for sale, I don't know how I'll buy it. A sheriff doesn't make much money. Maybe Wrightman will give me a loan." He suddenly smiled. "But enough of our problems. You two don't want to hear about that. What time are you getting married, and are Alison and I invited?"

"Of course you are," Jodie replied. "We stopped at the parsonage on our way into town, and Reverend Smith will meet us at the church at seven o'clock." Her wine glass was half full; she quickly downed it, bounded to her feet, and exclaimed, "I don't have much time left to bathe and dress. I wouldn't want to be late for my own wedding." Cade had remained seated; she leaned over and kissed him lightly. "I'll see you at the church. Aunt Doris is certainly going to be surprised when I tell her she's about to attend a wedding." She turned to leave.

"Jodie, wait a moment," Alison said. "There's something you should know. I saw your aunt this morning. Last night, Mr. Daniels asked her to marry him. She accepted, and is already packing to move into his home. They plan to marry early next week."

"That's marvelous," Jodie replied.

"There's more," Alison told her. "Laura and Dirk left this morning for Santa Rita. They eloped."

Jodie was dumbfounded. "Laura and Dirk? Their romance bloomed awfully fast!"

"Your aunt was incredulous. But after she got over the shock, she seemed resigned. In fact, she confessed that she was relieved Laura wouldn't have to move in with her and Mr. Daniels."

Jodie's eyes shone brightly as an idea suddenly crossed her mind. However, she wasn't ready yet to share it with anyone. She turned to Riker and asked, "Who's watching Edwards?"

"He's gone. The sheriff from Abilene picked him up this afternoon."

"Did he leave the thousand dollar reward?"

Cade tensed; he watched Jodie closely.

"He left the money," Jonas replied. "It's at the jail, locked in the safe."

"When you come to the church, bring it with you."

Her request surprised Riker. "Are you afraid someone might break in and steal it?"

"Maybe," she said evasively. Again, she kissed Cade, then hurried outside, for she was eager to get ready for her wedding.

Riker, his expression puzzled, asked Cade, "Why is she so set on getting that money tonight?"

"That's her getaway cash, her security, and her way of telling me that she hasn't changed a damned bit!"

"Cade," Alison began, "what are you saying?"

"I'm saying that Jodie is plagued with doubts. I thought she had overcome them, and that she had complete faith in our love. But apparently her problems go much deeper than I realized." He picked up his wine glass and took a big drink. "Let her stash away the thousand dollars. What the hell? I've done everything possible to convince her that I'll always love her. There's nothing more I can do. Maybe after we've been married a few years . . ."

Cade stood and placed money on the table to cover dinner. "I need to get a room at the hotel. I'll see you two at the church."

His thoughts were troubled as he left the restaurant. He wanted Jodie to marry him with no reservations and to have complete trust in his love for her. But, evidently, it was not to be.

He took his horse to the livery; then, seeing that the mercantile was still open, he went inside. He hoped to find suitable clothes for tonight. Luckily, he found a pair of black trousers and a blue shirt that fit perfectly. He took his purchases with him to the hotel, paid for a room, ordered a bath, and went upstairs.

* * *

Doris was overjoyed when Jodie told her that she and Cade planned to marry at seven o'clock. She helped her niece choose a wedding dress from her wardrobe. The delicate gown was snowy white, except for a pink ribbon that laced the bodice and bordered the garment's flowing hem. The bathtub was filled, and as Jodie bathed and washed her hair, her aunt talked happily about her engagement to Mr. Daniels. She rambled on for a long time before abruptly changing the subject to Laura's elopement. She voiced a little concern that the romance had happened so suddenly. She was also troubled that Dirk might prove to be irresponsible. After all, the man didn't have a very good reputation.

Jodie's nerves suddenly tightened, and a feeling of apprehension passed over her. Dirk! Her mind had been filled with so much that she had temporarily forgotten about Dirk hiring Breed to kill Emmett and Garth! She couldn't keep such knowledge to herself! Now that Breed was dead, Dirk might very well hire someone else. Emmett had a right to know that his life and Garth's were in danger. She dreaded breaking such terrible news. She found herself feeling sorry for Emmett; learning that his son wanted him and Garth dead would be a heartbreaking blow. She decided to tell him tomorrow.

She suspected Laura of marrying Dirk for his money, and now he would most likely be penniless, for Emmett would undoubtedly disown him. She wondered what that would do to their marriage.

She willfully cast the Bradleys and Laura from her mind—this was her wedding night and she was not about to let anything put a damper on her happiness.

Chapter Thirty-One

Following the ceremony, everyone went to Jodie's home, where Doris served cake and coffee. Cade and Jodie were anxious to be alone; nevertheless, they stayed and politely visited for nearly an hour. Deciding it was time to leave, Jodie went to her room and packed a bag. She and Cade planned to spend their wedding night in his hotel room.

Before leaving, Jodie, with Cade at her side, went to Jonas and Alison. She asked Jonas for the thousand dollars.

He had the money with him, and he gave it to her.

She looked at the bills for a moment, as though they held her undivided attention, but her mind was not really on the money. She was thinking about what she intended to do with it. With a large smile, she handed the bills back to Jonas, saying, "This is my wedding gift to you and Alison. I know you two need a house, and this house belongs to Mayor Wrightman. Papa only paid rent. But this money can help you buy it. I'm sure the mayor will agree to sell. Aunt Doris is moving out next week; then you and Alison can move in. The furniture belongs to me; you two are more than welcome to use it."

"I can't take this!" Jonas remarked, indicating the bills. "A thousand dollars! It's too much!"

"But I want you to have it."

Cade didn't say anything, but his arm went about Jodie's waist, drawing her flush to his side.

"I'll pay you back," Jonas said. "A little at a time."

"You don't have to."

"That's the only way I can accept this money."

Jodie conceded; after all, Riker had his pride.

Leaving, Jodie and Cade strolled toward the hotel hand in hand. Although their wedding had been small, hurried, and over with quickly, Jodie couldn't be happier.

"I'm very proud of you," Cade murmured.

"Why is that?"

"For giving Jonas and Alison the thousand dollars. At the restaurant when you insisted that Jonas bring the money, I thought . . ."

"Did you think I wanted the money in case our marriage failed?"

He smiled lamely. "I hate to admit it, but that's exactly what I thought."

"I have complete faith in you and in our love. Believe me, I truly do."

"I know that now, and I'll never doubt you again."

"Cade," she began, her tone apprehensive. "Tomorrow I want you to ride out to Emmett's ranch with me."

"Why do you want to go there?"

She told him that Dirk had hired Breed to kill Emmett and Garth. "I don't see how I can keep that information to myself. Now that Breed's dead, Dirk's liable to hire someone else. Emmett has a right to know that his life and Garth's might be in danger."

"You're right; you have to tell him. Furthermore, if you don't say anything it's the same as covering for Dirk."

"I would never do that. Dirk should pay for what he did. I always knew he was worthless, but I never imagined he was capable of hiring someone to kill his father and brother! I'm sure Emmett will disown him, but he deserves a more severe punishment."

They changed the subject, and happily discussed their future as they completed the walk to the hotel. They hurried upstairs and to Cade's room. He unlocked the door, placed Jodie's bag on the floor, then swept her up into his arms. He carried his bride over the threshold, and placed her gently on her feet. They kissed passionately, clinging to each other as though they never intended to let go.

Cade released her reluctantly, lit the bedside lamp, then brought her bag inside and closed the door.

"Why don't you step outside and have a smoke?" she suggested.

He looked at her with puzzlement. "Why would I want to do that?"

"So I can slip into my nightgown."

He grinned. "Why? I'll just take it off of you."

She gave him a persuasive nudge toward the door. "Appease me, darling. Come back in fifteen minutes."

"Fifteen minutes?" he groaned. "I don't know if I can wait that long."

"Force yourself."

"See how you are?" he teased. "We've only been married a little over an hour, and you're already telling me what to do."

"Get used to it," she joshed.

He opened the door. "I'll be back in fifteen minutes— on the nose. Not one minute longer."

"I'll be ready," she replied, her twinkling eyes promising a night of passion.

The moment he closed the door behind him, Jodie hurriedly slipped out of her dress. She delved into her bag and removed a white nightgown. The finely-weaved fabric was designed to temptingly silhouette a woman's body. Her father had bought the nightgown last year in Albuquerque and had given it to her on her birthday. She had never worn the gown. She had put it back to save for her wedding night.

She placed the delicate gown on the bed, and as she lightly brushed her fingers over the soft fabric, her mother's wedding band, worn on her left hand, caught her eye. There had been no time for Cade to buy a ring; therefore, Jodie suggested using her mother's ring. Cade had offered to buy her one at the first opportunity. However, she had declined, for she preferred to keep her mother's gold band. Furthermore, Cade had placed this ring on her finger as he claimed her as his wife, and she was not about to change it for another one.

She removed her undergarments, slipped into the gown, then took her brush from the bag. Going to the mirror, she brushed her curly locks until they shone with silky highlights.

Returning to the bed, she lowered the lamp's wick to a romantic glow. She then drew back the covers, propped the pillows against the headboard, and lay down.

A moment later, Cade checked the door, and finding it unlocked, he came inside and pushed in the bolt. He paused as his eyes raked his lovely bride.

Jodie, poised in bed, with her chestnut tresses splayed across the pillow, and her delicate gown gracefully defining her sensual curves, was a beautiful sight to behold.

Cade moved slowly to the bed, his gaze never leaving the beauty that awaited. He sat on the edge of the mattress, looked deeply into her blue eyes, and murmured, "I'll remember this moment if I live to be a hundred. No amount of time could dim this memory; it's stamped into my mind forever. You'll always be as beautiful to me as you are right now."

"Even when I'm old and wrinkled?"

"You'll never be old and wrinkled in my eyes. You'll always be my bride."

A trace of tears blurred her vision, for his words had touched her.

He leaned over and kissed her lips softly. "I love you, Mrs. Brandon."

She suddenly smiled pertly. "I think you should undress, get in bed, and show me how much you love me."

"There you go again, telling me what to do," he said with a grin.

"Well, if you'd rather not come to bed, I suppose we could find something else to do." She eyed him teasingly.

He raised a brow. "Well, you've had a spanking coming for a long time."

"Don't you dare!" she exclaimed, laughing lightly.

"That was a mistake—don't ever dare me."

"Will you please get undressed and into bed? Can't you see your wife is dying to make love to you?"

"In that case . . ." he said, standing, and unbuttoning his shirt.

Jodie watched admirably as her husband disrobed; she found his physique perfect—though lean, his frame was tightly-muscled. She lifted her gaze to his face. He was strikingly handsome. His dark blue eyes, black hair, and well-clipped moustache lent him a roguish charm that was irresistible.

When he stood before her fully unclothed, she moved over and gave him room to lie beside her.

He drew her body tightly to his, and seized her lips in a wild, hungry caress. She responded with untethered desire, her senses throbbing with the feel and need of him.

Eager to have her naked body pressed to his, Cade drew her to a sitting position, grabbed the hem of her gown, and lifted it over her head. He dropped it beside the bed, then eased his bride down onto the mattress, settling beside her.

His mouth swooped down on hers, and she fully returned his ardor as she pressed her thighs against his male hardness.

Unleashing their desire, their hands roamed boldly over each other's flesh, their intimate caresses setting fire to their passion.

Slowly, tantalizingly, Cade's mouth moved down to her breasts, his tongue tasting and circling her taut nipples, arousing her to even greater heights.

Her body, burning with desire, yearned for a conqueror, and she urged his lips back to hers. As she kissed him with total abandonment, she slid her frame beneath his. "Now, darling," she whispered throatily. "I can't wait any longer. I must have you deep inside me."

"Jodie . . ." he groaned, his tone husky with passion. Lifting her legs and placing them about his waist, he penetrated her in one quick thrust. They lay still a moment, relishing their joining and the intense pleasure spreading through every nerve in their bodies.

Cade began to move inside her, and she met his every thrust with equal fervor. Ecstasy, now all-consuming, engulfed the newlyweds, carrying them to a spiraling, breathless completion.

Their wedding night was filled with passion, for they never really slept, but dozed, awoke, and made love until the break of dawn. They finally fell sound asleep as the sun's morning rays filtered into the room, its reddish glow falling across the bed, where the lovers lay entwined in sated slumber.

The newlyweds slept late, and it was past noon before they left town to ride to Emmett's ranch. Although the day was warm, a refreshing breeze made the journey a pleasant one.

Emmett and Garth were home; they had company—Bill Lawson. Jodie was pleased to find that Bill was doing so well. He told her that his wound was still a little sensitive, but otherwise he was as good as new.

The Bradleys and Lawson were surprised to learn that Jodie and Cade were already married. The men extended their good wishes. Bill, however, experienced a pang of regret—he wasn't fully over Jodie, and had a feeling he would never really recover from losing her.

Emmett entertained his guests in the parlor, which was decorated tastefully and expensively. The furniture was solid oak; the floor-length drapes were made of the finest material, and costly paintings adorned the walls.

Coffee was served, and the conversation turned to everyday affairs. However, Emmett figured Jodie and Brandon didn't come here to discuss things like the weather, the cost of cattle, and the Apache situation.

"Did you ride all the way out here just to tell me you were married?" Emmett asked Jodie, leading into her reason for being here. She was sitting on the sofa beside Cade. Bill was seated in a chair that matched Emmett's; a small table separated the chairs. Garth was standing in front of the unlit hearth.

Jodie looked from Emmett to Garth, then back to Emmett again. She dreaded breaking such startling news. God, she wondered, how do I tell them that Dirk wanted them dead? She decided on a direct approach, for there was no way to soften the blow.

She began by giving a full account of the last couple of days. She explained that Alison and Jonas had been taken hostage; she also included Dirk's involvement. She recounted her abduction and that Breed decided to take her to the Comancheros' hideout.

"While I was Breed's prisoner," she continued, "he told

me that Dirk offered him a thousand dollars to kill you and Garth. The Apaches, however, killed Breed. But Dirk might hire someone else. I thought you should know that your life and Garth's could be in danger."

Emmett's face paled. "I . . . I don't believe this! Breed must have lied to you."

"Why would he lie?" Jodie asked. "There was no reason for him to tell me something like that if it wasn't true. He planned to leave me with the Comancheros, then come back and kill you and Garth."

"No," Emmett groaned. "I can't . . . I won't believe this!"

"Well, I can believe it!" Garth remarked angrily to his father. "I don't find it difficult to believe Dirk would hire Breed to kill us. Dirk's never had a conscience. And he doesn't give a damn about you or me. I'm sure there's nothing he'd like better than to inherit this ranch, sell it, and go to San Francisco. Living in San Francisco is all he ever talks about."

"For God's sake, Garth! He might want to go to San Francisco, but not at the cost of our lives! Besides, he's now married to Laura Talbert. She's a gentle and compassionate lady, and will be a good influence on Dirk."

Bill cleared his throat hesitantly. "Emmett, earlier when you told me that Dirk and Laura eloped, I thought maybe I should tell you about Laura, but I decided not to stick my nose where it didn't belong. However, on second thought I think you should know that Laura will not be a good influence on Dirk. After Jodie and I parted company, I began to see Laura. I mistook her for a lady, and was actually quite smitten with her. While I was convalescing, she tried to seduce me with the expertise of a harlot. She believed I would ask her to marry me. I honestly think the woman was after my money. She's looking for a rich husband, and Dirk was the best she could find. Don't mistake Laura for a lady; she's no better than a harlot."

Emmett turned to Jodie. "Laura's your cousin. You must know her very well. Do you think she married Dirk for money?"

"I don't know," she replied.

"Then let me rephrase my question. Do you think she's capable of such deceit?"

Jodie answered candidly, "Yes, I think she is."

"Damn it, Pa!" Garth said furiously. "Laura isn't the issue here! It's Dirk! That sorry bastard hired Breed to kill us! What do you intend to do about it?"

Emmett sighed heavily, pathetically. Although it tore him to pieces, he had to admit to himself that Breed hadn't lied. He had always known that his younger son was worthless, and thought of no one but himself.

At that moment, as though on cue, the front door opened, admitting Dirk and his bride. They weren't surprised to find Jodie and Cade, for they had stopped to see Doris on their way to the ranch. She told them that Jodie was now married to Cade, and that they were visiting Emmett. Dirk was disappointed to learn that Breed was dead. But he didn't remain disgruntled very long; he'd simply hire someone else to kill Emmett and Garth. Hired killers were not that hard to find.

A large smile was on Dirk's face as he and Laura stepped into the parlor. But his smile faded at his father's stern expression.

Emmett waved a hand in the direction of his study. "Dirk, I want to talk to you in private."

"Are you upset because Laura and I eloped?"

"Just come with me," he said. They left the parlor and walked down the hall to the study.

Jodie and Cade, along with Lawson, quickly made their excuses, told Garth good-bye, and went outside. They mounted their horses and rode away. Bill headed toward his ranch; Jodie and Cade started back to town.

* * *

Dirk, intimated by the silent rage in his father's eyes, stood stiffly, nervously shifting his weight from one foot to the other. He had never imagined that his elopement would anger Emmett so severely.

The study door suddenly opened, and Laura barged inside. Standing beside her husband, she placed a supportive hand on his arm. She looked at Emmett. "I know you wanted to speak alone to Dirk, but now that we're married, we have no secrets from each other. Whatever you have to say to Dirk, you can say to both of us." Like Dirk, she thought Emmett's anger was due to their elopement. She was sure she could soothe her father-in-law, and make everything all right.

"Very well," Emmett said. "Since you two have no secrets, you won't mind learning that Dirk hired Breed to kill Garth and me."

Laura gasped.

Dirk's knees grew so weak that he tottered. He wondered how his father had learned about Breed. He suspected that Jodie was somehow involved. After all, she had been with Breed.

"You . . . you don't believe I'd do something like that, do you?" Dirk asked his father.

Emmett regarded his son closely. Guilt was written all over his face. Dirk had always been a poor liar. "Yes, I believe you hired Breed," he said, his tone calm, yet blatantly frigid.

"I . . . I didn't do it, Pa! I swear I didn't!" Dirk's voice whined like a child's. "I'd never pay someone a thousand dollars to kill you and Garth! You're my family!"

"How did you know it was a thousand dollars? I never mentioned the payoff."

Dirk had trapped himself. He sighed miserably. He was caught, and there was no way out. Unable to face his father, he lowered his gaze to the floor and stood sheepishly.

Laura, however, was stunned. She was also enraged. Dirk had ruined everything!

Emmett went to his safe, opened it, and withdrew a small stack of bills. He handed them to Dirk. "There's enough money there to get you and Laura to San Francisco. I want you to leave on the first stage. I never want to see your face again. You are no longer my son, and your name will be taken out of my will—immediately. Go upstairs and pack your clothes; I'll have a wrangler take you to town so that you can catch the afternoon stage."

"But, Pa—" Dirk pleaded.

"Get out of my sight!" Emmett shouted furiously. "Now, before I wring your worthless neck!"

Dirk fled the study.

"But what about me?" Laura asked Emmett. "I didn't know about Breed." She wondered if she could gain Emmett's sympathy. "I never dreamed Dirk was so evil. I'll have my marriage annulled." Taking Emmett unaware, she leaned against him as though she were about to faint. She intentionally thrust her thighs to his, as her full breasts pressed against his chest.

Her seductive ploy didn't work, and pushing her back so firmly that she almost lost her balance, Emmett said coldly, "You and Dirk deserve each other!"

"I . . . I don't understand."

"Then I'll make it perfectly clear. Bill Lawson told me all about you." With that, he brushed past her and left the study, closing the door with a solid bang.

Laura, her dreams crushed, covered her face with her hands and wept loudly.

* * *

Cade was at the sheriff's office, but Jodie and Doris were home when Laura returned with Dirk, who insisted on waiting outside in the buckboard. Laura told her mother that she was leaving right away for San Francisco, but refused to tell her why. Doris followed her into the bedroom, and as Laura packed a suitcase, she pleaded with her not to leave so quickly.

Finally, giving up, Doris went to the parlor. Jodie was there, and Doris told her that she couldn't imagine why Laura and Dirk were leaving so suddenly. Jodie knew why, but she wasn't about to tell her aunt what had happened. There was nothing she could do about it, and it would only upset her more.

Jodie went to Laura's bedroom. She was finished packing, and was closing her suitcase.

She eyed Jodie hatefully. "I suppose you know everything; you always do!"

"I know about Dirk and Breed. But I wasn't sure if you knew."

"Oh, I know all right! Dirk's an idiot!"

"Then why are you leaving with him?"

"Because I don't want to stay here! What would I do? Move in with Mother and Mr. Daniels? God forbid! On the way back to town, I thought everything over very carefully. I want to go to San Francisco! The town is full of rich bachelors, and I intend to marry one."

"Aren't you forgetting something?"

"What's that?"

"You're already married."

"Not for very long. Once I'm in San Francisco, I'll find a way to get rid of Dirk!"

"Yes, I'm sure you will. I'd feel sorry for Dirk, but he isn't worth it."

She picked up her suitcase. "Mother can store the rest of my things. I'll send for them once I'm settled in San Francisco. The stage will here be soon, and I can hardly wait to be on it. I don't ever intend to see this two-bit town again!''

Taking her suitcase with her, she left without bothering to tell her cousin good-bye; that, of course, was fine with Jodie.

Epilogue

Three Years Later

Jodie sat beneath a huge pecan tree, its full-leafed branches shading her from the warm Texas sun. She was sitting in the front yard, ensconced in a cane rocker, and was gently rocking it back and forth as Doris, spotting her from the veranda, decided to join her.

Two more chairs were placed beside Jodie's, and as Doris sat down, she remarked, "Honey, I am so impressed with your home. You and Cade have done very well."

"When Cade first brought me here, we lived in a log cabin. But building a new home was very important to Cade, and this house was finished before our first anniversary."

The one-story home, white adobe with a red tile roof, was designed with a Spanish accent. A front veranda, supported by intricate posts, ran the entire length of the house. Inside, the spacious home was tastefully decorated. Cade had given Jodie a free hand, and she had done a remarkable job: their home was filled with comfortable furniture, brightly colored drapes and rugs, and several paintings that reflected the western culture that she and Cade loved so much.

Today was Jodie's and Cade's third wedding anniversary, and they were throwing a big barbecue. Invitations were sent to Doris and her husband, and to the Rikers. Hernando and Antonio were also invited. Jodie and Cade were delighted that they were all able to make the journey. Although Alison and Jonas had visited their home before, this was Doris's and her husband's first time here. It was also Hernando's and Antonio's first visit.

Doris and her husband, Carl, had arrived this morning, and Doris hadn't really had time to talk to Jodie. Now that they were alone, she heaved a deep sigh, and said, "The last time I wrote to you, I told you that Carl and I were going to San Francisco to try to find Laura." Doris's daughter had corresponded when she first moved to San Francisco, but gradually her letters had tapered off, and eventually she stopped writing.

"We got back to Crystal Creek three weeks ago, and your invitation was waiting for us," Doris continued. "I saw no reason to write about our trip when I would be seeing you soon. I talked to Alison the day we returned. I didn't say anything to her about Laura. I was too ashamed. But I did tell her about Dirk. I suppose she told you that he's dead."

"Yes, she did. She said that he was killed."

"He was killed in a fight over Laura."

"How do you know this? Did you find Laura?"

A trace of tears came to Doris's eyes. "Yes, I found her, and she told me what happened to Dirk. But Carl and I combed the city from one end to the other before we finally located Laura." She reached over and grasped Jodie's hand. "She's a prostitute! She's working in one of those awful houses! Oh Jodie, how could she have done this to herself? I raised her properly, didn't I?"

"Don't blame yourself, Aunt Doris. You did everything you could for Laura."

"Carl and I only saw her for a few minutes. She didn't want to talk to us, and I could tell she resented us being there. Not because she was ashamed; she was angry that we dared intrude in her life. She told me that she never wanted to see me again and that I should mind my own business. She still dreams of catching a rich husband. Can you believe that? She actually thinks some wealthy bachelor will visit that terrible house, fall hopelessly in love with her, and ask her to be his wife. I told her that rich bachelors do not marry prostitutes. That was when she ordered me to leave, and said she never wanted to see me again."

"I'm sorry, Aunt Doris. I wish I could say something to make all this easier for you."

"Now, don't you start worrying about me. I'm fine. Carl and I are very happy. He's a wonderful man. I told Laura if she ever needed me, she knew where she could find me. Carl agreed with me. He's willing to help her if she ever turns to us."

Jodie didn't say anything, but she seriously doubted that Laura would ever turn to her mother and stepfather. She would stay in San Francisco and hold tenaciously to her impossible dream.

Alison came outside, and seeing Jodie and Doris, she moved to join them. She walked slowly, for she was heavy with child.

"How are you feeling?" Doris asked her.

Sitting in the extra chair, she answered, "I've never felt better." She brushed her fingers lightly over her swollen stomach. "I only have three months left, and I'm getting very anxious." A bright twinkle shone in her emerald-green eyes. The sadness that had haunted her eyes was now gone, supplanted by happiness and hope for the future. Pregnancy agreed with her, and she had never looked more becoming.

Alison turned to Jodie. "When I woke up from my nap, everyone was gone. Did I miss something?"

"Not a thing," Jodie replied. "The men are behind the house checking the meat in the barbecue pit."

Alison smiled. "Does it take five men to check one pit?"

"It would seem that way." She suddenly caught sight of Antonio rounding the corner of the house. "Here comes one of them now."

He strode over to the ladies, and sat on the grass close to Jodie's chair.

"How's the meat coming along?" Jodie asked him.

"Fine," he replied. "But I decided too many chefs spoil the broth. Besides, why would I want to stand around a cooking pit when I can keep company with three such lovely ladies?"

Jodie smiled warmly. "You have always been a charmer, Antonio."

He reached into his pocket and withdrew a cheroot, asking the women if he could smoke. They had no objections. He lit the small cigar, then turning to Jodie, he remarked softly, "I've never seen Cade so happy or so content. Señora, you are very good for him."

"We're good for each other," she replied. "How is Hernando? I mean, he seems all right, but he must be hurting inside."

"Sí," he murmured. "Felisa's death saddened him. I think he was starting to truly love her. She came down with a fever, and the doctor couldn't save her. She has been gone now for six months, and Hernando is over his grief. He has his son, and is a very doting father. He lives for that boy."

"How are Lucinda and her husband?"

"They are fine. Lucinda is expecting a child in the autumn."

"It looks as though the chefs are through checking the meat," Alison said, for the men had come into view.

Carl and Hernando were ahead of Cade and Jonas, for they were able to walk a little faster. Hernando's son, Ricardo, who was now a little over three years old, could match his father's and Carl's leisurely strides. However, behind them, Jonas and Cade moved much more slowly, for the eighteen-month-old girl holding Jonas's hand, and the sixteen-month-old boy clasping Cade's hand, held their fathers to a slow pace.

A smile radiating with love and happiness spread across Jodie's face as she watched her husband and son making their way to her and the others. The child was a tiny replica of his father, his hair coal black and his eyes sapphire blue.

When everyone was grouped beneath the tall pecan tree, the men sitting on the ground, and the children playing within their parents' reach, Jodie allowed her eyes to sweep over the small congregation. She gazed at Doris and Carl Daniels; she loved her aunt dearly and had always been fond of Carl—she had known him all her life. She was glad that they had found each other and were happy together.

Next, she turned her gaze to Alison; Jonas was sitting at her feet. Their daughter toddled over and plopped herself into her father's lap. The child, inheriting her parents' good looks, was exceptionally beautiful. Jodie knew how much the child meant to Alison and Jonas, and how thrilled they were that Alison was expecting again. They had both lost children, and had suffered unbearable grief. But their love for each other, their daughter, and the baby on the way, had given them a new lease on life. Jonas, who had remained sober for three years, was still sheriff of Crystal Creek, and he had bought Jodie's former home from Mayor Wrightman. He and Alison were happy living in Crystal Creek, and they had no intention of leaving.

Jodie's gaze went to Hernando, who was sitting beside Antonio. Father and son's relationship had strengthened during the past three years. Hernando had put his bitterness behind him and had forgiven Antonio for deserting him so many years ago. Ricardo had helped bring them together, and they both loved the child, as well as each other.

As Jodie turned her gaze to Cade, she missed catching the adoration in Hernando's eyes as he glanced her way. He quickly veiled his feelings, for he knew she was deeply devoted to Cade. Hernando loved her unselfishly, and her apparent happiness pleased him. His thoughts floated to Felisa; he had learned to loved her, but only as the mother of his son. He sighed softly—maybe someday a woman with Jodie's vitality, beauty, and spirit would come into his life.

Jodie watched as her son scampered to Cade and began climbing onto his back, asking for a piggyback ride. She laughed merrily as, giving in, Cade hoisted the child onto his back, stood, and trotted about the yard, his son giggling at the top of his small lungs.

"Cole has Cade wrapped around his little finger," Doris said to Jodie, watching father and son romping playfully. "It's a shame your father didn't live to see his grandson. He'd be pleased that you named the child after him."

At that moment, Cade's uncle, who had been with the wranglers on the range, rode up to the house. He dismounted, chuckling as he watched Cade entertain Cole. He joined the others beneath the pecan tree, and said to Jodie, "I told the wranglers to call it a day in about an hour, come back, wash up, and help us eat all that beef." He gestured toward Cade and the child. "A sight like that does my heart good. I'm sure glad I lived to see Cade get married and know the joy of havin' a family."

Jodie smiled warmly at the man, who bore a strong resemblance to his nephew. Like Cade, he had black hair, but it was streaked with gray, which matched his full beard. She had grown to love Uncle Charlie, and she knew he felt the same way about her. Cade trotted back, lifted the child from his back, and sat down next to Jodie's chair. Cole was now content to sit quietly in his father's lap.

As Jodie's gaze once again swept over each individual, a feeling of total happiness rose inside her. This was a wonderful moment—a wonderful day—for she was surrounded by loved ones and loyal friends. She was thankful for her good fortune, and for the good fortune of those around her.

Jodie, dressed for bed, drew back the covers and fluffed the pillows. Although she was tired, her mind was wide awake. The day had been delightful, and she had enjoyed every minute of it. She was glad her guests intended to stay until next week, for she wanted to see more of them.

Cade, who had left the bedroom to check on Cole, returned, closing the door behind him. He carried a small gift-wrapped box, which he handed to Jodie. "Happy anniversary, darlin'," he murmured, his eyes twinkling with love.

Excited, she quickly tore off the paper and opened the box. Inside was a cameo brooch with matching earrings. "Oh, Cade!" she exclaimed. "They're beautiful!"

"Are you sure you like them? The jeweler said I can return them if you aren't pleased."

"Pleased? I'm ecstatic!" She flung herself into his arms. "Thank you, Cade. Your gift is lovely."

He kissed her deeply, drawing her body flush to his.

She suddenly pushed out of his embrace. "Your gift was too big to wrap. I hid it in my wardrobe." She placed her present on the dresser, then hurried to show Cade what she had gotten him. It was a western saddle.

"Thanks, darlin'," he said. "I'm glad you remembered I needed a new saddle."

She laughed gaily. "Remember? How could I forget? You've been hinting for a saddle for the past two months."

"Was I that obvious?"

"I'm afraid so."

He took her back into his arms. "Well, I might have hinted a little, but I didn't know for sure if you got my meaning."

"As if I could have missed it."

"I love you, Mrs. Brandon. And these past three years have been the happiest years of my life."

"Mine too," she murmured. "Cade, I have another present for you."

"Another?" he questioned. "Do I have a bridle to go with the saddle?"

"No, it's not a bridle. It's much better than that." She took his hand and placed it on her stomach. "Your gift is in here—another son or a daughter."

He smiled widely. "That's definitely better than a bridle. I hope this one is a girl and looks just like you. But if it's a boy, I'll still be the happiest man alive. We can always try again for a girl."

"If this one is a girl, does that mean we'll quit?"

"Of course not. Then we'll have to try for a little brother. She'll already have a big brother. But we won't be able to stop there, for then we'll have to get her a little sister, so she won't be the only girl."

Jodie laughed merrily. "Cade, this is too confusing. Maybe I should have gotten the bridle, after all."

Suddenly, he swooped her up into his arms, carried her to bed, and laid her down carefully. Anticipation glinted his eyes as he murmured, "I have another gift for you too." He had on his robe, for he had undressed for bed before leaving to check on Cole. He untied the sash; underneath he wore nothing, for he always slept in the nude.

His desire was apparent, and Jodie said with a bewitching smile, "I've been waiting all day to receive this gift."

He lay beside her, pressing her body close to his. "I love

you," he whispered, before seizing her lips in a rapturous kiss that set fire to their passion.

Marriage hadn't dimmed their desire; it was still as strong and as fiery as it had been on their wedding night. Their unending need for each other ignited into a leaping flame as their kisses grew more demanding, and their caresses became more urgent.

Their bodies fused into one, and engulfed in their exciting union, they fanned the flames of love until ecstasy, complete and all-consuming, carried them to passion's ultimate rapture.

They lay entwined in each other's arms, basking in the afterglow of their union, which had left them breathless and wonderfully fulfilled.

The bedside lamp was still burning; Cade reached over and turned the wick until the flame went out. He got up, opened a window, and drew aside the curtains, admitting soft moonbeams. Returning to bed, he brought his wife's body snugly to his.

"I love you, darlin'," he whispered, before closing his eyes and giving in to sleep.

Jodie smiled contentedly, for she knew Cade would always love her, and that she would never stop loving him. Their love was everlasting. She nestled her head on his shoulder; familiar sounds drifted in through the open window—the soft whinnying of corralled horses, the periodic mooing from cattle grazing nearby, and guitar music coming from the bunkhouse.

These sounds that were now a part of Jodie's life had a lulling effect, and she soon fell asleep cuddled in her husband's loving arms.

YOU WON'T WANT TO READ
JUST ONE—KATHERINE STONE

ROOMMATES   (0-8217-5206-5, $6.99/$7.99)
No one could have prepared Carrie for the monumental
changes she would face when she met her new circle of friends
at Stanford University. Once their lives intertwined and became
woven into the tapestry of the times, they would never be the
same.

TWINS   (0-8217-5207-3, $6.99/$7.99)
Brook and Melanie Chandler were so different, it was hard to
believe they were sisters. One was a dark, serious, ambitious
New York attorney; the other, a golden, glamourous, sophisti-
cated supermodel. But they were more than sisters—they were
twins and more alike than even they knew . . .

THE CARLTON CLUB   (0-8217-5204-9, $6.99/$7.99)
It was the place to see and be seen, the only place to be. And
for those who frequented the playground of the very rich, it
was a way of life. Mark, Kathleen, Leslie and Janet—they
worked together, played together, and loved together, all behind
exclusive gates of the *Carlton Club.*

*Available wherever paperbacks are sold, or order direct from the
Publisher. Send cover price plus 50¢ per copy for mailing and
handling to Penguin USA, P.O. Box 999, c/o Dept. 17109,
Bergenfield, NJ 07621. Residents of New York and Tennessee
must include sales tax. DO NOT SEND CASH.*